Spa

Will she b...

Three passionate novels!

In March 2008 Mills & Boon bring
back two of their classic collections,
each featuring three favourite
romances by our bestselling authors...

SPANISH AFFAIRS

A Spanish Vengeance
by Diana Hamilton
A Spanish Honeymoon by Anne Weale
His Brother's Son by Jennifer Taylor

BRIDES BY BLACKMAIL

The Blackmail Marriage
by Penny Jordan
The Greek's Blackmailed Wife
by Sarah Morgan
The Blackmail Pregnancy
by Melanie Milburne

Spanish Affairs

A SPANISH VENGEANCE
by
Diana Hamilton

A SPANISH HONEYMOON
by
Anne Weale

HIS BROTHER'S SON
by
Jennifer Taylor

MILLS & BOON
Pure reading pleasure

*Harlequin Mills & Boon Limited,
Eton House, 18-24 Paradise Road, Richmond, Surrey TW9 1SR*

SPANISH AFFAIRS
© by Harlequin Enterprises II B.V./S.à.r.l 2007

A Spanish Vengeance, A Spanish Honeymoon and *His Brother's
Son* were first published in Great Britain by Harlequin
Mills & Boon Limited in separate, single volumes.

A Spanish Vengeance © Diana Hamilton 2003
A Spanish Honeymoon © Anne Weale 2002
His Brother's Son © Jennifer Taylor 2002

ISBN: 978 0 263 86121 1

05-0308

*Printed and bound in Spain
by Litografia Rosés S.A., Barcelona*

A SPANISH VENGEANCE

by

Diana Hamilton

MILLS & BOON
100 YEARS
of pure reading pleasure.

100 Reasons to Celebrate

We invite you to join us in celebrating Mills & Boon's centenary. Gerald Mills and Charles Boon founded Mills & Boon Limited in 1908 and opened offices in London's Covent Garden. Since then, Mills & Boon has become a hallmark for romantic fiction, recognised around the world.

We're proud of our 100 years of publishing excellence, which wouldn't have been achieved without the loyalty and enthusiasm of our authors and readers.

Thank you!

Each month throughout the year there will be something new and exciting to mark the centenary, so watch for your favourite authors, captivating new stories, special limited edition collections…and more!

Diana Hamilton is a true romantic and fell in love with her husband at first sight. They still live in the fairytale Tudor house where they raised their three children. Now the idyll is shared with eight rescued cats and a puppy. But despite an often chaotic lifestyle, ever since she learned to read and write Diana has had her nose in a book – either reading or writing one – and plans to go on doing just that for a very long time to come.

Don't miss Diana Hamilton's exciting new novel, *Virgin: Wedded at the Italian's Convenience*, out in April 2008 from Mills & Boon® Modern™.

CHAPTER ONE

A *DEEPLY* unsettling mixture of frazzled nerve ends and sizzling excitement was making Lisa Pennington feel decidedly queasy.

Long fingers fumbled in her envelope purse, searching for a tissue to mop the perspiration from her face. She was sweating like a foundry worker. She tried to convince herself it was down to the heat of the Spanish evening sun and told herself to snap out of it. She'd end up looking a real soggy mess if she didn't pull herself together. And that mustn't happen.

She had to look good, cool and calm, if only to counteract Ben's reaction. So she'd pulled out all the stops, and dug out her make-up bag. The creamy foundation toned down the tan she'd acquired during the last eight weeks, while silvery eye-shadow emphasised the size and shape of her inky-blue eyes, and scarlet lipstick gave her the illusion of courage.

She'd slopped around in shorts and cool cotton tops all through this holiday but this evening she was wearing a dress in silvery-green silk, sleek and hopefully sophisticated. She couldn't be seen in the newest, smartest hotel in the whole of Marbella wearing any old rag.

Tomorrow she, Ben and Sophie would be returning to England. By tomorrow everyone would know what

Diego's intentions were. She quivered, assailed by a fresh onslaught of nervous tension.

Diego. Oh, how she loved him—she couldn't describe how much! In the last seven weeks he had become her whole world, the focus of every thought, of every breath she drew. And he loved her; she knew he did. The knowledge was pure magic. Tonight he would make his intentions plain. Why else would he have suggested he meet with her and her holiday companions in the disco bar of the exclusive hotel? He knew how close Ben and Sophie were to her, twin offspring of her father's business partner. The three of them had always been mates, especially after the death of her mother four years ago when they had taken her under their loving, protective wings.

Lisa crossed her fingers, praying that the coming meeting would go smoothly, that Ben wouldn't come out with something Diego's Spanish pride would never let him forgive. It would be unbearable if the three people she loved best in the world were at daggers drawn.

Straightening her shoulders, feeling the long silky fall of her silver-blonde hair brush against the bare skin of her back, she risked a sideways glance. Ben, strolling at her side, was seemingly intent on watching the expensive cars cruising the elegant sea front. He wasn't looking at her but she knew his bluntly good looking features would be clenched with displeasure if he did turn in her direction.

At twenty years of age he was only two years her senior yet he sometimes acted as if he were her grandfather! Lisa sighed, remembering his stinging comments when, in order to explain why she'd spent little time with him and Sophie, she'd had to confess that she'd met someone.

Flushed with the wonder of finding the love of her life here in Spain when she hadn't really wanted to be here at all, when she had intended spending her gap year back-packing around Europe, she had given his name, 'Diego Raffacani,' adding unnecessarily, 'He's Spanish.' Holding the fact that he was the most gorgeous-looking human being ever to walk the planet very close to her madly beating heart.

Ben had shot her the underbrow look that told her she was in for a lecture. 'How old is this guy? And I presume that, as you spend every day together, he's out of work?'

'Then you presume wrong!' Lisa's pointed chin shot up defensively. 'Diego works most evenings in one of the hotel restaurants down in Marbella—that's why he's free to spend his days with me! And, if you're really interested, he's twenty-two.'

Only four years her senior and so darkly handsome, so lithe and physically perfect that her heart ached just to look at him.

'So you've been picked up by a Spanish waiter,' Ben delivered drily. 'What a cliché!'

Unforgivably, Lisa giggled because, technically, Ben was spot on. She'd thought back to that day over three weeks ago. She'd spent the first week here dutifully tagging along with her friends. Descending from the hills where their rented ex-farmhouse holiday home was situated in the hired four-by-four. Doing what Ben and Sophie enjoyed. Playing golf, window-shopping, sipping coffee outside one of the trendy cafés, exploring what they could of the exclusive and highly fashionable nearby Puerto Banus area.

That particular day she'd cried off, the glitz beginning to pall, preferring to spend some time exploring the surrounding hilly back country on foot, comfortably clad in shorts and a matching acid-yellow T-shirt and sensible trainers. The buzzing of a motor scooter—a Vespino, Diego called it—was a warning that came too late. They had met on a bend in the steep, narrow track. Lisa had fallen backwards on to a carpet of wild herbs and the handsome young Spaniard had braked the scooter to a stone-spitting, slithering sideways halt.

Leaping across the narrow space, he'd gently helped her to her feet. So yes, he had quite literally picked her up! Looking into the concerned dark eyes, the proud, almost unnerving, aristocratic-looking features, at the tall bronzed perfection of a sensationally honed male clad just in patched cut-off denims that clipped the hard, narrow jut of his hips and a black vest top that had faded to grey, she had been utterly transfixed, her heart jumping up into her throat then spiralling down again to play havoc in the region of her stomach.

Their eyes had held as he assured himself she was unhurt—his questions couched in soft, only slightly accented English—gleaming black fringed with heavy thick lashes sending unspoken heady messages to wide inky-blue, the strong, steadying hands that curved around her slim shoulders transmitting a sensation that was a slow, unbearably sweet aching deep inside her.

That was how it had begun. And she would never again pour scorn on the idea of falling in love at first sight.

Ben had heaved a worried sigh, watching her as she made the morning coffee and Sophie, putting freshly picked peaches on a dish precisely in the centre of the breakfast table, had said lightly, 'Every girl's entitled to a holiday romance once in her life— provided things don't get out of hand.'

'They haven't, have they?' Ben put in quickly, his frown deepening.

As if she'd tell him! And no, they hadn't. Diego's kisses and caresses had sent her up in flames, the wanting a sweet wild torment inside her, but he had always pulled back at the critical moment, his voice soft and sultry as he had explained, 'You are very young, *querida*. One day you will be my bride. Until then, my angel, I value your purity above all else.'

'Is that a proposal?' Her voice was shaky with passion, her throat thick. He was all she had ever wanted; it was like a fairy tale.

'But of course, *querida*. You are my angel. I truly love you.' A gentle forefinger traced the outline of her lush lips, making her tremble. She could hardly speak through the rip-tide of ecstatic happiness, but managed a breathless, 'When?'

'When the time is right, *amor mio*,' he answered lightly, 'When you graduate from university—'

'That's years away!' she punched out, wriggling

out of his arms. He'd offered her heaven and now she could see it slipping away like water down a plughole.

He took her hands. 'There is no ending to our love; time won't alter that.' Warm, dark eyes smiled into hers. 'I too have things to do. Time will pass quickly, I promise. You will have vacations and I shall tell you where I am and you shall come to me.' His smile widened to a teasing grin. 'You have a rich daddy who will pay for your air fares!'

She dragged her hands away and sulked for the rest of the day. If he loved her as much as she loved him he wouldn't want to wait. Marrying her this minute wouldn't be soon enough!

But lying awake that night she'd formulated the perfect plan. She'd return to England at the end of their holiday as planned, square it with her father, who was remote enough not to mind what she did as long as she didn't bother him, and spend what was left of her gap year here with Diego. And at the end of the year they would have become so close, so loving, he wouldn't be able to face letting her go.

'Nothing to say for yourself?' Ben's question pulled her back into the farmhouse kitchen that day, almost four weeks ago. He accepted the mug of coffee she'd poured for him. 'I suppose you've told him who you are.'

'Of course he knows who I am!'

Ben's comment made no sense until he expounded, 'That your father is joint proprietor of a monthly glossy. That we publish *Lifestyle* among other less upmarket magazines. That our families are not short of cash.'

'There speaks the accountant!' Lisa derided gently. Ben had just finished a business accountancy course and on their return to England at the end of their holiday was to join the accounts department at *Life-style*.

'No,' Ben came back mildly. 'There speaks an old friend who is concerned for your happiness. Marbella is a hot spot of wealth; it attracts con men and hangers-on like flies. Men who latch on to rich women for what they can get out of them. Has your Spanish waiter wheedled anything out of you, by any chance?'

'Of course not!' But Lisa was aware that her cheeks burned with guilt. He hadn't wheedled that expensive watch out of her, she mentally defended. Far from it. He'd lost his own, explaining that the strap must have broken without him noticing it when he'd glanced at his naked wrist to check whether it was time for them to start heading back from the little secluded beach he'd taken her to.

That evening, while Sophie and Ben had been admiring the million dollar yachts in the marina, she'd slipped away and bought him a replacement, knowing he hadn't much money to spare. A waiter's wage wouldn't be anything to write home about and he needed a watch. 'And Diego doesn't like Marbella—' She wisely changed the subject. 'We never go there—he says it's too flashy, not the real Spain at all. We explore quaint little hill villages and off-the-track beaches.'

She loved Ben like a brother but was close to hating him for implying her beloved Diego was only interested in her for what he could get out of her. No way would she explain about the gift of that slim gold watch.

'So when do we get to meet him?' Sophie, the peace-maker, took her place at the table and reached for a crusty roll and the honey pot.

No answer, because there wasn't one to give. She'd once suggested a foursome—she'd wanted him to meet her best friends—but Diego had asserted that he was a selfish man and wanted her all to himself.

And now they were on their way to meet him at last—at his suggestion. Ben's comment had been a dry, 'He picked the most expensive joint he could find. I wonder who'll end up paying for the drinks and the meal!'

They were nearing the venue, the white futuristic hotel overlooking the gentle curve of the palm-fringed beach. Lisa's heart swelled. It would be all right; it had to be! Ben would take back every insulting insinuation when he realised what a super guy Diego was.

In a way she could understand his reservations. Ever since they'd been children he'd looked out for her. He still did, and that probably had something to do with her tiny stature—five-two, small-boned, delicately slender and wide-eyed. If she'd been built more like Sophie, tall and big in the bosom and hip department, he might have had more confidence in her ability to look out for herself.

Not that his opinion would make any difference to the way she felt about the man she was determined to marry. But she didn't want to quarrel with Ben; she was too fond of him.

'Hey, you guys—come and look at this!' Sophie cried. She'd been indulging in her favourite occupation, window-shopping, and was several yards behind them, her nose pinned to the window of a glitzy boutique. 'Would my bum look big in this?'

Ever willing to indulge his twin, Ben turned to retrace his steps, smiling, and Lisa stood where she was, too wound up to ooh and ahh over whatever it was Sophie was coveting.

Glancing at her platinum Jaeger-Le-Coultre watch, an eighteenth birthday gift from her father who thought that material things made up for a lack of any overt signs of parental affection, she noted there were still thirty minutes to get through before they were due to meet Diego. It felt like a lifetime.

The town was beginning to gear up for the evening, more people strolling the pavements, wanting to see and be seen, more flash cars cruising. One car in particular caught her attention. A bright scarlet drop-head sports job driven by a glamorous creature who looked as if she'd just materialised from between the covers of a high fashion magazine. But it was her passenger who drew her widening eyes—Diego? Surely not!

Diego, his thick dark hair expertly groomed, wearing classy casual chinos and an open-necked sleeveless shirt in a matching cool stone colour that accentuated the warm olive tones of his skin instead of the beat-up shorts and vest tops she was used to seeing him in.

The sports car growled to a halt, parked illegally outside the sort of jeweller's where the atmosphere would be too rarefied for ordinary mortals to breathe in, and Diego removed his arm from the back of the driver's seat and exited.

He had obviously smartened himself up for his meeting with them at the hotel and he looked good enough to eat, the darling! Like them, he was half an hour early. The classy female must have given him a lift. She was probably resident at the hotel where he worked, had recognised him as the waiter who serviced the table she regularly used and had picked him up.

The explanations flashed with comforting swiftness through her mind, though the phrase 'picked him up' did have uncomfortable connotations, thanks to Ben.

About to call his name, wave to attract his attention, she was morbidly glad she hadn't when he strolled round to the other side of the car, opened the door at the driver's side and helped the glamorous creature out, holding her hands. And not letting them go.

She was gorgeous. In spiky high heels, she was three inches short of his six-one, the hem of her silky black dress way above her knees, the costly fabric clinging to every curve of her eye-popping body, her bare arms glinting with, it seemed, half a ton of gold bracelets.

Jewelled hands slid from his fingers and snaked up to cup his face as he leaned towards her, saying something, his lips curved in the teasing smile Lisa knew all too well. Her heart stopped beating as the woman leaned right into him, bestowing kisses on one lean hard cheek and then the other before tipping her glossy head back, laughing up at him then leading him by the hand into the exclusive interior of the jeweller's shop.

As her heart crashed back into action Lisa went hot all over, then cold. Icy cold. Her breathing erratic, she felt giddy. There had to be a perfectly feasible explanation for what she had just witnessed. Anything else was unthinkable. Her dazed brain tried to find one.

Instead it spitefully reminded her that classy customers didn't go around kissing their waiters unless there was a high degree of intimacy between them. Then it made her recall her disbelief and disappointment when, the day before, he'd told her he wouldn't be able to see her that morning.

'Things to do,' he'd said, 'but we'll be meeting up in the evening.'

If she'd been a couple of years younger she would have thrown a tantrum. As it was, she'd been very adult about being deprived of his company on what he thought was her last day in Spain. She had meant to surprise him when she returned after she'd persuaded her father that she was going to spend her entire gap year holed up in Marbella. So she'd merely nodded, 'See you then,' as if not seeing him during the day didn't bother her.

Did 'Things to do', mean finding her replacement? If so, he'd hit the jackpot!

She shivered, swallowing down the sick feeling inside her, hating herself for thinking such a thing was possible. She rubbed a clammy hand over her forehead. It was all Ben's fault. He had put the idea of charismatic, handsome young Spaniards sucking up to wealthy lone female holiday-makers for what they could get out of them into her head.

'Practising being a statue?' Sophie slipped an arm under hers. 'You should have seen that suit! It was gorgeous but Ben said black wouldn't suit me and I'd have to live and sleep in it for fifty years to get my money's worth!'

'Typical boring accountant!' Lisa sniped, still annoyed with him for making her doubt—if only for a moment—her darling, adorable Diego.

'Now you know you don't mean that,' Sophie scolded mildly as they slowly, arm in arm, approached the wide flight of steps that led up to the hotel foyer. 'You know he can't help being practical any more than you can help being a dreamer. And cheer up, do. Such a long face! I can't wait to meet your Diego. It looks like he's serious about you if he wants to see me and Ben—your minders—on your last night in Spain!' She gave Lisa's arm a tiny, reassuring squeeze. 'I've told Ben not to say a word out of place; you know how protective he is of you. And I told him Diego probably wants to ask his permission—in the absence of your father—to visit you in England.'

Or to get a free slap-up meal and plenty to drink as a final perk. Lisa hated the disloyal thought that sprang into her head just as much as she hated her inability to prevent it forming. And loathed Ben for putting it there in the first place. She ousted it firmly. Diego wasn't into fancy food and wines. He'd always come provisioned with a picnic lunch on their days together. Crusty bread, olives, fruit and bottled water. Simple, cheap and wholesome.

'We're a bit early,' Ben commented as he caught up with them on the steps, eyeing the impressive smoked glass revolving doors.

'So?' Sophie shrugged. 'So we sit in the foyer, cool down and people watch.' She pushed through the doors and Lisa followed, wishing the dragging minutes away, desperate to ask Diego what he'd been doing with that devastatingly beautiful woman, why he'd let her kiss him, why they'd disappeared into that jeweller's together. Desperate to hear an entirely acceptable explanation.

And time, perversely, seemed to pass even more slowly in the air-conditioned space. All cool marble floors and stately columns, chandeliers and hushed opulence. Seated in matching pale jade-green uphol-stered chairs around a low table, Lisa had her back to the main area but Sophie was avidly scanning the languid comings and goings of the wealthy patrons.

'Now, how's that for an invitation!' Sophie gig-gled. 'Over there, by Reception—turn round and take a look. It's his lucky day!'

Lisa obliged. Anything to pass time, to stop her friends from wondering what was wrong with her, why she was wearing what they'd teasingly describe as her Tragic Face.

Diego and that woman!

Lisa shuddered with disbelief and a pain that wrapped icy fingers round her heart. What she was seeing wiped out every beautiful moment of the last weeks. Her eyes filled with tears. She blinked them away. One of his hands rested on the sexy curve of her black-silk-clad hip while the other flipped the lid of a small jeweller's box closed and slotted it into his pocket. A gold signet ring to match the watch she had bought him? Had the fabulous dark-haired woman already kitted him out with the classy casuals he was wearing?

Stretching up on her high spiky heels, the owner of the scarlet sports car reached up to whisper in his ear. Whatever she said made him grin, that wide slashing grin that said he was happy. She knew it so well!

A slender gold-dripping arm was lifted, beringed fingers dangling a room key in invitation, just before she turned and swayed away towards the bank of lifts, sexual confidence in every movement of those endless legs and delectable body. Diego watched her, still grinning, then turned and sauntered over to Reception.

'Steamy, or what?' Sophie hissed and Lisa had to summon every ounce of will-power to make her face blank as she turned back to face the others.

Ben kept glancing impatiently at his watch and Lisa said, trying not to sound as if her world had just fallen into ugly little pieces, 'Let's go and find a drink; I'm sick of sitting here.'

She shot to her feet to stall any protests from Sophie who was clearly enjoying her people watching session. And Ben followed suit but insisted on finding the disco bar, even though Lisa was convinced that Diego wouldn't turn up. Why would he, when he obviously had better prospects lined up? The betrayal was so immense she couldn't bear to think about it and she couldn't drag the others away from this place without confessing that Ben had been right about Diego.

Tapas and heavy beat music. Lisa demanded champagne. She would have asked for something strong enough to dull the piercing ache that stabbed through her heart—whisky, maybe—but she knew Ben wouldn't oblige. Convent educated by nuns strict enough to make your eyes water, treated like a vaguely annoying house guest by a father who had never taken much interest in her when she was home, Ben still tended to regard her as a delicate flower in need of perpetual care and attention.

'Yes, let's let our hair down,' Sophie put in when she noticed Ben's eyes gravitate to the soft drinks dispenser. 'It is our last night.'

Lisa drained her glass in two long thirsty swallows and sneaked a refill when Ben wasn't looking. He was peering at his watch.

Already ten minutes after the appointed time. Diego wouldn't be coming. Lisa was psyching herself up to tell them why, admit that Ben had been right about her Spanish waiter, drinking her second glass like water to dull the pain when Ben, watching her put the empty glass down on the tiny table, grinned at her. 'Dance, Lise?'

She wanted to dance about as much as she wanted to sit in a barrel of hot tar but anything had to be better than sitting here, getting tipsy, wanting to cry and doing her best not to, wanting to get her hands on Diego and strangle him after asking him how he could be so cruel.

She took Ben's hands and got to her feet. The floor dipped and heaved so, instead of dancing opposite him like the other couples, she clung on to his shoulders and was grateful when he clamped his hands around her waist to steady her. He raised his voice above the level of the thumping music and lectured, 'Squiffy, Lise? That will teach you not to drink a glass of champagne in five seconds flat.'

Two glasses, did he but know it! A hysterical giggle, halfway to a sob, caught in her throat. About to bury her head on his wide shoulder and confess everything, she saw Diego arrive. He said something to his glamorous new girlfriend who gave him a conspiratorial wink before sashaying off to the bar.

How dared he? How could he? Lisa knew she was about to be horribly sick. But she mustn't! Her fingers dug into Ben's shoulders. The pain in her gut was unbearable. Think about something else.

Revenge.

Show him! Show him that she wasn't a silly little girl with the smell of the schoolroom still lingering around her; that she wasn't the type to cry for a month because she'd been conned by an expert.

He was now standing a scant three feet away, his beautiful eyes lightly hooded as he watched her. What was his intention? How did such guys operate? Would he tap her on the shoulder, wish her a pleasant flight tomorrow, then join his new prey at the bar?

Or would he simply ignore her?

Well, he wouldn't ignore this—without giving herself time to think—her misery was too great to allow coherent thought—she lifted her hands, pulled Ben's head down and kissed him as if she were auditioning for a part in a blue movie.

And while Ben was trying to recover, his face brick-red, she looked into Diego's suddenly ferocious black eyes and lashed out, 'Go away! You're cramping my style!' and watched him turn abruptly on his heel, his mouth hard, his shoulders rigid, as he walked over to his new woman. Lisa thrust her knuckles into her mouth and bit them. She wanted to run after him, take it all back, beg him to make everything all right again.

But she knew she couldn't. The fairy tale romance was over, the ecstatic days when two hearts had seemed to beat as one had turned into a sordid nightmare.

She turned to Ben, her face white. 'Take me home. He won't be coming. I can explain. But not now. Take me home!'

CHAPTER TWO

SOMEONE was watching her. Lisa could actually and physically feel the dark power of unknown eyes on her. Nothing like the vaguely patronising glances she had endured all evening from the great and the good who were here in this glamorous setting to support and, far more importantly, be seen to support a fashionable charity.

She could feel the intensity of that look as it bored between her silk-clad shoulder blades. Feel the watchful, coldly cutting contempt.

It was unsettling, eerie.

A cold shiver flickered through her.

It was all in her imagination. It had to be!

Annoyed with herself, with the weariness that was making her prey to fanciful imagery, she did her best to dismiss it. She was overtired, that was all. It was obviously time to make tracks.

In her capacity as Sub for the Social Editor, as well as her own recently acquired title of Fashion Editor, she had noted the names and titles of those with the highest profiles and details of what the women were wearing. Neil, her snapper, had the shots. She'd dig him out from wherever he'd sloped off to and tell him to call it a day.

She was so tired her legs were having difficulty bearing her slight weight. If things at *Lifestyle* went on the way they were she'd find herself subbing for every department and working right round the clock eight days a week. Experienced editors were leaving in droves. Rats deserting the sinking ship, as her father said every time a letter of resignation landed on his desk.

The noise of high society at play had given her a pounding headache and she couldn't wait to get back to the peace and quiet of her flat. Trouble was, she was a round peg in a square hole and knew it. Perhaps that was responsible for the manic sensation of despising eyes following her every movement. She was transposing her own inner feelings on to a non-existent entity.

Of course no one was watching her, despising her! Why on earth would they?

Slender in her understated black sheath dress, she straightened her wilting spine and headed for the lavish buffet. Found Neil, as she'd thought she would, scoffing canapés as if he hadn't eaten for a fortnight.

'I'm off,' she said, shaking her head at his offer of wine. 'We've got all we need.' Though whether the tumbling circulation figures would be boosted by the feature in next month's issue was highly debatable.

Neil's brown eyes roamed her pale face. 'You look bushed. You should find yourself a proper job!' He abandoned the food in favour of a glass of red wine. 'Hang on a sec and I'll give you a lift home. I take it I'm invited to your engagement bash tomorrow night?'

'Of course. The more the merrier.' Lisa smiled then, her first genuine smile of the evening. A comforting warmth flooded through her, swamping out the unsettling sensation of being watched.

Dear Ben. She'd do her best to make him a good wife. No grand passion for either of them and that, they'd decided, was actually a bonus. There would be no ephemeral highs or debilitating lows in their relationship. They had discussed it, accepted it—embraced it, even. A safe marriage, a secure one, affection and respect on both sides was all either of them wanted. She didn't know about Ben but she guessed he was too pragmatic to harbour strong emotions; and as for her, well, the events of five years ago had put her right off the concept of passionate love. She would never again feel so deeply about anyone as she once had for the Spaniard. Which was a blessing. The stronger the emotions, the greater the hurt.

Unnervingly, the feeling of being watched came back again with a vengeance. She hated it; it scared her. It swamped all those comforting thoughts of Ben and the life they planned together.

She was out of here, home to get some much needed rest before her imagination ran away with her completely! 'I'll pass on that lift.' It was an effort to speak. 'I'll grab a taxi. See you.'

It was an even greater effort to turn. And impossible to stem her gasp of shock as she saw him. Cold black eyes watching her.

Just as she remembered him but with breath-snagging changes—a haughty elegance that made him seem older than his twenty-seven years, his dark, perfectly crafted suit adding to the intimidating effect, oozing the cool self-assurance of a man wholly at ease with himself.

The handsome features were arrogantly cold, the black eyes narrowed and intense as they raked the pallor of her face.

'Diego!' His name escaped her on a shaky huff of breath and everything inside her descended into chaos as he acknowledged her with a cool, dismissive dip of his dark head, turned on the heels of his immaculate, hand-crafted black leather shoes and walked away from her through the bejewelled, designer-clad chattering masses as if he didn't care to sully himself by any verbal contact.

Sophie was sprawled out on the sitting room sofa in the shoe box flat they shared near Clapham Common, her attractive face suffused with an enviable inner radiance until she glanced up on Lisa's arrival. 'God, you look awful!' She hauled herself into a sitting position. 'What happened? Did Neil make another pass at you? Shall I phone Ben and get him to go round and slap him?'

Lisa's mouth twitched. As usual, Sophie was completely OTT and she needed that to help her get the main event of the evening—seeing the man she had once believed to be the love of her life again—in proper perspective.

'No, nothing like that, thank heavens!' She lobbed her handbag to the floor and draped herself on to the armchair with the dodgy springs. 'These high society charity bashes are a complete pain.'

'Entirely your own fault,' Sophie pointed out unsympathetically. 'You should never have let yourself be talked into joining the staff. They tried to twist my arm too, remember, but I stuck out for my chosen career in physiotherapy.'

Lisa shrugged and kicked off her shoes. It was old history. She'd never got to university. On her return from Spain, joining her father in the service flat near the magazine's head office, he'd asked her to re-think her future.

The publishing company was in difficulties. They were in the process of downsizing, selling off or closing down the stodgy middle-of-the-road titles, concentrating on the flagship *Lifestyle*. They all had to tighten their belts. It was all hands on deck and loads of other clichés. It was her duty to join the staff—at peanut wages—and do what she could to help turn things around.

At the time she'd been too emotionally exhausted to stand up for what she wanted, in no state to really know what she did want any more.

'I expect you're right.' Lisa removed the battery of pins that kept her long blonde hair smoothly away from her face and was debating whether to tell her old friend of her sighting of Diego Raffacani when she noticed the champagne bottle and two flutes set out on the low coffee table. An arched brow tilted in Sophie's direction.

Sophie blushed then giggled. 'James proposed this evening. And I accepted.'

Lethargy entirely forgotten, Lisa leapt to her feet to give her friend a bear hug, settling beside her on the sofa, tucking her legs beneath her. 'That's the best news I've heard for longer than I can remember!' Sophie had been dating the attractive young GP for over a year and was madly in love with him. 'I'm so happy for you! Tell me more!'

'He's joining a practice in the West Country—all lovely and rural.' She stretched over for the bottle. 'He got called out, would you believe—so you're going to have to celebrate with me. I don't want to get squiffy on my own!'

The cork ricocheted all round the small room. 'We're going to have to house hunt down there,' Sophie confided excitedly. 'I can just see myself as a country doctor's wife—I'll have loads of babies, join the WI, put my name down for the church flower rota and wear tweed skirts and those green quilted waistcoat things. And hats! With pheasant feathers!'

'An unlikely scenario, if ever I heard one.' Lisa grinned, accepting a flute of bubbles, firmly dismissing the wish that she could be as excited over her own wedding plans as being well out of order. She and Ben weren't into high romance and magical, ephemeral flights of excitement. Companionship, mutual support... 'So when's the big day?' She rapidly blanked out another wholly unwelcome pang of envy.

'Three months. I'll be a midsummer bride.' Her eyes opened very wide. 'We could have a double wedding! That would be fantastic. Ben could move in here with you. It's time he got his act together and left the parental home.'

It was a possibility, Lisa mused as she listened to Sophie chatter on about wedding dresses, bridesmaids and honeymoon destinations.

Ben had mentioned a wait of a year after the official engagement announcement tomorrow. And he shared the family home in Holland Park for purely practical reasons. The money saved on rent and his keep was accumulating nicely. But when Sophie moved out she, Lisa, would still have to find the rent for this flat, so it would be both practical and sensible for Ben to share it as her husband.

After the second glass of champagne Lisa forgot practicalities and seemingly out of nowhere found herself blurting, 'He was at the charity bash tonight. Just as I remembered him, yet different.'

'Who?' Sophie, in mid flow over guest lists, refilled their glasses.

'Diego.'

How easily the name she hadn't mentioned since that dreadful night slipped from her tongue. How easily the sound of it brought it all back—the heartache, the anger, the sheer gut-wrenching misery, all the emotions she'd believed long dead and buried.

Fuelled by Sophie's blank look and an unaccustomed rapid intake of alcohol, she offered, 'Spain. You remember. That holiday you and Ben insisted on giving me?'

'Of course!' Sophie banged the side of her head with the heel of her hand. 'The handsome waiter you thought you were madly in love with, the one who dumped you on that last night—the snake! What a small world—and what was he doing mixing with that lot?'

'I've absolutely no idea.' Lisa put her glass down on the table, not really knowing why she'd started this, struggling to work out why she needed to talk about him. A catharsis maybe? An emotional release, setting her free from the pain of betrayal that had been buried deep within her psyche.

'He looked a million dollars—well, let's say he looked as if he'd regard that amount as small change. I guess his social-climbing career must have taken off in a big way.'

She had to say it, punch what he was firmly into her brain, paint him black so that never again would she—would she what? Still remember, still yearn, still dream about him?

'Blooming gigolo!' Sophie snorted. 'I hope you gave him an earful!'

'We didn't speak.' Just a single word. His name spilling from her lips.

'Probably just as well,' Sophie conceded. 'In your place I'd have probably walloped him and caused huge embarrassment all round. Now, let's forget about the wretch and talk about something nice— what are you planning on wearing for your party? I thought I'd wear the green satin—James says it turns him on...'

The Holland Park house looked at its festive best. Most of the guests were waiting when Lisa arrived. Flowers everywhere, filling the elegant rooms with the perfume of spring. Until her mother's death her parents had lived in a house similar to this, a scant five-minute walk away. She'd been at boarding school, barely fourteen years old, when the dreadful news had come.

Only after the funeral when her father had coolly informed her that he would be selling the family home, moving into a flat suitable for a man on his own, had the full enormity of her loss hit her. Her mother had loved her and now the sweet, gentle woman, who'd been completely dominated by the much stronger personality of her husband, was gone. Without consciously thinking it out she had naively believed that she and her father would now draw closer together in their mutual grief. But he was distancing himself even further, if that were possible, a fact brought home when he told her, 'The Claytons suggested you spend your school holidays with them. You've always got on well with the twins and Ben and Sophie will be far better company for you than I ever could be.'

Lisa closed her eyes briefly, willing the unwanted sadness of memories to leave her. This was a happy occasion, for pity's sake! Finding a smile, she handed her wrap to a waiting maid, who must have been hired for the evening, and went to find Ben.

The rooms were just comfortably crowded. Even so, her progress was slow, waylaid as she was by friends, colleagues and perfect strangers—invited by the elder Claytons, she guessed—who offered congratulations.

Items of furniture had been pushed to the edges of the rooms or removed entirely and a sumptuous buffet had been laid out on the long dining room table, attended by smartly uniformed waiters. Ben and his parents were grouped by one of the tall windows, seemingly in private, earnest conversation. A conver-

sation which ended abruptly when Lisa reached Ben
and touched the sleeve of his dinner jacket to claim
his attention.

'Is something wrong?' she asked, her silky brows
drawing together. All three of them looked strangely
worried but Honor Clayton denied immediately, 'Of
course not! How nice you look, dear. Doesn't she,
Ben? Is Sophie with you? How like you two girls to
be late!'

'She's waiting for James. He's picking her up at
the flat and bringing her here. She wanted them to
arrive together.' Lisa tucked her hand beneath Ben's
arm. 'I gather you've heard her news?' She knew
Honor had. She'd been there when Sophie had put
the phone down after speaking to her mother, seen
the wry twist of her mobile mouth, the slight shrug
accompanying the upward roll of her eyes.

Honor lifted her heavy shoulders in a gesture of
resignation. 'Of course. But do I see her as the wife
of a humble country GP?' She did her best to smile.
'Time will tell, I suppose.'

'She's very happy,' Lisa said gently. Her future
mother-in-law was a snob but she meant well. She
would never forget the rather self-conscious hearti-
ness with which the older woman had received her
on those long ago school holidays after her mother's
death.

Young as she'd been at the time, she had instinctively known that Honor hadn't the words to console
the motherless child of her husband's business partner
and had resorted to booming exhortations: 'Now
twins, find something jolly to do with little Lisa—no

'slouching about indoors and getting bored and miserable! There are plenty of things to do in London. Cinemas, parks…'

Into the edgy silence that had fallen following her last statement—though why the family should be uneasy about a guy like James being admitted to their ranks, Lisa couldn't begin to fathom—she asked, 'Where's Father?'

Again the odd sensation of unease. Arthur Clayton glanced initially at his son and then his wife. He spoke for the first time since Lisa had joined them. 'He's with our top advertiser in the study. He shouldn't be long. It's not ideal—a private family celebration and all that. But apparently his time in the UK is extremely limited.'

'And we've been nattering away for far too long,' Honor said bracingly. 'Time to circulate. Come, Arthur! You can make your speech as soon as Lisa's father appears—and I presume he'll want to say a few words of his own to mark the occasion. Everyone here knows, of course, but we have to make the engagement official.' Smiling fixedly, she dragged her husband into the main reception rooms and Lisa asked, 'Something's wrong, isn't it, Ben? At first I thought your parents were unhappy about Sophie's wedding plans. But it's not that, is it?'

'Problems over advertising revenue,' he confessed, keeping his voice down, uneasy about being overheard. 'But nothing for you to worry about, old thing. Is that dress new? It looks as if it cost a fortune.' He changed the subject, not wanting to pursue it there, a slight frown pulling his brows together as glanced at the elegant creation she was wearing. A slip dress in pale coffee-tinted layered chiffon decorated with swirling patterns of toning sequins, the bodice held up by narrow sequined straps.

Her fingers slid away from his arm as she waited for the unwarranted spurt of anger to die down. He had always been ultra careful about money, she knew that and, far from irritating her, she had seen the character trait as vaguely amusing. She didn't expect him to change, of course she didn't, but it would have been nice if he'd complimented her on her appearance before niggling about how much the dress had cost.

Dismissing her reaction as absurd—they didn't have the type of relationship that demanded sloppy compliments—she gave him a slight smile of conspiracy. 'It's hired for the evening—but don't tell anyone!'

She accepted the reward of his grin, the warm hand that slid around her tiny waist, with a small curve of her lips, a dimpling cheek. But there was more. 'Don't patronise me, Ben. If we have money problems I should know about them.' Number crunching was his department, not hers; he didn't interfere with her editorial input, but this was different.

Ben hunched his shoulders uncomfortably and for a moment Lisa believed he wasn't going to enlighten her. Then he shot her a wry glance. 'We didn't want to worry you. After all, your father might talk him round.'

'Who?'

'The top guy at Trading International. He's threatening to withdraw the company's advertising.'

'And that's serious?'

'You bet your sweet life it is! High fashion leather wear, the *Los Clasicos* range of jewellery, wine, gourmet cheeses, luxury hotels and apartments worldwide. Withdraw that lot and we're up the creek without a paddle.'

'That bad.' Lisa sucked her lower lip between her teeth. Shouldn't she have seen this coming? What major advertiser would stick with a magazine with circulation figures in slow and seemingly unalterable decline? 'What chance is there of Father talking him around?'

Ben shrugged. 'God knows!' He drew her away from the window. 'I shouldn't have told you—don't let it spoil our evening, Lise. If everything goes pear-shaped and *Lifestyle* folds, we'll be OK. With my qualifications and your experience we'll find other work. Hold that thought while we mingle.'

Smiling, chatting, doing her best to act as if all was right with her world, Lisa felt hollow inside, her eyes straying continually to the study, where her father was trying to persuade a hard-nosed business mogul not to pull the plug. Many of the guests tonight were on the staff of *Lifestyle*. By this time next month they could all be out of work, her father and Arthur Clayton looking into the bleak face of failure.

How could Ben possibly expect her to dismiss all that from her mind and console herself with the thought that he and she would be OK?

He couldn't be that selfish, could he? She shook her head in instinctive negation. Of course not. He'd only said that in an effort to cheer her up, not wanting their special evening to be spoiled for her.

As she accepted a flute of champagne someone put into her hand she saw her father and her heart banged against her breastbone.

It was impossible to tell from his expression whether or not he'd been successful. As always, her father kept his feelings to himself.

Silence fell, as if the sheer presence of the man had commanded it. When he spoke, talking of his happiness at the further cementing of the relationship between the two families, the words went in one ear and straight out of the other. And when Ben slid the diamond hoop on her wedding finger her face ached from smiling and the growing applause, the chorus of Ooohs and Aaahs, the glasses raised in cheerful toasts, slid past her consciousness, leaving no ripples at all.

All she was aware of was her father's stern features, the rigid set of his shoulders. He was standing just beyond the chattering group surrounding her and Ben. One tight-jawed sideways inclination of his head had her murmuring her excuses and threading her way towards him.

Taking the champagne glass from her fingers he said, 'You are needed in the study.'

'Me?' Lisa noted the impatient tightening of his thin mouth at what he would see as her idiotic questioning of his perfectly plain statement and to deflect the sarcastic comeback she knew from experience was in store for her she hurriedly asked, 'How did it go? Ben told me there were problems.'

What could the big-shot want with her? An assurance that she had a pile of must-read, breathtakingly fascinating articles in her in-tray? The sort of stuff that would guarantee a huge upsurge in readership? As if! Anything remotely startling or contentious would be immediately scotched at editorial meetings by the partners.

Skirting her question, Gerald Pennington remarked coolly, 'As I said, you seem to be needed. As far as I can tell, all you can do is try not to make matters worse. It shouldn't take long and then you can enjoy the rest of your evening.'

Yeah, right, Lisa thought resignedly as she went to answer the summons. Her hand on the study door, she paused for a moment, psyching herself up to deliver the spiel of her life. If she could make the future editorial input sound really cutting edge maybe she could swing the balance in their favour. Though 'cutting edge' didn't gel with anodyne accounts of boring society gatherings or fashion articles aimed solely at the seriously wealthy.

If she messed up her father would never forgive her. Not for the first time she wondered why she bothered to try to please him, why she wanted what she had never had—the warmth of his approval.

Wrinkling her neat nose, pushing her relationship with her father to the back of her mind, she straightened her spine, plastered a smile on her face and walked into the study.

And he was there, leaning against the edge of Arthur Clayton's desk, his long, immaculately trousered legs crossed at the ankles, black eyes cold and hard, narrowed on her face.

Her stomach jumped in shock. 'There has to be a mistake.' Her voice sounded echoey through the buzzing in her ears. She took a step backwards, one hand outstretched as she felt for the door. Coming face to face with Diego Raffacani last night had been bad enough, stirring painful memories back to life. But here—posing as a major advertiser—

'No mistake, I assure you. Sit down, Miss Pennington.'

He edged fully upright, feet apart, long-fingered hands resting on narrow hips, the jacket of his suit parting to reveal a matching waistcoat smoothly clinging to his powerful torso. The picture of sartorial elegance—no sign of the slightly shabby, casually dressed and ultra laid-back Spanish lover who had broken her heart.

The formality of his address helped her to pull herself together. It had been a long time. Too long to allow memories to live, festering away in the dark, rarely visited regions of her mind. If he had changed—and she only had to look into that hard, classically handsome face to know that he had—then so had she.

She watched him take Arthur's swivel chair behind the desk, her heart thumping at the base of her throat. He still moved with the same inborn grace and she couldn't help remembering how she had adored watching him.

Lisa took the chair opposite and sat, her hands loosely clasped together in her lap. Seeking the defence of outward composure, her voice commendably calm, she asked, 'So you now work for Trading International?' reining back the snide comment that it was a big step up for a humble waiter. For everyone's sake she couldn't afford to rub him up the wrong way, even though she still longed to wring his neck for what he had done to her!

'Since my father's retirement, I am Trading International.' He placed his elbows on the arm rests of the chair he was using, steepling his fingers, the tips lightly touching his wide, sensual mouth, narrowed eyes watching the disbelief and then the obvious shock flicker across her face.

The face of an angel. The smile of a siren. And the sensitivity and morals of an alley cat!

She was more beautiful than he remembered, the delicate perfectly formed body still unbelievably sexy.

Five years ago he could have taken that body, it had been his for the asking. He narrowed his eyes, black gleaming through the enigmatic, heavy sweep of his lashes. Five years ago he had denied himself the sensual pleasure of the ultimate possession of the bewitching temptation of her. Now, one way or another, he was going to have her. Take what he wanted for as long as he wanted it, learn the secrets of her delectable body then toss her back where she belonged.

Dropping his hands, he leaned further back in the chair, idly pondering the pleasure of removing the clasp that maintained the sophisticated upsweep of her hair and seeing the silvery silky mass tumble down to the creamy skin of her naked shoulders and the gentle, inviting curve of her breasts.

His accent was slightly more pronounced than was usual, his tone smooth as cream, he imparted, 'I have a proposition to put to you, Miss Pennington...'

CHAPTER THREE

'YOU can't mean that!'

It was appalling, utterly crazy! As propositions went it was totally unbelievable—she must have misheard. Either that or Diego Raffacani had gone stark staring mad!

Her wildly churning emotions swept away the last fragile pretence of composure and Lisa pushed herself to her feet, then wholeheartedly wished she hadn't. Her body was trembling so badly she was swaying on her kitten heels. Her breath shortened and her inky-blue eyes widened, darkening to black as she watched him get to his own feet and move around the desk to stand beside her.

Her nostrils flared as she inhaled the scent of him, the heat of his body. Her mouth ran dry and her heart began to pound as she stared up into the lean powerful face, watched the sinfully sensual line of his mouth as he asserted, 'I meant every word,' and dropped back into the chair she had vacated as her knees finally buckled beneath her.

'Why?' Her voice croaked as her mind skittered back and forth over everything he'd said. It was impossible to keep a sensible or decisive thought in her head for more than a nanosecond.

'Because you owe me.' His teeth glinted white. 'Five years ago you were more than willing. But out of respect for your youth and what I then believed to be your inexperience I held back. You proved yourself unworthy of any man's respect.' His hard, beautiful face was rigid with contempt. 'I loved you but you threw it back in my face—that was my reward for my unselfish consideration. It is now time to pay your debt to me. Six months, or maybe even three, should be enough to get you out of my system.' There was a glint in his eyes, a twist to his mouth that sent a waterfall of ice skittering down her backbone as he drawled, 'If you prick a Spaniard's pride then you sit back and wait for the inevitable vengeance.'

Lisa shuddered as a knot of something tight and hot claimed her stomach. She raised her shaky hands to cover her mouth, fighting to come to terms with what he was demanding of her. Grappling to make some sense of the situation, she seized on one solid fact and accused, 'You said you were just a waiter. And all the time you were rotten rich! You lied!'

His mouth flat he turned away from her. 'I didn't lie to you. You simply made your own interpretation. You were happy to amuse yourself with what you saw as a no-account stud. You were at a loose end and looking for a cheap holiday romance. You wanted sex. I didn't oblige so you eased your frustration by sleeping with the man I now know to be Ben Clayton.'

'For pity's sake!' Hot colour swept her face. 'I was only dancing—how dare you?'

Resuming his seat on the opposite side of the desk, he slashed his hand imperiously, cutting off any further words of self-justification. 'You were crawling all over him, kissing him. And if you don't recall what you said to me, I do.'

Lisa cringed away from the savage glitter of his midnight eyes. Of course she remembered. She remembered every word they had ever said to each other. And, as for the last vile words she had ever spoken to him… Well, she had no defence, certainly none that he would listen to. Prick a Spaniard's pride…

'The offer's on the table,' he said with a snap in his voice that made Lisa feel as if she'd just been pronounced terminally ill. 'You live with me, lie with me, pleasure me until you bore me. In return I will not cancel my company's advertising and use one of your competitors. I will even buy in, bring in new blood to gloss up *Lifestyle*'s dull image, bring it back to success. If you refuse, as is your right, of course, then—' With a slight shrug of those impressive shoulders he allowed the threat to hang in the air—air that now seemed to be suffocatingly thick and heavy.

Lisa couldn't breathe. Her brain wasn't functioning as it should. She could only hear the words that had burned themselves into her mind—'lie with me, pleasure me'—and only wonder with helpless self-loathing at the way the responsive heat pooled between her thighs and a piercing awareness made her whole body tremble. After all this time he could still reach her. How many times had she told herself that he wasn't worth wasting a single thought on? Millions! And yet she only had to be near him—

'I've only just got engaged,' she pushed out between suddenly unbearably sensitised lips, knowing that he would regard the statement as irrelevant.

'Break it.'

He got to his feet, large, lean and intimidating. But so utterly gorgeous her mouth went dry as she looked at him, searching for the man he had been, the man she had fallen so helplessly in love with.

'I'll call on you tomorrow morning. Early. For your decision.'

Diego strode out of the room, closing the door behind him with an emphatic snap. Lisa shuddered, wrapping her arms around a frame that seemed about to shake itself to pieces. Bereft of his presence, the room felt cold and hollow. But then, she thought shakily, he had always generated an atmosphere so vital the air around him was charged with stinging sexual energy. Unfortunately nothing had changed in that respect.

She felt sick with nervous tension. What Diego had asked—demanded—of her was impossible! Quelling the uncomfortable knowledge that he need only have used a kind word, confessed, with regret, that he had been two-timing her all those years ago, then the impossible would have turned into the opposite, she gave herself a savage mental shake.

Like the arrogant swine he obviously was he was accusing her of being in the wrong. True, she had behaved atrociously. But she had been too young to cope with his betrayal with any dignity at all. She'd had too much to drink, been borderline hysterical...

'So, how did it go?'

Lisa nearly leapt out of her skin. She'd been

drowning in her own tortured thoughts and hadn't heard Ben enter. He placed a hand on her shoulder. 'I saw Señor Raffacani leave—now, why does that name ring a bell?' He hunched his shoulders, dismissing it as unimportant. 'Don't suppose you talked him out of withdrawing his advertising account with us?' he queried defeatedly. 'The Dads couldn't get anywhere with him, apparently.'

At the wry resignation in his tone Lisa scrambled to her feet. His brows peaked in enquiry. He carried no sizzling sexual aura around with him. Just stolid, quietly comfortable normality. For the first time ever she wanted to fling herself into his arms and beg him to save her from the old treacherous longings Diego had woken within her. But they didn't have the kind of passionate relationship that would make that possible. For years now she'd tried her best to appear coolly sophisticated, in control. He would hate it if she went to pieces.

Her eyes stung with tears and she bent to adjust a strap on one of her shoes to hide them. Dear practical, sensible Ben would be mortified if he thought she was even considering—for one split second—prostituting herself to save the magazine.

But she wasn't, was she? she adjured herself silently. No way! Not ever! She straightened, willing herself to appear normal. 'We can't talk about it now. Later. We can stay another half an hour then you can take me home and we'll discuss it.'

A look of incredulity spread across his pleasant features. 'The Dads will want to know what he said to you, you know they will. We can't just walk out of our own party. People will think it's odd, to say the least!'

'No, they won't.' Lisa sighed resignedly, pointing out, 'They'll think we're like all newly engaged couples—panting to be alone together.'

'Don't be crude, Lise—it doesn't suit you.' His frown deepened. 'And why all this cloak-and-dagger stuff? Either the guy's going to finish with us, or he isn't. A straight yes or no will do.'

Ignoring his reprimand—there had been no driven eagerness in their desire to be alone together so he wouldn't understand what she'd been getting at—she tucked her hand beneath his arm and explained heavily, 'It's not as simple as that. Raffacani made a proposition. With strings attached. I need to tell you about them, in private, before everything comes crashing down round our heads.'

That earned her a puzzled glance but stopped him arguing and they rejoined the party. And for the entire fifteen minutes or so while they mingled and chatted Lisa's head felt as though her brains had been scrambled, the hopelessness of the situation making her stomach cramp and her heart bang against her ribs.

She had it in her power to save her colleagues' jobs, ensure them a brighter, more secure future. One word from her would prevent Arthur Clayton and her father from looking into the bleak face of failure. She owed them something, didn't she?

A light hand on her shoulder had her tensing her spine but it was only Maggie Devonshire, the Picture Editor. 'Caught you at last!' Her kindly face beamed with pleasure. 'I'm so happy for both of you—two young things starting out together, that's so beautiful!' Ready tears misted her tired hazel eyes. 'Show me the ring.'

As Lisa put her hand into the older woman's her own eyes stung. Maggie was one of the best; she bore her troubles with fortitude and grace. Her son had suffered brain damage at birth; Billy had the mind of a four-year-old in a young man's body. Because Maggie's husband had walked out on her many years ago she coped on her own, delivering Billy to the day care centre on her way to work, collecting him on her way home. And never one self-pitying word. If she lost her job she would never find another. In her midfifties all she could hope for would be something low paid and menial—cleaning offices, maybe.

A clammy chill spread over every inch of her body as Maggie, her admiration of the diamond hoop voluble, released her hand and confided, 'It was lovely of you to invite me but I really must be off. Billy's spending the evening with a neighbour. I don't want to impose on her good nature. You never know, I might need her again. A handsome millionaire might ask me out to dinner!'

As she turned away with a light self-mocking laugh Lisa put an unsteady hand on Ben's arm. 'Let's go,' she murmured thickly.

Could she barter her body for the sake of the magazine and the jobs it provided? And why did thinking about exactly what that would entail send dark heat surging through her veins?

She would have to return Ben's ring. How hurt would he be?

Could a short affair—how long would it be before Diego decided she bored him?—leave her anything other than deeply humiliated?

Even more deeply humiliated than she felt right now, she decided, angry with herself as her skin began to flutter and her heartbeat quicken at the mere thought of making love with Diego Raffacani.

'You will do as he asks?'

Slumped on the sofa, the coffee she'd made cold on the table in front of him, Ben had listened to all she'd had to say in heavy silence. Now he waited for an answer to his question.

Lisa, pacing back and forth, driven by a gripping inner tension, couldn't find one and only came to an abrupt, shocked standstill when Ben stated flatly, 'You want to. You still want him. Five years ago you swore you were madly in love with him. Sophie and I thought it was teenage infatuation. None of us knew who he really was and I put the worst possible interpretation on the whole thing. I thought he was stringing you along for what he could wheedle out of you.' His shoulders hunched in a wry shrug. 'When he didn't turn up that night I assumed that was the end of it, but it obviously wasn't.'

'He did turn up,' Lisa admitted unhappily, wondering why Ben wasn't furiously angry over Raffacani's proposition, vowing to kill the other man if he ever came near her again. Wondering, too, why his pragmatic response didn't hurt her.

Gingerly, she perched on the edge of the sofa beside him. 'That last night he turned up with a totally fabulous woman—rich as Croesus, by the look of her.' She didn't mention those earlier sightings; there seemed little point. 'I was sick with jealousy. I wanted to pay him back. So I kissed you, remember?'

'Do I!' He shifted uncomfortably. 'You shocked me rigid. That sort of behaviour in a public place was so unlike you. It was months before I could feel really easy in your company after that.'

Ignoring the evidence of his streak of prudery, Lisa confessed, 'Diego was standing right behind us. I said something really vile to him. That's why he's put such impossible strings on his rescue package. To punish me. I hurt his precious pride.'

Ben swung his head round to look at her. Something about that look told her he was resigned to letting her go, she thought in a panic, knowing that even though they weren't in love with each other he represented emotional safety. 'Not impossible, surely? You obviously hurt more than his pride,' he said gently. 'Five years is a long time for a man like him to carry a torch.'

'Don't be ridiculous!' Lisa dismissed sharply. 'I told you—he wants to punish me.'

'And you want that kind of punishment?'

'Of course not!' she denied, her cheeks going hot at the thought of the kind of punishment Diego could dole out.

'Then why didn't you tell him straight out to sling his hook? Why feel you had to discuss the situation if you were unwilling to go along with it? And don't repeat all that other stuff—saving *Lifestyle* and all that. If it folds it wouldn't be the end of the world.

The Dads would sink into comfortable retirement and I could find other work in my field, no problem—'

'And what about the others? Their jobs would go. And Maggie—what would she do?' she interrupted heatedly, incensed that he should put her concerns down to hot air and a sneaky desire to do exactly what Diego had suggested.

'People are made redundant every day,' he pointed out. 'They don't starve to death. They manage. And, as for Maggie, she's nearing retirement age. She'll receive a worthwhile pension.'

He huffed out his breath and got slowly to his feet. 'Admit it, Lise. You'd be a willing sacrificial lamb. You and I never pretended to a grand passion. If, deep down, you're still in love with your Spaniard, then go to him. But be honest about it, don't dress it up as anything other than a need to be with him at any cost.' He put his hand on her shoulder and gave it an affectionate squeeze. 'Think about it and be honest with yourself. And, if you do decide to do as he asks, you have my blessing. I don't go for all that hearts and flowers stuff, you know that. Even so, I wouldn't want a wife who was secretly yearning for another man. It wouldn't work out.' He gave her a last gentle smile. 'Keep the ring as a symbol of my regard for you.'

Lisa never was sure how long she sat there after Ben walked out. She was frozen with shock. How easily he'd let her go. How pertinently he'd put his finger on the heart of the matter. She still wanted Diego, was still in love with the handsome, charismatic young Spaniard who had broken her heart all those years ago

She had never regarded herself as a fool, but she did now.

Wearily, she dragged herself to her room, unwilling to face Sophie. Closing the door behind her, she leant against it, pressing her fingertips to her throbbing temples.

Diego would demand her decision in the morning.

Would she be strong enough, sane enough, to tell him to get lost? Leave *Lifestyle* to its ignominious fate. As Ben had pointed out, it wouldn't be the end of the world if the magazine folded; saving it would just be her excuse to justify her actions. A willing lamb to the slaughter.

Or would she go with him, lie with him and pleasure him? Take what she could of him and bear the pain and shame when it was over? Could she resist the wicked temptation?

Exiting the taxi that had brought him from the central London hotel he was using, Diego instructed the driver to wait. This wouldn't take long.

Despite his immaculate cashmere overcoat he shivered, blamed the miserable English March weather and set his jaw grimly. The unprecedented stinging, shivery sensation deep inside him had nothing to do with her answer.

It was down to the depressing weather, the grey streets and buildings, so unlike his vibrant, colourful homeland that it made his very soul shake inside him.

Or he'd caught flu—that would explain the band of perspiration that was chilling on his forehead.

His long mouth quirked wryly. He was turning into a hypochondriac now!

Shrugging that distasteful notion aside, he pushed open the door of what had once been an elegant Regency townhouse and was now converted into tiny flats. The unfurnished hallway was bleak. Someone's bicycle leant against the banisters of the uncarpeted stairs. His heart jumped like a landed fish as he began to mount them but he refused to let the possibility of a negative answer to his proposition take root in his mind.

Five years ago, when he'd truly loved her, she'd been greedy for sex, he reminded himself forcefully. It had taken all his self-control to deny her. He'd known his own mind, wanted her as he'd never wanted another woman, but she'd been young and impressionable and he'd needed her to be as sure as he was. Out of respect for her he'd denied himself the rapture of making love with her, so on that last hateful night she'd set her sights on Clayton, dismissing the supposedly penniless waiter as if he were dirt beneath her dainty feet.

Greedy for sex then—nothing would have changed over the intervening years. No problem there, then. Giving in to his demands for retribution would be no hardship as far as she was concerned—with the added, not inconsiderable bonus of the financial security engendered by the renaissance of *Lifestyle*. That would be important to her. Despite her initial, and understandable, shocked protests she'd had all night to think her way round his proposition. Lisa Pennington would always come out in favour of what was best for her.

He had her! He was damn sure of it!

His hands flexed into fists as his body leapt and hardened at the remembrance of her eager, passionate responses all those years ago. How he'd adored her, the blind witchery of falling truly in love for the first time in his life making him romanticize her, believing her to be an angel sent from heaven for him alone.

Cretino!

He gritted his teeth. Reaching the second floor landing, standing before the door to the flat she occupied, his mind darkened with an unaccustomed flicker of self-doubt.

Clayton.

Had she already given the poor guy his marching orders? Was he even now nursing a broken heart? He remembered, all too clearly, exactly how he'd felt that night five years ago. That night and countless sleep-deprived others. The pang of sympathy shook him. Then, determinedly, he dismissed it.

Lisa Pennington was a hussy. In the long run he'd be doing Clayton a huge favour.

He lifted his hand and pressed the doorbell.

CHAPTER FOUR

HER usually welcome morning tea tasted vile. Lisa put the cup down on the cramped breakfast bar; she couldn't stomach another drop.

She hadn't slept, hadn't expected to. And how early was 'early'? she asked herself agitatedly.

At least Sophie wouldn't be around when Diego arrived for his answer. It had been well after three when she'd heard the other girl's exaggeratedly careful progress to her bedroom, so she'd probably sleep in until eleven or even later. It was Sunday, after all, the day they usually spent relaxing, tackling the most pressing chores, catching up on the gossip.

She moved to the sitting room, restless. There would be nothing usual about today.

Crunch time.

Her heart lurched.

Would she? Wouldn't she?

Tugging her aubergine-coloured sweatshirt down over her jeans-clad hips she gravitated to the mirror that hung over the blocked-off fireplace. What she saw did nothing for her self-assurance. She looked like a twelve-year old, she decided, sighing with disgust.

The baggy top swamped her delicate curves. She looked flat as a board. Her hair scraped back off her face, held into her nape with a limp ribbon, looked dull and lifeless. As did the dark-ringed eyes that stared mournfully back at her.

Quelling the sudden impulse to go and do something about the way she looked, she turned and paced back to the kitchen. She had no wish to impress him. In fact, if she looked like a rag doll who'd been left out in the rain he might decide he wanted nothing to do with her and take back that shameful proposition, take the decision she'd been wrestling with all through the wretched night right out of her hands.

Perhaps if she ate something the horrible shaky feeling inside her would go away. But one look at her cooling cup of tea made her feel queasy and she scotched the idea of trying to eat anything, jumping like a scalded cat when the doorbell rang.

He was here!

And she still hadn't decided what answer to give him. Ben had made her take a long hard look at her motivations for even considering, for a single second, Diego's blackmailing proposition. The conclusions she'd drawn had told her uncomfortable things about herself. She knew what she wanted but couldn't convince herself that it would be right for her or for Diego.

A shriller, more persistent ring of the doorbell had her scurrying out of the kitchen on legs that felt as insubstantial as cotton wool. The noise would wake Sophie and that would be disastrous. She was going to have to pick her words carefully when she told her best mate that her engagement to her beloved twin was off. And explain why. Ben wouldn't put himself through the humiliation of marrying a woman who, so he'd decided, was still in love with another man.

Her hands were shaking as she opened the door and met Diego's impatient dark eyes. Her breath locked in her lungs and a sharp, catching sensation invaded her stomach. No man had the right to be so out and out gorgeous, so—so shatteringly male. Once she had rejoiced in his masculine perfection—now the slightly older, tougher version scared her witless!

Wordlessly she stood aside to allow him to enter, noting the elegantly styled coat he wore with the care-less arrogance of a man born to such luxuries.

Once, in those long-ago days of heady loving, she had believed him penniless, scraping a meagre living while she had come from a well-heeled family. His imagined near poverty hadn't bothered her a jot; now his obvious wealth gave her the shivers. Her once adored Diego was a stranger.

Watching him slide his eyes dismissively over the mediocre contents of the sitting room, she searched for something, anything, of the charismatic young Spaniard who had claimed her loving heart for his own during that long, glorious summer five years ago. And found none. Nothing in his narrowed-eyed in-ventory of her appearance, not a flicker on that lean, hard face to remind her of the way he had once loved her.

Had seemed to love her, she reinforced tiredly. Nothing about the younger Diego Raffacani had been as it seemed. In that bleak moment she reached her final decision.

'Well?'

The harsh monosyllable made her stomach turn right over. Long fingers drew back his cuff as he consulted his watch in a gesture she was sure was meant to intimidate her into blurting an immediate answer. The watch he wore wasn't the one she had given him. That had been slim and gold; the one he wore now was dark and chunky. So why did that hurt so much?

Grabbing on to the last ragged remnants of her composure, she said thinly, 'It looks cold out. I'll make coffee.' Letting him know this was her home and she wasn't about to be intimidated into anything. But really, she silently admitted with painful honesty as she walked back into the tiny kitchen, it was to put off the time when she would sell the magazine down the river, lose her colleagues their jobs. It was on her conscience but, as Ben had said, it wouldn't be the end of the world.

The underlying reason for her delaying tactics, of course, was more visceral. Once she'd told him where to put his 'proposition' she would never see him again. It shouldn't hurt, shouldn't make her feel empty and only half alive. But it did.

As the door closed behind her Diego made a determined effort to get his head straight. Seeing her this morning, pale and waif-like, bereft of the classy dress she'd been wearing the night before, her milky skin innocent of make-up, he'd experienced a near savage need to take her out of her dreary surroundings, take her to the sun, pamper her, care for her, see those huge drowning inky-blue eyes come alive, laughing and vital. Smiling for him as once they had used to, making him feel like the luckiest man in the world.

How crazy could a man get?

Despite appearances, she was as vulnerable as an armoured tank. He wouldn't let a pang of misplaced compassion rob him of a vengeance he'd been planning ever since he'd learned that *Lifestyle* was sliding unstoppably downhill.

Lisa Pennington could look out for herself, could take a man's love and throw it back in his face. He had no doubt she'd frittered her time away at university, batting those fabulous lashes at any male student who took her fickle fancy.

Gritting his teeth against the invasive spurt of anger—not jealousy, of course not—he paced the narrow room. Had she finally decided to marry that poor sucker, Clayton, because she'd seen him as a meal ticket? Probably. By the look of her surroundings she wasn't doing well financially. Nepotism had undoubtedly been responsible for her finally ending up on the magazine.

Despite her engagement, she would ditch Clayton. Having sex without love wouldn't be a problem for her, would it? He knew her track record. Even at just turned eighteen she'd been greedy for it and when he'd behaved honorably, out of love and respect for her, she'd turned to the nearest male who would oblige. Clayton.

Grimacing, he cursed under his breath. Memories of that last night still haunted his dreams. But he had her now; he was sure of that.

Denying the restless energy that was forcing him

to pace the cheap carpet he sank down on to the armchair. He closed his eyes, savouring the victory to come, the final and definitive act of removing her from his system, leaving him free at last to find pleasure, satisfaction and contentment with a woman who would be worthy to share the rest of his life, give him children.

There was no way Lisa Pennington would turn his offer down. With *Lifestyle* thriving again—and he could make that happen—her doting daddy could be relied on for fat handouts and she wouldn't have to worry about working for her living.

He liked his coffee strong, black and sugarless, she remembered as she placed a single earthenware cup and saucer beside the cafetière on the tray. Her hands were shaking. Courage, she told herself as she pulled in a sharp breath and walked out of the kitchen. Get it over with.

Maybe she was being selfish in letting *Lifestyle* fold but, as Ben had pointed out, no one would starve. The staff would find other work and Maggie, her main concern, would receive a pension.

The other way, selling her body for Diego to use until he tired of the game, would do her irreparable damage. And she knew it wouldn't do Diego much good either. Oh, right now he thought revenge would taste sweet, she understood that. But somewhere behind the coldly handsome mask he wore there had to be vestiges of decency. He would end up hating himself for what he had done.

Or would he?

He hadn't behaved decently five years ago, had he? Thinking of the woman he'd been with turned her stomach. And yet he blamed her for what had happened and was hell-bent on punishing her!

She paused in the act of pushing the kitchen door open with her foot, her brow wrinkling. Was his conceit so great that he couldn't bear the idea of a mere woman—any woman—giving him the brush-off, even if he'd already found her replacement?

Or could there possibly be an innocent explanation for the way he and the glorious creature he'd been with had been behaving?

Unconsciously, she shook her head. She'd seen what she'd seen, hadn't she? Of course, with hindsight, knowing who he really was altered the scenario. He'd had no need to prey on wealthy women for what he hoped to get out of them financially.

It was a mess. Her head was a mess. She couldn't think straight!

A nudge of the door and she was through. Her breath caught in her throat and stuck there. He was sprawled out on the chair with the broken springs, his eyes closed. He looked so beautiful and strangely, heart-stoppingly vulnerable. In that moment it all came flooding back. All the depth of love she'd once felt for him. Still felt for him?

The fine hairs on the back of her neck prickled as her heart swelled inside her breast, a bitter-sweet pain that took her breath away. And then, as if her involuntary gasp had alerted him, his eyes snapped open. In that unguarded moment, as their eyes met, soul to soul, she stopped fighting the inevitable and said, a shake in her voice, 'I'll do what you want me to do,' because she finally knew she couldn't bear to turn her back on him, lose him, not again.

His eyes on the sudden flush of colour on her face, Diego snapped to his feet. A shock of something hot and insistent raced through his taut body. He had her! Had he ever doubted it? Hadn't he known that the lazy, avaricious minx would always take what she would see as the easy option?

The only acknowledgement he dared allow himself was a brief dip of his dark head. Reaching in an inner pocket, he produced a card and wrote rapidly on the back. 'My mobile number. The address of my hotel. Be there tomorrow evening at eight. We will discuss our itinerary over dinner.'

Insouciantly, he dropped the oblong of pasteboard down on the coffee tray she'd prepared and turned away, reminding himself fiercely that he was no longer the eager besotted fool he'd once been, firmly battening down the primal instinct to take her in his arms and claim some of what he was owed. Feel the sweetness of her lips beneath his own, feel the heated response of her beautiful body. That could wait. No need to display the eagerness that would give her power over him.

Watching him walk to the door, Lisa's eyes were pinned on his wide shoulders and the back of his gleaming dark, proudly held head. She wanted to call him back, tell him she loved him—she'd believed she'd stopped, but she now knew she hadn't—and explain exactly why she'd acted as she had all those years ago.

But his arrogance, his hardness, his curt, almost disdainful acceptance of her submission stopped her. As far as he was concerned this was his due, a hard man's revenge. He would view any protestations of love with cynical distaste.

As the door closed behind him she stuffed her fist between her teeth and felt the tears course hotly down her face.

Leaving the normal Monday morning editorial meeting, Lisa was waylaid by her father's secretary. 'He wants you in his office. Now. And don't worry.' She grinned, seeing the younger woman's distraught expression. 'He's actually in a really good mood today!'

It wasn't her father's mood that was worrying her, Lisa thought distractedly as she walked to his office. It was everything else!

Telling Sophie yesterday of the broken engagement had been a nightmare. Sure, she'd dressed it up as best she could, explaining that having seen Diego again she'd realised she still had feelings for him and marrying Ben wouldn't be fair or right. She'd skipped the blackmail bit simply because since talking to Ben she'd understood that saving the magazine was not what this was about; it was irrelevant.

And since Diego had walked out she'd been having second thoughts. Throughout the day she'd stared at his mobile number until the figures had danced and blurred in front of her eyes, trying to decide whether to phone him and tell him she'd changed her mind.

If he'd shown some emotion, smiled at her even, then she might be feeling differently. Had he taken her hands as he always had done in the past when they'd met, brushing his warm lips slowly over her knuckles before turning them over and placing a lingering kiss in each palm, she would have been ecstatic.

When she'd changed her mind and agreed to what he'd asked she'd felt that they'd only need to touch each other for all the old magic to swamp them both again. But he hadn't touched her and she'd been a real fool to think they could go back to the way it had been because none of it had been real.

So, as it was, she felt insulted. And stupid.

His mobile number was printed indelibly on her mind. She would phone the moment she returned to her office and, hopefully, disguise the hurt in her voice when she told him she'd changed her mind.

Her father was staring at the view from his window. He turned when she entered, a rare smile on his craggy face as he announced, 'You might as well clear your desk today. Under the circumstances there's no need for you to work out your notice. Raffacani has everything in hand.'

Already! 'You've spoken to him?' Lisa felt for the back of one of the chairs that fronted his massive desk.

'He's only just left. He demanded an emergency executive meeting first thing this morning.' His tone was admiring. 'Not one to let the grass grow under his feet. I like that; it augurs well.'

For whom? Lisa asked herself sinkingly as she sat and watched her father take his seat behind the desk, his cold eyes scanning her pale features as if seeing her, really seeing her, for the first time. 'I had no idea you knew each other. Raffacani explained everything. How the two of you met in Spain, how he lost sight of you, and your agreement to spend some time with him in Andalusia.'

He permitted himself another slight smile. 'Play your cards right, convince him you'd make the perfect wife, and you'll be set for life. Mind you, Arthur was cut up. Ben's had his nose knocked out of place—yours was probably the shortest engagement on record. But, as Raffacani's package includes heavy investment, restaffing at the higher editorial levels, he soon came round.' He gave her a judicious look. 'I imagine his rescue package is down to you. I don't want to know the ins and outs of it but I can tell you this—you've actually made up for not being the son I always wanted. Good girl!'

So she had finally won his approval! Lisa swallowed the threatened tears. But at what price? No use telling herself it didn't matter, that she had learned to live with his indifference. All her life she'd wanted his warmth, his approval, his recognition that, despite not being a son, she was flesh of his flesh, his child. It was a need she couldn't shake off in the time it took to take a breath. And to give him his due, she rationalised, he didn't know the true story.

The phone call to Diego wouldn't be made. Couldn't be made, not now. He'd withdraw his rescue package. Her father would blame her. He would hate her!

The little black dress was earning its keep again tonight, was Lisa's self-admittedly ridiculous thought as she paid the taxi off and entered the foyer of one of London's most exclusive hotels.

Anything to stop herself thinking of the humiliation that lay ahead.

She'd showered and dressed like an automaton, coiling her hair up on the back of her head and fixing seed pearl ear studs into her lobes. Sparing with her make-up, she surveyed the finished result with the bleak satisfaction of knowing she looked cool, remote and untouchable. Her Ice Maiden Look, Sophie would have joked if she hadn't still been too miffed with her to speak to her at all.

'I've always thought of you as my kid sister!' Sophie had muttered at her yesterday. 'And my best friend—and it was going to be lovely having you really in the family. And don't forget, it was me who brought Ben up to scratch. I told him to propose to you to keep us all a nice cosy family!'

Lisa hadn't known that. But it made sense. Ben would have thought long and hard about what his twin had suggested and come down on the side of expediency.

He hadn't a romantic or adventurous bone in his body and if he wanted to marry at some stage, start a family, it might as well be with his father's partner's daughter. They were very fond of each other, always had been, knew each other inside out. And after the regrettable interlude with the Spanish waiter she had never put a foot wrong, never even dated. What could be better?

She sighed deeply. She knew the way his mind

worked and could furnish the internal conversation he would have had with himself.

And now she had lost Sophie, her best friend, and Ben too. The three of them would never be as close again. And when Diego had finished with her, tossed her aside like a used tea bag, she would have nothing and no one.

No pride, no self-respect. No job. And all because she had suffered a moment of sheer madness, thinking she and Diego could recapture what they had once had. His attitude as he'd acknowledged her submission had brought her back to sanity.

His room number in her possession, she took one of the lifts. Stiffening her spine, she drew in a deep breath as it stopped at the floor she wanted. She would match his mood, beat for beat. If he could be hard and disdainful, then so could she, curt to the point of rudeness, too, if that was the way he was going to play it. Keeping emotional distance was her only self-defence. Second time around a broken heart would be impossible to mend.

His great wealth had bought him the power to wreak vengeance but that didn't mean he had to gain any kind of satisfaction from it. If he wanted her to have sex with him—making love didn't come near to describing what this sordid bargain was all about— then she would keep her side of the hellish agreement. But he wouldn't enjoy having sex with a lump of wooden indifference.

That would be her revenge!

CHAPTER FIVE

LISA was oblivious of the sheer opulence of Diego's hotel suite; she didn't move more than a foot inside the door he'd opened to her hesitant rap. She didn't smile and she certainly couldn't speak.

She didn't look at him and kept her eyes on the patch of the soft cream carpet directly in front of her feet. But she was so stingingly aware of him her head was swimming, her heart banging wildly against her breastbone. She kept her teeth clamped tightly together. If she relaxed the iron grip they would start chattering with nervous tension.

Was he expecting her to go to bed with him tonight? That would be her side of the bargain, wouldn't it? Her stomach jaunted off on a roller coaster ride of its own at that thought and she emitted a low driven groan.

'Don't slouch.' The lightly accented drawled injunction dragged her back to her senses. She was supposed to be giving him the same cold treatment he'd given her, wasn't she? Not acting like a cringing victim waiting for the axe to fall.

She raised her head slowly, injecting ice into her inky-blue eyes. It was a real struggle to maintain a haughty, indifferent expression when looking into that lean, darkly handsome face and admitted to herself that he would only have to say one kind word to have her melting like a snowflake on hot coals.

Inching her chin higher as the cool narrowed assessment of his beautiful eyes made her pulses jump, she ignored the butterflies in her stomach and drawled as flatly as she could manage, 'Father tells me you've already got your side of the bargain moving.' A slight, resigned shrug. Could she come across as sophisticated and blasé? She had no idea. But she'd give it a try.

'We may as well get my side of it over, too.'

That less than enthusiastic statement should let him know she'd put their arrangement firmly into the boring business category, emotions totally absent.

'If that's an invitation I'm not overwhelmed with joy.' His handsome mouth hardened. *Por Dios*, but she was as hard as nails! But he had expected that, hadn't he? She didn't turn a hair at the idea of using sex as a bargaining tool. Five years ago he'd fallen fathoms deep in love with a sweetly generous, innocent angel. What an act she'd put on!

She was still as lovely, though. Perhaps even more so. Her eyes could still make his soul shake, his body sting with desire. And he would have her, but on his terms, not hers. He would make her beg...

Taking a pace back, he made a small gesture to a table set in front of an enormous window that gave a glittering view of the vibrant, brilliantly lit city. 'I would prefer our relationship to be civilised, so we start as we mean to go on,' he imparted levelly. 'To that end, dinner is already ordered and while we eat we will discuss our future arrangements.'

Ending that cool statement of intent, Diego placed a hand lightly on the small of her back and encouraged her in the direction of the elegantly laid table as the trolley from Room Service arrived, dexterously handled by an impassive-faced waiter.

Lisa was wearing the dress she had worn to the charity function, he recognised. Sexy. Silk. An understated design that hinted tantalisingly at the delicate curves and intriguing hollows of her divine body. He could feel the warmth of her under his palm, the way the silk slid against her body as she moved, and his groin ached fiercely. Had they been alone he would have dragged her into his arms...

And spoiled his plan to make her be the one to beg, go down on her knees and beg until she had no breath left and then, and only then...

The moral was, don't touch. Not yet. Removing his hand smartly, he stepped ahead and held out a chair for her and took his seat opposite, furious that his control over his libido was worse than shaky where she was concerned.

Watching, as stony-faced as she could get considering how his touch had affected her, Lisa envied his urbanity as he approved the wine he had ordered to go with whatever it was the waiter had put on her plate. Diego was clothed in a pale grey suit that shouted class, a white shirt with faint pale grey stripes that accentuated the dusky olive tones of his skin and the permanent five o'clock shadow that had always made her want to run her fingers over the firm set of his jaw.

Still did! Lifting her fork as the waiter withdrew

from the suite—she wasn't remotely hungry but pushing the no doubt delicious food around gave her something to do—she challenged, 'I believe you want to discuss my temporary status as your mistress.' And hoped the business-like tone made him feel as wanted and desirable as a giant black slug in a plate of salad.

But the only effect was a vague upward drift of one slanting black brow, a dismissive, 'The status of mistress is way above what I have in mind for you.' He lifted his wine glass. 'Can I take it that you have a current passport?'

That put-down cut her up. He really did despise her, didn't he? But her voice was sharp as broken glass as she answered his question. 'Of course. Why?'

'We leave for one of my homes in Spain at the end of the week. In the meantime I'll be tied up with lawyers and the ins and outs of putting my man in place to drag *Lifestyle* into the twenty-first century. We won't meet again until early on Friday morning when I pick you up on my way to the airport.'

Lisa shouldn't be poleaxed by that announcement but she was. During that morning's interview with her father she'd been so taken aback by the speed of Diego's movements, the way he'd spiked her guns when it came to changing her mind because she couldn't bear to lose what she'd never had before— her father's approval—she hadn't absorbed the import of his '…your agreement to spend some time with him in Andalusia'. The fact that he'd told her to clear her desk hadn't cut much ice, either. If clued-up editors were to be brought in no one would want her around because she'd be like a fish out of water.

Now her stomach performed one of the spectacular lurches that were becoming all too frequent since coming into contact with Diego Raffacani again. Here in chilly, early spring London she could maintain an indifferent façade. Just. And with supreme difficulty. But back in Spain with him, where it had all started, she wouldn't be able to survive the bitter-sweet pain of it.

Laying down her fork, her eyes clashed with his. It took only a moment to subdue her twanging vocal cords and remark tautly, 'Correct me if I'm wrong, but you said nothing to me about my going to Spain. I thought—'

'Thought a couple of quickies while I'm here in England would pay off the debt,' Diego interrupted drily, his long fingers tightening around the delicate stem of his wine glass. 'Not so. When you recompense me for the way you behaved five years ago it will be at a place and time of my choosing.'

And the little minx wouldn't be acting as though making love with him was a mundane and necessary task like sorting the washing. She would be as willing and eager as she had been five years ago, her sweet lips gasping for the fulfilment he had withheld out of genuine love for her. And when she was on the point of disintegrating he would take her, burn the frustration and anger that had been his private demon for far too long right out of his system. And dump her. Let her know for once what rejection really felt like.

Noting the sudden dark colour that stained his slashing cheekbones, the dark glitter of his eyes beneath the thick fringe of lashes, Lisa tried to block the images of her being used as a cheap sex toy right out of her mind and decided that the time had come to put the record straight. Then, surely, he would re-consider? And let her go. Maybe with an apology and a contrite promise not to withdraw his offer of in-vestment in the magazine.

But did she really want that? the part of her she privately despised commented edgily. Didn't she still hunger for him, despite pretending the opposite? Didn't some perverse and childish hope prod her into fantasising about him falling in love with her? Really falling in love this time, not whiling his spare time away with a silly little teenager, telling her what he thought she wanted to hear because it amused him to see her fall headlong under his spell. Not meaning a single word of it because he spent his evenings, not working as he'd said, but making whoopee with a gorgeous, sophisticated female from his own exalted class who really knew how to please her man.

No, she owed it to herself to wriggle out of his wicked bargain if she possibly could. Owed it to what was left of her self-control and dignity, she vowed, fervently hoping she believed herself. Clutching the bowl of her so far ignored wine glass, she questioned, 'Don't you think we should talk about it?'

The slight upwards drift of one dark brow was the only expression on that lean and dangerously hand-some face. 'I believe we have been.'

'No, not that. Not the terms and conditions,' she dismissed thickly, horribly conscious of the hot colour creeping over her skin as the reminder of exactly what he expected of her jumped into her mind with the force of a nuclear explosion. 'But why you're still so angry with me over what happened that night all those years ago. It's a long time to bear a grudge, Diego.' She spoke softly, willing him to listen, to at least understand that the blame wasn't hers entirely. 'I know I acted like a total idiot, but—'

'*Basta!* I have no wish to listen to the tissue of lies you've had time to dream up!' Black eyes glittered with savage contempt. 'You may look like an angel but you lie like the devil!' he informed her with deadly intensity. 'I saw what I saw, I heard what I heard—*perdición*!' He got to his feet, pushing back his chair, looming over her.

Lisa flinched, cut to the heart that he should hate her quite that much. Her eyes swam with unwanted tears as he reminded more levelly, 'The past is a distant country. Forget it. Concentrate on the future, on paying your dues, and, when that is done, it too can be forgotten.'

And she would be forgotten. Just like that! Lisa, too, sprang to her feet. He was cruel. Hard. And the hope that their relationship could develop into a mirror image of what it had been bit the dust. How could she have been so stupid to have fantasised that it might? He had changed out of all recognition.

Facing him, her inky eyes swimming as they collided with his, she acknowledged that he might not have changed at all. Had he always been this callous? The loving front of five years ago just that. A front, assumed for his own careless amusement?

'I hate you!' she spat with driven vehemence.

'Ah! That is good.' A slow, deliberate stride

brought him round the table to her quivering side, the slightest of smiles curving a mouth that was far too kissable for her own good. Two strong and almost painfully gentle hands cupped her face, setting up a chain reaction that made her tremble with far more than outraged anger and deep hurt. 'Any strong emotion is preferable to indifference, is it not?' Then he did what she'd been secretly hoping and dreading in equal measure.

He kissed her.

The effect of that wide sensual mouth on hers set off a volcanic explosion deep inside her, pulsing the ripples of aftershock right through every nerve and vein in her body. Had her matching his hungry urgency with a driven desperation that shattered her into launching herself against his powerful frame, looping her arms around his neck, her avid fingers tangling in the soft midnight darkness of his hair.

He tasted of hot male passion and she couldn't get enough of him. He was all she'd ever wanted, the only man she'd ever loved. Her body melted into him, her breasts peaking with open invitation, her lips matching his ravaging assault.

Her lips were still tingling, her knees shamefully shaky, when a short time later Diego handed her into the taxi he'd summoned to take her home. Her mind was still sickened by the ease with which he'd held her away from him when her response had threatened to get way out of hand. His coolly delivered, almost uninvolved comment that it was time she went home and a reminder that he'd call for her on Friday morning around seven-thirty was still ringing in ears that burned with shame. All capped off with the flatly delivered threat that he'd find her if she should be misguided enough to flee. It was a timely reminder of the humiliation he would dole out if she ever again was unguarded enough to demonstrate how she hungered for him.

An hour later she fell into bed still in a state of deep shock. Mostly induced by what her own behaviour had revealed about her. Diego Raffacani was a cruel blackmailing louse. So arrogantly sure of himself that he out and out refused to listen to a word she had to say in her own defence. He'd called her a liar and that alone should have put her off him for several lifetimes. But no, oh no! What had she gone and done? Shown him how needy she was, eager and straining against him, possessed by a frantic hunger for him.

She was still in love with him. She sobbed into her pillow. He was the only man she had ever loved. Far from being the promiscuous tramp of his imagining, she was still a virgin. Ben, the only other man she'd ever been involved with, had never inspired this wild yearning.

There had to be something drastically wrong with her if she could be in love with a man who was entirely without scruples or conscience. A man who intended to take her to his bed as an act of revenge, who had convinced himself that the blame for the way she'd insulted his precious pride, when she'd been too young to realise what she was doing, was hers entirely.

The immediate future looked bleaker than the lunar landscape. Lisa had no idea how she would survive it.

His car, a low sporty model, was waiting at the airport, delivered there by his Spanish minions, Lisa deduced grumpily, her spiky mood the legacy of a mostly sleepless night as she'd tried and failed to come to terms with what she was letting herself in for, the alarm clock ringing spitefully just as she had been finally dropping off. Her mood was not lightened by the sight of Diego arriving precisely at seven-thirty.

'Ready?' he enquired briskly, looking as if he'd had the benefit of a full eight hours sleep, a revitalising shower and a hearty breakfast.

'I haven't finished packing.' A lie. She hadn't started. Ever since that evening at his hotel suite she'd been hoping that something would happen to make him call this whole thing off. But he hadn't miraculously lost his memory and she hadn't broken a leg!

'Then I suggest you get on with it. The taxi is waiting. If you are always this disorganised I'm amazed that you held down any sort of job at all, even one manufactured by a doting father.'

Her irritation level rose a thousand-fold. What did he know? 'Dad doesn't dote!' she snapped and stamped into her bedroom to drag things out of drawers and cupboards and stuff them into a small suitcase.

Ever since then he'd been irritating the life out of her. Throughout the ride to the airport, the business of checking in and the flight itself he had been coolly polite and dutifully attentive. As if she were a virtual stranger he had found himself dragooned into escorting, when in harsh reality she was the woman he was callously blackmailing into becoming his temporary mistress.

Sub-mistress, she amended on a spurt of irrational anger. Though why she should object to the irrelevant point of being regarded as too low to be afforded even the slightly denigrating title of mistress only went to show what a muddle her mind was in. Whereas he, drat it, was calm and collected, single-minded, determined on one thing only—to take her to his bed and punish her for damaging his precious pride.

And then get rid of her.

Now, with the airport an hour's drive behind them, Diego asked, 'What did you mean when you said your father didn't dote?'

Lisa dragged her eyes from the alarmingly twisty narrow road that snaked up into the mountains and fastened her gaze on his impressively chiselled profile. It was the first personal remark he'd made since they'd entered the waiting taxi back in London.

Shrugging slightly, she returned her attention to the view. Now and then she caught the glitter of the sea and, unlike London, the air cocooned her in welcome warmth. 'I meant precisely what I said.' Her relationship with her father was something she wasn't prepared to discuss and, turning the subject, she asked, 'So where are we going? How much further?'

Diego's shoulders tautened as he handled the tortuous hairpin bends with practised ease. Who the hell did she think she was kidding? She would have been spoiled rotten from birth. What father worth the name wouldn't slavishly lavish all his attention on such an outwardly bewitching little charmer, even more so after she'd been left motherless at a relatively tender age?

A memory from five years ago, as clear as all the myriad others that had haunted him for so long, assaulted him. The day he found he'd lost his watch. She'd held hers out to him. The thing would have cost a small fortune. And when he'd commented she'd simply shrugged. 'My father's birthday gift', as if it were a mere trinket.

The spoiled brat had been given a responsible job on the magazine staff even though the whole enterprise was going pear-shaped and what had been desperately needed was an experienced editor. The fabulous dress she'd been wearing at her engagement party must have cost another small fortune, the wherewithal doubtless supplied by doting daddy.

And that sparked a different train of thought.

'How did Ben take the broken engagement?' He'd noticed the absence of the diamond hoop. He noticed every damn thing about her. He remembered his own desperate pain when the spoiled brat had as good as told him to shove off and wondered, guiltily, if Ben Clayton had felt the same, wondered if his initial thought, that he'd actually been doing the poor sucker a favour, still held water.

'That's not really any of your business, is it?' Lisa dismissed edgily. How could she tell him that hers and Ben's would have been a passionless marriage, based on nothing more exciting than long-standing affection and mutual respect? That Ben had been wise enough to predict that even that kind of marriage couldn't survive if one partner were still in thrall to a long-ago lost love?

'And you haven't answered my question,' she reminded him snappily. 'I have a right to know where you're taking me.'

Fully expecting him to tell her she had no rights at all and to continue prodding about her broken engagement—did the cruel streak in him want to hear that Ben had been devastated, suicidal?—she was stunned when he answered equably, 'To my favourite hideout. It used to be a monastery. The family rarely uses it these days. The area isn't frequented by hordes of tourists; its beauty and tranquillity remain intact. Unlike Marbella,' he added drily. 'You will find no beautiful people, no glitzy shops, fabulous yachts or smart hotels to claim your attention. You will give it all to pleasing me.'

She should have kept her mouth shut, Lisa recognised sickly. Whatever she said he managed to come back with something designed to put her down.

The next days or weeks promised to be a nightmare of humiliation and pain, she acknowledged, the hauntingly beautiful landscape lost in a sudden blur of stingingly hot tears.

CHAPTER SIX

LISA couldn't fault the beauty and comfort of Diego's preferred hideout. Built centuries ago of mellow golden stone, the former monastery commanded an impressive view over fertile valleys, thickly wooded slopes and tantalising glimpses of the sparkling blue sea between towering mountain crags.

She couldn't fault Diego's behaviour, either, she told herself edgily as she paced the flagged stone terrace in the soft dawn light.

She almost wished she could.

She would have better understood where he was coming from if he'd done as she had expected and taken her to his bed that first night. She might not have liked it—she might have liked it far too much, she corrected with painful honesty as her restless feet brought her to the end of the terrace—but at least she would have understood it.

What she was at a loss to puzzle out was why she'd been given her own suite of rooms. Beautiful, restful rooms that he had shown no inclination to visit. Why, during her nearly four whole days here now, he'd done nothing more alarming than treat her as a house guest. He had joined her for meals, during which his conversation had entranced her against her will— witty, perceptive and at times, hardest of all to bear, cool and painfully impersonal. And all the while he had seemed to look straight through her, not really seeing her at all.

Between meals he'd taken himself off to his study, explaining courteously that he had much work to get through, leaving her to her own devices. Her own thoughts.

Her hands tightened on the warm stone of the balustrade. She knew what he had planned for her, what she was expected to be. So what was he waiting for? Why was he behaving like a great jungle cat, stalking a prey he was not yet hungry for yet never really letting it out of his sight?

Her whole body was tingling with sexual tension, her mind edgy, her nerve-ends as jumpy as a flea on a griddle.

'Quite the early bird. Couldn't you sleep?'

The unexpected soft laid-back drawl made the hairs on the back of her neck stand to attention, made her heart leap to her throat and jump about like a frightened trapped animal.

Lean hands on her shoulders turned her to face him. As always he looked spectacular, she noted with feverish tension. Dressed this morning in stone-coloured chinos with an olive-green lawn shirt tucked into his narrow waistline, his shatteringly masculine features were bland, but instead of looking through her as usual his sultry black-fringed eyes were making a slow, devastating inventory of her quivering frame.

This close he was dynamite, always had been. Lisa tried to smother an inrush of sobbing breath as she felt the betrayal of her peaking breasts beneath the checked flannelette shirt she was wearing over an old pair of jeans. His eyes on her body felt like a physical caress. A caress he was denying her.

Because he'd changed his mind and he no longer wanted to touch her?

A hand lifted from her shoulder in answer to the unspoken question that glittered in her eyes, long tanned fingers brushing the fall of her hair away from her face. The backs of his fingers lingered slightly, seductively, scorching her skin.

She was hot all over, so hot, burning up, fiery heat pooling between her thighs, making her legs shake. She was trying to make her face as expressionless as a lump of stone but, in spite of the effort she was making, could he guess what he did to her? He slowly dropped both hands and remarked lightly, 'Breakfast awaits. Pilar saw you were up and about and thought we might prefer to eat in the courtyard. Come.'

Her unfortunately mesmerised eyes on the length of his legs, on his seemingly indolent stride as he led the way, Lisa felt on the point of collapse when she took her seat in the central courtyard, shaded at this time of the morning from the rapidly increasing heat of the sun.

White doves called sleepily from the trees that overhung the high stone walls and the scent of a myriad flowers perfumed the air. In any other circumstances she would have revelled in this much perfection.

Ever the attentive host, Diego poured juice for her and passed her the fruit bowl. Lisa, selecting a peach she had no appetite for, tried not to scream.

If today were to follow the pattern of all the others

since she'd been here he would make light conversation while they ate, suggest a walk she might like to take before the real heat of the day, and then excuse himself politely and spend his time shut away in his study.

And she would play the part she had assigned herself, give a bored, dismissive shrug, as if she couldn't care less, and wonder how long she could keep up the act of total indifference.

Asking why he was spending as little time as possible with her was quite out of the question. It would let him know she was hankering for his attention. Desperate for it, even. His twenty-four-hour-a-day intimate attention! It was the reason he'd brought her here in the first place, wasn't it? she thought wildly to excuse her shameless longing to be held in his arms, to have his mouth create havoc with hers, to…

'We'll drive down into Marbella this morning,' Diego imparted as he laid his napkin down. 'You appear to have packed nothing but heavy jeans and shirts.' A censorious glance at the perspiring pallor of her overheated face. 'Suitable for doing the weekend chores in chilly London but not for this climate, this ambience.' He poured them both a second cup of coffee as he stated, 'I'll buy you the right clothes.'

Too dazed by his intention to spend time with her just when she'd been agonising over his four day long disinclination to do any such thing to say a word, Lisa struggled to think of a single thing to say.

Was this the beginning?

Her heart began to race, her breathing going haywire, colour flooding her face. Obviously, the workaday stuff she'd shoved so carelessly into her suitcase wasn't turning him on. What did he have in mind? Pelmet-sized mini-skirts, black fishnet stockings, six-inch heels and minute crop tops decorated with purple sequins?

Hadn't he as good as said he'd treat her like a hooker, the title of temporary mistress being far too good for her in his haughty opinion? Was he expecting her to dress like one too?

The idea was so absurd she didn't know whether to laugh or to cry, just stared at him instead, her pale cheeks blooming with pink, aware that her mouth had dropped open but unable to do anything about it.

Replacing his coffee cup on its saucer with a clatter, Diego got to his feet, noting her wide-eyed, open-mouthed look of pleasure with grim distaste.

Greed.

It was the first genuine emotion she'd displayed since they'd arrived here. She'd looked edgy or bored during their carefully rationed meetings. He'd only had to mention buying her a few new outfits to have her lighting up like a Christmas tree. But what else had he expected? he asked himself tersely before telling her flatly, 'Manuel's bringing the car round. I'll see you on the forecourt in ten minutes.'

Ten minutes to get her racing heartbeat back to normal, to calm herself sufficiently to face what appeared to be the next stage of the game.

Because he was playing games, she told herself agitatedly as she exchanged the checked shirt for a marginally more attractive ribbed cotton sweater in a shade of deep raspberry pink and hurriedly applied a toning lipstick. What else could explain the way he'd left her largely to her own devices, never once mentioning the real reason for her being here, much less acting on it?

Today he intended to spend time with her. Today he'd touched her, his hands on her shoulders, his fingers brushing the skin of her cheek as he'd pushed her hair back from her face. The second stage of the game was obviously about to begin.

Which didn't do her pulse rate any good at all, she recognised as she scraped her hair back in a ponytail, acknowledging that she, too, was playing games. Affecting indifference, boredom even, was all very well but she had the sinking feeling that she wouldn't be able to keep it up for much longer because he was turning out to be a real expert when it came to winding her up.

A fact amply demonstrated by the easy way he talked to her as he drove, giving her a potted history of the former monastery, explaining that his grandfather had bought it many years ago, had it restored by experts and turned into a tasteful home without losing any of the atmosphere. 'But my parents rarely use it; they find it far too isolated. If I didn't love it, come here whenever I can, keep on a skeleton staff, it would fall back into dereliction.'

As he talked his features softened, coming to vibrant life. Lisa swallowed thickly, averting her eyes from the intimate warmth of the sideways glittering glance he bestowed on her.

This was Diego as she remembered him. The Diego she had fallen in love with. Charming, vital, fascinating. And dangerous, she reminded herself on a tingling *frisson* of unstoppable sexual excitement.

The narrow road was descending through a thick belt of woodland, the air just slightly cooler, which hopefully went some way towards excusing the shiver that racketed through her.

'Scared?' he asked softly, his eyes knowing as he glanced at her, his long mouth curving with what looked suspiciously like male satisfaction as he gave his concentration back to the twisting tarmac.

Lisa knew what he was talking about. But no way would she admit to being affected in any way at all by his far more intimate, softer attitude. 'Not at all,' she murmured drily. 'You drive well, so why should I be scared? Just chilly, that's all.'

His open grin told her he didn't believe a word of it. Even beneath the trees the cooler air was still soft and warm. No one could possibly feel chilly!

'But of course,' he murmured tauntingly. 'What else could make you shudder to the soles of your pretty little feet?'

It was time she straightened things out between them, put a stop to this cat and mouse game of his, Lisa fulminated inwardly. Against all common sense she might still secretly and hopelessly love the wretch but she hated the way he seemed to be manipulating her.

As they approached the outskirts of the coastal playground of the seriously wealthy she told him, 'I wasn't thinking straight when I packed. I'd forgotten the huge difference in climate, even at this time of year. My fault,' she admitted stiffly, wishing she hadn't been in such a contrary, ill-tempered mood when she'd thrown just any old thing into her suitcase. 'And I'll buy my own clothes, thanks all the same.'

A couple of cotton skirts and tops would be as much as she could afford. Marbella wasn't the place to come if you were shopping on a budget, she decided wryly, thinking of her tiny bank balance and the fact that she had no job to go back to.

'I wouldn't hear of it,' Diego stated firmly as he found a parking spot. Turning to her, he slid an arm along the back of her seat, deft fingers finding the narrow ribbon that pulled her hair starkly back off her face and removing it. His voice was now a soft velvet purr, making her tremble. 'At the risk of sounding incredibly vulgar, I can afford it. Particularly as the doting daddy isn't with us to pick up your bills.'

'Don't!' Lisa snapped, hot colour flooding her cheeks. The ribbon was disappearing into his trouser pockets; to try to take it back would result in an unseemly tussle which she, of course, would lose. And she'd had more than enough of his mind games. 'If you mention my supposedly doting father one more time I'll—I'll hit you!'

Hard fingers fastened around her wrist as she attempted to scramble out of the car, pulling her back to face him. One ebony brow arched as he murmured, 'Hit me and I'll retaliate.' His eyes dropped to the kissable, trembling pout of her mouth and lingered there. 'But not with physical violence. There are other, pleasanter ways of subduing a woman.'

A stab of satisfaction forked its lightning way

through his body. He'd left her to stew for four whole days and nights, keeping her on an emotional knife-edge. Her veneer of indifference was cracking up and he was going to make it crumble to dust.

A slow smile curved his mouth as his words brought the frost back into those huge inky-blue eyes, her lips tightening in mute rebuttal. She was fighting her corner with every atom of her will-power but before too long he would have her as weak as a kitten, begging him to end the impasse, clinging to him, her body on fire for him and only him.

As his loins tightened Diego wiped out that train of thought and slowly released her wrist, frowning at the band of reddened skin. 'A long cold drink's in order before we hit the shops.'

And he would foot the bill for clothes that would be more comfortable and do justice to her ethereal loveliness, in spite of her unexpected refusal to let him. A refusal that was surely just lip-service to the conventions? Easily forgotten in the face of the slightest pressure?

Pondering that, he joined her on the pavement. She was wearing the strap of her shoulder bag across her body. It lay diagonally between the pert perfectly shaped breasts that were lovingly shaped by the softly clinging pink cotton of the top she'd changed into. The worn denim of her jeans moulded the curve of her hips, the rounded temptation of her thighs.

He snapped his eyes away. *Cristo!* She was pure temptation. Before he knew it he would be the one down on his knees and begging! That was not part of his plan. She, not he, would abase herself, plead with him—not the other way round!

Fifty yards brought them to the nearest pavement café. He led her to a table shaded by an arbour of vines with a panoramic view of the glittering blue sea. Ordering Buck's Fizz for Lisa and plain orange juice for himself, Diego allowed the atmosphere between them to settle before probing something that was beginning to puzzle him.

'Tell me something, Lisa,' he murmured when he noted the signs of the beginnings of relaxation in the easing of her tense shoulders, the way her fingers now lay loosely around her thirstily emptied glass. 'Why do you get so angry whenever I combine the words daddy and doting in the same sentence?'

'Because you don't know what you're talking about,' Lisa came back without heat. That drink had been delicious, dissolving her annoyance, bringing the ghost of a smile at the thought that anyone could imagine that Gerald Pennington had fond fatherly feelings for his small, insignificant daughter.

'Then why don't you enlighten me?' A click of his lean fingers brought a waiter with a fresh glass of Buck's Fizz to the table. Diego watched the look of surprise and pleasure cross her lovely face and waited until she'd taken the first appreciative sip before pressing softly, 'I like to know what I'm talking about. It gives me more—' he paused a moment before adding with self-mocking solemnity '—more *gravitas*.'

Her brilliant eyes swept up to lock with his and she giggled softly, just as he'd intended. Diego felt a pang of self-dislike as he remembered that she'd eaten nothing for breakfast, merely mangling the peach she'd taken. Then brushed it aside. He wasn't aiming to get her drunk, just relaxed enough to rid her of that slightly edgy indifference.

'Well—' Her slim shoulders lifted in a careless shrug. She took one more sip then decided to leave the rest. She was beginning to feel light-headed and that wasn't a good idea around Diego Raffacani. She needed all her wits about her.

Pulling in a tight breath, she told him, 'My father showed little interest in me while my mother was alive and even less after her death. When I was home from boarding school I was farmed out on to his partner's family—that's why I'm so close to Sophie and Ben.'

Lisa sucked her lower lip between her teeth, her eyes clouding with regret. Had been close, she mentally amended. Not any more.

Seeing her sudden distress, Diego frowned. His instinct was to take the small slender hands that were lying on the top of the table and enfold them with his. He denied it with difficulty.

'Maybe he was grief-stricken after your mother's tragically early death, but wanted you to be able to move on,' he suggested even-handedly, trying to understand why a man with a needy, fragile girl-child could farm her out to someone else. Where he came from people looked after their own. Family was of the first importance.

Lisa pulled a derisory face. 'You obviously don't know my father!'

Fishing for sympathy, the stock-in-trade of a spoiled brat?

Diego stated softly, 'Maybe not. But I do know he gave you expensive gifts and eventually, probably because he could think of nothing else to do with you, put you in a responsible position on *Lifestyle*. Did you get your degree, by the way?'

The illusory mists of his seemingly gentle interest cleared from Lisa's eyes. If that wasn't scorn in his deep voice then she was a monkey's uncle!

'The only thing he ever gave me was a book token each Christmas—and a watch for my eighteenth, and he didn't even choose it himself; Honor Clayton let slip that he'd asked her to pick something out. And, as for getting my degree—I didn't get the chance, did I?' she shot back at him. 'As soon as I got back from Spain he told me the publishing empire had shrunk to the size of a small island—*Lifestyle*! He asked me—more or less commanded, now I come to think of it—to give up my university place and join the staff, dogsbodying, trying to learn the ropes. All hands on deck and everyone pulling together is the phrase I remember.'

'And you were happy with that sacrifice?' Diego wanted to know, a slight frown pulling his slanting ebony brows together.

Her mouth set stubbornly. 'No. Just flattered that for once he was noticing me, wanting something. Of course I agreed. I wanted to please him, didn't I? I wanted him to value me.'

Diego felt his breath lock in his lungs. Her lovely eyes had flooded with moisture. His own eyes nar-

rowed as he watched her blink furiously, drag in a
breath and essay a tight smile as if to signify she'd
said too much, revealed too much.

'Shall we go?' As she began to get to her feet,
Diego captured both of her hands and held her.

'In a moment.'

Her hands felt so small within his. The delicacy of
her bone structure had aroused all his protective instincts five years ago, left him in awe of her fragile
beauty. As his eyes narrowed on the exquisitely mod-
elled features, the soft mouth that trembled slightly,
he could feel it happening all over again. The need
to cherish and adore.

If she was telling the truth about her relationship
with her father, and he was pretty sure she was, then
he had misjudged her, he acknowledged heavily.

Had he misjudged her in other ways? Should he
listen to what she had to say about that dreadful night
without cynically presuming that whatever she said
would be a tissue of lies?

If he confessed what his conscience was belatedly
telling him—that he'd been wrong to give her no option but to break her engagement, come to Spain with
him—then maybe, just maybe, they could start all
over again. The spark was still there; it had been playing havoc with him since meeting up with her again.
And they were both older and wiser.

Then the small, passive hands came to life, the
slender fingers curving around his, and the effect was
electrifying.

He said thickly, 'And did he? Value you?'

Lisa couldn't answer. Simply stared into his lean,

dark, shatteringly gorgeous face. Holding Diego's
strong warm hands knocked all the breath from her
body, made her quiver with a thousand memories of
how it had been for them in those far off days when
she'd truly believed he'd loved her as passionately as
she'd loved him. She wanted to be back in that beautiful magical time with a fierce longing that pushed
everything else right out of her head.

She gently withdrew her hands from his and felt
the loss of physical contact like a pain. She tried to
concentrate on what he'd been asking her.

'He gave no sign of it,' she said at last, sadness
darkening her eyes.

Diego leaned over the table, the dark glitter of his
eyes pinning her to the spot. 'What kind of man is
he?' he asked rawly.

'I honestly don't know,' she answered truthfully.
'He never let me close enough to find out.'

'Yet you agreed to my demands, broke your engagement and, presumably, hurt the man you were
supposed to be in love with, just to save the business
and future financial security of a man who, from your
account, showed very little parental interest in you.'

Put like that, so baldly, didn't explain her lifelong
need to earn her father's approval and once having
got it how she hadn't wanted to let it go.

Lisa shook her suddenly aching head. She wished
she hadn't emptied that first glass so rapidly, wished
she hadn't started this. 'It wasn't quite like that. You
make me sound really hard-hearted. Ben and I never
loved each other.'

Automatically, she glanced down at her ringless

finger. 'We've always been fond of each other and I suppose we just drifted into the idea of marriage.' A tiny shrug. 'Actually, it was Ben who convinced me that letting *Lifestyle* fold wouldn't be the end of the world for our parents, or for the staff. That I could tell you where to put your "demands" with an easy conscience.'

But she hadn't, had she? A tide of warmth spread through the entire and towering length of Diego's body as he stood up from the table and held out his hand to her. Which must mean she had come because she wanted to. Which, in turn, meant that she still felt something for him. *Madre de Dios!* If the past could be forgiven, the bitter years erased, then...

'I was on the point of phoning you,' she told him as they reached the sun-drenched pavement and fell in step. 'And telling you I'd changed my mind and the deal was off, when my father told me he'd already had a meeting with you. I don't know what you said to him but he'd got the idea that your rescue package had everything to do with our knowing each other in the past.'

Her mouth curved in a wry smile, aware that her tongue was still running away with her. 'He told me I'd finally made up for not being the son he'd always wanted. Call me a fool if you like—I probably deserve it. But I couldn't tell him the whole thing was off and have him go from being indifferent to me to actively hating me, could I?'

Suddenly, for Diego, the sun went in. His blood ran cold then burned with fire. *Imbécil!* Had he no more sense than he'd had five years ago? Of course she hadn't agreed to come because she still wanted him, cared something for him!

She'd as good as sold herself to him for a period of time to earn her father's approval.

He put his jealousy of the other man—her own father, for pity's sake—down to anger, gritted the hard clean line of his jaw, the bitterness flooding back, and decided to take full advantage of what he'd bought and paid for.

Lisa.

CHAPTER SEVEN

EVERYTHING had changed; she knew it had. The smallest shake of the kaleidoscope and a new pattern emerged. Pausing at the head of the wide stone staircase, wearing the ice-blue chiffon slip dress Diego had picked out for her, Lisa pinned down the defining moment.

It had come when she'd explained exactly why she'd agreed to his blackmail, back in Marbella that morning, when Buck's Fizz rapidly hitting an empty stomach had loosened her tongue.

To an onlooker the change in him might have been too subtle to cause comment. But to her, finely attuned to everything about Diego Raffacani, it had hit her like a ton of bricks.

Autocratic didn't come near to describing the way he'd stalked the pavements as if he owned the whole town and everyone and everything in it. His dark head high, his handsome face wearing the slightly contemptuous, highly assured expression of a man who knew his smallest whim would be immediately and fawningly catered to, he had ushered her through the plate glass doors of a high fashion boutique, the exclusive sort that had made Lisa feel immediately awestruck and very out of place in her worn jeans and bright pink top.

And she had simply, weakly, let it all happen.

Attended by a tall, pin-thin gushing thirty-something with a permanent soulless smile, Diego had lounged back in a silk-covered baroque-style chair while garments of unbelievable style and quality had been paraded for his lordly nod of approval.

Two hours later a fresh faced youth, wearing a formal light grey suit and an aura of his own importance, had carried an armload of classy carriers and boxes to Diego's car. Lisa had thought let him waste his money if he wants to, and almost had hysterics.

After a late lunch during which little was said and even less eaten they had begun the long drive back to the old monastery. Gripped with a strange foreboding, due to the new cold-edged authority she detected in him, the sense that he saw her as a mere puppet, bought and paid for and designed to perform whenever he pulled the strings, she couldn't regret having opened up to him, not only about her relationships with her father and Ben but her reason for agreeing to his demands in the first place.

It had been a release of sorts, she decided as she began the lonely journey down to the main dining hall. And it was high time Diego opened up too. Ever since they'd met up again they had both been skirting around too many secret thoughts. Condemnatory thoughts coming from both directions, she supposed. Whatever, it would be better if they were spoken.

Manuel had carried the mountain of carriers up to her rooms on their return and Diego had broken his silence to tell her, 'Wear something beautiful. Tonight we eat in the formal dining hall and I like my possessions to be easy on the eye.'

His possession!

Earlier today that would have made her shudder; now she was able to take it in her stride. And she'd done as he'd asked, picked out this dress from the dozens of garments that Rosa, Manuel's pretty wife, had taken from the tissue-packed carriers and hung in the walk-in wardrobe.

High heeled court shoes covered in a matching ice-blue silk gave her much needed extra height. She'd brushed her hair until it fell around her shoulders like a pale blonde waterfall, caught back from one side of her face with a tiny jet clip, and gone to town with her make-up.

He couldn't accuse her of being an eyesore, although by the time she'd finished with him he'd probably accuse her of being a pain in the neck. Things couldn't go on as they were. And tonight she was going to make damned sure that they didn't!

Previously they'd taken their meals in the inner courtyard or in the small, homely breakfast room that overlooked the front terraces and the sweeping views of the mountains. If he'd chosen the formality of the great dining hall to humble her he wasn't going to succeed, she vowed as she opened the heavily carved double doors.

It was an impressive room by any standards, the carved vaulted ceiling soaring way above, lit by massive wrought metal chandeliers, the frescoed walls punctuated by narrow arched windows, the immense glossy-as-glass table set with two places, one at either end.

Biting back the flippant comment that they would

need walkie-talkies to converse with each other, Lisa walked forward, high heels tapping out a confident tattoo on the wide polished boards. Diego rose from the carved chair at the head of the table, a glass of what looked like whisky in one hand.

Dressed formally, he all but took her breath away. Elegant, immaculate and as cold as charity.

During his measured approach his heavily veiled eyes made a lengthy assessment, from the silky fall of her hair, over slender shoulders that the narrow straps of her dress left bare, the pert swell of her breasts and down to the slender length of legs made elegantly longer by the just above the knee hemline and spiky heels.

It was difficult not to squirm beneath that expressionless scrutiny but Lisa just about managed it, nearly sagging with relief when he dipped his head, maybe in approval, maybe not, and turned to walk to a plain oak side table set near the hooded hearth where logs burned brightly against the evening chill of this immense stone room. Then she stiffened when he returned with a flat leather-covered box in his hands and told her, 'Not knowing what colour you would choose to wear, I decided diamonds would be the safest selection.'

The diamonds glittered with cold fire from their bed of faded blue velvet. Appalled, Lisa's eyes widened as he lifted the choker of magnificent stones in an elaborate white gold setting and moved behind her to fasten it around her neck.

Her vow to remain steadfastly calm and sensible

flew out of her head as she jerked away and blurted, 'I don't want them!'

'You're not getting them, believe me. They are on loan for this evening only. To complete the picture and give me the pleasure of looking at outward perfection.'

Smarting under that deliberate put down, Lisa stood like a stone when he brushed her hair aside and fastened the choker around her neck. Move by so much as an inch and those strong hands would pull her back to him again. The touch of his hands would start her shaking all over. Already, knowing that those long fingers were just a hair's breadth away from her skin as he dealt with the tricky clasp, a tingling sensation spread all the way through her.

The bracelet came next. A double row of fine stones in an exquisite setting that matched that of the choker. Diego said flatly, 'The family jewels my mother finds too old-fashioned for her tastes are kept in the strong room here. She sometimes picks through them when she and my father visit. She says it gives her something to do.'

Diamond studs with tear-shaped droppers completed the suite. The backs of his fingers brushed the heated skin of her cheeks as he fixed them in place. When he stood back a pace to survey the finished result Lisa, even though her face was flaming as the result of that light, erotic touch, got a little of her own back as she asked with manufactured brightness, 'How often do they visit? Shall I meet them?' knowing that in his present mood of icy dignity the question would affront him.

'Hardly. There are women a man would be happy to introduce to his parents. Patently, you are not one of them,' he replied, a honed edge to his voice, and she knew she'd been right in her assumption and didn't care because, after what she had to say to him tonight, he wouldn't be able to hurt her any more.

At least that was what she told herself as Rosa and Manuel arrived to serve dinner, but when Diego held her chair out for her and murmured softly for her ears only, 'I will have something beautiful to look at while we eat. The sight of you will give me pleasure,' she wasn't so sure. He could hurt her simply by being himself, a man who was loved and loathed in equal and utterly confusing measure. Did she want to give him that kind of pleasure? The cool, objective pleasure of a man who had acquired an expensive artefact. Like the diamonds, a possession to be admired occasionally then locked away again and forgotten. Certainly not the pleasure of passionate possession. And that did hurt although she did her best to convince herself that it shouldn't.

Between them, Rosa and Manuel served the baked scallops, poured wine, brought quails with herb dressing and roast vegetable salad, poured more wine and finally left them with coffee and little dishes of cream-filled profiteroles and tiny baskets of fruit.

'You should kit them out with roller skates,' Lisa said with forced lightness, an attempt to counteract the unnerving effect of having his eyes on her throughout the seemingly interminable meal. 'They'd get from one end of this mile-long table much quicker.' She said it partly to amuse herself but most of all to let him know that all this formal splendour, the king's ransom of diamonds on her neck her arm and in her ears, wasn't impressing her at all.

No reaction. Diego leaned against the elaborately carved back of his chair, his hands lightly placed on the armrests, his eyes still on her, considering. So she said firmly, 'I'm leaving in the morning. Even if I have to walk. Do what you like about the rescue package you put together. This unpleasant charade is beginning to bore me and I've decided that if you pull out of your side of the bargain I can put up with my father's displeasure. After all, I've endured it, or something very like it, for all of my life.'

She hadn't meant it, any of it, had only said it to jolt him out of this new unbearably autocratic coldness. She didn't want to leave until they'd talked over the wrongs of five years ago. He didn't know she'd seen him with that beautiful woman, witnessed so painfully how they'd been together, so he couldn't know her subsequent bad behaviour had been down to a heart that was shattered and twisted with jealousy.

It was time the truth came out. All of it. He'd stopped her, back in London, by saying he wasn't prepared to listen to a 'tissue of lies'. Somehow she had to force him to hear her side of the story.

The sudden unwelcome thought that he might be just as bored by the charade as she'd said she was and would immediately agree to her leaving, chilled her for a moment, but the bleak smile he gave her, the softly spoken, 'If you go, I'll follow. If you hide, I'll find you,' froze her to the very core of her being.

For all the softening of his voice it sounded menacing but she wouldn't let it throw her. She said brittly, 'I'm sure there must be a law against that sort of harassment. And there's no law that says I have to stay here. However—' she took a last sip of her wine to bolster the nonchalant image she was desperate to portray '—I'll stay if you agree to answer one or two questions. But not here—it's far too formal. I'll be in the courtyard if you think you can go along with that.'

How she got out of that room without falling down she would never know. And she didn't know if he would follow, either. But he did, unnumbered, nerve-scratching minutes later.

He had shed the jacket of his dark immaculate suit and the sleeves of his white shirt were rolled up above his elbows, his black tie discarded. In the pale moonlight he dazzled her with his physical perfection, with the careless arrogance of the way he moved.

He had taken his time before joining her but at least he looked far more approachable, Lisa decided thankfully, monitoring the shiver of excited anticipation that quivered down her spine at the thought that at last they could go some way towards sorting out the past, putting it behind them.

But she changed her mind, realising that nothing concerning him could ever be that easy when he walked over the moon-bathed flagstones to the table beneath the sheltering, shading branches of an ancient fig tree and drawled, 'Let's get one thing straight, shall we? You may ask questions but I may not choose to answer them. And you stay here until I say you may go.' He put the bottle and glasses he carried down on the table. 'Sit where I can see you.' He indicated a seat facing the vine-covered wall and miraculously the area was flooded with soft light.

He must have pressed a hidden switch, Lisa thought distractedly as the diffused light of concealed uplighters and downlighters glowed through banks of lush foliage. He was obviously in no mood for a heart-to-heart, no mood for closure.

Diego Raffacani was still pulling her strings, she thought sinkingly as she sat where he had said she must. And, to her shame, she was actually letting him.

Determined to do something about that degrading state of affairs, she sat up very straight and said, 'You're treating me like a criminal. You heap the blame for what happened five years ago entirely on me. But consider this—you lied to me from the first time we met. So what does that make you?'

A liar, she answered inside her head, her eyes lowered as he calmly poured wine into both glasses, pushing one of them across the table to her. And the only man she had ever loved. After him, no other man could hope to hold her stupid heart in the palm of his hand—and she still wanted him, warts and all, she acknowledged unhappily.

She wanted her Diego back, back the way he had been in those ecstatic days when they had been falling in love with each other. But it wasn't going to happen. Not a chance. He had not been what she had thought he was. Now she was seeing him in his true colours. And still wanting him, for her sins!

He lowered himself into the seat opposite hers. That was better because six foot plus of looming, magnificent, sexually charged manhood was more than she felt she could possibly cope with. But it made little difference to the lurching sensation around her heart because, whereas she was illuminated, he was in shadow.

It was impossible to read his expression, make a stab at guessing what he was thinking. His voice was just slightly amused as he came back with, 'As a criminal you're getting five star treatment without receiving your punishment. I really wouldn't complain if I were you. And—' his voice hardened '—I have never lied to you, so don't insult me by saying I have.' He lifted his wine glass and reflected moonlight shimmered and danced as he idly swirled the contents. 'But that's what women do, isn't it? When they're cornered they fling out patently absurd counter-accusations.'

'You must have known a few really weird women,' Lisa replied quietly. If she allowed her voice to rise by the merest fraction she would go out of control, start to rant and rave. 'So you can take back that sexist remark and explain why you told me you were a humble waiter when all the time you were sickeningly wealthy.'

She picked up her own glass. Her hand was shaking. She put it down again before she disgraced herself and spilled the lot. Diego, leaning well back in his chair, remarked, 'You decided I was a humble waiter. I told you, quite truthfully, that I spent almost all of my evenings working in one of the hotel restaurants. You see, my tarnished angel, how I remember every word we ever said to each other? The hotel we were to meet in on that last night was the latest in the family chain. My father, being a sensible man, insisted that I had hands-on experience of each branch of the varied business enterprises. I was acting night manager at that time.'

Lisa's eyes filled with emotional tears. She couldn't help it. Her crazy heart seemed to turn to mush. He'd obviously meant to be scathing and he didn't realise what he'd just unwittingly given away—that he, too, had remembered every word they'd ever said to each other. That wouldn't happen, would it, if he'd thought of her as just a casual fling, something to amuse him and boost his inflated male ego?

She must have meant something to him... 'Why didn't you tell me who you were?' she asked shakily. 'I told you all about myself. What I mean is, I answered every question you ever asked. Why did you let me go on thinking you were scraping a living waiting on tables?' She had believed a lie and he had let her. He must have been laughing at her misconception, thinking she was a real fool. That really hurt. She had been open and frank with him and he... 'Why were you so sly?'

'Why do you think?' Diego countered grittily. 'And I'd prefer the word sensible to sly.' He put his emptied glass on the table top and Lisa blinked the recent moisture from her eyes and narrowed them at him through tangled damp lashes.

A single glass with dinner was all she'd ever seen him take but this evening he was drinking steadily. To drown his guilty conscience over his foray into the world of blackmail? Or was he seeking Dutch courage before he meted out the punishment he'd mentioned earlier? So far he'd shown no sign of wanting to have his wicked way with her!

Barely breathing at the thought of that, Lisa found it difficult to concentrate on anything else and had to force herself to tune in to him when he told her edgily, 'Since I turned seventeen I've been hunted down by females with their eyes on the main chance.' A brief silence, loaded with cynicism, then more softly, almost as if he were talking to himself, 'I rather liked the idea that you thought I was just an ordinary guy.'

Was that a hint of a smile in his voice? Lisa couldn't be sure, but hoped it was. And, prince or pauper, no one could ever call him ordinary.

And then, of course, he spoiled it all by drawling, 'You were very young. Both in years and experience. I would imagine it takes a little time for a girl to learn how to be more discriminating—financially speaking, that is—with her sexual favours.'

Still mooning over his liking her because she'd thought he hadn't got two pennies to rub together, it took Lisa several seconds to work out the implication of what he'd just casually tossed at her.

He was calling her a gold-digger!

He obviously hadn't believed a word of what she'd said about her reasons for finally agreeing to his callous proposition. He thought she'd jumped at it for what she hoped she could get out of him. Lazing around in the sun, waited on hand and foot, fabulous food, beautiful new clothes. Borrowed jewels!

She would rip the dress from her back if she could bring herself to stand in front of him in nothing but her underwear! As it was his hateful diamonds could go, she told herself in a fury of hating him for thinking she was the lowest of the low, for making her carry on loving him when he really and truly and thoroughly despised her!

Her face flaming with hectic colour, she jumped to her feet and dragged the fabulous bracelet off her wrist. The earrings followed, tossed carelessly down on the table. She would have thrown the whole lot over the edge of the terrace, to get lost in the sweetly flowering shrubs, if she hadn't known he'd stand over her with a stick while she grovelled on her hands and knees until she'd found them—even if it took ten years!

The choker was a different matter. Frustrated, angry tears spiked her lashes and coursed unheeded down her cheeks as she struggled with the awkward clasp, her soft mouth compressing into a hard straight line as if that would somehow ease the problem.

'Allow me.' Diego shifted lazily to his feet and came to stand behind her. Lisa stiffened as his deft fingers removed the choker. Every last one of her senses were unbearably sharpened when he was this close. She was achingly aware of the warmth of his body, of every breath she took, of every quickened heartbeat. A faint trembling invaded her body and she choked back a sob as, his task finished, the necklace tossed on the table, his hands cupped her shoulders as he turned her to face him, the look of male superiority swiftly turning to a slashing frown.

'I didn't mean to make you cry.'

Lisa saw his broad chest expand as he sucked in a

hollow breath. She bit down hard on her quivering bottom lip as he stroked the tears away with his fingers. Gentle fingers. Too gentle. She could feel a fresh deluge of shaming tears building up behind her eyes.

She was angry with him, furious, for bunching her in with a whole load of greedy gold-diggers, wasn't she? So why did she want to bury her head in that broad chest and sob her heart out?

'Please don't,' Diego muttered thickly as he ran a finger over her tightly compressed lips. A driven groan was wrenched from him as her mouth instinctively softened in unstoppable response, parting on a breathless loss of sanity as her glimmering eyes lifted to meld with the melting darkness of his and absorbed the messages he was sending out.

'Kiss me!'

Had that husky entreaty come from her or from him? Lisa didn't know or care as his dark head lowered, his long sensual mouth covering hers with a sweetness that made her dizzy, made her knees buckle beneath her with the wonder of it. Clinging to him, she ran her hands over the wide span of his shoulders as she pressed herself into the lithe length of him.

This was what she'd been wanting, aching for. The release from the tension of these last days came swiftly, with a cocooning sense of safety, of coming home to where she belonged after long sterile years of exile.

And then he deepened the kiss, his body taut and demanding, drugging her with an erotic expertise that harmonised with the sultry warmth of the night. Beneath her questing hands she felt his body shake and, even as his lips still ravaged the willing moistness of her mouth, his long hands swept the narrow straps of her dress off her shoulders then slid with shaky, barely contained impatience, to cup her naked breasts.

Desire, naked and unashamed, swept through her on a hot, wild tide. 'Kiss me!'

This time she knew the honeyed command had come from her, knew the intoxication of pure incandescent joy as his dark head bent to take one straining nipple between his lips and then the other. Her back arched in ecstasy, her head falling back on her neck, her fingers digging into his skull, through the thick dark softness of his hair as she held him to her.

With hot, muttered words in his own language, Diego found the delicate zipper at the back of her dress, heard the slither of silky chiffon as it pooled at her feet. With his hands on either side of her tiny waist he raised his head and held her minutely away from him, drinking in the loveliness of her.

Tiny white briefs hid her sex. Her skin gleamed like mother-of-pearl in the moonlight. Her eyes, darkened by the desire that thrummed between them, glowed for him.

Only for him…

He had to believe that…

With a smothered groan he lifted her slender pale arms from around his neck, scooped her up, holding her tightly against his racing heartbeat and carried her to his bed, where she belonged.

CHAPTER EIGHT

PALE, pure moonlight bathed Lisa's beautiful body in silvered washes as he lowered her on to his bed, the dark cover accentuating the ivory loveliness of her limbs and the silver gold of her hair, those long silky tendrils spread around her.

His heart racing, Diego straightened, his fingers moving to his shirt buttons. His hands were shaking. His body was aching for her. Just her. Only ever her. His pale, glorious angel.

He'd waited so long. Too damned long!

A soft breeze from one of the many open windows set deep in the ancient stone walls feathered over his skin as he dropped his shirt to the floor, his eyes never leaving the deep pools of hers.

Moonlight made a mystery of her. He snatched in a breath. His lungs tightened. He was about to solve that mystery.

She was his!

A tiny gasp alerted him to the fact that her eyes had broken his hypnotic hold on her and were drinking in his partial nakedness, sweeping achingly slowly across the breadth of his shoulders, down to the tightness of flat stomach muscles. A nerve jumped at the side of his hard jawline as she raised her pale slender arms to him, her lips parting on another intake of breath.

110

Without having to think about it, he took her out-stretched hands in his and brushed his lips over the backs of her fingers, turning them over to place lingering kisses in her tender palms, just as he had always done when he'd greeted her way back in that time so long ago when love had been young and infinitely precious, the most precious thing in the world for him.

'Diego—'

Just his name, emerging from her lips on a rawly breathy sigh that could have been the desperate plea he'd been waiting for. His heart seemed to swell to twice its normal size within his chest cavity, making him breathless as his impatient, unsteady hands dropped to the waistband of his trousers and dealt summarily with the zip.

And *Madre di Dio!* Did she know what her eyes were saying to him as they rose, limpid dark pools full of yearning neediness, to lock again with his?

Leaning over her, he touched her soft lips with the tips of his fingers and she parted them with immediate, telling response, her long lashes drifting closed over those beautiful sultry eyes.

He lowered his tight, throbbing body on to the bed beside her, hot masculine pleasure flowing through him in a wild unstoppable tide as she turned to him, those delicate naked limbs reaching for him, holding him, her arms around his body, her legs entwined with his, her gloriously sexy mouth raised to his.

He wanted to lose himself in that mouth, in that exquisite body. The need was raw and primitive, but 'Slowly, my angel,' he murmured thickly, needing to savour this moment, the forerunner of the climax that had haunted his mind for far too long, savour this timeless moment before the blessed release from private nightmares of anger and frustration.

Even so, he could no more stop his hands from sweeping down the length of her body, sweeping away the tiny briefs, the final barrier between them.

He heard her soft intake of breath, felt her body shake with fine tremors as the instinctive, urgent arching of her hips met his full arousal and he knew the sting of desire was building in her, unfettered, hot and greedy, meeting his own.

His hand on the seductive curve of her hips pressed her closer and lightning forked through his loins as she moved against him, her sweet mouth trailing feverish kisses along the length of his throat.

Diego dragged in a harsh breath. This was what he'd wanted, wasn't it? Lisa's wantonly willing body in his bed, pleasuring him, washing away the years of anger and bitterness.

And yet— He wanted more. Far more than the primeval act of mating. He had no idea where the sudden need had sprung from but the power of it was an insistent beat in his brain.

Feeling her skin against his skin, the heated urgency that was melding them together, two bodies as one, had wrought a change in him, a shift in his underlying emotions. This thing—the path to revenge he'd put in train—was debasing both of them.

Knowing he could be an all-time loser, committing himself to frustrated needs, no earthly chance of redemption, Diego levered himself up on one elbow, his eyes narrowed solemnly on her lovely face.

His voice flat with the knowledge of what he was about to do, the outcome uncertain, he told her, 'The game's over, Lisa. You've kept your side of the unworthy bargain I forced on you—coming willingly to my bed—and I'll keep mine.' He shifted his weight slightly, putting an unwanted space between them and hating it, craving the ultimate closeness which now might never come. 'The magazine's safe. Your father won't have occasion to lower his new found good opinion of you.' He dragged in a harsh breath, his stomach hollow. 'And you're free to go back to your own room right now, if that's what you want, and back to London as soon as we can arrange a flight. Just say the word.'

Shock froze Lisa's body, wiped out her vocal cords. He didn't want her! She was offering and he was saying no thanks! His sole and despicable intention had been to humiliate her.

Struggling helplessly to work out what was happening here, she scoured his shadowed face with desperate eyes but found no answer, merely enigma. His moods could change faster than a teenager's. Marbella this morning. And now this.

Now that he'd proved to himself that he could bring her to the point of writhing about on his bed, naked and frantic for his love-making, he was throwing her out like the worthless object he had decided she was!

'You are one vile human being! Do you know that?' burst from her on a wild tide of really loathing him. Limbs flailing, humiliation exploding inside her, Lisa tried to struggle off the bed, get as far away from the monster as she possibly could.

'*Tranquilo.*' Two gently determined hands curved round her shoulders, pressing her back against the pillows. A smile mellowed his voice. 'Allow the vile human being to finish.'

At her seething snort of outrage and ineffectual struggles the smile vanished, leaving his voice ragged. 'I want you to stay. Believe me, I want it more than anything else. But only if you want it too. Without threats hanging over your head, Lisa. You don't owe me anything and if you stay with me it must be of your own free will. Otherwise, when we make love it will be meaningless. Do you understand what I'm saying?'

Poleaxed into speechlessness, Lisa lifted her hands to cup his beloved face. Her heart was suddenly so full she was sure it was about to burst. He wanted her to stay with him; he'd said so with a sincerity that made her heart ache. He wanted to make love with her, not just have sex. And he wanted it to mean something!

He did care about her. It was obvious, wasn't it? Her breath exhaled on an emotional sob. She wriggled forward, reclaiming the small unendurable space he'd put between them. Maybe he was remembering the wonderful magical times they'd shared all those years ago, was regretting having played around, one girl for the daylight hours, one for the evening. Maybe...

Expelling a driven moan, Lisa dragged his head down to hers and kissed him with a wild hunger that drew an answering blisteringly passionate response. Only when the need for breath became imperative was she able to tell him what was in her heart, her voice no more than a whisper as she confessed, 'I want to stay. I want you, Diego, I want everything back the way it was.'

'That can't happen, my angel,' Diego denied wryly, one hand gently caressing her fine-boned shoulder. 'The past can't be reclaimed, no matter how much we wish it could be. We are both older and hopefully wiser. All we can do,' he said thickly, 'is concentrate on the present.' His hand slipped lower, resting possessively on the throbbing peak of one breast then sliding to the other, the hot pleasure almost more than she could stand as her whole body was invaded by a desire so intense it shocked the breath out of her body.

'You are so beautiful. I ache for you!' His voice was ragged with emotion, more heavily accented than she had ever heard it. 'I have dreamed of this,' he confessed rawly, the touch of his hands as he explored her willing body slow and sensual, blowing her mind, making her writhe against him, her breath coming in frantic gasps until he held both her hands above her head and murmured softly, 'Patience, my angel. I am a possessive man and I will give pleasure such as you have never known.'

His black eyes smouldered with male intent. 'After tonight there will be no room in your mind for any other man.'

There had never been any other man, Lisa thought dizzily and wondered whether she should tell him,

then gave up on all brain functions as his lips eroti-
cally travelled the path of his exploring hands.

She'd been a virgin; he was sure of that. She might
have been a flirt and a tease, but she hadn't been
promiscuous. She hadn't even slept with Clayton;
he'd stake his life on it.

Looking down at her fragile, fine-boned body as at
last she slept, Diego's heart swelled with an emotion
he couldn't name. The triumph of male possession?
A release from the devils of the past?

Love?

Love. His mouth compressed wryly. He'd loved
her once, adored her, put his angel on a golden ped-
estal. And look where that had got him! His days of
romanticising fallible womanhood were long gone.

Yet she was ineffably special; he was too honest
to deny that.

Tenderly, careful not to wake her, he drew the
silken cover over her body, as graceful in sleep as she
always was awake, and eased himself off the bed.
Fingers of dawn light were creeping into the room.
Each climax had been more stunning than the last. He
had never known anything like it but, in spite of all
that sensual overload, he was bursting with vitality.

A long walk was called for. Something to tax his
body and leave his mind free to work out his feelings,
let him see the future—if there could be any future
for the two of them, he amended—more clearly.

Lisa woke to floods of sunlight. She could hear the
doves calling in the courtyard below, a soft sweet

sound that matched her mood perfectly. Releasing herself from the tangle of the silky cover she wriggled over and stared at the empty space beside her.

Diego was already up and about. It didn't matter that he'd left her to sleep alone. She vented a dreamy sigh. He could change his mood more often than he changed his socks and that didn't matter either.

She knew what she knew.

What he felt for her went far deeper than simple male lust; she knew it did. Hadn't he offered to let her go before things went any further, hadn't he admitted he wanted her to stay, but only if she wanted it too? And throughout the long, ecstatic night he'd made love with such passionate tenderness, as if she were the most precious thing in the world!

It couldn't possibly get any better or any more revealing of his true feelings than that, could it?

Slipping out of bed, she hugged her arms around her body. She was actually squirming with happiness inside. She felt intoxicated by it. Despite what he'd said, they could recapture the past. And if he still went on denying it then she'd have to make sure to change his mind!

The embarrassing problem of getting back to her own rooms, naked, without being met by Rosa or Manuel, was solved when Diego walked into the room moments later. He was carrying something over his arm; she didn't register what because she only had eyes for him, for his heart-wrenching gorgeousness.

Those dark eyes were intimately warm, his slow smile infectious, and the way the fine cotton of his sleeveless shirt clung to the wide span of his shoulders, those long legs clothed in narrow-fitting sand-coloured jeans, made her legs go hollow, her tummy tighten with intense physical need.

Feeling the rosy peaks of her breasts swell and tingle, her pale skin bloomed with warm colour as his eyes made a languid tour of every naked inch on display.

Her eyelids drooped, she could hardly keep them open and her breath was coming in ragged little gasps. She loved him so, wanted him until she went weak and boneless from the tips of her toes to the top of her tousled head.

Diego walked towards her and then past without so much as touching her. Lisa's face fell a mile but her dismay was swiftly forgotten when he laid garments she vaguely recognised from the stuff he'd splurged out on yesterday down on the bed and turned to her, grinning wickedly over his shoulder.

'I've been retrieving last night's careless scatterings.' He straightened up, his feet planted apart, his soft, slightly breeze-ruffled black hair gleaming in the shafts of sunlight, his eyes smiling for her. 'We left your dress and a fortune in diamonds in the courtyard, remember?' A slanting brow quirked. 'Now, I don't mind the staff putting two and two together but I thought you might.' His mobile mouth curved. 'The diamonds are back in the safe and your dress is back in your room.'

And after that he'd tramped the hillside, getting his mind straight and not liking himself. He could only describe his behaviour as appalling. He'd verged on an unprecedented and shameful temper tantrum after she'd admitted that holding on to her father's approval was the only reason she'd agreed to his unholy proposition. So, not recognising what was actually happening to him when it smacked him squarely in the face, he'd set out to punish her.

He'd been falling in love with her all over again and had been too stiff-necked and blinkered to admit it to himself. He didn't care how badly she'd behaved in the past. *Madre di Dios!* She'd been little more than a child at the time!

'And this—' a lean tanned hand indicated the clothing he'd put down on the bed, drawing a steadying breath to get himself back on track '—is for you to dress in after you've showered.' He glanced at her enquiringly. 'So, breakfast in half an hour?'

At her mute nod he dipped his head understandingly and came to her, where her feet felt rooted to the polished boards, his hands thrust firmly in his trouser pockets. 'I know.' His voice lowered with husky understanding. 'But if I touch you we'll never leave that bed. And I've got plans for today. There's a cove I know of, not more than a hour's drive away. No one ever goes there. It will be just the two of us.'

He wanted to take her in his arms, feel that beautiful body trembling with need against his own, kiss her until they both forgot what planet they were on, wanted it so much that he didn't know how he managed to get himself out of that room.

But how could he talk rationally to her when they were in the throes of making love—which was what would happen if he stayed in the intimacy of the bedroom with her—naked and utterly desirable as she was?

Couldn't be done.

On the secret silvery beach, just the two of them and all the time in the world, he could open his heart to her. They could disregard all that had happened in the past and plan for the future. A long and happy future together. If she'd have him, if she could fall in love with him all over again.

And if she was having any trouble in that direction he'd make it happen for her just as it had for him, he decided with a surge of fierce Spanish possessiveness before he turned his mind to more practical matters and stalked off to find Rosa to order a lavish picnic hamper.

A tender smile on her face, Lisa couldn't move for quite some time. They were to spend the day together. Not like yesterday when he'd stalked around with a face like thunder, spending money on her as if it were an unpleasant but necessary duty. Not like the days that had gone before when they'd met only briefly at mealtimes, either. But together, really together, and loving too. Well, she was almost certain about that.

Almost.

With a guilty squawk, realising time was flying, she showered in his bathroom and scurried back to the bedroom to get into the clothes he'd so thoughtfully brought in here for her.

Gossamer fine underwear, just panties, no bra. Her face bloomed with frankly delicious lustful pleasure because the top he'd provided was definitely provocative—a fine cotton, much the same colour as her eyes, sleeveless, cut to reveal her shoulders with a sexy V neck and tiny buttons down the front. She could just imagine him undoing them, slowly, one by one.

Before those mind pictures could get the better of her she stepped into a floaty cream-coloured skirt and thrust the hem of the top under the narrow waistband, then used Diego's comb to restore her hair to its normal sleek, beyond-shoulder-length waterfall.

She was nervous as a kitten faced with a bristling Alsatian, she admitted as she stepped into the strappy sandals that completed the outfit, frightened of what the future might bring.

What if Diego saw the future as the few weeks, or mere days even, before he had to get back to his busy working life? Nothing more than a stolen interlude of fabulous sex with a very willing woman? And then: goodbye, it's been nice getting reacquainted, see you some time. Maybe.

She took a deep breath to calm herself down, told herself to stop being paranoid—she really meant something to him, didn't she?

Of course she did!

To stop herself from dwelling senselessly on the worst case scenario, she decided to spend a few minutes before joining him for breakfast taking stock of his room in daylight.

Unlike the room she'd been given, it was almost austere, dominated by the huge bed. Highly polished floorboards, no softening colourful rugs. A cavernous wardrobe, heavily carved with what appeared to be exotic fruits and vine leaves, and a solitary desk set against the wall between two of the tall windows.

Gravitating towards it, she noted the angled lamp, the pens in a horn beaker, suggesting that when he was here he sometimes wrote letters or jotted down memos for his staff before retiring for the night.

A photograph in a plain silver frame. A handsome middle-aged couple. His parents? Running her fingers over the frame, Lisa wondered if she'd ever get to meet them and tried to block out the memory of his scathing, 'There are women a man would be happy to introduce to his parents. Patently, you are not one of them.'

That had been before they had made love and found each other again. Things were very different now. Of course they were, she assured herself staunchly.

A smaller frame was half hidden behind the photograph of the smiling middle-aged couple. Curiously, Lisa slid it out into the light. And her heart literally stopped. Then crashed on. She would never forget that fascinatingly sensual face. The face of the woman she'd seen him with all those years ago. Feeling nauseous, she pushed it roughly back out of sight.

He wouldn't still keep her photograph near his bedside if she'd been simply a young man's fling, part of his wild oat sowing period, would he, part of a promiscuous past he would rather forget. She had to be someone really special to him. The knowledge left Lisa feeling cold and frightened. Had she got everything wrong? Was her heart to be broken all over again? And could she hope to survive it?

Had he married this vibrantly lovely creature? Was that why he kept her photograph beside that of his parents, part of a family group? Was he being unfaithful to his wife, treating her, Lisa, as nothing more than a piece of unfinished business?

He was used to cheating on women, wasn't he, as she knew to her cost. She should have remembered that.

Her hand flew to her trembling mouth to smother a cry of pain, the suspicions crowding in, thick and fast. And why, in the name of all that was holy, hadn't she thought to ask him, way back in London, if he was married?

She swung out of the room. It was an omission she was about to remedy. The last time, when faced by evidence of his perfidy, she had cut him brutally out of her life without telling him why.

This time it would be different.

CHAPTER NINE

CALM, at all costs she had to remain calm, Lisa repeated to herself as she trod the upper corridors of the ancient monastery, heading for the stone stairs that would take her down to the magnificent great hall.

There could be a perfectly reasonable explanation why that photograph was in Diego's bedroom, though she couldn't for the life of her think of one. But she loved him, didn't she, even if he turned out to be the selfish bastard, ruthless and cruel, that was being conjured up by all these unwanted suspicions.

Some women—herself probably first among them—were their own worst enemies! She wished she could turn love off, like a tap, but knew she couldn't.

She could have married dear, safe, trustworthy Ben and spent her life on an even keel, avoiding the shattering peaks and troughs of being madly in love with a man she couldn't trust as far as she could throw him. She desperately wanted to trust him but how could she?

Pausing on the first floor landing to allow her racing heartbeat to decelerate, she leant against the cool stone window mullion. She was going to be sensible and calm about this, not rush in hurling accusations which might be unfounded.

She was no longer a naive eighteen-year-old, fresh from a convent schoolroom, she reminded herself

snippily. They were both, as Diego had stated, older
and wiser. She would have to try harder to believe in
him, in spite of the haunting memories of what had
happened all those years ago.

She knew she'd been a darn sight longer than the
half an hour Diego had given her. Nevertheless she
lingered for a further few moments, her attention
drawn now by a bright yellow low-slung sports car
parked at a skewed angle on the gravelled approach
at the front of the building.

Diego had a visitor, she deduced on a flash of irritation. What a time to pick! The planned confrontation would have to be put on hold. Which might not
be such a bad thing, she reflected on consideration,
beginning the final descent to the ground floor. It
would give her more time to cool off and recover
from the shock of finding that woman's framed photograph in Diego's bedroom.

She had no appetite for breakfast, usually taken in
the courtyard, but if there was any of Rosa's excellent
coffee left and still drinkable she could certainly do
with a cup.

Suddenly the idea of sitting in the peaceful seclu-
sion of the courtyard strongly appealed. Breathing in
the warm scented air and listening to the melodic
sound of the doves, the fountain playing into its stone
basin, the rustle of the soft breeze in the leaves of the
old fig tree while she waited for Diego to deal with
his visitor was exactly what she needed.

Such tranquillity would surely help her to come at
the situation from an adult direction?

The quickest way to her objective was through the

outer door in the library, rather than the french doors leading out of the small salon she normally used. Funny how she was finally learning her way around this maze of a building at precisely the time she might have to leave nursing a badly broken heart.

But she wouldn't think about that. Not yet anyway. It was far too negative, she informed herself tartly as she pushed open the heavy oak door. First she had to hear what Diego had to say. She might have got entirely the wrong end of the stick, which begged the question that she might have badly overreacted five years ago.

And that was the last sensible thought she had because what Diego had to say on the subject of the silver-framed photograph became academic when she saw that the subject herself was sitting at the table beneath the fig tree with floods of tears running down her beautiful face. Diego was seated opposite, leaning forward, holding her hands in both of his, talking to her, his actual words indecipherable from this distance, but the tone of his voice soothing and quite definitely placatory.

Something he said must have angered the beautiful young brunette. It happened so quickly that Lisa, rigid with the shock of what she was witnessing, could only flinch with disbelief as the other woman sprang to her feet, bristling with anger, her voice hysterically shrill. The only word she was able to pick out of the tirade of Spanish was *Perfidia!*—and wasn't perfidious one of the words she'd used herself to describe the man who'd betrayed her with this very woman five years ago?

Lisa's eyes frosted over, her stomach tying itself in knots, as she watched Diego immediately get to his feet and capture the other woman's gesticulating hands. Then, with a few murmured words—silver-tongued, lying excuses?—he pulled her into his arms and held her there, tenderly pressing her glossy dark head against his wide shoulder, rocking her gently back and forth until gradually moving her towards the door to the house.

As they disappeared inside Lisa pressed her knuckles against her mouth to stop herself from crying out. She had no idea what was going on but from where she was standing those two were very far from being casual acquaintances! The suspicion that the other woman was either his fiancée or his wife returned with a force that made her feel ill.

The only way to discover the truth was to confront them and ask. And the only way to get her leaden legs to move was to try to assure herself that this was just some misunderstanding, something that looked definitely iffy on the surface, hiding a perfectly innocent explanation. After last night it just had to be that. She wasn't going to go on torturing herself by thinking anything else. Well, was she?

Shaking inside, Lisa found herself in the great hall. The ancient stone walls seemed to freeze her right through to her bones instead of creating the usual welcome cool ambience. The silence lay like a heavy weight on her shoulders. Now she was about to begin her search for Diego and the other woman she didn't think she had the courage.

If what she couldn't help suspecting turned out to

be the truth she didn't think she could bear it. Not after last night when his love-making had made her feel like the most beautiful, desired and loved woman in the world.

Adrenalin pumping, she almost leapt out of her skin when Rosa, soft-footed in her comfy old plimsolls, appeared at her shoulder. Her pretty features had concern and condemnation written all over them. Her normal smile was notably absent. Disconcerted, Lisa told herself not to be a coward; she had to get this sorted out, of course she did. She stated, 'I'm looking for the *señor*. Do you know where he is?'

A quick frown clouded the big brown eyes. 'I am to take to them coffee and cognac and leave—*solo*—' She struggled with her rudimentary English. 'You leave also. Is bad thing when the beautiful Isabella find husband have other woman. Much explosions! The *señor* needs to be—*privado*. So you leave also?'

Leave. It was the only option, Lisa decided hollowly as Rosa disappeared to meet Diego's request for coffee and brandy. Barely able to move for the feverish pain that invaded every inch of her body, she dragged herself upstairs to the rooms she'd been given.

To allow herself to be conned by Diego once had been a dreadful mistake. To allow it to happen twice should be a capital offence!

That she hadn't known he was married was no excuse, she castigated herself wildly as she closed the door to her bedroom behind her and sagged weakly back against it, nausea a coiled knot in her stomach. She should have damned well asked.

She should have known. A man so gorgeous, sinfully sexy and rotten rich would have been snapped up years ago.

Isabella—as Rosa had named her—had obviously discovered that he had a woman holed up here with him in his self-admitted private hideout, the place the family rarely visited, where his sins, for sins they were, could be hidden.

But someone must have blown the whistle—Rosa, through a sense of family loyalty?—and the wronged wife had appeared to confront him. Demanding explanations was out of the question; she saw that now, she thought on a wave of draining exhaustion. His poor wife had enough to contend with without coming face to face with Diego's latest bit on the side.

Feeling dreadful for her part in this sordid shambles, Lisa walked unsteadily to the hanging cupboard to drag her clothes out. Just the things she'd brought with her—she never wanted to set eyes on the expensive gear he'd bought her again.

In a minute she'd change out of the pretty skirt and sexy top she was wearing. But first she had to make sure she had everything she needed. Her head was in a dreadful daze, her brain consumed by her awful discovery. If she didn't take herself firmly in hand she could well land up at the airport without the essentials, hysterical and not knowing what the hell she thought she was doing!

Tipping the contents of her handbag out on to the bed beside her suitcase and the untidy heap of clothing she'd tossed there, she sifted through what the average male would classify as junk—combs, lipstick, tissues, sundry keys, a battered appointments diary, a clutch of old letters and postcards from friends—and located her passport and her wallet. She would use her credit card to take care of the flight home but, unfortunately, she would need to beg a lift to the airport.

Would Manuel be willing to drive her? There shouldn't be too much difficulty about that, she decided sickly. Hadn't Rosa insisted she leave? The Spanish woman might be disgusted by her but she would make sure her husband facilitated that sensible outcome, if only to see the back of her.

Her fingers shaky, she carefully slotted her passport and wallet into the zipped compartment where she would know where they were, and was beginning to shovel everything else back any old how when Diego walked in.

His beautiful face was grim. His wife had obviously been giving him a hard time. Serve him right! Lisa thought, trying to ignore the stab of pain that pierced her already mangled heart. She hadn't wanted to set eyes on him again but now that she had she wasn't going to let him see how devastatingly upset she was.

'What the hell are you doing?'

'What does it look like?' Lisa muttered fiercely, wanting to strangle him. 'And there's no need to snap. It's your fault if your wife's been reading the riot act, so don't take it out on me!' She grabbed the packet of tissues and something rolled off the bed. 'Rosa, in her wisdom, told me to leave so that's what I'm doing. Eminently sensible under the circumstances, wouldn't you say?'

Straightening abruptly after automatically stooping to retrieve the object that had dropped from the bed, Diego drew a sharp breath in through his teeth. Black brows meeting, he demanded, 'Run that by me again. Why the hell should Rosa tell you to leave? By what right? And what wife? I don't have a wife!'

He sent her a dark, exasperated glance and Lisa sank down on the bed and vented a huge sigh that seemed to come up from the soles of her feet.

So that was the way he was going to play it. Lying creep! With the patron saint of liars and deceivers on his side—or patron devil, more likely—he must have persuaded the hysterical Isabella to return to whence she had come, in double quick time. Made her believe there was no other woman holed up here with him, that he was here alone to commune with nature, or some such other unlikely story.

But she wasn't that gullible. No way! 'Right,' she said through gritted teeth and shot to her feet. 'Wait here,' she growled and stalked out of the room, red flags of furious disgust flying on her cheeks as she headed for his rooms, hearing his firm footsteps following as he disregarded her instruction and came after her.

She'd wanted a few minutes on her own, away from the man she was tempted to do serious damage to. But at least this way she'd have to stay a few minutes less in this place.

Swooping into his bedroom, she homed in on the framed photograph and whipped round to face him.

He towered over her, bemusement coupled with the irritation of a man reaching the end of his tether writ large on his too-handsome features.

'This—' Lisa stabbed a forefinger at the lovely smiling face 'is the woman I saw you with in Marbella on that last evening. You were all over each other. Even Sophie said you were a real steamy couple!'

He was looming over her, his expression that of a man who had been hit over the head with a rock, but that didn't fool her, not for a single instant. 'And I found this—' again a stab at the picture of the wronged Isabella '—this morning after you'd spent the night making love to me!'

When this hatefully necessary confrontation was over, she'd probably be stupid enough to cry herself to sleep every night for a year but right at this moment anger was fuelling her blistering attack.

'I came looking for you to ask for an explanation of your obvious on-going relationship with her and there she was, having hysterics, and you were—were—' Words almost failed her in her furious need to lash out at him, but she ploughed on raggedly, 'Cuddling her and stroking her...' Her voice rose to an anguished wail. 'And Rosa told me that Isabella had exploded because she had found out you had another woman. And then Rosa told me to leave.'

Struggling to make sense of the disjointed statements that were issuing from that lushly desirable mouth was like wading through a thick fog and then emerging into bright sunlight. Diego's mouth curved with immense inner satisfaction. She was behaving like a jealous virago. *Bravo!* It had to mean she cared for him!

With one hand he reached out to take Isabella's portrait from her and became aware of something digging into the palm of the other. He opened his fist on the glitter of the hoop of tiny diamonds he'd seen her wearing on the night of her engagement party.

He dragged in a breath. It didn't mean a thing. He held it out to her. Lisa, her face going bright scarlet, snatched it and felt awful. Ben had told her to keep it as a memento of their affection and what had she done? Carelessly dropped it into the messy and cavernous depths of her handbag!

Knowing Ben it wouldn't be worth much materially, but it was worth a great deal as a token of friendship and abiding affection that had been in place for most of their lives.

Cursing herself for not taking proper care of it, she slipped it on her finger for safe-keeping and Diego, watching from suddenly narrowed eyes, told himself that her wearing another man's ring didn't mean anything, either. She was almost incandescent with rage and fierily beautiful with it and now that everything had slotted into place he couldn't blame her.

As she made to stalk past him, out of the room and, presumably, given her assumptions, out of his life, Diego clamped both hands on her slight, stiffly held shoulders and swung her round to face him.

Inky-blue eyes dealt him a slaying glance and Diego grinned. Under the circumstances it probably wasn't the wisest thing to do but he couldn't help it.

She was already bristling like a wild kitten and at any moment she would use her claws!

As a small hand rose to slap the grin off his face he captured it, slid an arm around her tiny waist and deftly deposited her on the bed, quickly joining her.

'Will you stop mauling me?' Her full lower lip jutted petulantly and the temper had gone out of her voice, replaced by grumpiness. Her breathing was short and rapid, Diego noted on a tidal wave of tenderness. And something else, he decided, as desire steamed in his blood. Was she, too, remembering what had happened for them last night in this bed? She looked fantastic. His fingers itched to undo those tiny buttons down the front of the sexy top she was wearing, to slide beneath that gauzy skirt, to claim her as his own for all time because he point-blank refused to spend the rest of his life without her…

'Mauling you isn't what I had in mind,' he affirmed thickly and felt her shudder. He stopped there, hauling himself back to the present situation.

Briskly clearing his throat, he got back on track. 'From your verbal assaults I think I've worked out what's sent you up like a volcano.' His eyes, as they rested on her defensively prickly profile, went soft with compassion. He ached to take her in his arms and make her believe he loved her, had never stopped, but he had to sort out this mess first.

'Isabella—the girl you obviously saw me with in Marbella, the girl in the photograph—is my sister. That last night, when I'd asked to meet your friends, I'd planned to explain who I was and introduce you to the only member of my family who was in Spain at that time—my parents being on an extended visit to relatives in South America.'

Disconcerted by that statement, Lisa sneaked a sideways glance. He looked really sincere. But apparent sincerity was the stock-in-trade of the con artist, wasn't it?

Huffing out a sharp breath, she returned her gaze to the uncontentious consideration of her feet. She wanted to believe him and sitting beside him on this bed wasn't the best idea in the world.

'Isabella and I met up in Marbella. She insisted on going with me when I chose the ring I intended to give you. And if you saw us and decided she was all over me, well, I guess you could have got that impression. Lisa—' he cupped her chin and turned her to face him '—my sister has been a drama queen since the day of her birth, completely over the top! She was so excited that her adored brother had gone and fallen in love, was about to get engaged, and she was determined to celebrate every inch of the way.'

He felt his bones melt as her soft lips quivered, the deep blue pools of her eyes misting over. His voice was unsteady as he mentally begged her to believe in him implicitly. 'And that same headstrong nature had her setting out in the early hours of this morning to find me, vowing she'd left Cesar, her big-shot lawyer husband, because he was having an affair with his newly appointed personal assistant.

'Utter nonsense, of course.' The ball of his thumb gently stroked away a glistening tear drop. 'I calmed her down and phoned Cesar, who was worried witless. Apparently, a so-called friend of Isabella's had told her that Cesar had been seen in one of Seville's grandest restaurants with his dazzlingly lovely new assistant when he'd told her he was working late. Well, that was exactly what he was doing, having a working dinner with an important client. His assistant was there to take notes. Nothing else. Cesar adores Isabella. The idea of cheating on her would never cross his mind.'

'That's what I did all those years ago, didn't I? Overreact. I spoiled what we had. I decided you were a penniless waiter, the sort who preys on well-heeled females for what you could get out of them,' Lisa confessed mournfully after a long beat of silence, feeling really guilty for the bad names she'd called him inside her head and sick at heart at the thought of what she'd done.

She sniffed miserably. Five years ago this fantastic man had loved her, had chosen a ring to make their engagement official and she'd ruined everything, thought the very worst of him, not giving him the opportunity to say a word, just opening her big mouth and sending him away.

'Don't cry.' Diego got to his feet to reach for a tissue from the box on the night table. Wordlessly, he handed it to her and stood over her, watching as she dabbed her eyes then pulled the soggy tissue into tiny little pieces. She was the picture of misery. His heart kicked with compassion. He knew exactly what she was feeling. He, too, savagely regretted the misunderstandings of five years ago, the barren wasted years.

But the moment passed. Brooding over what

couldn't be changed was a fool's game. Only the future mattered. As soon as Isabella was safely on her way back to Seville he would have all the time in the world to convince this adored, delicately lovely creature that he loved her more than life itself and ask her to be his wife—go down on his knees and beg if necessary! But until then... 'Can you remember how Rosa asked you to leave?' he enquired briskly of the silky crown of her drooping head. It was the one thing that was still puzzling him. His staff weren't in the habit of telling his guests what to do.

Lisa's thoughts were still on the way her awful behaviour had driven this fantastic man away. Not only that of five years ago but this morning too. He was proud and honourable; he wouldn't relish the idea of being thought of, firstly, as some sort of gigolo and then as a cheating, sneaky husband. Last night she had really believed he cared for her, that they could put the past behind them and start over. Right now he would be despising her, or thinking she was completely insane. He would want to see the back of her as soon as possible.

'You can't remember?' Diego asked with a decisive bite.

Lisa shivered. He was out of patience with her and she couldn't blame him. 'Oh, that.' She recalled his question and mumbled, almost word for word, what Rosa had said, then gasped with surprise as his strong hands fastened around her waist and pulled her upright.

'Rosa has some difficulties with the English language. I'd asked her to bring coffee and brandy and then make sure that Isabella and I were left alone, and to pass that message on to you with my apologies. I needed time to quieten her down and contact Cesar. She didn't mean you were to leave the house.'

Lisa nodded, helplessly acknowledging that she was pretty damn good at getting her wires crossed. And driving a huge wedge between herself and the man she loved to distraction.

'Right,' Diego said flatly, for the first time in his life wishing his sister hadn't followed the habit of a lifetime and come running to him whenever something happened to upset her. He wanted her out of the way, well out of it, to begin his campaign to get Lisa to agree to marry him. 'Let's get you looking less like a wet weekend, then go and keep Isabella company.'

Impersonal hands smoothed her hair off her face while he was telling her, 'Cesar's already on his way to collect her. He's bringing one of his junior clerks to drive her car back. He refuses to let her get behind the wheel when she's in a state, which,' he admitted drily, 'she mostly is. Either deliriously happy, high as a kite, or down in the rock-bottom dumps.'

His mouth tightened as he tucked the wandering hem of her top back into the waistband of her skirt. The touch of her skin scalded him. *Dio!* He didn't know how he stopped himself from taking her in his arms and smothering her with burning kisses. He would make up for it later, when they were alone.

Lisa noted the compression of his beautiful mouth and the chilling fact that there was no reaction to the small intimacy. She bit down hard on her lower lip to stop herself from weeping. The magic they'd re-captured last night had clearly gone and was lost for ever, swept away by her not trusting him and thinking the sort of things about him that no man could be expected to ever forgive.

'In the meantime we could all use some breakfast.' He made a terse after-you gesture in the direction of the door and Lisa exited, trying not to look as down as she felt.

Watching the unconsciously sensual sway of her hips as she walked out of the room Diego smothered a groan. Part of him wanted to haul her back and open his heart to her, confess that he couldn't rest until she'd given her word that she would spend the rest of her life with him.

But the more sensible part insisted that he would need more than a few rushed minutes to convince her that despite his sordid and shamefully dishonourable attempts at revenge he did truly love her.

A decision he would later deeply regret.

CHAPTER TEN

THEY found Isabella sprawled out on a padded sunlounger on the terrace. As Diego's shadow fell across her she half opened her dark sleepy eyes and murmured plaintively, *'Tengo mucha hambre!'*

'Speak English, *cara*. We have a guest.'

There was no mistaking the affection in his tone, in stark contrast to the snippy way he'd been speaking to her, Lisa recognised wretchedly.

'We are all hungry, breakfast has been delayed for too long,' he chided gently as he took his sister's slim hands and helped her to her feet. 'Isabella, meet Lisa Pennington,' he introduced smoothly, his smile for his sister.

Feeling like a spare part, Lisa met Isabella's wide smile and returned it feebly. There was no sign now of that earlier hysterical anger, just a warm look of curiosity on that vivacious face.

'Hola! Lo siento—I forgot—no Spanish! You are English, yes?' She tucked her arm through Diego's, her curvaceous body in flame-coloured linen pants topped by a white silk blouse gracefully relaxed as she gave Lisa a warm assessment. 'You are the secret one, my brother, to hide your guest here away from prying eyes!'

Her sultry eyes, glinting with mischief, found Lisa's. 'So tell me, how did you do it? Diego's so off

140

women it's painful. It's lovely to see he can be as human as the rest of us—and wicked, too! Tell me, is my big brother truly wicked?'

'Lisa's father is a recently acquired business partner. She is part of the same enterprise,' Diego cut in repressively. 'You said you were hungry.' He curtly dismissed the subject of Lisa's status. 'So why don't we eat?'

Give Isabella the merest hint of a romance in the offing and she would be merciless, as he remembered only too well. The outrageous teasing and non-stop questions when he'd invited her to Marbella to meet his intended fiancée five years ago had tried his patience to the limits. He and Lisa had to sort things out for themselves. And they needed to be alone.

'Oh, just business,' Isabella said disappointedly as Diego steered her back towards the house. 'How horribly boring.'

Lisa followed on leaden legs. Diego was cutting her out of his life, that much was painfully obvious. But what else could she have expected after the things she'd accused him of? His Spanish pride wouldn't forget such insults to his integrity.

She had woken to a day that had seemed to be so full of promise, sure that they could reclaim the joyous, loving happiness they had both thought they'd lost. Now there would be no lazing about on the beach he had spoken of, no making love, no talking, no way of discovering if he really did still care for her.

Her shoulders slumped and not even the Spanish sun burning into her back could thaw the ice that was forming around her heart. If he had started to believe that there was still something very special between them, then she'd certainly put paid to that by opening her big mouth on a spate of wild accusations. It certainly looked that way from where she was standing and she couldn't come out with it and ask, not with Isabella around.

Following the other two, Lisa took her place at the table in the small salon where Rosa had produced dishes of scrambled eggs and mushrooms, the usual crusty rolls with a choice of fillings, cured ham, crisp sweet tomatoes, cheese and anchovies.

'I am dying of hunger!' Isabella declared theatrically, opening her starched white napkin with a flourish. 'All my own fault, of course. I couldn't eat a thing after I believed my darling Cesar was betraying me with another! How could I have been so silly? He will be so cross with me. I shudder!'

She didn't seem exactly fazed by the prospect, Lisa thought tiredly as she took a roll she didn't want and began to crumble it on her plate. Diego didn't appear to have much appetite, either. He just sliced a tomato up on his plate and drank several cups of coffee.

Rousing herself to make an effort—it was entirely her own fault that Diego had washed his hands of her so she had to accept it and not wallow in self-pity and sit here like a mute lump of misery—she asked over-brightly, 'What time do you expect your husband, Isabella?' She guessed that Diego would remain politely distant with her until they were alone again, then arrange for her own departure in double quick time.

'Diego?' Isabella had polished off the eggs and was piling a roll with thin slices of ham. 'What do you think? Mid-afternoon?'

'Maybe sooner.'

Dio! The sooner the better! If he'd had his wits about him earlier he'd have told Cesar he'd drive his scatty wife back to Seville himself. At least he'd have been doing something constructive. Instead of just sitting around waiting, carefully not looking at Lisa because when he did he had a battle royal on his hands, wanting to pull her into his arms and kiss her until she agreed to be his wife. He could have insisted she came with them, so that she'd have no opportunity to leave, as she'd been on the point of doing.

Edgily, he pushed back his chair and got to his feet, his hard jawline grim. Isabella dabbed her mouth with her napkin and said, 'Are you in a bad temper? Am I being a nuisance? Do tell if I am.' She tilted her head coquettishly, her accompanying smile saying she couldn't believe she could possibly have any nuisance value to anyone. 'If you and Lisa want to have your business meeting, or whatever, then please go ahead. I won't listen if it's supposed to be secret!'

'My discussions with Lisa can wait,' he answered tersely. Taking up that suggestion, whisking Lisa away for a bogus business meeting in the library, was more than tempting. But he couldn't trust his inquisitive, easily bored sister not to barge in on them. Probably at a critical moment. So he'd just have to curb his impatience, grit his teeth and wait it out.

He said, 'I'll ask Rosa to take fresh coffee to the courtyard. I'll join you there shortly.'

Watching his smooth stride, the proud angle of his handsome head as he walked from the room, Lisa felt her eyes blur with tears. She knew what form the discussion he'd mentioned would take.

Would he accept her heartfelt apologies? Probably. With a formal, chilling courtesy. But all the grovelling apologies in the world wouldn't change a single thing. The damage had been done. His current attitude towards her, the way he deliberately refused to even look at her was proof of that.

'Pouff!' Isabella patted her slender midriff. 'I eat too much. I soon will burst! Shall we do as ordered?' She tucked her arm through Lisa's as they both rose from the table. As they strolled together to the inner courtyard Lisa knew that under any other circumstances she would have enjoyed this woman's lively company. They might have become really good friends.

Pausing by the central fountain, gently splashing into the shallow stone basin, Isabella dabbled her fingers in the cool water. 'I am always telling Diego he must have a pool put in this place. At least then there would be something to do.' She shrugged her elegant shoulders. 'But he always tells me something so modern wouldn't fit the whatever you call it—*ambiente*.'

'Atmosphere?' Lisa supplied gently. 'I think he's right. There's something so timeless about this ancient place. It would be a pity to spoil it. '

'Then I am outnumbered! Diego must be right when he calls me a barbarian!' Her wide white grin was stunningly unrepentant. 'But of course he has the swimming pool at his so modern home near Jerez. I am surprised he didn't invite you there for your business meeting. Or book you into a hotel, one belonging to our family, naturally, as is usual with his business associates.'

The dark eyes were dancing with sardonic little lights but Lisa managed a throwaway shrug as if she didn't understand what Isabella was getting at. But of course she did. She obviously had her doubts about her brother's assertion that Lisa's presence here at his isolated and private hideaway had something to do with her father's business.

The water danced with flashing lights. The sun beat down on her head. The paving stones seemed to tilt beneath her feet. The scent of the flowers that rambled over the old stone walls and billowed from the dozens of planters was suddenly overpowering. Lisa raised an unsteady hand to her temple. She was feeling strangely dizzy. She should have forced herself to eat something...

'Oh—you are engaged to be married?'

Did Isabella sound disappointed? Not possible, surely? She had to be imagining it. Lisa's aching brow pleated as the other girl took her hand and examined Ben's ring. She had forgotten she was wearing it. It was nothing like as grand as the huge emerald Isabella sported next to her wide gold wedding band.

'So when is the big day? Are you soon to be married? To an Englishman back home? Or to someone else, someone I might know?' the Spanish girl enquired archly.

'Sorry?' Lisa's eyes clouded as she attempted to

sift through the spate of questions with a brain that was suddenly assaulted by a headache of unprecedentedly vicious proportions.

'Are you to marry your Englishman soon?' Isabella persisted as Rosa appeared at the far side of the courtyard to deposit a tray of fresh coffee on the table beneath the fig tree.

'Yes,' Lisa stated as firmly as she could, given the way she was feeling—all wobbly and feeble, her head pounding. It was a silly weak lie, of course, but it should stem the spate of eager intrusive questions. Saying no would involve explanations about the broken engagement, her reasons for still wearing her ex-fiancé's ring, explanations that she didn't feel up to making right now. She felt with draining misery that she would never want to talk to anyone about anything ever again.

'Move into the shade.' Diego's command was ferociously taut. The sound of it, right behind her, made Lisa jump out of her skin.

Had he heard that stupid lie? More than likely. Her heart lurched downwards at the speed of an out-of-control lift. But she could explain later, of course she could. She twisted her head, seeking his eyes, but he was already walking Isabella to the table.

If he had heard, and he must have done—she'd spoken the lie firmly and he wasn't deaf—it certainly wasn't bothering him one little bit. He was smiling and looking sveltely relaxed as he held out a chair for his sister. As far as he was concerned she could go and marry the devil himself. She had never felt so utterly wretched.

Diego's face ached from smiling and responding to Isabella's idle chit-chat. And his heart ached because of what he'd heard.

She couldn't still be planning to marry Ben Clayton. He wouldn't let it happen! He must have got hold of the wrong end of the conversation. They couldn't have made love with such passion, tenderness and beauty if she'd been in love with another man.

Lisa wasn't that kind of woman.

Unless… The unwelcome thought darkened his soul and made his blood run cold. Unless they'd cooked something up between them.

Faced with the failure of the magazine, their parents facing a mountain of debts, both of them about to lose what they probably thought of as their inheritance, not to mention their jobs, he could almost hear Clayton telling her, Do this for us, for our future. Do what he wants, lie back and think of *Lifestyle* flourishing again. And when he throws you out we'll marry anyway.

Utter nonsense!

He wouldn't let himself go down the tortuous track Lisa had followed earlier when she'd believed Isabella was his wife. In view of what Rosa had said to her he could understand why she'd jumped to that conclusion. Coupled with the misconceptions of five years ago he could understand and forgive.

But she'd been kissing Clayton as if she couldn't wait to jump into bed with him.

He wished he hadn't had to remember the torrid

scene that had left him feeling so shattered, the shock quickly turning to bitterness and anger.

In any case, she had never been to bed with Clayton. He knew that for a fact. She'd been a virgin; he'd stake his life on it.

She'd been angry enough to slay him where he stood when she'd accused him of being married. If she was in love with Clayton, if together they'd hatched up the plan to part him from a sizeable chunk of money, then the fact that he had made her his bit on the side wouldn't anger her so much, would it?

Dio! If he didn't haul her away to somewhere private within the next few minutes he'd go loco! He needed everything straightened out. He had to know if her feelings for him ran as deep as his did for her.

Brooding eyes rested on her for longer than he'd allowed himself thus far. Sideways glances, swift and quickly away again, had revealed her—unusually— adding dollops of cream and several spoonfuls of sugar into her coffee. And she'd drunk thirstily of the jug of iced water Rosa had provided. She'd been worryingly pale when she'd joined them in the shade but, thankfully, she looked marginally better now.

He loved her so much—he adored her. His heart turned over. She was listening to Isabella's rapturous descriptions of the delights of Seville, predictably focusing exclusively on the best boutiques, restaurants and night spots. The Plaza de Espana, the Giralda, the lovely gardens of the Maria Luisa Park not rating a mention. Lisa was doing her best to look interested, smiling, inserting the odd comment or question when she could get a word in but her beautiful eyes were troubled.

Time to butt in, make his excuses to Isabella and take Lisa some place where they wouldn't be disturbed. To the coast, as he'd originally planned. Isabella could kick her heels here until Cesar arrived. A just punishment for the earlier histrionics that had come within a whisker of ruining his life!

Lisa could feel Diego's eyes on her. She felt her cheeks go pink, tried to concentrate on what Isabella was chattering about, blissfully unaware of any undercurrents, and couldn't. Wondering what he was thinking, she gave a start of surprise as Rosa appeared with a portable phone extension and handed it to her.

'For me?'

Stupid question! Why else would Rosa bring the phone to her?

Her stomach lurched sickeningly. She had insisted Diego left a contact number with her father in case he wanted to get in touch with her, just for a chat, but secretly aware that he wouldn't. As far as he was concerned, if his daughter was out of sight she was out of mind.

Her hand was shaking as she took the instrument. Had something terrible happened to him? The headache that had eased while she'd been sitting in the shade came crashing back.

She spoke her name on a near whisper and heard Sophie's voice—loud, clear and riven with tension.

'Ben's been in a traffic accident. They're operating on him now. And the last thing he said before he went through to theatre was, 'Ask Lisa to come. I need to see her.' So you'd better forget what you're doing over there...' Her old friend's voice curled with contempt. 'And get back here. You owe him that much. We thought he was dying, and he still might, and I don't think it's a coincidence that a man who was always an ultra careful driver should turn into the opposite after he'd been dumped, do you?'

Too shocked to speak, Lisa's lips moved wordlessly. She could hardly take it in. Dear Ben, the lifelong friend who'd been looking out for her for years, might be dying! He mustn't!

Crisply, Sophie named the London hospital he was in then snapped, 'Say something, why don't you? Even if it's only sorry!'

Lisa snatched in a breath, anxiety making her voice thin. 'Tell him I'll be with him as soon as I can. I'll get the first available flight back. And tell him to—' her words wobbled emotionally '—hang on in there and—and wait for me.'

If he died it would be like losing a brother. And Sophie, who had been like a loving sister to her, would always lay the blame on her.

She scrambled to her feet, the phone slipping from her nerveless fingers. Trying to keep the panic out of her voice, she told the wide-eyed Isabella, 'Excuse me, I have to go.' She shot a glance in Diego's direction, noted that he'd picked up the phone and was saying something to Sophie, and fled to her room.

Once there she had to take deep breaths and really force herself to think straight, get a grip. Someone would have to drive her to the airport or arrange for a taxi. And, more importantly, she would have to say goodbye to Diego and explain what was happening.

Although, as he'd been speaking to the distraught Sophie, he would already know. There wouldn't be a problem with him. From his recent attitude towards her, he would have packed her off home as soon as he decently could in any case. This crisis merely meant that she'd be leaving a few hours earlier than he'd anticipated.

The very thought of saying goodbye to Diego made her want to throw herself on the bed and cry her eyes out. Courtesy of her nasty suspicious mind she had lost him, she knew that. Tears coursed down her pale cheeks as she began to push the things she'd thrown down on the bed earlier into the waiting suitcase.

She would have liked to have had the opportunity to apologise, to tell him she would regret everything—from her awful behaviour five years ago to the latest tantrum of suspicious abuse—for the rest of her life.

The thought that the little box she'd seen him push into his pocket in that hotel reception area had contained the ring he'd meant to give her had her hating herself. A huge sob built up inside her, venting as Diego walked into her room.

Her heart juddered to a halt and then rushed on in a panicky catch-up exercise. He looked so tense, his dark eyes glittering, his wide shoulders rigid. He was so perfect. And she'd lost him! Another sob exploded within her chest and, before she could tell him how much she regretted everything, Diego said flatly, 'I was sorry to hear the bad news. You and his family must be terribly anxious.'

The predictable words of sympathy increased the pain even more. Guilt stabbed at her heart, reminding her of how selfish she was being—crying because she'd lost whatever chance she might have had of Diego falling back into love with her when her dear friend was fighting for his life back home.

Memories of Ben's many kindnesses, the way he'd always been her ally, taking her firmly under his wing after her mother had died and her father had as good as abandoned her, came rushing back. She might have shared Sophie's amusement at his old-fashioned pedantic ways but there had always been an underlying staunch affection.

Diego, his sensational features flatly expressionless, asked, 'Do you love him?' The stark guilt of thinking only of her own utter misery regarding her fraught relationship—ex-relationship—with the man she would love for the rest of her life had the words, 'Of course I do!' tumbling in a driven wail from her tremulous lips.

His eyes glittering with pain, Diego turned. He had had to know and now his worst nightmare was staring him in the face.

How long would she have kept the pretence up? Coming willingly to his bed, even after he had told her, in a crisis of conscience, that she was free to go. How long, if the co-author of their plan to make a fool of him, take him for all they could get—the man she admitted she loved—hadn't called her back from what he must have believed was his deathbed?

Reaching the door, he turned back. The sight of her tears for the man she loved sent a cold shaft of pain through the centre of his heart. The last words he would ever say to his cheating fallen angel were, 'Manuel will drive you to the airport. Take your case down. He will be ready when you are.'

CHAPTER ELEVEN

SHE'D been fortunate with her flight but even so it was late when the taxi deposited her outside the hospital. Praying Ben had come through the operation successfully, Lisa dragged herself and her suitcase towards the main building on legs that felt too limp to hold her.

Even if he was well enough to have a visitor it was too late to see him now but she could find out how he was. Surely someone would tell her, even if she wasn't a close relative.

If Diego had been with her he would have got all the information going. He was that kind of man. He had natural authority. Her heart gave a painful twist. She had to stop thinking of him, beating herself up over what had happened; if she didn't she would go to pieces.

Nearing the double automatic doors she saw them slide open in front of the Claytons—Honor, Arthur and Sophie—who were exiting together. Lisa's heart banged frantically inside her ribcage.

After Sophie's phone call she knew they were blaming her for what had happened. She had to face them as bravely as she could. Automatically, she straightened her shoulders as they walked towards her, her heart clenching with compassion when she saw Honor's red-rimmed eyes and Sophie's drooping mouth.

'How is he?' Anxiety streaked her voice; she was dreading having to hear the worst.

'The operation was successful, thank heavens. He'll probably walk with a limp for the rest of his life but he won't lose his leg.' It was Ben's father who answered. His voice was heavy with strain and his big shoulders were slumped.

'He will be all right, though?'

'He is sleeping. We were only allowed to look in on him for a few moments,' Ben's mother put in. Honor Clayton looked a decade older than the last time Lisa had seen her at the engagement party. 'Tomorrow, all being well, we will be able to see him for a few minutes longer. It was, was—' she stumbled over the words '—good of you to come so quickly.'

Lisa shivered as a chill wind flicked her skirt against her body as she dipped her head in wordless acknowledgement of Honor's thanks, suddenly aware of the way she was dressed.

She had meant to change into practical jeans and a shirt but she hadn't had a coherent thought in her head after Diego had simply walked out on her, not giving her a chance to say she was deeply sorry for everything. In the light skirt and skimpy top she wasn't dressed for a chilly spring evening in England.

'Well, we can't stand out here getting cold.' It was Honor who rallied. 'We've persuaded Sophie to stay with us until Ben's over the worst. You must, too. You can use your old room.'

Lisa instinctively shook her head. How could she

accept their hospitality when they blamed her for being the indirect cause of Ben's accident? They were
going through enough without having to endure her
surely unwanted presence.

'Please come.' Sophie spoke for the first time. 'We
want you to. Really we do.'

Inky-blue eyes met tearful hazel. 'Honestly?'

Sophie nodded vigorously, too choked to speak,
and Arthur settled the matter, taking her suitcase and
dropping a hand on her shoulder. 'Let's get to the car.
There's no point hanging around here. There's nothing we can do. What we all need is a stiff drink.'

For all her school holidays after her mother's death,
and that first year when she'd been working at *Lifestyle*, this room had been hers. It hadn't changed at
all. The same pretty wallpaper, matching curtains and
bedcover, the same white scatter rugs here and there
on the pale blue fitted carpet.

She'd expected it to be quite different, for Honor
to have altered the young-girl decor after she and
Sophie—to Ben's irritation—had made a bid for in-
dependence and moved into the rented flat.

Somehow it didn't seem right that anything could
remain so completely unchanged when her whole life
had altered so drastically.

She opened her suitcase, looking for her washbag.
She felt so tired, so emotionally drained, she scarcely
knew what she was doing.

It had been a busy, emotional evening. While
Arthur had fielded a spate of phone calls from people
anxious to learn how Ben was, she and Honor had

retired to the kitchen to heat soup and make toast while Sophie had located her father's single malt and given them all a more than generous tot.

The conversation, inevitably, had centred on Ben's accident. 'Apparently, he overtook a lorry on a blind bend and met a van sideways on.' Honor shuddered violently, her hand visibly shaking as she lifted the glass to her lips. 'As the police said, if he hadn't managed to swerve at the very last moment it could have been so much worse. The van driver was relatively unscathed. But Ben wasn't wearing his seatbelt. I simply can't understand it. He's always been a sensible driver.'

Inevitably, Lisa had met Sophie's eyes. She knew what her old friend thought. But the other girl compressed her lips and shook her head, tears flooding her eyes.

After the scratch meal at the kitchen table Sophie had pushed back her chair, glancing at her watch. 'James should be back by now. He's been to the Practice Manager's leaving do. He said he'd back out of it, but I told him not to. There was nothing he could do to help Ben. But I promised to phone and give him what news there is.'

Smothering a yawn, Sophie had left the kitchen and, after helping Honor load the dishwasher, Lisa had excused herself and gone to her old room.

And wished she hadn't. Downstairs, with the others, while the talk had been all of Ben and the dozens of concerned family friends who had phoned, her mind had been kept occupied by thoughts of the anxiety these good people were trying to handle.

Now, alone, her thoughts returned to her own misery. She knew it was selfish but she simply couldn't help it. What was Diego thinking of her? Had he believed the stupid lie he must have overheard? Had he misconstrued her distress on hearing of Ben's accident?

Naturally, she'd been distressed. Ben was a very dear friend of longstanding. But Diego hadn't known the full story or understood how wretchedly guilty Sophie had made her feel, piling on the sense of responsibility, increasing her need to get back to England immediately because the badly injured Ben had been asking for her. He hadn't known, or been able to understand, because he hadn't given her the opportunity to explain anything at all.

Or didn't any of that merit room in his head? Had he already decided he wanted nothing more to do with her after what she'd accused him of? Remembering the distance he'd put between them after she'd confessed to her unthinking overreaction it seemed the more likely scenario.

In any case this anguished introspection wasn't going to make anything better, was it?

'Can I come in?' Sophie, after a moment's hesitation, thrust herself into the room and two seconds later Lisa was being grabbed in a bear hug. 'I'm so sorry, Lise! What I said on the phone was hateful! Will you ever forgive me?'

'Forget it,' Lisa said with the little breath that was left in her lungs. 'I have. You were upset—'

'No, I was hateful!' Sophie denied vehemently, releasing her, standing back a pace, her eyes brimming.

'I was upset—distraught, more like it—but that didn't mean I had to lay a guilt trip on my best friend!'

Best friend!

The first warmth she'd felt since she'd woken this morning stole round her heart. Lisa gave Sophie a gentle shove that deposited her at the end of the bed and plonked herself down on the pillows, her legs tucked beneath her. Just like old times, gossiping half the night away, she thought with a clutch of gratitude at her heartstrings.

'When I thought my twin was going to die and Dad asked me to get the number from your father and phone you and tell you Ben had been asking for you, I simply let rip and lashed out. I was about to lose my brother, or so I thought, and you were swanning around in the sun with your Spanish hunk. It was unfair and wrong and I'll never be able to apologise enough.

'I was fed up with you when you broke your engagement.' Sophie gave a noisy sniff. 'I'd wanted you to be sort of cemented in our family. But Ben did explain at the time, after you'd decided to take off for Spain, that you and he had been going to settle for a dead boring marriage—my description, not his. No passion.' She was twisting the hem of her sweater between her fingers, her eyes downcast. 'Then you met up with the only real love of your life again and bingo!' She raised red-rimmed apologetic eyes. 'I'm crazy in love with James, so I do understand what happened.'

'Shut up!' Lisa said gently, swallowing a lump in

her throat. At least she had her best friend back and that was a lot to be thankful for.

Sophie asked, 'How's it going with your Spanish hunk? We thought he might have been coming with you. We got the guest room ready, just in case. Mum was determined to get you to stay with us here and not be alone in our miserable little flat.' She gave a tiny sigh. 'I expect you'll be haring back as soon as Ben's out of danger.'

Lisa firmly changed the painful subject. 'Never mind all that. Let's talk about you and James. Tell me, how's the house-hunting going? Is everything still on track for a midsummer wedding?'

No way could she discuss what had happened between her and Diego. Maybe she'd be able to confide in her friend later, when the pain of it was a little less savage. But not now.

It was two days before Ben was allowed visitors for longer than a few minutes. On the third morning he'd been moved out of ICU and into a private room and his parents and his twin visited for half an hour and reported good progress. Confined to bed with a cage over the lower half of his body, he was getting bored and cranky which, Honor said happily, meant he was well on the mend.

The atmosphere lightened dramatically and when Lisa left for the early evening session Sophie and Honor were preparing a celebratory meal of roast beef and Arthur's favourite apple pie. Her father had made daily phone calls to the Claytons to keep up to speed over Ben's progress. He'd spoken to her once, just to say he'd heard she was back and hoped Raffacani wasn't too put out by her departure. He hadn't suggested they meet. Lisa hadn't expected him to and for the first time in her life had no room in her heart for disappointment.

Lisa approached Ben's bedside with some trepidation. She couldn't imagine why she had been uppermost in his thoughts when he'd thought he might be dying. But she kept a smile on her face and it widened when she announced with genuine pleasure, 'You're looking a whole heap better than I thought you would.' She bent to kiss his cheek, laying the flowers she'd brought on his bedside locker.

'You shouldn't have bothered.' He indicated the bright bouquets in vases on every available surface. 'You only needed to bring yourself.'

'Right.' Lisa took her time locating a chair and bringing it to the bedside. *In extremis*, he had called out for her and he was going to tell her why. She dreaded hearing he had been deeply in love with her all along but had done the decent thing and stood aside when he rightly concluded she was in love with another man. Truly, she had never wanted to hurt him.

He had never given the smallest sign that that was the case, though. She would never have agreed to marry him if she'd thought for one moment that he was madly in love with her. But some people were experts when it came to hiding their feelings.

'Well, I'm here now,' she said quietly as she sank down on the chair. 'So why did you ask to see me when you thought you might die?'

He shot her a shame-faced look and too quickly

denied thinking any such thing. 'Who said anything about dying? Other people might have been weeping and wailing and thinking the worst but I knew I'd be OK,' he said, not really convincingly. 'Got a lot to live for, haven't I?' His voice strengthened with relief as he informed her, 'I only got a smashed up leg— they've put metal pins in it—the rest of the injuries were pretty small beer, apparently, so I was luckier than I thought I was. No, the timing might have been a bit off, under the fraught circumstances, but I'd been going to ask your father for the phone number. I hadn't got around to it and it was playing on my mind.'

His hand reached for hers and gave it a friendly pat. 'I'd been worrying about you and I wanted to find out if you were OK, that Raffacani was treating you right. I had a pretty good idea of your feelings for him, but I was a bit unsure about him. I mean— a guy who would tell you, Come and live with me, or else—it made me more uneasy the more I thought about it, I guess.'

He gave her a wry smile. 'I've got too used to looking out for you. And the habit sticks. I wanted to let you know not to be afraid of coming back if things weren't working out. I would make the Dads give you a job on the staff again so you wouldn't need to be afraid of being out of work. And, knowing you, I knew you'd be feeling you wouldn't be welcome. I admit the folks were cut up when I told them the engagement was off. I explained why—though not about Raffacani's threat to cancel all his advertising—

and they came round. I wanted to let you know that
we'd all welcome you back, if the need arose.'

'You're a good friend, Ben. The best,' Lisa said
huskily, her eyes filling emotionally. She blinked rapidly and noticed his increasing pallor with a stab of
guilt for allowing him to say so much. 'I should go;
you're beginning to look tired. I've kept you talking
for too long. I'll visit tomorrow if it's OK with the
family.'

She got to her feet. As well as tiring him she knew
that the natural progression from what he'd already
said, bless him, would be to question her about her
relationship with Diego.

Her non-existent relationship.

She wasn't yet up to discussing it with anyone, not
even her dearest friends, without making a complete
and utter fool of herself.

But Ben twisted his head on the pillow. 'Stay. I get
so bored! They won't come to throw you out for at
least another ten minutes.'

He looked so aggrieved she didn't have the heart
to leave. But she had to keep the conversation away
from her ruined relationship with Diego somehow.

So, sinking back on the chair again, she said
quickly, 'Then you've got ten minutes to explain why
you've started to show boy racer tendencies. Sophie
and I always complained that you drove like an old
granny on her way to the shops! No one can understand why you did what you did.'

Ben pulled a face, clearly embarrassed. 'It won't
happen again, believe me! At the time of my accident
my mind was away on another planet.'

On another planet? She said softly, 'That's not like you, Ben. You always have your feet well grounded.'

'Don't I know it!' His face turned fiercely red, alarming Lisa until he told her, 'I never thought I'd go and fall in love, but one look at her did it. It shook me rigid!'

'Ben!' Happiness for him brought the first real smile for days to her lips. 'Good for you! Who is she?'

'Sarah Davies.' He spoke the name with hushed reverence. 'You won't know her, of course. She's one of the high-flyers Raffacani brought in. She edits the gardening section—we're broadening out, not just concentrating on way out fashions very few could wear or afford and society functions of no real interest to the majority of readers.'

'And does she feel the same?' Lisa steeled herself to ask. The last thing she wanted was to see him hurt. A man who up until now had staunchly pooh-poohed the idea of romantic, passionate love could be hurt so much more than a man who had been regularly falling in and out of that state since his teens.

Ben shrugged, wincing as a minor chest injury protested. 'How would I know? Though when I finally plucked up the courage to ask her to have dinner with me she did look pleased. It was to have been the night of the accident, would you believe? My mind just wasn't on what I was doing. I was all knotted up, wondering how I should play it—no practice in that sort of thing, as you know. And there I was, knocked sideways by a big white van! I guessed I'd well and truly blown it, until this came.' He tipped his head in the direction of a get well card prominently displayed on the locker. 'Read what she's put and tell me what you think.'

'That she's holding you to that dinner date and hoping to visit you as soon as she gets the nod,' Lisa affirmed after reading the cheery message. She got up and put the card in his hands. 'I don't think you've blown it. In fact I'm sure you haven't.'

Leaning over, she put a careful kiss on his forehead. 'And, as for how to play it—don't even think about it. Just follow your heart and do what it tells you.'

Diego paced the terrace, the moon-silvered stone walls of the ancient monastery behind him offering no refuge from his tortured thoughts.

There had been no closure. Their brief time together had been meant to heal old wounds but had opened up new ones, wounds so raw and painful he could neither sleep at night nor rest by day.

He'd told himself he could put it all behind him, forget her, get on with his life. It hadn't worked. He didn't want to return to his home in Jerez, or get back to work, or stay on here.

He wanted to be with her. With Lisa. He needed her. Whatever her faults, he had to have her in his life, convince her he could make her happier than Clayton ever could.

And to accomplish that he had to do something about it. He had to go and get her, make her see they were meant to be together. It had been fated ever since he'd lifted her to her feet on that mountain track five years ago and first looked into her beautiful eyes. He'd been a lost man ever since and was damned well going to find himself again. With her. Only her.

Swinging on his heel, he stalked back into his favourite home, took the stairs two at a time and began to pack the few things he'd need. First thing tomorrow he'd be on the first available flight to London.

CHAPTER TWELVE

THE flocks of butterflies in Lisa's stomach began to beat their fluttery wings as the hired Seat climbed to the upper reaches of the twisty mountain road.

She was doing the right thing. She was! She had to hang on to that belief or she would find herself turning round in the next pull-in she came to and heading straight back to Seville.

A detailed map of the area was spread out on the passenger seat but she'd only really needed it at the start of the journey from the airport. It was as if she had an internal homing device that was drawing her back towards the man she loved.

Easing the car round a particularly tight bend she recognised the glimpse of spectacular scenery—the mountainside dropping to a deep river valley, the huddle of white-washed houses far below enclosed by the verdant greenery of vines, citrus trees and olives.

As the road widened slightly it began to descend and the butterflies cranked up their annoying activities, her neck and shoulders ached with tension and, despite the car's air-conditioning system, Lisa began to sweat. Another mile, maybe two, and she would reach the monastery. And Diego.

But she was doing the right thing!

Reaching the Claytons' Holland Park home after visiting Ben yesterday evening, the words she'd said to him had echoed with startling, inescapable clarity inside her head.

'Just follow your heart and do what it tells you.'

She had stood as still as a stone on the doorstep, listening. And her heart had told her to return to Spain, find Diego, and tell him how much she loved him. The voice was clear, insistent.

Her body had glowed—every vein, every nerve end, every muscle and sinew responding to the inescapable tug of him, as if he were calling to her from his remote mountain hideaway.

Now she was seeing the almost mystical experience of the evening before in a more grounded way. Diego might not be still at the old monastery. But Rosa and Manuel would be able to tell her where she could find him; they would give her the address of his home near Jerez and his place of business.

And she knew that when she eventually ran him to earth her admission of love might well leave him cold; he might simply tell her he wasn't interested. That was something she would have to accept.

Even so, she was doing the right thing. There was a smooth, untroubled logic to it. Things left undone, important things, didn't bring a peaceful mind. Ben had shown her that.

Soon after his accident, when he'd thought he might not make it, he'd said he needed to see her. He'd wanted to make sure she was all right, to tell her to come back home if things weren't working out for her, that she'd be welcome, no hard feelings. He hadn't wanted to leave the assurances unsaid.

And life was notoriously precarious. If something

happened either to her or, heaven forbid, Diego, before she'd put the record straight there would be no peace, no closure.

Tears were wetting her face when she eventually switched off the ignition on the forecourt. Briefly closing her eyes, she gave herself a few moments to quieten her mind before mopping the dampness away with a tissue, exiting and stretching her cramped muscles. She took a deep breath and walked steadily over the sun-baked slabs towards the main door.

Her mouth ran dry and her heart banged savagely against her ribs. Would he refuse to let her cross the threshold? Refuse to listen to what she had to say? Had she come on a fool's errand?

Don't even think about it—don't accept defeat until it's inevitable. Think of something else, or don't think at all!

The late afternoon sun burned through the thin cotton of her blouse. But at this time of year the evenings in the mountains would be decidedly chilly. Had she packed a sweater? Did it matter?

'*Señorita!*' The great door swung open and Rosa's pretty face was wreathed in a beaming smile. Lisa gulped and did her best to return it.

'I heard the car. So it is you—you stay?'

Lisa tucked a heavy strand of hair behind her ear, took a steadying breath. 'I'm not sure.' And wasn't that the truth—she could be thrown out in two seconds flat. 'But I'd like to speak to the *señor*. If you'd tell him I'm here, please.'

'Come—' Rosa ushered her into the cool vastness

of the great hall. 'I fetch Manuel. He has the good English. I have not so good.'

Not a bad idea at that, Lisa thought as she lowered herself into a heavily carved chair beneath the tall window flanking the door, wishing the flutter of internal nerves wasn't making her feel quite so nauseous. There had been too many misunderstandings in the past; they could all do without any more. Though she'd have thought that a simple request to tell Diego she was here would have been easy enough to understand.

By the time Manuel put in an appearance Lisa was pacing the floor, mentally climbing walls, about to go in search of Diego herself because this waiting, this not knowing what her reception would be was killing her.

Twirling on her heels she faced him, nerves pattering. Soon now she would see her love—

'Rosa tells me you have come back from England to meet with the *señor*.' His swarthy features were sympathetic. 'But he is not here. He left very early this morning before it was light.'

'I see.' The tension drained out of her, quickly replaced by a dull sense of frustration. Nothing to get in a panic about, though. She had half-expected it, mentally prepared herself for this eventuality, hadn't she?

She'd missed him by a whisker.

'Then perhaps you could give me addresses of where I might find him?'

He seemed to consider her request for a long moment, then grinned. 'Perhaps I do better! Rosa is making coffee for you. She will bring it to small salon and I will make the phone calls. It is better to know for sure he is home—he might have gone anywhere in the world—his business affairs take him to many places.'

Sickening thought!

Impulsively, Lisa reached out to touch his arm as he began to leave her, her eyes unknowingly full of stark inky appeal, the hand that clutched his arm shaking just a little. 'I'd love coffee. It's been a long drive. But may I have it in the kitchen with Rosa?' She didn't want to be alone to agonise over the very real possibility that Diego was even now on his way to the other side of the world.

'Certainly.' His dark eyes were kind. 'Come with me. You drink coffee and I use the telephone.'

The main kitchen was cavernous with a vaulted stone and timber ceiling and a huge open fireplace. Nevertheless the atmosphere was surprisingly home-like, with hams, strings of onions and dried herbs hanging from the massive beams, the aroma of coffee drifting like a blessing.

Manuel said something to his wife in rapid Spanish as she turned from the huge gleaming range, a cafe-tière in one hand.

'*Ciertamente!*' Rosa smiled in response to what-ever her husband had said, setting the coffee on an immense wooden table near a bowl of yellow roses, plucked, Lisa guessed, from the many blooms that perfumed the courtyard. 'All of us will drink! You will please to sit, *señorita*?'

Taking the chair indicated, Lisa sat and closed her

tired eyes for a moment, the quiet, comforting atmosphere helping her to wind down just a little. Rosa
fetched three bowl-shaped coffee mugs and a plate of
sticky almond pastries and Manuel consulted a list
pinned up by the wall-mounted phone and began at
last to dial.

Drinking the welcome coffee and queasily refusing
the pastries, Lisa wished she could understand
Manuel's side of the conversations that ensued as he
dialled at least three separate numbers. Diego was obviously proving harder to track down than she had
hoped.

A point punched home when he walked back to
take his mug of coffee from the table, shrugging his
shoulders fatalistically.

'I called the *señor's* office first. He has not been
there. His sister hasn't seen him since she left here
with her husband and his housekeeper gave us the
only clue we have.' He spread his free hand as if to
indicate the clue was sadly worthless. 'The *señor*
phoned to his home at mid-morning to say to cancel
the dinner he had arranged to give his parents next
week. Is all. He didn't say where he was going, only
that he had no idea when he would return.'

It was another perfect morning but Lisa couldn't begin to appreciate it. Something inside her had died.
Diego could be anywhere in the world. True, she'd
asked Manuel to ask Diego to get in touch with her
when he saw him next. But she wasn't holding out
much hope that he would bother to respond. He was

getting on with his busy, successful life. He didn't need her in it.

Yesterday, the afternoon had been drawing to a close, the shadows lengthening on the mountains, when she'd thanked Rosa and Manuel for their help, hardly able to hide her misery, and made to leave.

But Manuel had firmly argued against her driving back to Seville, pointing out that she had already had a long journey from England, that it would soon be dark, and Rosa could quickly make the bed up in the room she'd had before. It would be no trouble, he'd insisted.

So she'd stayed the night, giving in because she had no energy left to fight for her own way—her need to get away from this beautiful place where she had been, so very briefly, happy and hopeful. Staying overnight had been sensible, she supposed, but she wished she hadn't slept late after the initial long restless hours.

Hurriedly, she stripped her bed and repacked the few overnight things she'd needed and carried the case down to the hired car.

She'd already said her goodbyes and thanks to Rosa and Manuel and while she'd been eating the very late breakfast the pretty housekeeper had insisted on making for her, Manuel had offered to try again to track Diego down for her.

He could telephone the *señor*'s parents; why hadn't he thought of that before? There was a slim hope. The *señor* didn't answer to them for what he was doing but they might know where he was. Though he doubted it. Hadn't the *señor*'s housekeeper had to give them his message? Which meant he hadn't spoken to them himself, didn't it? Nevertheless, for the *señorita*'s sake, he would try.

But the phone was dead. A problem with the line; it often happened, the Spaniard said with a shrug of resignation. So even the final slim hope of making contact with him was gone. There was nothing to keep her here.

Starting the engine, she said her silent farewells. There would be no closure and she'd just have to live with that. Get on with her life, just as he was doing.

Diego forced himself to slow down as the road twisted sharply, the wheels spinning on the loose surface. He wasn't suicidal; he was merely in a desperate hurry!

He vented a vehement string of oaths, his hard profile clenched. Everything was conspiring against him. He remembered what he'd told Lisa five years ago. He'd said his love had no ending and had meant it. Still did.

But finding her and proving it, demanding that she give him a chance to make her understand that she could find happiness as his wife—not Clayton's—was turning out to be a problem of nightmare proportions.

It had been mid-afternoon yesterday when he'd arrived at her flat. No answer. A phone call to her father had given him the information that she was staying with the Claytons in Holland Park, just until Ben was out of danger. The older man had sounded defensive, almost as if he were reluctant to let him know where his daughter was or what she was doing.

The taxi that had taken him to the Holland Park address had been frustratingly slow through the heavy traffic. Sophie, his rival's twin, had answered his summons, peering behind him. 'Where's Lise?'

'That's what I'd like to know.' Still sitting at Clayton's bedside, mopping his brow, feeding him grapes and kissing him better? The thought made him furious.

'She isn't with you, then?'

'Obviously not.' He had a hard time of it, hanging on to the very last thread of his rapidly dwindling patience. 'Why would she be?'

'Because she flew out to Spain this morning to see you. She said you had unfinished business. Look, she didn't put me in the picture, but she did say she didn't know when she'd be back. Ben's making good progress so I suppose she feels she doesn't need to be here now.' She widened the door aperture. 'Won't you come in?'

What the hell for? had been his initial, ill-mannered answer, happily unvoiced. He made himself smile. 'No. No, thank you.' And then, as if on an afterthought, 'Is Lisa's engagement to Ben still on?'

Sophie stared at him as if he'd been speaking double Dutch, then denied, 'No, of course not. I would have thought you, of all people, would have known that.'

Which had left him with a lot to think about. Just as he had come to London to find her, she had flown out to Spain to see him. Their planes had probably passed in mid-air, going in opposite directions! That surely had to mean she hadn't written him off as the uncaring boor he must have appeared during the final hours they'd spent together.

And her engagement to Clayton was still off. So why had she told Isabella she was soon to be married to the man whose ring she wore?

He must have taken his leave of Sophie but he couldn't remember having done so. He remembered walking further down the street, hailing a cab to take him back to the airport and using his mobile to phone Manuel to tell him to keep Lisa where she was until he got back.

The line was engaged. It was still engaged twenty minutes later. He tried again when he was dropped off at the airport and nearly exploded with frustrated fury.

The line was dead. The phone at the monastery was out. Finding him gone, no one knowing where he was, Lisa would have made tracks.

He had two options. Sit on the Claytons' doorstep until she decided to return. Or get back to Spain, hoping she'd still be there, waiting for him. Even if she'd left, which seemed more than likely, she might have told his staff where she was heading—directly home, or not.

There was too much adrenalin pumping round his veins to allow for inaction. He booked the last remaining seat on the early flight out to Seville then took himself off to the arrivals hall to wait for the late night flight in, hoping she might have been on it.

She wasn't.

And now he was wishing the last few miles away, undoubtedly looking like something the cat had dragged in, hoping against hope that she hadn't already left the monastery.

His thoughts grimly occupied, he had to stamp on the brakes to avoid a head-on collision with a Seat being driven the other way. As it was they were bumper to bumper. *Cristo!* Some people weren't fit to be behind the wheel; the driver had taken the tight bend at a maniac speed!

And there was no way he could pass; the road was too narrow. The other driver would have to back up, pronto. He was in a hurry!

His jawline set, shadowed with an overnight beard growth, he slid out of the car, took two stormy paces and his heart stopped.

Lisa!

His heart crashed on then melted as he watched her open the door at her side and slowly swing her long legs to the ground. She stood, lifting her face to him. She was pale, those beautiful eyes shadowed, her hair tumbling down in wayward tendrils. Her soft mouth quivered as their eyes meshed. He had never loved her more.

His driving aim to kiss that look of uncertainty from those haunted eyes, those trembling lips, had him landing one hand on the bonnet of his car and vaulting over the obstruction. Only one pace was necessary to bring him to his heart's desire. One forceful pace and he was holding her in his arms, fiercely pressed against his heart, groaning thickly as he felt her delicate body shake.

Then she slithered even closer into him, winding her arms around his neck, lifting her lovely face to his. There were tears in her eyes. His heart jerked. There must be no sadness. Not for her, not ever again. He would not allow it!

'Diego—'

'Hush,' he commanded thickly. 'No words. Just this—' He lowered his head to kiss her.

Lisa knew she was in heaven. Joy leapt through every vein and sinew and all the cells in her body were on fire as she kissed him back, her hunger matching his as she strainingly attempted to writhe closer even though that was not possible.

Their bodies were welded. She could feel the heated hardness of him through the barrier of their clothes. Lightning exploded inside her.

One of his hands was tangling in her hair. She could feel him shaking with the intensity of the passion that was claiming them both as reluctantly he dragged his mouth from hers and stated raggedly, 'You will marry me. You will forget Clayton, forget you ever knew him. If he weren't already lying injured on a hospital bed I would have beaten him to a pulp!'

He planted a kiss on her startled mouth, impressing his forceful decision. Lisa gurgled with laughter and kissed him back, only to find his dark head rearing away, a ferocious glitter in his dark eyes. 'This is no laughing matter. You are mine and I am a possessive man. I mean what I say. I propose to you and you giggle!' Violently insulted male pride bristled from every pore. 'But this time,' he uttered darkly, 'you do not leave my sight until I have my wedding ring on your finger. And not even then.'

'No problem. You won't be able to get rid of me,' Lisa assured him, a soft smile curling her mouth. 'And leave poor Ben out of it. I was engaged to him for a few hours. I have no intention of marrying him. There is no need to be jealous, and your proposal leaves a lot to be desired,' she added with teasing severity, safe now in the mind-blowing knowledge that the love of her life wasn't lost at all; he'd just been mislaid for a while.

His lean hands tightening on her shoulders, one black brow rose as he questioned, 'Then why did you flaunt his ring in front of me, tell Isabella that you would be marrying him soon?'

At least she had the grace to blush, Diego conceded, magnanimously deciding that he had already forgiven her for not knowing her own mind at that time. Hadn't she come back to Spain to find him and although she hadn't formally accepted his proposal— and how did it leave a lot to be desired?—she hadn't been able to hide the way she felt about him when he'd kissed her.

Her colour receding as she recalled just how dreadful she'd felt that last morning, her glance was direct as she offered contritely, 'It was stupid of me. But at the time it seemed the easiest way to shut her up. You were treating me as if I were a nasty smell and I was so miserable, so sure you wanted nothing more to do with me after the things I'd accused you of, I couldn't face explaining that I was only wearing the ring for safe-keeping. Your sister would just have asked more questions—'

'Isabella hasn't known how to keep silent since the

day she first learned to talk,' he acknowledged. 'Even so, you couldn't wait to leave me when you knew he'd been injured and when I asked if you loved him you said you did. You can't begin to imagine how that made me feel.'

'Oh, I can!' she whispered emotionally, lifting her hands to touch his lean and handsome face. 'When I thought you'd turned your back on me my whole world fell apart, my darling. And I do love Ben. But like a brother. Not as I love you.'

He pulled in a breath. His stunning eyes glittered as he commanded, 'Say that again. Say you love me!'

'Why else do you think I'm here? I knew I couldn't go through the rest of my life without telling you how deeply I love you.' Her voice wobbled. 'But you weren't here. Where were you?'

Completely consoled, Diego trailed loving kisses down the length of her throat. 'In London,' he murmured thickly. 'Looking for you. I, too, had to tell you that I loved you more than my life.' His lips encountered the top button of her cotton blouse. Slightly unsteady hands lifted to slip it out of its moorings, then stilled. With a supreme effort he controlled the fierce need to make love to his beautiful darling right here and now.

'We are blocking the road, my angel. We must go.' The lightest of kisses on her unbearably sensitised lips. 'Wait in my car. I will move the Seat.'

No sooner said than he was behind the wheel, reversing the little car in a cloud of dust. And within moments he was striding back to where she was frozen to the spot, immobilised by the utter magic of what was happening. Diego loved her! She was to be his wife! Welded to his side for the rest of their lives! How could anything in the world possibly be more wonderful?

All macho confidence, Diego opened the passenger door and gently eased her poleaxed body inside, strapping her in with cool efficiency before walking round to get behind the wheel, telling her, 'It is parked in a pull-in. And there it may stay,' with a calm disregard for the need to get it back to the hire firm at the airport. 'You, my most precious love, are going nowhere. And this time I keep you here with love. My bad behaviour is a thing of the past.' His hand on the ignition key, he turned to her, his eyes drenched with tenderness. 'For five years you haunted me. When I saw how I could take what I believed was my right to vengeance, I took it. Can you forgive me?'

'I can't blame you for thinking bad things about me,' Lisa confessed earnestly. 'Five years ago I behaved like a spoiled brat. I'd seen you with this fabulous woman. Twice. Once going into a jeweller's, and again in the hotel foyer. I thought you'd dumped me for her, that you hadn't meant it when you said you were in love with me. I—' her voice almost disintegrated '—I took my own childish form of revenge.'

'*Querida*—' His hands took hers, pressing kisses into her palms. 'That is all forgotten. But I need to hear you say you forgive me for my truly vile treatment once I had you to myself. I wanted you like crazy and I knew you weren't indifferent to me. So I decided to let you stew, wondering when you would have to fulfil your part of the hellish bargain. Increase the sexual tension until you begged me to make love to you. How can you love such a monster?'

'How can I stop?' she replied, sincerity spilling from her eyes. 'Besides, you gave me the option of leaving when it came right down to it, remember? So you can't be all bad!'

And with that assurance he gave her the slashing grin that had always had the power to turn her knees to water and started the engine.

It was growing dark, a soft amethyst light stealing over the mountains. Lisa, watching for the first faint stars from the terrace, wondered where Diego had got to.

She'd bathed and changed as he'd suggested, dressing with immense care in one of the beautiful dresses that she'd never expected to see again. A honey-coloured silk shift that made the most of her slender curves, her hair loose around her shoulders, her make-up as perfect as she could manage given that her fingers, all the cells in her body, were trembling with delicious anticipation.

'Come.' He was behind her, his hands lightly on her shoulders as he turned her to face him. She hadn't heard him approach. Her heart leapt.

'You are so beautiful,' he announced with betraying huskiness, beautiful himself in a formal white jacket over a pristine shirt and those narrow black trousers that made his sex-appeal positively killing.

Dreamily, she allowed herself to be led back

through the silent house. And only when he opened
the door to his bedroom did her love-drenched eyes
sparkle with delight.

The softly lit room was full of flowers—someone
must have denuded the garden and the courtyard!
There was champagne on ice and hauntingly sweet
music coming from a hidden tape deck.

Wordlessly, he led her to the bedside where the
satin covered pillows had been heaped to resemble a
throne. He eased her down then with a flourish went
down on one knee and took her hand.

A dark flush emphasising his slashing cheekbones,
his voice deep with emotion, he asked, 'Lisa, will you
marry me if I ask, leaving nothing to be desired?'

Her throat closed up. Speechless at first, her heart
feeling as though it had no option but to burst, she
lifted the hand that was gripping hers so tightly and
kissed the back of each of those strong lean fingers
with fevered intensity until she was able to whisper,
'Yes! Oh, yes, my darling!'

Several breathless minutes later, after the throne-
like position of the heaped pillows had been thoroughly disturbed, Diego eased himself away from her
and slipped a ring on her finger. The beautiful sap-
phire gleamed in the soft light. 'This is the ring I
chose for you five years ago. It is now where it be-
longs.'

Her eyes brimmed with delirious tears and Diego
took his time over kissing them away, only stopping
when her fingers clamped around his wrist and she
stated happily, 'You didn't throw it away.'

'Throw what away, my dearest angel?'

'The watch.' She'd seen the glint of gold.

For a moment he looked discomfited. Then he grinned, kissed her with swift passion and confessed, 'I have always worn it. Only when I got to London on my mission of vengeance did I replace it with some cheap horror bought from the airport duty free shop. If you'd seen it you would have known that you had been in my heart, had never left it. At the time giving you that knowledge was not on my agenda.'

'I see.' Her eyes sultry, Lisa trailed kisses down from his temples to his sensual mouth. 'So what is on your agenda now, I wonder.'

His mouth smiled beneath hers as his body pinned her back against the tumbled pillows. 'I'll give you three guesses, my dearest darling.'

A SPANISH
HONEYMOON

by

Anne Weale

Anne Weale was still at school when a women's magazine published some of her stories. At twenty-five she had her first novel accepted by Mills & Boon. Now, with a grown-up son and happily married to her first love, Anne divides life between her winter home, a Spanish village ringed by mountains and vineyards, and a summer place in Guernsey, one of the many islands around the world which she has used as backgrounds for her books.

CHAPTER ONE

La mujer sin hombre es como el fuego sin leña.

Woman without man is like fire without wood.

THERE were nights when Liz couldn't sleep.

Memories…regrets…doubts…unfulfilled longings…elation at breaking free…panic at her recklessness; all these fizzed about in her brain, like the firecrackers the village boys let off in the street on *fiestas*, and made sleeping impossible.

When this happened she would get out of bed, make a mug of herb tea and, unless it was raining, which was blessedly seldom in this benign climate, climb the outside staircase to the flat roof where she dried her laundry and sunbathed.

One night she was up there, gazing at the moonlit mountains surrounding the valley, when she was startled by noises. They came from the big house that had its front door on the next street up the hillside on which the small Spanish village of Valdecarrasca was built.

Named after the fig tree in a corner of its walled garden, the big house was called La Higuera. Its rear windows overlooked the rooftops of the terrace of much smaller houses on the street below, where Liz lived. But as La Higuera had been empty since her arrival, six months ago, she had almost forgotten that, some day, its owner would return and her flat roof would no longer be as private as it had been up to now.

The first intimation that someone had arrived was the rattling sound of the *persianas* being rolled up, releasing a glow of light from each of the ground-floor windows.

5

Liz's instinctive reaction was to leap up from the lounger, hurry down the staircase and disappear into her house before anyone at La Higuera noticed her.

Standing in her unlighted kitchen, she waited to see if the blinds hiding the upstairs windows of the big house would be rolled up. It might not be Cameron Fielding, the owner, who had arrived. Sometimes, she had been told, he lent the house to his friends.

To many of the foreigners living in or around the village, Cameron Fielding was a household name. Liz had never heard of him until she started living in Valdecarrasca. Nor, from what she had been told, did she like the sound of him. However, being a fair-minded person, she took some of the more scandalous stories with a pinch of salt.

Whoever it was who had arrived at La Higuera must have come without Alicia being notified, she thought, as she watched and waited.

Alicia was the portly Spanish lady paid a retainer to keep an eye on the house while it was empty, and to air and clean it before anyone used it. According to village rumour, she was supposed to do this once a month so that it was always in order. In practice, so Liz had heard, she did it only a day or two before Mr Fielding or his guests were expected.

This time, it seemed, she had been caught napping. To Liz's certain knowledge, Alicia had not set foot in the place for months, which meant that every horizontal surface would be thick with dust and the rooms would have a musty smell.

Wondering if tomorrow Alicia would find herself out on her ear, Liz saw one of the upstairs *persianas* being hauled up by the stout tape that reeled the slats into a box at the top of the window. Many village houses, including her own, still had the old-fashioned wooden-slatted blinds that were pulled up by cords into a roll that remained visible. But La Higuera had been altered and modernised.

The person who had lifted the blind was a man but, because he was silhouetted by the lights in the room behind him, all she could see was that he was tall and broad-shouldered, with dark hair. In fact he looked like a Spaniard. Although many of the elderly locals were short and often bandy-legged, owing to an inadequate diet in the years when Spain was a poor and backward country, the younger Spaniards had much better physiques and were as well-built as their contemporaries in other parts of Europe.

Then a second person came into view, a woman. As the man, whoever he was, stood looking out at the moonlit valley, she moved close behind him and put her arms round him. Immediately he swung round to return her embrace. Liz saw his head bend towards the girl's and, for quite a long time, they engaged in what was clearly a passionate kiss.

It was still going on when, almost as if some sixth sense told him they were not as private as they might expect to be in a small Spanish village at one o'clock in the morning, he reached out an arm towards the side of the window. The next moment Liz's view of the embrace was blocked by the pair of curtains whose draw-cord he must have pulled.

Feeling as guilty as if she had been caught watching something far more intimate than a kiss, Liz drew the kitchen curtains and felt her way to the light switch. Then she made another cup of tea and took it up to her bedroom, intending to continue reading the book on top of the stack on her night table.

But, like a love scene in a movie or on TV, what she had seen had stirred up the powerful yearnings that, as they had no hope of being realised, she did her best to keep battened down.

She was also curious to know if the man in the bedroom at La Higuera was, in fact, the legendary womaniser whose amorous exploits provided so many titbits of gossip for his fellow foreigners to relish.

'...a different girlfriend every time he comes here,' was one of the allegations Liz had heard about him.

'Not what you could call handsome, but *madly* attractive...my goodness, yes, as attractive as the devil and *totally* without morals. Still, as he isn't married, can you blame him for grabbing his opportunities?' was another comment that had stuck in her memory.

Liz, who had had her childhood and teenage years blighted by a man of the same stamp who *had* been married, was disposed to dislike all philanderers. She had no time for people who treated sex as a game. She despised them all.

Despite a disturbed night, she was up at her usual early hour the next day. Brushing her teeth in the bathroom, she thought for the umpteenth time how different she looked today from the way she had looked on arrival, pallid-faced and drawn after a cold and wet northern European winter and a succession of head colds caught while commuting from her home in the outer suburbs to her workplace in central London.

Now, even after a disturbed night, she had three times as much vitality as she had ever had in England. She had never been a beauty. Her dark blue eyes and her clear skin—once pale but now lightly tanned—were her best features, counterbalanced by a disastrous nose and a rather unfeminine chin.

In her other life, as she had begun to think of it, she had adapted her hairstyle to a conservative version of whatever was the prevailing fashion. Here, to save money, she had given up going to the hairdresser and let it grow to a length she could tie back or pin up. Her basic colour was mid-brown. In place of professionally-done highlights, these days she had only sun streaks, helped by rubbing selected strands with a cut lemon. There was always a lemon to hand because there was a *limonero*, that bore fruit all year round, growing in her little back yard.

After a quick hot shower, she dressed in a plain white T-shirt, a navy blue cotton skirt and navy sneakers. Later she was driving to the weekly produce market in a larger village a few kilometres away. She had planned, immediately after breakfast, to spend half an hour working in the walled garden of La Higuera.

In the same way that Alicia was supposed to look after the

interior of the house, the previous owner of Liz's house, an elderly Englishwoman called Beatrice Maybury, had undertaken to take care of the neighbouring garden. Beatrice had asked if Liz would be willing to continue this work and Liz had agreed. She had always liked gardening, and the generous fee paid to her predecessor in return for an hour's work a week would be a welcome addition to her limited funds. At that time, of course, she had not known the kind of man the house belonged to. Beatrice had never mentioned his predatory tendencies. Perhaps she had been unaware of them since, by all accounts, she had kept herself to herself and not been part of the expatriates' grapevine.

After their late arrival, and whatever had followed that passionate kiss, it seemed unlikely the people staying at La Higuera would be up and about before mid-morning. Liz decided to stick to her plan and do some weeding and watering before they surfaced for the day.

She entered the property by a gate at the side of the house that, by way of a narrow passage, led down to the 'secret' garden at the rear. Most of the larger houses in the main part of the village did not have gardens, only patios. In the rest of Europe, a patio meant any paved sitting-out area. But in Spain it was an open area within the structure of a building. In Valdecarrasca, many of the houses too small to have a patio had a small garden or yard. But the garden behind La Higuera was the size of a tennis court.

Her first task today was to plant out some cuttings she had taken from a clump of silvery-grey artemisia and kept, in water, in a dark green wine bottle until they put out small roots.

She was on her knees by the narrow bed at the foot of the wall clad with variegated ivy that spilled over the top and cascaded into her own little yard on the other side, when a man's voice said, 'Hello...who are you?'

The question gave Liz such a start that she let out a muffled squeak and, in scrambling to her feet, almost overbalanced. He stepped forward, grabbing her arm to steady her.

'Sorry...I didn't mean to scare you. I suppose you thought the house was still empty. I got back late last night, or rather early this morning. I'm Cam Fielding, the owner. And you are...?'

She had known who he was immediately. 'Madly attractive' had not been an exaggeration. He was unquestionably the most attractive man she had ever encountered.

Last night she had taken him for a Spaniard and he did have some of their characteristics: the black hair and eyebrows, the olive skin that tanned easily, and the hawk-like features that often indicated Moorish ancestry. But although by no means all Spanish people had brown eyes, she had yet to meet one whose irises were the colour of steel.

'I'm Liz Harris,' she said, acutely aware of his grip on her arm and also of the fact that, under a white terry bathrobe, he was undoubtedly naked. Glancing downwards, she saw that his feet were bare, which was why she hadn't heard him approaching. Looking up again, she noticed his hair was damp. He must have just had a shower, come downstairs to make coffee and seen her from the kitchen window.

She had never been inside his house but Beatrice had described its layout so she knew that the two doors set close to each other led into the kitchen and the garage.

'Are you Mrs Harris's daughter...or her daughter-in-law?' he asked.

'Neither...I'm Mrs Harris.' She wished he would let go of her arm and move back a bit. At such close quarters his physical magnetism was uncomfortably strong.

He lifted an eyebrow. 'I see. I expected you to be much older...the same age as Beatrice Maybury. When she wrote that an English widow was buying her cottage, I assumed that you were contemporaries. How old are you?'

'Thirty-six,' said Liz, relieved that he had finally let go of her arm so that she could step back and widen the distance between them. It was rather a cheek to ask her age at this early stage of their acquaintance, she thought. 'How old are you?' she countered.

'Thirty-nine,' he replied. 'Was your husband much older than you...or did he die untimely young?'

'He was a year older. He died four years ago.' She had never met anyone who asked such personal questions so soon. Most people carefully avoided mentioning anything to do with her premature widowhood.

'What happened?'

'He was drowned trying to rescue a child in a rough sea. He wasn't a very good swimmer. They were both lost,' Liz answered flatly. Duncan's heroism was still a puzzle to her. He had been a cautious man, not one who took risks or chances. The courage and folly of his last act had been totally out of character.

'That makes his action even braver,' said Fielding. 'Were you living in Spain when it happened?'

'No, in England. We had stayed in Spain several times with his parents. They used to rent a villa to escape the worst of the winter. But I like the mountains better than the seaside resorts. Beatrice Maybury's brother—the one she's gone back to look after—knows my father-in-law. Mr Maybury thought my parents-in-law might like to buy her house. I came out with them to look at it. They didn't like it, but I did.'

'And how is it working out?' Fielding asked. 'The majority of the British expats in this part of Spain are retired...though the number of young working expats is building up, so I'm told. Do you have a job apart from keeping this garden in order?'

'I'm a freelance needlework designer...mainly for women's magazines. It's work I can do anywhere—thanks to e-mail.'

Her attention was distracted by colour and movement on the terrace built out from the house. The girl she had seen last night was coming to join them. Like Fielding, she was wearing a robe, but his was utilitarian and hers was designed to be more decorative than practical. Made of irregular layers of chiffon in sunset colours, it floated, cloud-like, round a spectacular figure of the kind displayed at movie premières and Oscar presentations.

'Cam...the fridge is empty. There's no orange juice,' this vision said plaintively, wafting down the steps that connected the terrace and garden.

'I know. I'll get some from the shop. I didn't expect you to get up until later.' He introduced them. 'Mrs Harris...this is my house guest, Fiona Lincoln. Fiona, this is my neighbour from over the wall. Mrs Harris keeps the garden in order.'

Liz removed the cotton gardening glove from her right hand. She was not surprised to find that Fiona had a limp handshake. She didn't look the sort of person who would shake hands firmly. Glamorous women hardly ever did, in Liz's experience. Perhaps they thought it was unfeminine to exert any pressure.

'I thought you had a maid to look after things,' Fiona said to Cam.

Despite not being dressed for the day, she was already fully made up, Liz noticed.

'I have a cleaning lady, but it doesn't look as if she's been in recently,' he answered. 'Do you know my home help, Mrs Harris? Is she ill or something?'

'Beatrice mentioned that you had help...someone called Alicia. But we don't run into each other,' Liz told him. 'I'm usually here before breakfast or in the late afternoon. I expect she comes in the middle of the day.'

'I know where she lives. I'll call round there. Now we'll leave you in peace while we get ourselves organised. Catch you later.' As they turned away, he put a possessive hand on the other woman's slender waist.

Watching Fiona leaning against him as far as the foot of the steps, Liz felt a moment of envy. She would have given a lot to have a man in her life against whom she could lean like that. At the same time she knew that a relationship such as theirs—she felt sure it wasn't 'serious' and would probably end as casually as it had begun—would not satisfy her.

She could never take a lover purely for physical pleasure, or be a temporary girlfriend.

The stairs to the terrace were narrow, with succulents growing in clay pots placed at the outer edge of each tread. Before mounting them, Fiona furled her floating layers of chiffon, wrapping the garment more closely around her and, in so doing, drawing Fielding's attention to the curves of her shapely bottom.

Watching him admiring it, Liz wondered how men like him and her father could be satisfied with making love to women for whom they felt no real affection or even liking. To her, the idea of going to bed with someone you didn't love was repugnant.

Because she had married so young, she had missed the sexual freedom enjoyed by most of her generation. Duncan had been her first boyfriend and her only lover. That she might marry again seemed doubtful. Unattached men of the right age were thin on the ground. And anyway did she want to marry a second time? Marriage was such a huge risk.

With a sigh, she resumed her planting.

After lunch, Liz went for a walk on the dirt lanes and narrow tarmacked roads criss-crossing the vineyards that stretched from the edge of the village to the far side of the valley. When she arrived the grapes had been tiny, no larger than orange pips. She had seen them grow and ripen until they were ready to be picked. Now the vine leaves were turning red or purple.

On the way back, she followed a lane that gave her an overall view of Valdecarrasca. Its clustered rooftops were dominated by the church and a sloping line of cypress trees leading up to the small white-walled cemetery where coffins were placed in banks of narrow vaults marked by their occupants' photographs as well as their names and dates.

Even for an outsider, it was a comfortable feeling to be part of a small close-knit community where each generation had been at school together and had many shared memories.

The rest of the afternoon was spent working on a design for a tablecloth and matching napkins for a 'garden lunch' feature scheduled for publication the following summer.

At six o'clock she went downstairs to fix herself a gin and tonic and started preparing the salad she would eat at seven. Some of the foreigners who lived here had adapted to Spanish meal times and had a *siesta* after lunch. For the time being, in her own home, she was sticking to the timetable she had always been used to.

She was about to halve one of the avocado pears that were so much cheaper here than in London, when someone knocked on her front door. To her surprise, when she opened it, she found Cameron Fielding standing on the narrow pavement outside.

'I hope this isn't an inconvenient moment to call. Do you have five minutes to spare?'

'Of course. Come in.'

She stood back while he ducked his head to avoid cracking it on the rather low lintel. Two of the things that had put her parents-in-law off the house were the absence of a hall and the lack of light in the room facing the street. It only had one small window guarded by an iron *reja* as was standard in Spanish houses whether they were palaces or cottages.

'Come through to the kitchen,' she said, after closing the door.

Fielding waited for her to lead the way. Perhaps it was the first time he had been here, she thought. Because Beatrice had been to his house it didn't mean he had been to hers.

But a moment later he corrected this assumption by saying, 'You've had the kitchen altered. It's much better now…much lighter.'

'Beatrice wasn't keen on cooking. I enjoy it,' said Liz. 'I'm having a *gin-tonic*.' This, she had read, was what trendy young Spaniards called what her parents called a G and T. 'Can I offer you one?'

'Thank you. Ice but no lemon, please.'

Liz fixed the drink and, with a gesture, waved him to the

basket chair in the corner. 'What did you want to see me about?'

'I've always suspected that not a lot of cleaning went on when I wasn't around. This unexpected visit has confirmed it. The house obviously hasn't been touched since the last time I was here.' His powerful shoulders lifted in a philosophical shrug. 'Well, that's not unusual. It happens in lots of countries where foreigners have vacation houses. Incomers are usually regarded as suckers with more money than sense. Cheers!' He raised his glass to her.

'Cheers!' she echoed. Was he going to ask her to take on the housework as well as the garden? Surely not.

'Alicia is not a bad worker when she gets down to it, but she needs keeping an eye on,' he went on. 'I was wondering if you would be willing to provide that supervision…to make sure she does what she's supposed to do. Also I'd like to have someone I can rely on to stock the fridge and maybe arrange some flowers. But perhaps you're far too busy with your own work to tackle anything more?'

Liz had been preparing a frosty answer if he asked her to take over the cleaning. Not because she considered housework beneath her, but because she resented him thinking her own work was little more than a hobby.

While she was rethinking what she had intended to say, he went on, 'By the way, it's obvious that you're doing far more in the garden than Beatrice did. I don't think I'm paying you enough. If you were willing to oversee Alicia's work, I'd be happy to increase your fee.'

He then suggested an amount, in pesetas. It seemed such a massive increase that, at first, Liz thought she must have made a mistake converting it into pounds. Even after six months here, she still tended to think in sterling except with small everyday transactions.

'If you feel that isn't enough, I'm open to negotiation,' he said, watching her with those curiously penetrating grey eyes.

'It's enough…more than enough. But I need time to think it over. I'm not sure I want to take on the double commitment. For one thing, my Spanish is still pretty basic. I get by with the man at the bank who comes from away, but the village people seem to have a problem with my accent. Do you speak Spanish?'

He nodded. 'Try out your Spanish on me.' He suggested some sentences for her to translate and, when she had done her best with them, said, 'You're coming along very well. Remember that the people here speak Valenciano, the regional language, from choice and Castilian Spanish to communicate with outsiders. Nowadays, with supermarkets everywhere, the expats who live near the coast can get by without learning any Spanish, and most of them do.'

'How did you learn the language?'

'My grandparents retired here after spending most of their lives abroad. My parents were also abroad a lot and I used to come here during the school holidays. Children pick up languages faster than adults do.'

'Was La Higuera your grandparents' house?'

'No, they lived on the coast, before it became over-crowded. When my grandfather died, he left their house to me. But by then it was surrounded by elaborate ''villas'' with swimming-pools, so I sold it and bought La Higuera for when I retire.'

Liz picked up the critical note in his voice. 'What have you got against swimming-pools?' she asked.

'In a country like this, with a chronic shortage of water, they're an unsustainable extravagance. The main blame lies with the planners who, up to now, haven't introduced legislation to make it obligatory for all new houses to have *cisternas* filled by rainwater, not mains water. People without *cisternas* should swim in the sea, or have very small exercise pools and swim against power-jets.' He finished his drink and stood up. 'We're here until Saturday evening. When you make up your mind, call me. The number is in the book.'

She saw him out. Returning to the kitchen, she was uncomfortably conscious that she would have liked him to stay longer. Yet, apart from his looks and his charm, what did he have to recommend him? Nothing. He was just like her father, a despicable charmer whose infidelities had caused her mother years of anguish. Even as a parent, Charles Harris had been unreliable, the pursuit of his numerous affaires often taking precedence over his paternal responsibilities. Though she hadn't discovered until later the reason why he broke promises to attend school plays and other functions.

Closing her mind to thoughts of past unhappiness, Liz washed Fielding's glass and put it away in a cupboard, as if removing the evidence of his presence would eradicate him from her thoughts. But, try as she might to concentrate on other matters, the impact of his personality, and the extra income he had offered her, continued to preoccupy her throughout her solitary evening meal.

It was the sort of wage that people paid for domestic and garden help in London, and no doubt he could well afford it. People who worked in television seemed to earn massive salaries. But was it right for her to accept it? It would certainly make a big difference to her somewhat straitened finances.

At eight o'clock, when Spanish telephone charges became cheaper than during the working day, she went up to the larger of the two small bedrooms which was now her workroom and where she used her computer.

After checking for incoming e-mails, her link with colleagues and friends now far away, she clicked on her Internet browser and went to a favourite website. The World Wide Web offered an escape from the problems of the real world. Sometimes she felt she might be becoming a Web addict, but at least it was a harmless addiction, not like taking to the bottle as some lonely widows did.

On Friday afternoon she rang his number.

'Cam Fielding.'

She would have recognised the distinctive timbre of his voice if he hadn't given his name. 'It's Liz Harris. If your offer is still open, I'd like to give it a try.'

'Splendid…that's excellent news. If you'll come round, I'll give you a set of keys and a quick tour of the house.'

'Now?'

'If it's convenient.'

When, five minutes later, he opened the door to her, he was wearing a coral linen shirt and pale khaki chinos.

Unlike her little house, his had a spacious hallway and a staircase with a beautiful wrought-iron balustrade that looked antique.

'Fiona is in the garden having a siesta,' he said, as he closed the door. 'We went to a nightclub on the coast. I hope our return in the small hours didn't disturb you.'

'A car wouldn't wake me,' she said. 'In the summer, when the nights were hot, the local dogs were a bit of a nuisance.'

He showed her around the ground floor. The windows on the street side were small, with protective iron *rejas*, but those on the south side had been replaced with tall windows with no *rejas* to obstruct the view of the mountains. There was a large kitchen with a big family-sized dining table at one end. Folding doors connected this to a living room lined with bookshelves and paintings. There was also a bedroom-cum-study lined with more books and, next to it, a spacious bathroom.

'This serves as the downstairs loo, and upstairs there are more bedrooms and bathrooms,' he told her. 'Let me give you a cup of coffee and then we'll discuss the new arrangements.'

The daughter and wife of men with no domestic capabilities, Liz was always surprised by men who knew their way round a kitchen and could keep themselves fed and laundered without female assistance. Whether Fielding's competence extended beyond making coffee, she rather doubted. Though perhaps it might if his life as a roving reporter for a television news channel had, from what she had heard, taken him to many of the world's trouble spots where hotel facilities were not always available.

'I expect to be down here more often in the next twelve

months,' he said, putting cups and saucers on a tray. 'How often, in your view, does the place need cleaning to keep it in reasonable order?'

Liz leaned on the rose marble worktop that divided the working part of the kitchen from the dining area. 'The kitchen and the bathrooms need more attention than the other rooms. I have no idea how efficiently Alicia cleans when she does clean. The most sensible plan might be for me to look in, say, every two weeks and suggest to her what needs doing.'

He gave her a smiling glance. 'I notice you say "suggest" not "tell". That sounds as if you have good management skills.'

Conscious of his charm, and resistant to it, she said, 'Most people prefer to be asked rather than ordered. That's just common-sense. For what you're prepared to pay me, I'm prepared to make sure that the house is always ready for occupation. Though, obviously, some notice of your arrival is important as far as stocking the fridge is concerned.'

'Give me your e-mail address and I'll give you mine,' he said. 'That way we can keep in touch easily. You'll find a notepad and pencils by the phone in the other room—' with a gesture towards the living room.

Liz fetched the pad and wrote her address for him. While waiting for the kettle to boil, he wrote down his for her. Then he spooned coffee powder from a jar of instant decaff into the cups, filled them with water and carried the tray to the table.

'I didn't buy Alicia's explanation of why the place was in a mess when we arrived,' he said. 'Hopefully, with you keeping an eye on her, she'll pull her socks up. If she doesn't, it may be necessary to find someone else. Perhaps you could make enquiries. I know a lot of the younger women have cars now and prefer to work in supermarkets and offices. But for the older women, without any transport, domestic work is still the only option.'

'I'll keep my ear to the ground,' said Liz. 'But it has to

be said that cleaning an empty house for an absent employee is not much fun. Alicia may buck up a lot if you're going to be here more often, and if I'm around to applaud her efforts. Housework is horribly repetitive and women who do it need to feel appreciated.' She was thinking of her mother, whose excellent housekeeping had never been praised or even noticed.

He changed the subject. 'Do you mix with the other foreigners round here? Have they been friendly?'

'Very friendly…and so have the local people.' But, as she had already learned in England, there was a world of difference between the life of a wife and that of a widow. The social world was set up for pairs, not singles.

The door to the terrace opened and Fiona joined them. She was wearing the briefest possible silver two-piece swimsuit. As Fielding rose, she said, 'Is that coffee? Can I have some?' Only as an afterthought did she toss a 'hello' at Liz.

For something to say, Liz asked, 'Did you enjoy your night on the town?'

'It was OK.'

Fiona's indolent shrug made her breasts do a jelly-like wobble in their silver cups. Probably most men would find her nudity enormously sexy, Liz thought. But would a discriminating man? Wouldn't he think she was overplaying her seductiveness. Still, presumably sex, and lots of it, was the only reason she was here. She didn't give the impression of being a great conversationalist. She was not even good at the small talk that strangers tossed back and forth in situations like this.

Liz drained her cup. 'I'd better be off. I have a lot to do today.'

'Hang on a minute.' Fielding handed Fiona her coffee, then felt in his back packet and produced a billfold. 'You'd better have some money on account…both to pay Alicia and for yourself.'

'That really isn't necessary. We can settle up next time you're here.'

'Certainly it's necessary. I might get my head blown off by a terrorist and then where would you be?' He handed her some twenty *mil* bills. 'Tomorrow morning I'll call at the bank and arrange for the payments into your account to be altered. You also need the extra house keys I had cut. They're in a drawer in the hall.'

Following him from the kitchen, Liz said, 'Goodbye, Fiona.'

Fiona did say, 'Bye,' but she didn't bother to mask her indifference with a smile.

She must be fantastic in bed for him to put up with her abysmal manners, thought Liz, as she marched down the street, the money in her pocket, the keys to La Higuera in her hand.

When Cam returned to the kitchen, Fiona said, 'She ought to get that nose bobbed.'

'What's wrong with her nose?'

'It's too big.'

'So is mine,' he said, rubbing the prominent bridge inherited from his great-grandfather, Captain 'Hawk' Fielding. His features had been similar to those of the Afghan tribesmen against whom he had played the Great Game on the North West Frontier, eventually dying a hero's death in Kabul in the early years of Queen Victoria's reign. Cam had often thought it was probably a gene from his adventurous forebear that had dictated his own choice of career.

'That's different,' said Fiona. 'On a man a big nose is OK. On a woman it's not.'

'I only noticed her eyes. They're the colour of speedwells.' Realising that Fiona might never have seen a speedwell, he added, 'They're small wild flowers...the bluest of blues.'

'She doesn't like you,' said Fiona. 'Or me. She was looking down her big nose at both of us. But it didn't stop her taking your money.'

'Why do you think she doesn't like us?' Cam could guess why, but he doubted if Fiona could.

'I expect she envies you,' said Fiona. 'You're famous and rich and successful, and she's a nobody living in a grotty little house with no money. I shouldn't think she'll ever get another husband.'

'You're a luscious piece, but you don't have a kind heart, do you, Fifi?' he said dryly. 'My reading of Mrs Harris is that she likes her little house, she doesn't want to shop till she drops, and she's still in mourning.'

Fiona didn't like it when he called her Fifi. There were several things about him she didn't like. He could be sarcastic, and sometimes she had no idea what he was talking about. But she enjoyed being envied by other women who would like to be his girlfriend, and he didn't expect her to do all the work in bed, like some of the men she had known. In fact going to bed with him was a treat. She was in the mood for it now.

She gave him her most alluring smile. 'I'm going to have a shower. Care to join me?'

In the night, without waking Fiona, Cam got up and went downstairs for some water. In his twenties and early thirties he had got through a lot of alcohol, but nowadays he drank less and less, knowing what happened to journalists who went on hitting the booze into their forties.

He was fit, and he wanted to keep it that way. He had drunk more this week, with Fiona, than he had for a long time. And he knew why. Because she bored him. When they weren't actually in the sack, he found her a dull companion. It had been a mistake to bring her. This wasn't her kind of place. She liked shopping and smart restaurants and places to dance. It had been selfish of him to deprive her of the things she enjoyed. She was a playgirl, but he was no longer a playboy. It was time to recognise that fact, to restructure his life accordingly.

After drinking one glass of spring water, he carried another upstairs. The bedroom was full of moonlight. It illumined

Fiona's unconscious face and the voluptuous curves outlined by the rumpled sheet.

Cam went to the window and looked out. Beyond the top of his garden wall was a row of Roman-tiled roofs, many tiles out of alignment, others speckled with lichen. Several of the houses were empty or used only for storage. There was only one flat roof, a conversion done by Beatrice Maybury.

Thinking about her successor, the buttoned-up Mrs Harris, he felt he had made a good move in appointing her to sort out his domestic problems. She seemed the conscientious type who would earn every peseta of the extra money he was paying her. She was certainly doing a much better job with the garden than Beatrice had.

At the same time he thought she was crazy to bury herself in a place like Valdecarrasca. Obviously, as he had said to Fiona, Liz Harris was still in mourning for her damned fool of a husband who had thrown away his life, and ruined hers, in a gallant act of madness. If his attempt had succeeded, he would have been a hero. Instead of which he was dead and she was condemned to a lonely future. He hadn't asked, but he felt sure there were no children. If there were, she wouldn't be here.

That she had accepted his offer, while privately disapproving of him, suggested that her work as a designer wasn't bringing in enough money. Not that she had shown her disapproval, but his job had made him an expert at picking up vibes. Like most 'good' women, she had a strict moral code that put free agents like himself and Fiona beyond the pale. Good women wanted everyone to live the way they did, the men in solid nine-to-five jobs like accountancy and the law.

But he had chosen a career that demanded he pack his bags at short notice and go to wherever the headlines were being made, usually somewhere bloody uncomfortable, from which there was always a chance he might not return. The casualty rate was high among war reporters and photographers. It wasn't a life to share with a wife and children. Some of his colleagues had tried, but usually it ended in divorce. It was wiser not to attempt it, or not until one retired. Which was what he was thinking of doing.

For almost twenty years he had run the gauntlet of violence in all the world's worst trouble spots and got through with only a graze from a bullet on his arm. His luck might not hold out much longer. Too many colleagues had died, or been badly injured, or resorted to dangerous forms of Dutch courage. It was time to call it a day and become a desk-bound presenter or, failing that, find some other way of earning his living.

He had a hunch the Internet held the key to his future and, if that hunch proved correct, he could live where he pleased, perhaps here in this peaceful village, so remote from the war zones where he had spent recent years that it might be on another planet.

Early one morning, a week after the *persianas* came down at La Higuera, Liz opened the Inbox on her e-mail program to find a message from Cameron Fielding. In the subject line, he had typed 'Congratulations on your website'.

Although the e-mail address she had written down for him was what was known as a dot com address, she was slightly surprised that he had bothered to check that the last part led to a website. But then she remembered he was a journalist, and curiosity was their stock in trade.

She read the main part of the e-mail he had written.

Dear Mrs Harris (or may I call you Liz?)
I've been looking round your website. I'm impressed. Maybe you should switch from needlework designs to website design. I'm told there's a big demand for good site designers. How about making a start by designing a site for me? If you're willing to have a crack at it, I'll be happy to pay you the going rate.
Think it over.
Regards, Cam.

Liz printed out his e-mail and put it in her bag to re-read later. Today was the day she drove down to the coast to attend the weekly meeting of the Peñon Computer Club at Calpe.

According to elderly people who had known Spain before the tourist invasion, when she was a little girl Calpe had been a sleepy fishing village. Now it was a large resort with many tall blocks of apartments, most of them holiday flats or the year-round homes of retired expatriates.

Liz didn't like Calpe but acknowledged that lots of people did, and it took all sorts to make a world. She did enjoy the club meetings, although most of the other members were old enough to be her parents or even grandparents. But their shared enthusiasm for computers made the age difference unimportant. One or two of the old men were inclined to ogle her, and one was a furtive groper. But she could cope with that.

After the meeting, she and Deborah, a divorcee in her late forties who kept in touch with her children by e-mail, had lunch at a Chinese restaurant not far from the port. It was close to the Peñon de Ifach, a massive rock, a thousand feet high, that reared out of the sea and was a mecca for rock climbers from all over Europe.

'Have you ever walked up the path that goes up the other side of the Peñon?' she asked her friend.

Deborah shook her head. 'I don't have a good head for heights. Living on the higher floors of some of the apartment blocks would worry me!'

'Me too,' said Liz. 'I should feel uneasy sitting out on some of those tiny balconies. But a penthouse apartment with a garden might be nice. The views must be wonderful.'

After lunch she drove back to Valdecarrasca where, having no garage, she had to leave her seven-year-old vehicle in the car park near the building that had once been a *lavadero*, a public laundry with a stream running through it. Since then the stream had run dry and today, so Beatrice had told her,

the water came from deep bore holes near a village at the far
end of the valley. Nowadays everyone had mains water and
washing machines but, in a country with little rainfall, the
ever-increasing demand for water could not be met indefinitely.

After changing out of her good clothes into everyday things,
she settled down to reply to Cameron Fielding's e-mail.

She didn't mind him calling her Liz, but she wasn't sure
she wanted to call him Cam yet. However, to start 'Dear Mr
Fielding' sounded rather stuffy in response to his informality,
so she stretched a point and started off.

> Dear Cam,
> I'm glad you like my website and I'm flattered that you're
> willing to entrust the design of your site to me. As I have
> never done any designing for other people, I have no idea
> what the going rate is. But I can find out, and perhaps we
> can discuss the matter further next time you come down.
> I should have to ask you a lot of questions before I could
> create a site that satisfied us both. What would the purpose
> of the site be?
> Liz.

After she had connected to the Spanish telephone company's freebie server, and sent the message on its way, she
had a spasm of doubt about the wisdom of becoming any
more involved with Cam Fielding than she was already.

From the first moment of meeting him, she had been on
her guard with him. That being so, was it foolish to take on
a commitment that, inevitably, would involve more contact
with him? Would it have been more sensible to politely decline his suggestion on the grounds that she had more work
than she could handle?

CHAPTER TWO

Entre col y col, lechuga

Variety is the spice of life

UNTIL Cam put the idea into her head, it had not struck Liz that there might be a better income to be made from designing websites than from her present occupation. A site commissioned by a 'name' as big as Cameron Fielding would certainly give such a venture a splendid start.

But would there also be a downside? Would designing a site for him involve a lot more personal contact than she wished for?

Cam's reply to her e-mail came into her Inbox the next time she logged on.

> Liz,
> In a couple of hours I'll be flying to the Middle East to cover the latest outbreak of hostilities. Hope to be back next week. Meanwhile I'll think about the kind of site I want. Maybe I'll be able to get down to V. for a night or two so that we can put our heads together and get the basics sorted out.
> Take care, Cam.

The phrase 'put our heads together' conjured up a degree of intimacy that she wasn't comfortable with. At the same time she was increasingly curious to see him in his public persona.

Beatrice Maybury had not owned a television set. She considered TV a waste of time. Liz had had a set in England but had not brought it to Spain, or bought a new set here. She preferred reading anyway.

She was certainly not going to ask any of the foreigners she knew if she could watch a news programme on the channel Cam worked for. That would immediately trigger more gossip on the lines of—'Liz Harris has taken a shine to the heart-throb at La Higuera, we hear. I wonder how long it will take him to get her between the sheets?' The thought of being the subject of lubricious speculations made Liz cringe.

It was in the middle of another wakeful night that she suddenly realised that his TV channel would have a site on the Web where she might find information about Cameron Fielding, foreign correspondent.

Although her computer was three years old, and not equal to handling the very latest technology, she could pick up the ordinary stuff. She sat up in bed and reached for the quilted dressing gown thrown over the footrail. The days were still mild and warm, but at this time of year there was a significant fall in the temperature after sunset.

With her feet tucked into cosy slippers, she went to her workroom and was soon online. It took only moments to find the website she wanted, and a few moments more to find a list of the channel's presenters and reporters.

When she clicked on Cam's name, up came a potted biography and a photograph. The sight of his face looking out at her from the screen had almost the same effect as when she had scrambled to her feet in his garden and looked into those amused grey eyes for the first time.

In an automatic reflex, she right-clicked with the mouse, bringing up a menu that included the option to save the picture to her hard drive. Then, not wanting to, yet compelled to continue, she saved the photograph in her My Documents folder where it would remain until she chose to delete it.

The bio at the side of the picture read:

Cameron Fielding is arguably the best-known of the élite group of internationally famous foreign correspon-

*dents who report world news for television. He has been
awarded the* CBE *for his services to journalism.*

*In a career spanning almost 20 years, Fielding has
worked for the* BBC, CNN, ITN *and* Sky News. *His reporting has won widespread critical acclaim and many
awards including the* Amnesty International Press Award,
the Reporter of the Year award *at the New York Festival
of Radio and Television, the* James Cameron Award *for
war reporting, and the* One World Broadcasting Trust
Award. *He has also won the prestigious* Emmy Award
*presented by the American National Academy of Television
Arts & Sciences.*

Below this was a question-and-answer interview.

Q: Where did you grow up?
A: All over the place. My father's career involved frequent uprooting. My passport is British, but I was born in
Hong Kong and spent my formative years in Tokyo,
Rome, Madrid and Washington DC, so I count myself a
citizen of the world.
Q: What was your first job?
A: I joined the BBC's World Affairs Unit after reading
Modern History at university.
**Q: What was the most memorable event you have
reported?**
A: I've covered a succession of memorable events:
Tiananmen Square in 1989; Baghdad and the Gulf War
1991; famine in Somalia 1993; the Soweto riots 1996.
Every year produces a major disaster. I wish the media
would focus more on mankind's achievements. I think being swamped with bad news depresses people.
Q: What are your worst and best qualities?
A: Worst: I'm impatient, especially with petty bureaucracy. Best: Probably tolerance.
Q: If you could travel backwards in time, what era

would you visit?

A: I'd like to have been the expedition reporter on Christopher Columbus's ship *Santa Maria* when, trying to reach the East by sailing westwards, he discovered the New World.

Q: What excites you and what depresses you?

A: I'm excited by the World Wide Web: I believe it has the potential to make life better for everyone. I'm depressed by self-satisfied, self-serving politicians.

As she re-read his answers to the questions, Liz was forced to admit that, had she known nothing about his personal life, the interview would have impressed her.

His childhood sounded far more exciting than hers. She had always longed to travel, but a possessive mother, shortage of money and falling in love with Duncan had conspired to prevent her from being anything but an armchair traveller. Now her wanderlust had diminished. From what she read, mass tourism and the popularity of back-packing had combined to make exotic destinations far less exotic than they had been when she was eighteen. The time to take off and see the world had been then, not now. As her grandmother had often said to her, 'Opportunity only knocks once'.

Liz shut down her computer and went back to bed. After she had switched out the light, for a while it was Granny she thought about. Granny had tried to dissuade her from marrying so young. 'You're not properly grown-up,' she had said. 'You've had no experience of life...or other men. There are more fish in the sea than Duncan.'

Knowing that her grandmother's marriage had not been happy, Liz had dismissed her advice.

But her last thought, before she slept, was not about Granny. In her mind's eye she saw the strong features of the man whose faced was filed on her computer.

Cam's e-mailed instruction, before his next visit, to have Alicia make up the bed in the room above the garage puzzled

Liz until, on her own next visit to La Higuera, she went upstairs for the first time. It then became clear that the bedroom where she had seen him kissing Fiona was a comfortable guest room and the room over the garage was his room.

The first thing that caught her eye was a portrait on the wall between the two windows, obviously placed there so that the light wouldn't fade it. It was an oil painting of a man in the regimental dress uniform of a bygone age. He had an early Victorian hairstyle, but otherwise it might have been Cam in fancy dress. There was a small engraved brass plaque on the bottom of the ornate gilt frame. She had to go close to read the small writing—*Captain Nugent Fielding, 1st Bombay Light Infantry.* Clearly the captain was Cam's ancestor.

There were family photographs around the room and many other personal possessions. She found it interesting that he slept here when he was alone, but used a guest room when he had a girlfriend in residence. What would a psychologist make of that? she wondered. That he didn't want his private space invaded by any woman? That he saw women purely as sex objects and therefore, like kitchen equipment and garden tools, they belonged in certain areas, but not in here?

It was twelve-forty-five and she was about to wash the fruit she was having for lunch when the telephone rang.

'Hello?'

'It's Cam. I just got in. What are you doing for the next couple of hours?'

'Nothing in particular, but—'

'Then we'll go out to lunch. There's a lot to discuss. I'll pick you up in ten minutes, OK?'

Taking her consent for granted, he rang off.

Liz flew upstairs to her room, whipped off her house clothes and scrambled into grey gabardine trousers and a grey and white striped silk shirt. Slotting a belt through the loops on the waistband, she stepped into suede loafers, then put on her favourite gold knot earrings, hurriedly slapped on some make-up and re-brushed her hair before pulling it through a black scrunchy.

It was only when she was ready, with a couple of minutes to spare, that she asked herself, What am I doing, making an effort to look good for a man I don't even like?

There wasn't time to consider the answer to that question because, remembering that once summer was past the interior of Spanish restaurants could sometimes be chilly if they didn't have an open fire, she had to whizz back upstairs and grab her red shawl.

She was running downstairs when she heard a knock on the door. She had thought he would pip his car's horn to alert her to his arrival, but when she stepped into the street he was waiting to open the door for her. Quickly, Liz locked up and slid into the passenger seat. No doubt it was part of a wom-aniser's armoury to have impeccable manners, she thought as he bent to pull the safety belt out of its slot and handed her the buckle.

'Thank you.' She tried to recall a previous occasion when a man had performed that small extra courtesy but could not remember it ever happening before.

'So what's new in Valdecarrasca?' he asked, as he got in beside her and pulled the other belt across his own broad chest.

'Nothing…as far as I know. How did your trip go?'

'I've been dashing around the world, covering outbreaks of mayhem, for too long,' he said, checking his rearview and wing mirrors before pulling away from the kerb. 'It no longer gives me a buzz, which means it's time to call it a day and find something more rewarding to do.'

'What have you in mind?'

'It would be fun to do a Gerald Seymour.'

'The name rings a bell but I can't place him.'

'He used to be a war reporter. Now he writes excellent thrillers.'

'Oh, yes…I remember now. My husband used to like his

books.' Not that Duncan had been a bookworm, but when they were going on holiday he would buy a thriller at the airport and often would still be reading it on the flight home.

'Unfortunately I don't think I have Seymour's imaginative powers,' said Cam, 'and, although there are exceptions, not many non-fiction writers make a comfortable living. By the way, the house is in the best shape it's been in since it was new. Your relationship with Alicia is obviously going well.'

'My Spanish is improving too,' said Liz. 'It's hard to get her to speak really slowly, but we're managing. I've started buying the Saturday edition of *El Mundo*. It has very good health and history supplements. It takes me all week to read them, but it's good for my Spanish vocabulary.'

'There are some Spanish novels on the shelves in the sitting room. If you want to borrow them, or any of the books, feel free,' Cam told her.

'That's very kind of you. If I do, I'll take good care of them.'

'If I had any doubts about that, I wouldn't have suggested it.' He took his eyes off the road for a moment to smile at her. 'I don't give many people the freedom of my library.'

The flattering implication that they were two of a kind, at least as far as books were concerned, was a small breach in her defences that she couldn't afford to let him repeat.

'If there are any wonderful restaurants around here, I haven't discovered them,' he went on. 'But Vista del Coll has a good view and the food is passable. Do you know it?'

'I've passed it. I haven't eaten there.'

'The clientele is an odd mix of elderly expats and Spanish workmen. At weekends and on *fiestas* it's packed with Spanish families. Young couples are reducing the number of children they have, but the different generations of the family still go out in a bunch in a way you don't often see in the UK,' he said. 'I like that.'

Liz made no comment. That she had no children, and probably never would have, was a sadness she had learned to live with. But sometimes, seeing other women with theirs, she felt an ache inside her.

It was only a short drive to the restaurant where, although it was early for lunch by Spanish standards, there were already several cars parked.

'Would you prefer to eat inside or outside?' Cam asked, as they mounted the steps to the terrace.

'It's such a lovely day, it seems a pity not to make the most of it.' Liz had left her shawl on the back seat of the car.

'That's my feeling too. How about there?' He indicated a table for four where they would both be able to sit facing the mountains.

Cam was drawing out a chair for her when the proprietor bustled out to greet them. Evidently he remembered Cam from previous visits and the two men—one short and rotund, the other tall and lean—had a conversation in rapid Spanish.

Then the other man gave a smiling bow to Liz and presented her with one of the two menus he was carrying.

'What about a drink while we're choosing what to eat?' Cam said. 'A glass of *vino blanco*, perhaps?'

'I'd rather have a glass of sparkling water.' She wanted to keep a clear head.

Cam's left eyebrow rose a fraction, but he didn't try to persuade her to change her mind.

The menu, she discovered, was set out in several languages. She read the Spanish page, keeping her finger in the English page in case there were dishes she could not translate.

With her bottle of spring water came a glass of white wine for Cam, a basket of crusty bread and a dish of *alioli* to spread on the bread.

'When I was in my teens, *alioli* was always made on the premises,' he told her. 'But then an increase in salmonella caused several bad cases of food-poisoning and restaurant hygiene regulations became a lot stricter. Now it's not home-made any more and doesn't have the same flavour.'

Liz sipped the refrigerated water and looked at the view. There was no denying that it was nicer being here, sitting in the sun with an interesting companion, than having lunch by herself at home.

'Were your father and grandfather journalists?' she asked, remembering what he had told her before, and what she had read about him online.

The question seemed to amuse him. 'Definitely not, and they didn't approve of my choice of career. They wanted me to follow them into the foreign service but fate decreed otherwise. Do you believe in fate?'

'I don't know. Do you?'

'No, actually I believe in chance. The chance that led me to break the family tradition happened in Addis Ababa...if you know where that is?'

'Of course...it's the capital of Ethiopia in north east Africa.'

'Your geography is above average. You'd be surprised by how many people I meet who have only the haziest idea where places are outside their own country. It happened during a vacation while I was at college. I was in Ethiopia when a munitions dump blew up, killing a TV reporter and leaving the cameraman and sound recordist without a front man. I persuaded them to let me stand in for the guy who was dead. I had beginner's luck. The reports we did were good enough to get me a place on the payroll as soon as I got my degree. How did you get your start?'

'As an office dogsbody. Then I worked up to being PA to the magazine's crafts editor. Needlework was my hobby. They were always short of good projects and they took some of my ideas. After a bit I was promoted to assistant crafts editor. I might, eventually, have succeeded her. But after... There came a point when I suddenly realised I hated the twice-daily commute and the whole big city thing. I'd had enough of northern winters and unreliable summers.'

'That's the way I feel. I'd like to spend nine or ten months of the year here, and the rest of the time networking in

London, New York and wherever else I needed to keep up my contacts. That said—' He broke off as the proprietor came back, expecting to take their order.

When Cam explained they hadn't decided yet, he gave an accommodating shrug and turned away to greet some new arrivals.

'We had better make up our minds. What do you fancy?' said Cam.

'I'd like to start with a salad and then have the roast lamb, please.'

'You'll have some wine with the meal, won't you?'

Liz nodded. 'I like wine…but I can't knock it back like some of the expats I've met.'

'Oh, the drinks party crowd.' His tone was dismissive. 'You find them wherever there's a large foreign community. People who live abroad fall into two groups. One lot thrives in a different culture. The other never feels really comfortable. Have you met Valdecarrasca's first foreign residents, the Drydens?'

'I've heard them mentioned. I haven't met them. He's an American, isn't he?'

'Todd is one of those cosmopolitan Americans who has spent more time outside the US than in it. He used to be something important in the oil business and then, in his forties, he had a heart attack and nearly didn't make it. They decided to downsize their lives and came to Spain, where Leonora discovered she had a genius for doing up derelict *fincas* and transforming them into desirable residences for well-heeled rain exiles.'

'They live in that house near the church with cascades of blue morning glory and purple bougainvillaea hanging over the wall, I believe?'

'That's right. Leonora bought it years ago, when they were living on the coast near where Todd's yacht was berthed. She bought up a lot of properties. Prices were much lower then. The hinterland was unfashionable. I expect you'll be asked to the Drydens' Christmas party. It's when they give new-

comers the once-over. Those who pass muster are invited
again. Those who don't, aren't. Leonora doesn't suffer fools
and bores gladly.'

'She sounds rather daunting,' said Liz.

'She's a doer,' said Cam. 'She has no patience with people
who aren't. She'll be impressed by your courage in coming
here on your own.'

'It wasn't courage. It was desperation,' she said lightly. 'I
was in a rut and I had to get out of it.'

Cam signalled to the proprietor, who came back and took
his order. When he asked, '...*y para beber?*' Cam turned to
her.

'Would you like red or white wine? Or they have a good
rosado, if you prefer it?'

'I'm easy,' she said, without thinking, and then wished she
hadn't. Not that he was likely to read the alternative meaning
into her answer. Or was he?

The order completed, Cam picked up her remark about
being in a rut. 'I feel much the same. I don't know if there's
any scientific basis for the idea that our bodies go through
seven-year cycles of change, but I think it's a good idea to
review one's life every ten years or so. I don't want to spend
my forties the same way I spent my thirties and twenties. It's
been a lot of fun, but now it's time for something new.'

The wine arrived. Here, Liz noticed, the usual restaurant
ritual of pouring a little into the host's glass and waiting for
his approval was ignored. It was taken for granted the wine
would be drinkable. This would have disappointed Duncan
and her father-in-law, who had both enjoyed the pretence of
being connoisseurs. It didn't seem to bother Cam.

When both their glasses had been filled, he thanked the
young waiter and said to her, 'Here's to us...an escapee from
the rat-race and a would-be escapee.'

Liz responded with a polite smile, not entirely comfortable
with a link that seemed tenuous, to say the least.

She was even less comfortable when, after they had both
tasted the wine, he proposed a second toast. 'And to your

new venture as a website designer…with me as your first
client.'

She put her glass on the table. 'I think we need to discuss
that before we drink to it. That's why we're here…to talk
business,' she reminded him.

'Certainly, but business goes better when it's combined
with pleasure, don't you think? For me, it's much more enjoyable having lunch with an attractive, elegant woman than
with a teenage or twenty-something techie who knows all the
IT answers but not much else.'

Liz decided it was time to put her cards firmly on the table.
'As long as it's clearly established that business is where it
begins and ends. You have the reputation of being a—' she
searched for the politest term for it '—an habitual ladies' man
and, in the last four years, I've found that a lot of men think
a widow is a sitting target. I just want to make it clear that
I'm not.'

As soon as she had made this statement, she felt she had
gone too far and the lunch, far from being enjoyable, would
be ruined by deep umbrage on his side and acute embarrassment on hers.

'I'm sorry if that sounded rude. It wasn't intended to. I
only want to avoid any…misunderstanding. It's not that I
have an inflated idea of my attractiveness. I don't. Compared
with Fiona Lincoln…' She felt she had said enough and left
it at that.

While she was speaking, Cam had leaned back in his chair,
watching her with an expression she could not interpret. Now
the flicker of a smile appeared at the corners of his mouth.

'It must be very annoying to have passes made that you
haven't encouraged,' he said mildly. 'You'll be relieved to
hear that I never do that. I only make passes at women who
indicate, beyond doubt, that they would welcome a closer
relationship—and not always then,' he added dryly. 'So now
you can relax, *señora*. If I tell you I like your clothes, it will
be a straightforward comment like saying that I like the

shapes of those mountains—' with a gesture at the craggy
crests to the south of the valley.

At this point, to her relief, their first course arrived. Liz's
salad was more imaginative than the standard Spanish restaurant salad that often consisted of lettuce, tomato, onion
and a few olives. Here, the chef had added hard-boiled egg,
grated carrot, sweetcorn and pickled red cabbage, the last
perhaps a concession to the taste of German patrons.

Cam had chosen *canelones* and they came in a small round
glazed clay dish, hot from the oven or, more likely, the *mi-
croonda.*

A combination bottle containing oil in one section and wine
vinegar in the other was on his side of the table, its surface
covered by a white paper cloth anchored to the undercloth by
plastic clips. Cam passed the bottle to her, and the pepper and
salt.

'Thank you.' Liz loved olive oil, especially the green-gold
first pressing that was not always provided in restaurants, although it was in this one.

Cam said, 'When my grandparents came to Spain it was
easy to get cooks and maids. They had a wonderful cook
called Victoria who didn't only cook the specialities of this
region but dishes from the other provinces. Spain is intensely
provincial and they all think their ways are the best.'

He spoke as if nothing had happened to disturb the ease of
their conversation. He broke off a piece of bread and dipped
it into the red sauce covering the three stuffed rolls of pasta
that were his starter. Putting the bread in his mouth, he chewed
for a moment, then gave a satisfied nod. 'This isn't out of a
bottle. Now…to business. You asked, in an e-mail,
about the purpose of my website. I suppose what I want is a
CV, but also something more than that…' He began to elaborate.

Their discussion of his requirements went on through the rest
of the meal, only occasionally interrupted by remarks on other
topics.

He had also chosen lamb for his main course and, when it was served, Liz said, 'One of the things I love about living here is going up to my roof and seeing a shepherd and his flock and his dogs passing somewhere near the village.'

'Have you noticed how they lead their flocks, not drive them? As a boy, I knew a shepherd. He was a gentle sort of guy who hated having to take his sheep to the *matadero*, the slaughter-house.'

'At least they enjoy their lives while they are alive,' said Liz. 'It bothers me when animals are kept in unnatural conditions. Do you eat out a lot when you're here? I'm sure Alicia would cook for you, if you wanted it.'

'I can cook, if I need to. Victoria taught me how to make a *caldo* and a *tortilla*. Sometimes foreign correspondents find themselves stuck in situations where they need practical skills as well as the gift of the gab.'

He topped up her glass, making Liz suddenly aware that the bottle was three-quarters empty and he hadn't had the lion's share. She had drunk more than she'd intended and must be careful to make this glassful last. She had never had enough to make her tight and wasn't sure what her limit was.

'I don't do puddings,' said Cam, when their plates were being removed. 'But don't let that put you off. The *flan* here is home-made, not served in a plastic pot.'

'I don't do puddings either. Too many calories. Why don't you eat them?'

'I'm a cheese man, and generally speaking the cheeses of Spain aren't wonderful. *Cabrales*, a goat's cheese wrapped in leaves, is good, but it's rare to find it in restaurants and you don't see it often in supermarkets.' His glance took in as much of her figure as he could see. 'You don't look as if you have a weight problem.'

'I don't, but I think I might if I didn't watch it. I walk on the lanes through the vineyards every day, but that, and a bit of gardening, is not a great deal of exercise. Most of the time, I'm sitting.'

'Talking of the garden, let's go back and have our coffee

there. I have some ideas for improving it that I'd like your opinion on.' He signalled for the bill.

In the light of his assurance that he never made passes without encouragement, and assuming he was a man of his word, Liz had no grounds for feeling uneasy about going back to his place for coffee in the middle of the day. It would have been different at night, but then it was most unlikely they would ever have dinner together. Nevertheless she did feel slightly uneasy. Mainly, perhaps, because he was agreeable company and she didn't trust herself to remain impervious to his charm if they were together too often.

When they reached his house, he said, 'Sit tight while I open the garage.'

He unlocked the metal up-and-over door and swung it open. Earlier, watching him eat, she had wondered how he kept fit. Inside the garage, she saw a mountain bike and a shelf bearing several pairs of heavy walking boots.

Before he closed the outer door of the garage, Cam unlocked the door to the terrace for her. She did not offer to help with the coffee but left him to deal with it while she went down to the steps to the garden and settled herself on one of the two park benches with metal arms and wooden seats. The bench at the west end of the garden was close to two huge lavender bushes that were in flower with a score of bees working on them.

She had sometimes sat on this bench for a few minutes at the end of her gardening sessions. She wondered what changes he wanted to make, and then her thoughts drifted back to the garden of the suburban semi-detached where she and Duncan had lived together for thirteen years, slightly more than a third of her lifetime.

Cam came down the steps carrying a folding table that he set up in front of the bench. Soon afterwards he reappeared with a tray. As well as the coffee things there were two liqueur glasses and a bottle on it. Liz's doubts about his intentions reactivated.

'I mustn't stay long. What are your ideas for the garden?' she asked.

Instead of answering the question, he said, 'What's your hurry? Why not relax for the rest of the afternoon?' He checked the stainless steel watch that circled his muscular wrist. 'It's past three o'clock now.'

'I want to type out the things we discussed about your website while they're still clear in my head.'

'I can save you the trouble. I'll send you a copy of my notes. Is it OK to send them as an attachment, or do you regard e-mail attachments in the same light as unprotected sex?'

She knew then that he thought her a prude, and perhaps she was, because, coming from him, even a joking reference to sex made her uneasy.

Forcing herself to sound composed, she said, 'I certainly wouldn't open an attachment sent by a stranger, or with come-ons like "Free" or "Win a million dollars" in the subject line. But I'm sure your computer is effectively virus-protected.'

'It's protected. How effectively I'm not sure. The hackers seem to invent new viruses faster than the anti-virus guys can pile up the barricades.'

While they were talking he had been pouring the coffee. After placing a cup in front of her, he put a glass alongside it and reached for the bottle.

'Not for me, thank you,' said Liz.

'You don't like liqueurs…or you don't like *poire William*.'

'I've never tried it, but I think any more alcohol might give me a headache.'

'You've only had three glasses of wine. That's not heavy drinking, especially with meat and two veg. Come on, let me give you a small one.'

'I don't want it, Cam. Please don't press me.'

'I shouldn't dream of pressing you to do *anything* you didn't want to.' He took the glass away from her cup and placed it next to his own, pouring a generous measure of the liqueur for himself. 'But your nervousness does make me wonder what you've been told about me. Am I accused of luring respectable women into my garden and plying them with potent liqueurs before attempting to have my wicked way with them?'

Liz grabbed the strap of the shoulder bag she had hung on the back of the bench. Jumping up, she said crossly, 'If you're going to take that tack, I'm going home...now.'

She was halfway to the steps when he hooked his hand in the bend of her elbow and stopped her. As, angrily, she swung to face him, he said, 'You're making a fuss about nothing. I was only teasing you.'

'I'm not amused,' she said hotly.

And then, as they faced each other, her indignation evaporated, replaced by a different and unfamiliar emotion.

For a long, tense moment they looked at each other and she saw his expression change from a smile to a look she could not define or describe.

All she knew was that, for several seconds, some kind of current was switched on and flowed between them.

Then he released her arm and said quietly, 'Come back and drink your coffee and let's talk about the garden.'

Dazed and disturbed by what she had just experienced, Liz returned to the bench and sat down. As if nothing had happened, Cam began to outline his ideas. Forcing herself to concentrate, she listened to him.

'The last time I was here, I went to a party in a garden where the owners had made clever use of a large piece of mirror glass. They'd placed it so that it appeared to be an ivy-clad archway leading to another garden. Do you think we could copy that here?'

Liz drank some coffee and thought about the suggestion. 'You would have to try it out with a small piece of mirror. I go to the *rastro* at Benimoro most Saturdays. I could probably pick up a mirror for a few hundred pesetas.'

'Could you? That would be great.' He explained his other

ideas, one of which involved getting a local builder to construct a walled bed for shrubs against the side of the terrace.

Eventually the conversation came to a natural end and when Liz got up to go he did not attempt to detain her.

She left by way of the house in order for Cam to give her a *Time* magazine he had bought for his flight down and thought she might like to read.

She had turned the corner into the short length of downhill street that connected his street and her street when she encountered a middle-aged woman she knew by sight who was holding a baby in one of the quilted bags in which recently born infants were often carried about.

By now Liz knew that baby girls could be recognised by the earrings they wore from soon after birth. The appropriate comment was an admiring, *'Qué guapa!'* if the child was female or, in the absence of earrings, the masculine form of the word meaning pretty or handsome.

Often the babies were beautiful only to their parents and grandparents, but this tiny boy was a charmer with large dark eyes and a mop of quite thick black hair. As Liz touched his petal-soft cheek with a gentle finger, a wave of sadness washed over her.

She controlled her feelings until she was safely indoors, but then the repressed emotion welled up again and she found herself in tears. It was most unlike her to cry. Perhaps it was partly reaction to the stresses of lunching with Cam. But mostly it was the reminder that in a few years it would be too late for her to have a baby of her own.

She had wanted to start a family two years after her marriage, though Duncan had been less keen. When she was twenty-five, after tests, her doctor had assured her there was no medical reason for her failure to conceive. At his suggestion, Duncan had undergone tests. The results had shown that the only way they could have children was by adoption, which her husband had not wished to do.

She was drying her eyes and pulling herself together when there was a knock on the door. She expected the caller to be the woman across the street who, if the postman left a package on Liz's doorstep while she was out, would take charge of it till she returned. But when she opened the door, it was Cam who stood outside.

'You forgot your shawl,' he said, handing it to her.

'Oh...thank you. I'm sorry you had the bother of bringing it down. Thank you very much.' Was her mascara smudged? Would he see she had been crying? Flustered, she closed the door.

Cam walked back to La Higuera wondering what had made her cry. She didn't seem the weepy type. He felt sure it had nothing to do with her angry flare-up in the garden. It would take more than that to reduce her to tears. Anyway, by the time she left that had been smoothed over.

He remembered that when, during lunch, he had asked her about her working life in England, she had spoken of the probability that she would have succeeded the crafts editor. She had started to say 'But after...' and then paused and begun again with 'There came a point when I suddenly realised...'

'But after my husband died...' was probably what she had intended to say but had changed her mind. Suggesting that, even after four years, remembering him still upset her.

Cam had never been in love, and in his world marriages seldom lasted. But he had not forgotten how lost his grandfather had been after his grandmother's death. He had enough imagination to guess what a devastating blow to Liz her husband's death must have been.

She was too young and attractive to live alone and, despite her making it clear that she wasn't in the market for an affair, should he have had that in mind, her body was ready for sex even if her mind rejected the idea of making love with anyone but her late husband.

The proof of that was in the way she had reacted when he stopped her walking out on him.

'I'm not amused,' she had stormed at him, and then something had sparked between them that he had recognised as mutual desire. Whether she had known what it was he was inclined to doubt. In four years of living as chastely as a nun, her senses atrophied by grief, she might have forgotten the buzz of physical attraction.

One of the Ancient Greek philosophers—probably Aristotle—had said that human beings had three basic motivations: hunger, thirst and lust. Liz was the kind of woman who would repudiate lust unless love was involved.

The idea that she could want a man whom she didn't trust would be repugnant to her. But for a moment or two she *had* wanted him, and he her. Not that he was going to do anything about it. You couldn't mix business with pleasure, and Liz was too much of an asset in her triple roles as gardener, Alicia's supervisor and the designer of his website for him to risk having a more personal relationship with her. Not that he wouldn't enjoy bringing her back to life and making her glow again. He could visualise how lovely she would be with her blue eyes sparkling with vitality instead of shadowed by unhappiness. But, at least for the time being, it was more important to establish a friendship, getting her to the point where she could take his teasing without getting uptight.

The day after Cam left, Liz went for her usual walk through the vineyards. Though the sky was blue, the air was cooler and the outlines of the surrounding mountains were more sharply defined than in warmer weather. Though in certain lights they seemed to merge with each other, there were seventeen mountains visible from the village. She was beginning to know them by name and keep their shapes in her mind's eye.

Her own house could not be seen from where she was walking, but La Higuera stood out from the smaller houses around it. When the *persianas* were down, the windows looked like closed eyes. She wondered how long it would be before Cam came again, and if he would keep in touch by e-mail or, now that she knew what sort of website he wanted, he would leave it to her to contact him.

She had not seen him again after he had brought her shawl back. He had said goodbye by means of a brief e-mail. By the time she read it, he was already on his way to Valencia airport.

The strange feeling she had experienced in his garden, while he had hold of her arm, continued to fidget her. She had never felt anything like it before, except occasionally when a passage in a book or a scene in a movie had started a quiver of excitement deep inside her.

But it had been anger she felt towards Cam, and how could anger change to that deep pulsing excitement in a matter of seconds?

She did not like the feeling that, however briefly, she had lost control of the situation and might not have resisted if he had chosen to…

Closing her mind to the thought of what might have happened, she promised herself she would make sure that all their future encounters were kept on a strictly business footing.

CHAPTER THREE

En la batalla de amor, el que huye es el vencedor

In the battle of love, he who flees is the winner

BY THE time Cam came back, a month later, the valley had changed.

Two days of strong west winds had blown away most of the vine leaves. Some of the old vines had been grubbed up and the reddish clay soil rotavated. Shepherd's purse was springing up in the spaces between the vines, attracting flocks of noisy little finches. There were also some white egrets flying about, Liz had noticed on her daily walks.

Notifying her of his arrival twenty-four hours beforehand, Cam had added a postscript—'I've had what I hope is a brainwave. Looking forward to talking it over with you.'

In his absence she had made good progress with the design and coding of his website. But whether it would come up to his expectations remained to be seen. She could have sent the documents for him to view on his Internet browser, but she wanted to see his facial reactions the first time he looked at them.

On the evening he was due to arrive, Liz went to the eight p.m. showing of an English language film at the cinema at Gata de Gorgos, a town nearer to the coast.

She liked going to a movie occasionally but, more importantly, she wanted to be out in case he rang up and suggested they dine together to discuss his brainwave. Rather than make excuses, which he might overrule, it was easier not to be at home.

Although she knew that, in Spain's big cities, people dined

48

as late as ten o'clock and the streets were still busy at midnight, this was not the norm in Valdecarrasca. When, coming home, she drove through the village, the square was deserted and all the houses in the main street had their shutters closed or their blinds down.

While the kettle was boiling for a cup of tea, she checked for e-mails. There was a message from Cam. 'If you're free tomorrow morning, could you come round at ten?'

Liz typed a one-word answer. 'Yes.'

As she logged off and closed down her PC, she was reluctantly aware that tomorrow was going to be a more exciting day than any since his last visit. It annoyed her that this should be so, but she couldn't deny it.

Next morning she washed her hair two days sooner than was strictly necessary. After breakfasting in her dressing gown and, aided by a dictionary, reading a page of a Spanish novel she had found on Cam's shelves, she went upstairs to dress. What to wear? Jeans and a sweatshirt? Or the kind of outfit she had worn to work in her previous life?

After looking through her wardrobe, she compromised between rustic casualness and city smartness by selecting the same gabardine trousers she had worn to lunch with him and a plain dark blue cashmere sweater bought in a sale. As a finishing touch she knotted a blue and grey kerchief round her neck with the ends above her left shoulder.

'Hello…good morning,' said Cam, as he opened the door.

The double greeting was one she had learnt to use with the Spaniards she met on her walks. But most of them were elderly men who might have exuded *machismo*, as he did, when they were younger but had long since lost it apart for a vestigial sparkle in the eye when she smiled at them.

'Good morning,' she said, rather formally, as she entered the hall.

'Coffee's on.' He gestured for her to precede him into the kitchen. 'Thank you for stocking the fridge. Here's what I owe you.' He indicated some banknotes placed on the kitchen counter where she had left the receipt from the supermarket.

'Thank you.' Seeing at a glance that the notes amounted to more than she had spent, Liz took her wallet from her bag. 'I'll give you your change.'

'No change is necessary,' he said. 'You forgot to charge for your petrol and your time.'

'I shouldn't dream of charging you for either,' she said firmly, putting down the change before she picked up his notes. 'I have to go shopping for myself. It's no trouble to pick up a few things for you occasionally.'

Cam gave her a thoughtful look. 'OK, if you insist. But what did that large piece of mirror glass you've found for me cost?'

'It was only a *mil*, but if it's not what you want I can take it back.'

'It's exactly what I want, and where you've positioned it is perfect.' He handed her a thousand-peseta note. 'It must have been an awkward thing to transport and put in place…or did you have help?'

'My car has a hatchback so it wasn't a problem getting it here. The man down the road, Roberto, saw me getting it out of the car and offered to help. I wondered if I ought to give him the price of a drink, but then I thought it was better not to risk offending him.'

'I'll buy him a drink and thank him next time I go to the bar,' said Cam.

'Which bar do you go to?' she asked, surprised that he went to either. The village bars were fairly rough-and-ready establishments with fruit machines and a TV permanently on, not the sort of places he was used to.

'I have a drink in both of them occasionally. The noise level is hard on the eardrums, but the gossip can be amusing. Most foreigners aren't aware of it, but the village is a hotbed of politicking and rivalries.'

'It must be great to be fluent in Valenciano as well as Spanish. I don't think I'm ever likely to achieve that. Even if I did, the women don't seem to use the bars. The older ones get together in small sewing-bees outside each other's houses.'

'Do you miss the company of women of your own age?' he asked, making the coffee.

'No, not at all. There are lots of special interest organisations run by and for the expat community. I could go to a different meeting every day, if I wanted. But the Peñon Computer Club is the only thing I've joined. I'm not like someone who has retired. I don't have hours of spare time to fill.'

'No, but we all need congenial company. Is the computer club fun?'

'It's very male-orientated,' she said, before it occurred to her that this might be a contentious comment to make to someone as manifestly masculine as Cam.

'In what way?' he asked.

'Men have an affinity with machines that I don't think most women do. The guys at the club love tinkering with their computers' innards. I would rather not know about what goes on inside the systems unit. I just want it to run as smoothly as the washing machine or the fridge. If something *does* go wrong, I want to be able to call an engineer to fix it, not have to do it myself.'

'I should have thought the guys at the club would be falling over themselves to come and fix it for you. Or are they the ones who have made unwelcome passes?' he asked.

'I haven't had any serious computer problems since I've been here. If I did, I wouldn't expect someone who lives on the coast to come trailing out here to help.'

'There must be youths in the village who could sort out any but the most complex problems for you. Ask Alicia if she knows any teenage computer buffs. There are bound to be some around.'

'I'm sure there are, but the language barrier would be even worse with technical matters.'

'Not necessarily. Like cars, computers work in much the

same way the world over. Shall we have our coffee on the terrace?'

When they went outside, she found he had put out two director's chairs, a dark green sunbrella and a camp stool to support the tray.

'I expect you like to sit in the shade. After last week's weather in London, I can't get enough of the sun,' said Cam. 'Do you mind if I take my shirt off?'

'Of course not.' Liz was beginning to wonder if, even sitting in the shade, she was going to be too hot in her sweater. The temperature inside her house was many degrees lower than on his sun-baked terrace. She should have put on a shirt.

Cam was unbuttoning his. She focused her gaze on the mountains to the south, and said, 'I'm very keen to hear about your brainwave. Do I gather it has to do with your website?'

'It will, if you think it's workable. But you may not.'

'Tell me about it.'

Without looking, she was aware that he was tugging his shirt free from his shorts. She had already taken in that his long legs were tanned, suggesting that, even if he hadn't been in Spain much this year, he had spent time in the sun elsewhere.

'I got the idea from a television advertisement that ran for a while last year, or maybe the year before,' he said. 'You may have seen it. I can't remember the product it was advertising, but it was a spoof dinner party and the guests included Marilyn Monroe, Albert Einstein and other celebrities whose names I've forgotten.'

'I didn't see it,' said Liz. 'But I did see an advertisement for a car which showed Steve McQueen apparently driving it years after he had died. Rather spooky, I thought... technology being able to resuscitate someone like that.'

'It is spooky,' Cam agreed, 'but also very clever. My idea has nothing to do with reviving the famous. What I have in mind is simply to interview six or eight interesting people about a particular subject and present the results as table-talk written in hypertext—that is with illustrations and links and perhaps sound clips. The overall title would be ''Cam Fielding's Dinner Parties'', each with a subtitle indicating the subject.'

'I think it's a terrific idea,' Liz said eagerly. 'Not complicated to do, and a wonderful draw to your site. Have you started making guest lists and choosing subjects?'

'Not yet. I wanted to see if you thought it was workable. I did do a quick Web-search to check if anyone else was already using the idea, but all I came up with was recipes and tips for holding real-world dinner parties.'

'I was going to suggest a search,' said Liz. 'If someone else was already doing it, that might have been a snag. Otherwise it sounds perfectly workable. My only concern is that you might do better to find an experienced professional designer to handle it for you, rather than an amateur like me.'

She was looking at him as she spoke. She couldn't fail to be aware that he was now stripped to the waist and she was within touching distance of the most beautiful male torso she had ever seen. His shoulders and chest must delight any sculptor in search of a subject epitomising strength and grace. His body was as far removed from beefcake as truly beautiful girls were in a class apart from the silicone-breasted bimbos of the soft porn magazines. She was gripped by a crazy and quickly controlled impulse to reach out and stroke the smooth brown skin covering the muscles cladding the perfectly proportioned bone structure.

'My feeling is that most of the so-called professionals in this relatively new area of mass communication are far too keen on flashy gimmicks,' said Cam. 'Did you bring your design ideas with you?'

'Yes.'

'Right…when we've finished our coffee you can give me a demo on my laptop. I do use it out of doors sometimes, but in this case it's probably better to go inside.'

Ten minutes later, with the laptop set up on the big table

in the kitchen, two chairs placed side by side and the *persiana* lowered so that sunlight would not fall on the screen, everything was in readiness for Liz to display her work to him.

She was accustomed to using a mouse, but Cam's laptop had a touchpad and, although she had tried one out at the computer club, she was not as adept as she would have liked to be. Also, although he had replaced his shirt when they moved indoors he had not bothered to button it and she was still disturbingly aware of his body.

She inserted the floppy disk, on which the documents that made up her design for him were stored, into the disk drive and, less expertly than she would have done with a mouse, transferred the folder she had named 'Fielding' to the laptop's hard drive where it would display faster.

She was seated on Cam's left with the edges of their chairs almost touching and their thighs parallel under the table. Before bringing up the opening screen, she said, 'As you'll see in a moment, I've designed areas that, if you like them and want to keep them, will need specially written text. For the time being I've put in place-holders. There you go...' This as she opened the website's homepage for him.

She had expected that he would move the laptop so that it was directly in front of him rather than, as at present, in front of her. Instead he rested his left arm along the back of her chair and, leaning closer to her, began to study the design.

Knowing that she wouldn't be comfortable staying like this for the ten minutes or longer that it might take him to navigate around the entire layout, Liz said, 'If it's all right with you, I'll make some more coffee.'

'Sure...go ahead.' As she rose, he gave her a glance that made her wonder if he suspected her real reason for moving.

From a more comfortable distance, by the worktop where the kettle was plugged in, she watched him become engrossed in what he was seeing on the screen.

What he was thinking as he inspected each section was impossible to tell. As the minutes passed, she found her insides beginning to knot with tension. So much depended on whether he liked it. If he did, it could be the beginning of a whole new phase of her life. If he didn't, many hours' work would have been wasted. Well, no, not totally wasted, she corrected herself, because she had enjoyed doing it. But the chances of her being able to sell her skills to anyone else of his stature were small.

The kettle boiled and Liz made two more cups of coffee, adding to his the amount of milk she had noticed he liked. She carried his cup and saucer to the table. Without glancing up, he said, 'Thanks.'

To her surprise, she saw that what he was looking at was the normally invisible code that most Web-surfers never saw and many didn't know existed.

'I see you've even spent time putting in meta tags,' he said.

'Because I think they're so important. Again they are only place-holders. You'll want to improve on them.'

Cam closed the screen showing the code and leaned back in his chair. 'I don't think they can be improved. The whole thing is brilliant...far better than I expected, to be honest, and way beyond anything I had visualised myself.'

Relieved and delighted by his praise, Liz reacted by saying, 'Really?'

'Yes, really. So what's the next step? Where do we go from here?'

Up to now she had not allowed herself to think beyond his reaction to the basic design.

'I guess the first thing to do is to register your dot com address, and then to decide who you want to host the site.'

'Can you handle the registration for me?'

'If you'll trust me with one of your credit card numbers.'

Cam frowned. 'Hmm...I'm not sure about that.'

For a disconcerting moment she thought he was serious. Then his cheeks creased in that dangerously charming smile that did things to her pulse-rate. 'I would trust you with *all* my card numbers. The world is full of con artists, but I don't think you're one of them. I'll write it down for you.' He rose from the table to use the notepad by the telephone. 'Here you are. Now, tell me who hosts your website.'

Liz told him, explaining the reasons for her choice.

She had noticed before that when Cam listened he gave his full attention to the person talking.

At the end of her explanation, he said, 'If they're good enough for you, they're good enough for me. Can I leave that to you as well?'

'By all means.'

'In that case the only thing left to settle is what I'm going to pay you. I've been looking into that and, frankly, I consider some of the fees being asked are lunatic. I suspect that a lot of people who haven't a tenth of your skills are trying to make some fast bucks from people to whom the Net is unknown territory.'

He then proposed a monthly retainer that was twice what she had expected he might be willing to pay her.

'In view of the experimental nature of this venture for both of us, I think we should try it for six months and see how it works out. At the end of that time we'll be in a better position to frame a more formal agreement. In the meantime, are you happy to go ahead on an informal basis?'

'Yes, perfectly happy. I think you're being generous. I'll do my best to merit your confidence in me.'

'Then let's shake on it.' He offered his hand.

The firm grip of his long strong fingers, and the effect that the physical contact had on her, reminded Liz that she was sealing an agreement with a man who, although he had brought her an unexpected opportunity to increase her income and break new ground professionally, was still someone whose values and standards were far removed from her own.

For the next hour they discussed the website in detail, both making notes. She had the satisfying feeling that, on this level, they could work well together.

She almost forgot about the personal level until, as the

church clock began to strike twelve, he said, 'I think we should celebrate our partnership properly. How about dinner tonight?'

Immediately Liz's alarm system went into red alert mode.

'I'm afraid I'm going out tonight,' she said untruthfully.

'Are you free on Thursday?'

'Thursday is my Spanish conversation class.' The class started at six and finished at seven but she saw no need to tell him that. In case he intended to ask if she were free on Friday, she said hurriedly, 'I think to celebrate now would be premature. Wouldn't it be better to wait until the website is online?'

'Perhaps you're right. That's a date, then. When the site is launched, we'll party.'

There was something in the way he said it that made her suspect he knew she was being elusive and it brought out the predator in him.

The church clock began to strike noon for the second time. 'Why does it do that?' she asked him, relieved to turn the conversation in a safer direction.

'I don't know. I must ask.'

'Perhaps Alicia would know,' Liz said, preparing to leave. 'Though she isn't much help with plant names. I asked her about the climber with the yellow flowers growing up the wall by your log store. It grows all over the place, but she doesn't know its name.'

Cam surprised her by saying, 'Its botanical name is *Senecio angulatus*. It comes from South Africa, I was told by a friend who's a botanist. How it came to Spain, who can say? I'll walk to the corner with you. I need to go to the bank.'

They parted at the end of the street where he turned in the direction of the grandly named Plaza Mayor and she in the direction of her house. Walking the short distance to her front door, Liz wondered if she had been stupid to wriggle out of having dinner with him. After all, he had assured her that he didn't make passes without encouragement. More to the point, why should he feel impelled to come on strong with a woman in her late thirties, who had never been more than averagely presentable, when there were luscious creatures like Fiona willing to go to bed with him?

During the evening Cam rang Liz's number. If she answered, he intended to apologise, in Spanish, for dialling the wrong number. However, as he'd expected, the number was engaged. She was at home, not out as she'd said she would be. Of course there was the possibility that whoever she had been going out with had been forced to call it off at the last moment. He thought it a lot more likely that Liz had been telling a lie to avoid having dinner with him.

There could be two reasons for that: she didn't like him, or she didn't believe his promise not to pounce on her. Cam did not expect the entire female sex to like him, but experience told him that this attraction was mutual. So why was Liz unwilling even to have dinner with him?

Could it be that, still grieving for her husband, she felt that even to have dinner with another man was a kind of infidelity?

For her own sake, she needed to be shown that grief, however profound, was an unnatural state for someone of her age. She was too young to live on memories of past happiness. It was time to put the past behind her. Why had she come to Spain if not to start a new life?

After heating up one of the ready-made pizzas she had put in his fridge, he booted up his laptop and took another look at the website she had designed for him. There was something almost uncanny about the way she had realised all his own half-formed ideas about how his place in cyberspace should look.

He was in bed, reading, when there was a call from London. Cam listened, agreed to what was required of him, and then made a call to Valencia airport to book a seat on the first flight to Schipol where an onward ticket would be waiting for him.

He didn't need to pack. For years he had lived with a grip containing all he would need to survive wherever his masters sent him. Until the end of the year, that would continue. But once his present contract expired he would be a free agent. Whether it was too late for him to change from a nomad to a settler he couldn't tell, till he tried it.

Finally, he set his alarm clock to wake him in time to drive up the *autopista* to Valencia. Then he turned out the light and, with the ease of long habit, settled down to sleep.

When, checking her e-mail next morning, Liz read, 'Gotta go! Not sure when I'll be back. Will keep in touch if I can. *Adios.* Cam,' she should have felt relief that a threat to her peace of mind had been removed, if only temporarily.

What she actually felt was dejection.

The night before, on the Spanish teletext news that she read to improve her vocabulary, there had been an item about more than sixty journalists being killed in various trouble-spots during the year. It seemed a horrendously high casualty rate and she couldn't help thinking how dreadful it would be if, just when he was thinking about retiring, Cam's luck ran out.

A week went by with no word from him. By now she had carried out his instructions to do with his website and could do no more till she saw him again.

One glorious morning, when the weather was warmer than many summer days in England, as a change from walking through the vineyards she decided to explore one of the old mule tracks that led into the mountains. Now that mules had been replaced by rotavators, such tracks were used only by walkers and botanists.

She took an orange and some chocolate. After walking uphill for an hour, she ate them sitting on a rock with a panoramic view of the whole valley. It was on the way back that the accident happened. Looking at the view instead of the track, she trod on a wobbly piece of rock, lost her footing, and fell. If she hadn't flung out her arm in an instinctive effort to recover her balance, she would have escaped with bruises. But her outstretched hand took the brunt of the fall and the jarring impact was so agonising that she thought she might pass out.

For a moment she lay in a heap, convinced she had broken her arm and wondering how the hell she was going to get herself down the mountain. Then, knowing that she must, however difficult it might be, she struggled back to her feet. Fortunately it was not her elbow or her forearm that was damaged, only her rapidly swelling wrist.

By the time she got back to the village, the pain was becoming alarming. She had heard that the village had a *practicante*, a medical assistant who gave injections and changed dressings. But she didn't know where this person was to be found, and the building that housed the doctor's surgery was open only in the morning. She could ask at the *farmacia*, but she felt she needed a cup of tea and perhaps a slug of brandy before explaining the situation to the chemist in Spanish.

Then, as she turned the corner of her street, she was astonished to see Cam talking to the woman who lived opposite. For a moment she almost burst into tears of relief.

The woman spotted Liz first and, tapping his arm, pointed to her.

'You're back,' she said, forcing a smile as they met on her side of the street.

'Your neighbour has just been telling me that you went out several hours ago—' He noticed the hand she was holding against her chest. 'Liz…what's happened? What's wrong with your wrist?'

'I think I may have broken it. I was out walking and I fell. Would you mind explaining to the chemist? I don't know the words to—'

'The *farmacia* will be closed till four-thirty. The chemist won't be there until later. I'll run you over to Denia. If it's broken, it needs to be X-rayed and put in plaster. But first it needs a cold compress and a sling. Come to my place and I'll fix you up.'

'I don't want to be a nuisance…' she began.

'Don't be silly. Come on.' He put an arm round her waist as if he feared that without support she might collapse, and indeed she did feel rather wobbly. 'Tell me what happened.'

Liz explained. 'It was my own fault. I should have been looking where I was going.'

'Yes, one of the rules of mountain walking is "look or walk, but don't try to do both",' he agreed. 'But it's one that we've all forgotten one time or another. What you need is a cup of tea and a couple of painkillers.'

'When did you get back?' she asked.

'Less than an hour ago. Lucky I did. You couldn't drive with your left hand out of action.'

'There's a taxi service in Benimoro. I can get them to take me to Denia.'

'Certainly not. You need an interpreter with you. When people are hurt, or ill, they can't think straight.'

'I feel such a nuisance.'

'Well, don't. I have nothing else to do.'

By this time they had reached his front door. Still keeping his arm round her, he fished in his pocket for his key.

Half an hour later, they set out for the coastal town where there was a hospital. By this time Liz was feeling better, though still in considerable discomfort. A couple of paracetamol tablets had dulled the pain, and her forearm and hand were now in a triangular sling that Cam had produced from a well-stocked first aid box. Before fixing the sling he had applied a cold compress, inside a plastic bag, to her now grossly swollen wrist. She had been impressed by his efficiency. The village doctor could not have done more.

The drive to the hospital took about forty minutes, first by winding back roads and then by a section of the main road that followed the east coast of Spain all the way from the frontier with France to the naval base at Cartagena and beyond. Roughly parallel with it, the *autopista* offered a faster alternative, but was only practical for short journeys if the access points were convenient, which in this case they were not.

'From what I've heard, there can be very long delays in the accident and emergency department. I'm afraid you may have to hang about for ages,' said Liz, when they were nearly there.

'That's no problem. There's a paperback in the glove box if I need it.'

At the reception desk in the hospital's A&E department, it was Cam who explained in his fluent Spanish what had happened. Liz's details were noted and they were instructed to sit down and wait.

Almost immediately Cam was engaged in conversation by the woman on the other side of him. First she asked him about Liz's accident. Then she recounted, in detail, the circumstances that had brought her, and her injured daughter, to the hospital.

Listening to their conversation, but understanding only about a tenth of it, Liz was impressed by the way Cam responded to outpourings that could not really be of great interest to him. Perhaps, she thought, it was his ability to tune in to the wavelengths of many different kinds of people, from high-powered politicians to someone like the little woman next to him, whose work-worn hands and cheap clothes indicated that she had lacked most of life's privileges, that made him such a successful journalist.

From time to time someone in urgent need of attention arrived and was whisked through the door leading to the treatment rooms. Inevitably this slowed down the rate at which those in the waiting room were told to go through.

More than an hour passed before Liz was called. Cam rose to accompany her but was not allowed to enter the treatment section. There followed another long wait before her wrist was examined and she was told that her wedding ring, now very tight because of the swelling, would have to be cut off. Done with a special kind of clipper, this was not painful. Then her wrist was X-rayed.

Greatly to her relief, she was told that no bones were broken but the wrist was badly sprained and would need to be put in plaster. Again, she had to wait before her wrist was wrapped in gauze and plaster applied to the upper side only. At last, three hours after her arrival, she was free to return to the waiting room.

She found Cam chatting to a young man in a blue boilersuit who appeared to have nothing wrong with him so presumably had come with a workmate. As soon as he noticed Liz, Cam excused himself to his companion and joined her.

'It's not broken, only sprained,' she told him. 'They've told me to see my doctor, to have the plaster removed, in ten days. I'm terribly sorry you've had this long wait.'

'It hasn't seemed that long. The guy I've been chatting to is a telephone engineer. I picked up some interesting stuff from him. You must be starving. Before we go back, let's have a snack and some coffee...but not in the hospital's cafeteria where the queue for service is probably as long as it is here.'

He put his hand under the elbow of her right arm and, with his other hand, pushed the exit doors open for her.

It was when they were in a nearby *bar-restaurante*, drinking coffee and waiting for slices of tortilla to be heated in the microwave, that Cam noticed the absence of her wedding ring and concluded it had been cut off. But he didn't remark on it, guessing that it would have upset her to have the symbol of her marriage removed. He knew that some women never took their wedding rings off from a superstitious feeling that to do so was bad luck. Liz didn't seem that type but, often, people's natures were not all of a piece. He had come across sensible, down-to-earth personalities who, on closer acquaintance, had revealed all kinds of unexpected quirks.

While they were eating the tortilla, he said, 'What are you doing for Christmas, Liz?'

'I'm going to the UK to stay with my mother. Why do you ask?'

'I'm spending it with some friends at a *casa rural* about forty kilometres inland. Do you know about the *casas rurales*?'

'Only that the literal translation is country houses and that there's one in our village run by an English couple. But I haven't met them.'

'In the context of places to stay in the Spanish countryside, they vary from houses to rent to small, simple hotels. The one where my friends and I have booked rooms is run by a French couple whose cooking is excellent. There are only six bedrooms, four doubles and two singles. I thought, if you had nothing better to do, you might like to come with us.'

'It's kind of you to think of it. I wish I could accept. I'm not looking forward to returning to English winter weather, or the hassle at Alicante airport.'

'Is your mother on her own?'

'No, my aunt shares the house with her since my parents separated. My father has moved to Florida with his American girlfriend.'

'My parents have split up too,' said Cam. 'They've both remarried people with grown-up children and grandchildren, so I don't feel it's necessary to play the dutiful son. Also I have my sisters to do the filial thing. Most years I've been abroad anyway. But if you are an only child, the ties are stronger.'

She said, 'Yes,' but made no other comment, and he had the intuitive feeling that it was her sense of duty rather than strong affection that was making her go back.

'Is it possible you'll have to cancel your plans and fly off somewhere this year?' she asked.

'Not this year. My contract has almost run out. I've made it clear I won't be available. You've booked your flight, I imagine? What day are you leaving?'

'I'm going for two weeks—December eighteenth to January first.'

'I'll run you to the airport.'

'I couldn't possibly put you to that trouble. You've done

enough for me already. I'll go on the bus, or maybe that
funny little train that runs between Denia and Alicante.'

'What time is your flight?'

'Not till early evening, so I have all day to get there.'

'I want to do some Christmas shopping in Alicante. Why
don't we go down in the morning, browse in the two big
department stores and have lunch at a restaurant I know? You
won't get a memorable dinner on the plane, that's for sure.'

She gave him one of her doubtful looks. 'I didn't think
men did Christmas shopping,' she said.

'Perhaps they don't if they have women to do it for them,
but I haven't,' said Cam. 'Have you been to Alicante? Like
Barcelona, it benefits from having a waterfront. Cities by the
sea never seem as claustrophobic as inland cities.'

'I've never been into Alicante, only passed it on the motorway,' she told him.

'Then why not grab the chance to explore it, with me as
your guide?' he said, smiling at her.

'All right…thank you…thank you very much.'

'Good, that's settled.'

That night, sitting beside the butane gas *estufa* that heated
her sitting room when she did not want to light the logs inside
the closed stove, Liz wished she was not committed to going
to London for Christmas. She would much rather have joined
Cam and his friends at the *casa rural*.

She wished she knew why he had suggested it. To be kind?
It didn't seem likely he would go *that* far out of his way to
befriend a newcomer to Spain, even one with whom he now
had a professional involvement. He was paying her well for
her services. Why would he feel the need to be friendly as
well?

The longer she knew him, the more he was an enigma she
could not fathom. Perhaps if she had not heard about his
reputation, and had not seen for herself the kind of woman
with whom he amused himself, she would have been able to
judge him on the basis of his behaviour towards her. But the

memory of him embracing Fiona by the bedroom window was hard to dismiss.

Remembering the last time Duncan had made love to her, Liz looked down at the bare third finger on her left hand and sighed. Perhaps it would be possible to have the break in the ring mended, but she did not think she would do that. Already her marriage seemed as distant as her schooldays.

In the following week, Cam called at her house every day to see if she needed help with tasks that were hard or impossible with only one hand in use.

After a week, rather than going to the doctor, Liz decided to take off the plaster herself. It was a simple matter of cutting through the gauze bandaging on the underside of her wrist.

The next time Cam called and found her using both hands normally, he said, 'I've been meaning to talk to you about the inadvisability of wandering around in the mountains on your own. Earlier this year, an artist I know had an unpleasant experience while she was painting somewhere on Montgo, the mountain to the north of Jávea. Some guy appeared and started exposing himself. She's twenty years older than you are, but it scared her and she grabbed her equipment and made a dash for her car. I think she panicked unnecessarily. Flashers aren't usually a serious threat to women's safety. But, that said, they can be alarming. The other hazard of solitary hill-walking is running into a herd of cattle, including some *toros*.'

'Surely not the bulls used in bullfights?' Liz exclaimed in surprise. 'I thought they were bred in the south of Spain, not in these parts.'

'The most famous herds supplying bulls to the top-level fights are bred in the south,' he agreed. 'But all over Spain there are less important *corridas*, and many local *fiestas* have bull-running. Certain streets are closed off and the youths of the town show off in front of the girls. I've seen those beasts in the mountains.'

'Goodness…how scary. I had no idea they were wandering around loose up there. I'd rather meet a flasher than a bull any day,' Liz said, with feeling.

Cam laughed. 'The cattle aren't wandering around loose in the sense you mean. They graze as a group and sometimes there's a herdsman with them. Personally I wouldn't walk through the middle of a herd. The cows can be dangerous if they have young calves. But it's easy enough to skirt round them.'

'What if you were going up a track and they were on their way down?'

'Then the thing to do would be to get off the track till they'd passed. Probably the wisest thing, if you want to explore the mountains, is to join a walking group. There are plenty of them. If you had sprained your ankle instead of your wrist, getting back to base could have been a problem.'

That night Liz had a strange dream in which Deborah, her computer club friend, persuaded her to take the train from Alicante to Madrid to do some Christmas shopping. On arrival, Deborah announced she had tickets for an important bull fight. Liz was reluctant to go. Although she knew that in Spain bull-fighting was regarded as an art form as well as a sport, she disliked the idea of animals being tormented for entertainment, even though the matadors also risked injury and death.

But Deborah overruled her objections and she found herself attending the fight at which the star turn was going to be a famous bullfighter called El Macho. When he appeared in the ring, he came straight to where Liz and Deborah were sitting. Looking up at Liz and speaking English, he said, 'You are the most beautiful woman here, *señorita*. If I bring you the bull's ears, will you reward me with a kiss?'

Before she could make up her mind what to answer, she woke up.

What disturbed her about the dream, and kept her awake for a long time, was that the matador had been Cam in a suit of lights.

The dream was still on her mind when, next day, she resumed her work in his garden. He had told her he was going to have lunch with a man who, during his professional life, had directed some fine documentaries and now, in retirement, lived somewhere inland from Gandia. Liz delayed her stint in the courtyard until she judged Cam had left the house.

To have dreamed about him troubled her. She did not want him invading her subconscious mind. Yet within a few minutes of thinking this, she found herself daydreaming about him: thinking how well a suit of lights would become him. As she knew from the pages of *Hola!*, the Spanish magazine which had inspired *Hello*, not all matadors were men of imposing stature, but even the short, stocky ones looked good in the traditional costume with its embroidered epaulettes, short jacket and tight-fitting britches.

Cam's broad shoulders and long legs needed no enhancement. They would set off the costume. In her mind's eye, she saw again him striding across the sand to the barricade in front of her seat, and the teasing glint in his eyes as he asked her to reward him with a kiss.

Stop it! she told herself angrily. Once before, a long time ago, her imagination had led her down dangerous paths into a world of misleading illusions. She was not going to let that happen a second time. For the rest of her life she would keep her feet firmly on the ground.

CHAPTER FOUR

Amar y saber, todo junto no puede ser

To love and to be wise are incompatible

ON THE day of her flight to England, they drove down the *autopista* to the provincial capital in Cam's new Mercedes. Previously he had rented cars, but now that he was going to be in Spain more often, he needed a car of his own.

Liz had never been a car-conscious person, but she had noticed Mercedes sports cars whenever they whipped past her because of their broad wheel-base and their look of being fast but safe.

'I like the sweeping curves of this road,' said Cam, as they headed south. 'There's a place on the shortcut from Valdecarrasca to the coast where you get a terrific view of the *autopista*, supported by tall columns, crossing a dry river valley. It's a masterpiece of engineering and artistry. In February, when the almond groves on either side of the backroad are in blossom, I must remember to photograph it for the website.'

'The almond blossom season is something I'm looking forward to,' said Liz. 'Spring in February is a concept that people who grow up in northern countries find it hard to get their mind round.'

'That reminds me, do you have a key-holder…someone in the village who could get into your house in your absence?'

'No, I don't. Should I?' she asked.

'It's a sensible precaution against unforeseen emergencies. The Drydens have a key to my house. If you like, I'll do the same for you. I don't suppose you have a spare key with you, but it wouldn't take long to get one cut in Alicante. One or both the department stores may have a key-cutting service.'

Sooner than Liz had expected, the city appeared on the skyline. Glancing at the speedometer, she realised that they had been travelling much faster than she had realised. The car's superior road-holding made it seem to be going more slowly than it was.

Although she had passed her test soon after her eighteenth birthday, and normally enjoyed being at the wheel, she would not have wanted to negotiate the streets of a busy city in a new and expensive vehicle. But Cam seemed unconcerned by Alicante's congested streets and one-way system. He drove along the waterfront, past the palm-lined pedestrian esplanade, before turning into the heart of the city where the pavements were crowded with fashionably dressed women and dapper men.

Living quietly in Valdecarrasca, Liz had forgotten what a city felt like. But in any case Alicante, under a cloudless blue sky with the sun shining, was very different from a typical December day in London. However, as far as the Spanish were concerned it was winter and many of the men were wearing smart overcoats and the women furs which here, it seemed, were still acceptable.

Cam parked the car in an underground parking lot belonging to El Corte Inglés, one of Spain's most famous department stores.

'I don't think they'd call it "the English cut" today,' he said dryly, as they entered the lift. 'A fashion journalist I know says the Germans have the edge for fine materials and tailoring. That's a very nice suit you're wearing—' with a downward glance at her classically simple fine wool jacket and skirt. 'Where was it made?'

'In Germany.' She would have travelled in something more casual but, because they were going to have lunch in the city, had decided to cut a dash. It was unlikely the suit would have many airings in future.

The last time Liz had gone shopping with a man had been with her father, an extravagant shopper who enjoyed chatting up pretty salesgirls. Duncan, indoctrinated by his mother, had regarded all shops as women's places. Uninterested in his appearance, he had even left it to Liz to pick out his suits.

She was curious to see what kind of shopper Cam was. Today he was wearing a long-sleeved light blue shirt and well-cut navy blue trousers with black socks and black calf loafers. On leaving the car, he had taken from the back seat a light-coloured sports coat. She knew by the way it fitted him that it had to be custom-made. No off-the-peg jacket would have fitted his shoulders and broad back so perfectly.

By lunch time they had toured the entire store and Liz had learnt a lot more about him. Unlike her father, he didn't flash numerous credit cards, nor did he ogle the female sales staff. It was they who looked appreciatively at him. Unlike her husband, he was obviously at ease in this environment, even on the fashion floors where he looked for gifts for the women he was spending Christmas with. He didn't ask Liz for advice, but picked out the presents himself, all of them things she would have been happy to receive.

At half past one, leaving their shopping to be picked up later, they strolled down to the esplanade she had glimpsed earlier. By now most of the benches were occupied by people chatting while others strolled back and forth. In a pavilion, a uniformed band played middlebrow music.

'Are you wilting? We should have had a coffee break,' said Cam. 'Our table is booked for two so there's time for a glass of wine in one of the pavement cafés, if we can find any free seats.'

'I'm not wilting. It's been great fun. What a beautiful pavement,' said Liz, indicating the tessellated marble surface they were walking on.

'Red, cream and black are the city's colours. This undulating design represents the waves of the sea,' he explained, looking towards the harbour.

He did not notice, as Liz did, a couple of expensively

dressed women both looking him over and exchanging a glance that meant the Spanish equivalent of 'I wouldn't mind spending time with him!'

It was an unwelcome reminder that, although they might think her lucky to have such a personable man in tow, in fact he was only being neighbourly and she wasn't the type of woman he usually escorted.

'Quick…I've spotted some empty chairs.' He grabbed her arm to steer her to a nearby café where people were drinking *aperitivos*.

'Where does your mother live, Liz?' he asked, after a waiter had taken his order. When she told him, he said, 'Never been there.'

'You haven't missed much. It's the epitome of everything that's boring about the outer suburbs.'

'To a journalist, nowhere is boring. Suburbia is full of interesting stories and people.'

'Not in the street where my mother lives,' Liz said dryly. 'Respectability is the watchword.'

He gave her a penetrating look. 'But what about your mother's daughter, who broke out and went to Spain? I could get a story out of her, couldn't I?'

The waiter came back with two glasses of champagne and some little dishes of *tapas*.

'Couldn't I?' Cam persisted.

'I suppose an expert journalist can make a story out of almost anything. But even you would find it difficult. Coming to Spain isn't particularly adventurous. Thousands of people do it every year.'

'Yes, but most of the expats are retired. For someone of your age to come is a lot more enterprising.' He picked up his glass. 'I won't say Merry Christmas because it doesn't sound as if it will be merry for you. Let's drink to the New Year…and to our new directions.'

'To new directions,' she echoed.

As she drank some of the pale golden wine, it occurred to

her that this was one of life's golden moments that she would remember when she was old.

The warm winter sunlight, the fronds of the palms stirred by a light breeze from the sea, the animated Spanish conversations going on around her, the personable man with whom she was sharing a table: all these combined to make a memory that would still be vivid half a century on, if she lived that long.

'Do you like *boquerónes*?' Cam asked, offering her a dish of pickled anchovies that, for easy eating, had been curled up and speared with toothpicks.

'Very much.' She took one. 'I like *albóndigas* too.' She looked at the small meatballs in a red sauce. 'Compared with Spanish nibbles, crisps and peanuts seem seriously boring.'

Presently, on the way to the restaurant, Cam produced from his pocket a rolled-up pale yellow tie. 'I'd better put this on. In the States, it's OK not to wear a necktie, as they call it, as long as you have a jacket. Here, except in the tourist resorts, they tend to be more formal.'

He threaded the tie under his shirt collar and tied it with the swift deft movements of long practice. Watching his lean brown fingers adjusting the knot, she felt a fluttering sensation that she recognised as excitement. She had read that champagne was an aphrodisiac, but surely one glass was not enough to kindle thoughts and feelings she would prefer to stay dormant? Closing her mind to them, she made herself pay attention to the shop windows they were passing.

Only a handful of people had arrived at the restaurant before them. While they were being shown to their table by the head waiter, they passed a table occupied by four Spanish businessmen of around Cam's age. Both the men seated on the outward-facing banquette gave Liz an interested glance that she felt was probably more attributable to her escort's charisma than to her own looks. Even off-screen, in a country where he wouldn't be widely recognised, Cam had the ineffable quality known as presence. When she was with him some of it rubbed off on her; waiters were more deferential, people who might have ignored her had she been alone looked at her with attention. It was a curious sensation to be caught in someone else's spotlight and she wasn't sure that she liked it.

By the time they had chosen their lunch and eaten their *montaditos*, the tempting morsels presented on little squares of toast, the restaurant was filling up with affluent Alicantinos. Seafood and savoury rice dishes were the mainstays of the menu here, and they both had a shrimp starter followed by *suquet de peix* which the head waiter translated as fisherman's pot.

'I hope you are going to let me share this,' said Liz, when Cam asked for the bill.

'Absolutely not,' he said firmly.

Seeing that it would be futile to argue, she said, 'Then at least let me contribute something towards the petrol and cost of the motorway.'

'I appreciate the offer…but no. I was going to come anyway. Your company has made it more enjoyable.'

It was said in a matter-of-fact tone, but she could not help feeling a glow of pleasure. 'It's been a wonderful meal. The whole day has been fun,' she said.

'Good. We must do it again.'

The rest of the afternoon passed as pleasantly as the morning. Soon it was time to drive to the airport on the southern outskirts of the city. There, in the car park, Liz transferred the presents bought for her mother and aunt to her suitcase and Cam wheeled it as far as the entrance of the departure section of the terminal.

There he set the case down and said, 'I'll say goodbye here. I may not be at home when you come back so I won't arrange to pick you up in case I can't make it.'

'You've been more than kind already. I'm very grateful. I hope you enjoy your stay at the *casa rural*. I *shall* wish you a Merry Christmas,' she said, smiling and offering her hand.

Cam took it, but then, to her surprise, he leaned forward

and brushed a light kiss first on one cheek and then the other. 'Goodbye, Liz. Take care. See you soon.'

He released her hand and turned away, striding across the road where coaches, taxis and cars were allowed to put down and pick up their passengers to where he had left the Mercedes in the car park.

Liz watched him go in a daze of surprise and uncertainty. Kissing on meeting and parting was widely practised in Spain, and many of the expat community had adopted the habit and exchanged social kisses with each other at every opportunity, to an extent that she found rather absurd. But she had not expected Cam to kiss her goodbye and, if she had, would not have expected the commonplace gesture to give her such a buzz.

Her parents had not been demonstrative with each other. She had never seen them embrace. Nor had Duncan and his family been given to affectionate gestures. As far back as she could remember, Liz had wanted to hug and be hugged but had adapted herself to the ways of the people closest to her. That was one of the reasons why not having a baby had been such a disappointment. With a child she could have acted on her impulses. Babies and toddlers enjoyed being cuddled and kissed.

Inside the terminal, she joined the long line of passengers waiting to check in for her flight. It was forty minutes before she reached the desk, was given her boarding card and could take the escalator to the departure lounge level where there was also a cafeteria and a shop selling papers and paperbacks. Liz had a look at the books but did not buy one as she meant to spend the flight planning the site she would need as a website designer. It would be separate from the site that showcased her skills as a crafts designer.

Having coffee in the café reminded her of the previous occasions when she had flown back to England from this airport. The first three times had been after holidays with her in-laws at the villas they had rented in Denia, Moraira and Altea. The last time had been after she had flown down to

sign the papers that made her the owner of Beatrice
Maybury's house.

At the outset, she would have preferred to go further afield,
to the Greek islands or to Italy. But Duncan, who had been
careful with money, had seen staying with his parents as a
useful saving. It had never crossed her mind that she might
one day live here. Or that a few years hence another man's
kiss on her cheek would make her heart beat as fast as when,
in her early teens, she had said shy hellos to the son of the
new people next door when he and she happened to be in
their parents' back gardens at the same time.

Presently, sitting in the departure lounge—perhaps the
only person there who was looking forward to the return
flight more than to the outward flight—Liz thought about
Cam's toast to 'new directions'.

The year that would soon be ending had been a momentous
one for her. Would next year be even more life-changing?

Her mother, Mrs Bailey, and her aunt, Mrs Chapman, were
both television addicts. The small set in the kitchen was
switched on before breakfast and, except when they were out
shopping, the big new set in the lounge remained on till they
went to bed. They planned their day's viewing as carefully
as people preparing for an expedition. When there was a gap
between their many favourite programmes, they filled it with
a video of a programme that had conflicted with something
they liked even better.

Television had taken over their lives, Liz realised. She had
no quarrel with that, if it kept them happy. But it drove her
mad. There were times when she had to escape by going for
a walk even though the weather was terrible.

She was herself an addict of another kind, she discovered,
during the first week with them. Without e-mail and the Web,
her life had lost an important dimension. After seven days
without a 'fix', she was driven to buying herself a laptop.

She justified this expensive outlay by telling herself that it
was unprofessional to depend on her desktop computer. She

needed to have a backup machine. But she knew that the real reason was that, if Cam e-mailed her while she was out of Spain, she wanted to be able to pick up his message and perhaps reply. That she could have accessed her mailbox from a cyber café was something she chose to ignore.

'Is it OK if I plug my computer into the telephone jack?' she asked her mother, after unwrapping the laptop in her bedroom. 'You aren't expecting any important calls in the next half-hour, are you?'

'The only person who rings me is you,' said Mrs Bailey. 'I don't know what the world's coming to. People are lucky to see their children once a year these days. Families used to be close.'

Liz was tempted to say, But now that I am here you don't want to talk to me. You're more interested in your favourite presenters' lives than in mine. But she knew that, even though it was true, to say so would hurt her mother's feelings. Instead, she said, 'It's nice that you and Auntie Sue are still bosom buddies. Not all sisters get on as well as you two.'

'We have to, don't we? If we relied on our children where would we be? You've gone off to Spain, and Sue's two hardly ever visit her.'

Between them, Liz's cousins had five children. 'You haven't room to put them up and they can't afford to stay at a hotel. Why not go and visit them…or come and stay with me?' she suggested.

'You know I'm not keen on flying.' Mrs Bailey caught sight of the clock. 'Oh…it's almost time for Oprah.' Her expression brightened. Of all her television idols, the American chat show hostess topped the list. 'Sue, hurry up, dear. Oprah's starting,' she called from the doorway.

Liz's homeward flight was delayed by two hours, but she didn't mind. She liked airports. It was drizzling when the plane took off from Gatwick, but the sun was shining at Alicante. She took a taxi to the coach station in the city and, after half an hour's wait, climbed on a bus that would drop her off at a town not far from Valdecarrasca. There she could call another taxi to take her the last ten kilometres.

She enjoyed the bus journey with its views of the mountains through the offside windows and nearside glimpses of the blue Mediterranean and the coastal towns.

'The topless towers of Benidorm,' Cam had said sardonically, as they drove past the high-rise blocks of the famous resort a fortnight earlier.

She had known it was a literary reference and in England had looked it up and found it was part of a poem about Helen of Troy.

Was this the face that launch'd a thousand ships,
And burnt the topless towers of Ilium?
Sweet Helen, make me immortal with a kiss!

Reading it, she had wondered if Cam would ever meet a woman who would have the effect on him that Helen, wife of a king, had had on the prince who abducted her. Was Cam capable of that kind of overwhelming passion?

She could not help being disappointed at receiving no e-mails from him during her absence. Now he was probably away, as he had said he might be. But even if he was not there, she looked forward to seeing the garden after a fortnight's absence. Her trip had proved one thing: the village was 'home'. Any lingering doubts about the wisdom of her decision to uproot herself had evaporated.

There was only one letter in the metal box attached to the wall beside Liz's front door. The envelope had no stamp. An unfamiliar hand had written 'Mrs Harris' and, in the bottom right-hand corner of the expensive envelope, 'By hand'.

Liz stuck it in the pocket of her jacket to be looked at after she had unlocked the front door and lifted her book-heavy suitcase over the threshold. When she and her luggage were inside, her first task was to open the curtains and let in some light. It was only then that she noticed a small parcel on the table that had not been there when she left home. For a moment or two she was baffled by how it could have got there. Then she remembered the spare key she had had cut in Alicante and given to Cam.

Wrapped in plain brown paper fastened with transparent sticky tape, the parcel was roughly the size of a 500 *gramos* box of *margarina*, but considerably heavier. Inside the outer wrapping were several layers of tissue that, unfolded, revealed an object that Liz had often admired when she saw it on the front doors of the more opulent Spanish town-houses.

Formed in the shape of a woman's hand emerging from a lace cuff, the brass doorknocker was clearly an antique, not one of the cheap reproductions she had sometimes seen for sale at junk markets. Probably this one had come from an old house that had been demolished. Cam could not have given her anything that would have delighted her more.

Taped to the back of the knocker was a card on which he had written—

Hope you like this. If so I'll fix it for you when I get back on Jan 4th. Happy New Year. Cam.

The news that in three days' time La Higuera would have its blinds up made her feel even more cheerful.

Valdecarrasca had two small general stores of the type that, in England, when she was a child, had been known as 'corner shops'. Like that of their now largely vanished counterparts in the UK, the village shopkeeper's livelihood was under threat from the supermarkets. But for the time being they were surviving and Liz made a point of using them.

It was not until after she had been to the shop run by Maria, a forty-something mother of several children, that Liz remembered the letter she had put in her pocket. She fished it out and slit the envelope. The letter inside was typewritten

but topped and tailed in the same elegant hand that had addressed the envelope.

> *Dear Liz (if I may?)*
> *Cam has told us how well you are looking after his*
> *garden. I am also an enthusiastic gardener. We are having*
> *a party for friends on January 4th and should be delighted*
> *if you can join us? Buffet supper. Smart casual. 8 p.m. If*
> *you can't make it, please ring me.*
> *Hoping you will be free, Leonora Dryden.*

The following morning, Liz put a note accepting the invitation in Mrs Dryden's letter box. For the rest of the day,
at odd moments, she wondered what she should wear.

It was Deborah, her friend at the computer club, who told
her about the nearly-new shop in Denia where the wealthy
expats who lived in the urbs on the coast disposed of their
cast-offs.

Liz had first heard someone say 'urb' while staying with
her parents-in-law. It was short, she discovered, for *urbani-
zación*, the Spanish word for the clusters of villas that had
sprung up like colonies of mushrooms wherever the land near
the sea could be built on and now were spreading relentlessly
inland.

'Why don't we go together?' Deb suggested. 'After we've
shopped, we can lunch. There's no point in taking two cars.
There must be somewhere on the main coast road where you
can leave yours for a few hours while we drive the rest of
the way in mine.'

The outing was a success. They both emerged from the
nearly-new shop with bulging recycled carrier bags. As they
finished lunch at a restaurant close to the sea's edge, Deborah
said, 'Let's not go back the way we came. Let's go by the
mountain road. You haven't been over Montgo yet, have

you? There's a lovely view from the flat bit on top of the seaward end.'

The mountain called Montgo, its skirts now dotted with villas, was a major landmark along this stretch of the coast. Liz had assumed the only way round it was on the inland side. She had not known there was a winding road over the mountain connecting the town of Denia with the neighbouring small port of Jávea. She wondered if Cam knew about it and supposed he must. Uneasily aware that thoughts of him kept popping into her head with increasing frequency, she was also conscious that the uncharacteristically dropdead dress she had just bought had been chosen to stop him in his tracks rather than to cut a dash with the Drydens or their other guests.

'I wonder if you'll meet anyone interesting at this party you're going to?' said Deborah, as she drove round the tight hairpin bends ascending the mountain. 'If there are any eligible singles in this area, I never meet them.'

'Do you want another man in your life?' Liz asked.

'I certainly don't want a dud like the last one I had, but I'm over that fiasco now and, yes, I'd like to try again. Chance would be a fine thing,' Deborah added dryly.

At the top of the mountain road, but still well below the actual summit, a byroad led to the lighthouse at the seaward end of the massive promontory. There Deborah parked the car and they got out and strolled about.

'I guess it's different for you,' said Deborah. 'If someone has been happily married and then lost their partner through an accident, as you did, it must take longer to recover than from a marriage like mine that started going downhill almost from the end of the honeymoon.'

Liz liked Deborah and valued their friendship. But she didn't really want to get into in-depth discussions about their personal lives. 'Maybe a slow decline is more painful than a sudden ending,' she said. 'I can't say that living alone for the rest of my life bothers me. I'd rather be single than married to the wrong person.'

'I'm not going to argue with that!' Deborah said emphatically. 'But hopefully I'm wiser as well as older. Next time I won't lose my head as well as my heart.'

Later, when Deborah had dropped her off near her own car, and she was driving back to Valdecarrasca, Liz thought how easy it was, on the basis of insufficient evidence, to make false assumptions about people. She had probably done it herself. Maybe one day she would correct Deborah's assumption about her. Or maybe not. Usually it was better to let sleeping dogs lie.

On the afternoon of the party, she gave herself a top-to-toe beauty treatment starting with a luxuriously long bath and finishing with a pedicure and manicure.

From time to time she looked out of her kitchen window to see if the *persianas* at La Higuera were up. At sunset they were still down. Perhaps Cam's return had been postponed for some reason.

Normally she picked up e-mails every two hours. At six o'clock the Inbox was empty. At seven, half an hour before starting to dress, she logged on and checked again. Nothing. Why should he let her know he wasn't coming? she asked herself. They were neighbours and business associates, not close friends. But she couldn't help feeling miffed that he hadn't made any contact since kissing her goodbye at the airport almost three weeks ago.

Before taking the new-to-her dress out of the wardrobe, she put on a new bra and briefs and a pair of sheer black tights. Then she spent twenty minutes putting on a party face and adding sheen to her newly washed hair with a tiny amount of wax spread on her palms.

Tonight was only the second time she had tried on the dress since Deborah's comment, 'That looks stunning on you,' had convinced her she had to buy it. Even second-hand, it hadn't been cheap. But, according to the shop's owner, the name on the satin label was that of a top German designer famous for mannishly tailored day clothes and glamorously feminine evening wear.

Carefully, Liz opened the zipper, and gathering the delicate folds of the exquisite fabric dropped them carefully over her head and helped them to slide down her body, the silk lining cool on her bare flesh.

When she looked at her reflection in the long mirror that was one of her additions to the house, she knew that tonight she was going to do something she had never done before. She was going to make an entrance.

The church clock was striking eight for the second time when she locked her front door and, with her red shawl protecting her upper body from the after-dark fall in temperature, walked to the Drydens' house, the sound of her heels echoing in the empty streets.

At that moment Cam's Mercedes was alongside the toll-booth at the *autopista* outlet nearest to Valdecarrasca. It had been a long day. Tired, and with things on his mind, he was not really in the mood for Leonora's chatfest. But he knew she had invited Liz and, as he was the only person she would know, he felt an obligation to show up. The Drydens' parties could be a bit of an ordeal for anyone who was shy or reserved and Leonora would be too busy hostessing to keep a close eye on the newest addition to what, by expat social standards, was a fairly glittering circle.

By the time he closed his garage door it was nearly eight-thirty and he needed a shower and shave. But he was used to quick changes.

The clock was starting to strike nine when he left the house. In Spain, many foreigners arrived late in the belief that it was the custom here. Normally punctual himself, when he gave a party he expected people to show up at or close to the time he had decreed.

Knowing that the door would be open, he chose not to ring the bell that would require someone to break off their conversation to admit him. Letting himself in, he unwound his cashmere scarf and tossed it onto a dark oak hall chest. Then he climbed the stairs to the first-floor living room that had even better views of the valley than his own upper rooms.

About thirty people were drinking and chatting, but the space was large and lofty enough to prevent the noise level from becoming annoying. He took a sweeping look round, recognising most of the faces but not all. He didn't know the man who was chatting up a woman with beautiful legs and a silky fall of hair that half hid her profile.

Then she turned slightly towards where Cam was standing, at the same time lifting her hand to tuck the hair behind her ear. As she made that quintessentially feminine gesture, he experienced two reactions. First he recognised her. Then he remembered the feel of her cheek under his lips and felt a surging desire to kiss her again, on the mouth.

Liz was listening to the man called Tony who was her hostess's house guest when, suddenly, she had the feeling that someone was staring at her.

'Let me get you another drink,' said Tony, taking her glass. 'I'll be right back.'

She thought it was actually he who wanted a refill. His departure left her free to glance round the room. She found that someone *was* staring. It was Cam, standing by the double doors, fixing her with such a strange intense look that, for the first time that evening since she had put on the dress, she felt her confidence falter and was shaken by nervousness.

He came towards her, not smiling but extending his hand. When she gave him hers, he turned it and kissed it. Straightening, he said, 'You look beautiful.'

'Thank you.' Her self-possession returned. 'I'm glad you got back in time for the party.'

'Who is the guy with the moustache?'

'He's staying with Mr and Mrs Dryden. He's a professor of linguistics.'

'Interesting?'

'Extremely. How was your trip?'

'The weather was vile…snow turning to slush. How was yours?' he asked.

'I was pleased to get back. You must be longing for a drink. Don't let me stop you heading for the bar.'

'Is that a diplomatic way of telling me I've arrived in the middle of a promising tête-à-tête that you'd rather was not interrupted?'

'Not at all. I think you'd have more in common with Tony than I do. Language is your stock in trade. I'm better with visuals than words. Here he comes now. I'll introduce you.'

Soon after the two men started chatting, Leonora joined them. 'Delighted you made it, Cam.' She gave him a glass of red wine and offered a dish of smoked salmon and caviare *montaditos* to all three of them. 'I hope you don't mind if I whisk Tony away. There's someone I specially want him to meet.'

'Leonora has the most efficient antennae of any hostess I've met,' said Cam, as she led the other man away. 'I'm sure she knew that, after a trying day, I would rather talk to my ravishing neighbour than to the most brilliant professor in the whole of the US.'

'You promised not to flirt with me,' Liz reminded him.

'I promised to wait for a signal. You can't wear a dress like that and not expect to receive compliments. You should emerge from your chrysalis and shake out your wings more often. Why hide those legs inside trousers?' He stepped back the better to admire them.

'How many drinks did you have on the plane?' she asked.

'None. I never drink on flights if I have to drive when I land. This is my first alcohol today.'

She remembered that, in Alicante, he had had champagne before lunch but not much wine with their meal, and he had not been driving back until several hours later.

'I wonder what time we're eating?' he said. 'I skipped the inflight meal and my stomach is starting to growl.'

'I think supper proper starts at nine-thirty, but there are masses of nibbles. Wait here. I'll fetch a selection.'

But when she attempted to leave him, he caught her hand and made her stay. 'I can wait another fifteen minutes.'

'Oh...I've forgotten to thank you for the door-knocker,' Liz exclaimed. 'It was such a lovely surprise...my best Christmas present.'

Cam was still holding her hand. 'Then how about showing your pleasure in the traditional way?' He leaned towards her, offering a closely shaven cheek.

She didn't want to but, without seeming ungracious, she had no choice but to comply with the suggestion. As she pursed her lips, intending the kiss to be very brief and light, he turned his head and it was their mouths that made contact.

Angry that he had trapped her into a public gesture that must, if anyone noticed it, give a misleading impression that they were on much closer terms than was actually the case, Liz jerked back and gave him a glare.

'That wasn't fair,' she muttered crossly.

Yet, even as she reproached him, all her senses were tingling and sparking in the same way that a hand that had gone to sleep started coming back to life when its blood supply was restored. Feelings almost forgotten, because it was so many years since they had been experienced, revived with disturbing force.

Almost twenty years on, she relived the misleading rapture of her first kiss and all the passionate, only dimly understood longings it had aroused in her.

'Life isn't fair,' said Cam, her hand still imprisoned in his.

'Ladies and gentlemen, supper is served.' The ringing voice of their host broke the tension between them.

Moments later, a voice said, 'Cam, darling...long time no see,' and a woman in a purple top and dangling amethyst earrings began an animated monologue about the dramas in her life that allowed Liz to extricate her hand and remove herself from his orbit.

By the time supper was over, she had decided that the only way to deal with him was to stay resolutely unfazed. He was

only trying it on. He wouldn't force himself on her. Not if
he wanted to keep her as his garden-minder and website designer.

She must cultivate a light-hearted, 'down boy' manner,
treating him like an over-exuberant dog. There was, she
thought acidly, no shortage of accommodating bitches to
waggle their tails invitingly at him. The woman he was talking to now was fifty if she was a day, but it was plain from
the other side of the room that she would be more than willing to have an enjoyable fling with him.

Liz and another guest were in their hostess's bedroom,
touching up their lipstick, when Mrs Dryden joined them.
With her slim athletic figure and thick blonde hair, seen from
behind she could pass for a much younger woman than she
was. But her wrinkles, her neck and her liver-spotted hands
indicated that she was in her late sixties or possibly older.
Clearly colouring her hair was the only artifice she was prepared to use to keep age at bay.

She was simply dressed in a black satin shirt and black
trousers with grosgrain ribbon down the side seams.

After chatting for a few minutes, she said, 'Liz, I have a
gardening magazine I think would interest you. Come to my
den and I'll find it for you.'

Her den was divided into three areas. On a large table
stood a sewing machine. In another corner stood an easel
with the charcoal outline for a portrait on canvas on it. There
was also a writing desk and, nearby, a comfortable sofa
backed by shelves for books and magazine boxes.

'Perhaps you already subscribe to *Gardens Illustrated*?'
she said, closing the door behind them.

'No, I don't.'

'If you like it, I can lend you all my back numbers. But I
thought the issue dealing with courtyards might give you
ideas for Cam's and your own. Do sit down while I look for
it.'

'Obviously you don't have a problem filling your time
here, Mrs Dryden.'

'Do call me Leonora. No, certainly not. My problem is the reverse…finding time for all my pursuits. Ah, here it is.' She handed Liz a glossy magazine. 'What a gorgeous dress you're wearing. Cam mentioned that you have connections with a women's magazine. Were you the fashion editor?'

Liz laughed and shook her head. After explaining what she had done, she said, 'Actually I found this dress in a second hand shop in Denia. When it was new it would have been too expensive for me. I can't understand its original owner not keeping it. I shall wear it for ever.'

'Alas, there will come a time when you won't be able to,' said Mrs Dryden. 'There comes a point when arms are better covered up. But it will be at least twenty years before you reach that stage. I often sigh over clothes that I could have worn at your age but can't any more. Still, I have kept my waist, which is something to be thankful for. Have you ever been painted?'

'Not since primary school when we all did drawings of each other,' said Liz.

'I should like to paint you in that dress. Could you spare the time? It would take several hours but we could split them into forty-minute sessions. I find that's about my limit for intense concentration.'

'I'd be happy to pose,' said Liz.

'Good: I'll call you next week and we'll look at our diaries. Now, I think we'd better rejoin the others. Leave the magazine under your shawl on my bed.'

When they returned to her sitting room, she introduced Liz to some people she hadn't yet met, their chief interest in life being Spanish wild flowers, particularly the native plants.

Several times, while she was with them, she noticed Cam moving about the room, doing his guestly duty of mixing. His popularity was obvious, not only with women but also, a little surprisingly, with the men present. But the fact that he was a womaniser didn't necessarily make him a poacher of other men's women, she thought. Anyway it was unlikely

he would pursue women past the first flush when voluptuous
beauties like Fiona were available to him.

Being an early riser and unaccustomed to late nights, by
half past eleven she was beginning to wilt. But as no one
else seemed ready to leave, she waited until an elderly couple
departed before seizing the opportunity of the Drydens' being
together to thank them for having her and say goodnight.

'Allow me to walk you home,' said Tony, appearing beside them as they were shaking hands.

Had Leonora signalled to him? Liz wondered. She said,
'Thank you, but it isn't necessary. I don't mind walking
through the village at night. There are no muggers here.'

'I will see Liz to her door,' said Cam, from behind her.
'Con permiso,' he added, with a glinting glance that challenged her to refuse permission.

CHAPTER FIVE

Galan atrevido, de las damas preferido

A bold lover is a favourite with women

'GOOD party, didn't you think?' he said, as they left the house.

'Very good. A lovely house. Great food. Lots of interesting people. But I don't know what they will make of my little cottage when I ask them back.'

'They'll like it. Money and status symbols mean nothing to the Drydens. What they value are brains and initiative…and good manners,' he added. 'I'm sure you will write to Leonora tomorrow, but guests who don't are not invited again. She's a stickler for the old-fashioned courtesies.'

'I do know how to behave in polite society,' said Liz, rather miffed by the possibility that his comment had been a hint in case she did not. 'When you have time to look through your snail mail, you'll find a note I wrote to thank you for your Christmas present.' He would also find the book she had bought for herself but decided to give to him.

'Are you still cross with me?' he asked.

'Not in the least. Why should I be?'

'Because I kissed you in public. It was only a peck…not enough to start any gossip.'

'Gossip doesn't need a solid foundation. It can start from nothing,' she retorted. 'But I should think my reputation is a good deal more robust than yours.'

'I agree with you,' he said carelessly. 'But gossip always exaggerates. I'm not as black as I'm painted. You have nothing to fear from me.'

'I didn't think I had.'

By the light of a street lamp, she saw the lines down his cheeks deepen, betraying amusement. 'You have a short memory, Liz. But I'm glad you've revised the opinion you held the first time we lunched. How about lunch tomorrow? I have another proposal I'd like to discuss with you.'

'It's my turn to stand you a lunch.'

'All right. We'll do it your way. What time do you want me to be ready?'

'Half past twelve, if that suits you. The restaurant is about half an hour's drive from here.'

By now they had reached her house. Liz had already taken her key from her evening bag. When Cam held out his palm, she put the key on it and watched him unlock the door. Would he try to kiss her goodnight? she wondered. Would she let him? Or would she resist?

She did not find out because he did not attempt it.

'Buenas noches…hasta mañana.'

When he spoke Spanish, even commonplace remarks like 'goodnight' and 'until tomorrow' sounded oddly caressing.

'Buenas noches.' She watched him turn and walk back the way they had come, his tall figure casting a long shadow ahead of him.

After the warmth of the Drydens' sitting room, her house felt like a dungeon. She hurried upstairs to the bathroom where a hot towel rail and an electric radiator, which she always switched on at sundown, provided a comfortable level of warmth. Her bedroom did not have a heater, but the bed itself would be cosy because she had put the electric blanket on before she went out.

Before she took off her dress, she looked at herself in the mirror behind the handbasin. 'You look beautiful,' Cam had said. No other man had ever said that to her. She had received lesser compliments, but never that ultimate accolade, and said in a tone that sounded as if he meant it.

In the morning, Liz regretted agreeing to lunch with Cam. She shouldn't have drunk so much wine. It had clouded her judgment, she told herself severely.

After hand writing a thank-you letter to Leonora Dryden, she typed and printed her weekly letter to her mother.

Describing the party, she wrote, 'One of the guests was a television reporter, Cameron Fielding.' She had not told her mother he lived in the village or that she looked after his garden.

Later she put the first letter in the Drydens' box and posted the second in the yellow box attached to a wall in the main square.

Cam was already in the street outside his house when she arrived in her car. He was chatting to one of his neighbours, a small woman dressed in black, a convention still observed by many of the older ladies. This one had bandy legs, usually a sign that their owner had been born in the Thirties when Spain's civil war had made worse the poverty endured by most of the population in the first half of the last century.

As she slowed down, Liz saw that Cam was listening with the same close attention he had given to the well-heeled guests at the party. Clearly, like his hosts, he did not rate people according to their social status but by a yardstick of his own. There were some things about him that she liked very much, Liz thought, as she stopped the car a few yards short of them.

Perhaps the old lady was deaf and had not heard the car pull up. She had been in full spate for several more minutes and might have gone on indefinitely when he said something that made her pause and turn round. From their gestures, Liz gathered that the old lady was apologising for delaying him, and he was assuring her no apology was necessary.

'I wish my Spanish was good enough to talk to people the way you do,' she said, when he climbed in beside her.

'It will be. Give yourself time. Señora Mora was telling me about her brother who, when times were bad here, emigrated to Argentina and did well for himself.'

That he knew the Spanish woman's name and didn't refer

to her as 'that old dear' sent him up another notch in her estimation.

When they were clear of the village, she said, 'Tell me about your new project.'

'If you don't mind I'd rather wait till we get to where we're going.'

'I hope it lives up to my friend's recommendation. I haven't been there before.'

'If we don't like it, we can always push on.' His tone was relaxed.

Half an hour later, they were the only patrons at a small country restaurant. This establishment was far more rustic than the one where he had taken Liz. Here, in the middle of nowhere, the place was run by a middle-aged woman and her mother. Inside the building were several long trestle tables, outside four metal tables. As it was a lovely day they chose to sit outside.

Cam filled their glasses from a jug of red *vino de mesa* they had seen filled from a cask inside the restaurant. 'It'll take them a while to cook our *paella* so I'll do my presentation now, shall I?'

'I wish you would. I'm seething with curiosity.'

'Have a swig of wine before I start. This could come as a slight shock.' He drank from his own glass. 'Mmm...this is good. I wonder where it comes from?'

'What could come as a shock?' Liz demanded impatiently.

'I think we should get married,' he told her calmly. 'When, last night, I called it a proposal, that's exactly what I meant. You and I have a lot to offer each other.

'Before you tell me I'm mad, let me explain my view of marriage,' he went on. 'I've seen a lot of marriages go wrong, including my parents', and a few that have been successful. The successful ones all seem to have a common denominator. They are basically intimate friendships between people prepared to make trade-offs. In marriages that last, both partners will give up something they want if it will benefit their partner. But it has to work both ways. It's no use one person making all the sacrifices.'

By now Liz was recovering from her initial stupefaction.

'I'm sure all that's true,' she said, 'but I can't relate it to us. We hardly know each other. We come from completely different backgrounds. We have different temperaments. We—'

He cut her short. 'Let's take those first three items and deal with the others later. You feel we hardly know each other. What does a woman need to know about a man before she marries him? Take five minutes to think about it and then tell me your conclusions.'

Wine glass in hand, he rose from his chair and strolled across the rough turf to where the land fell away so that from where she was sitting Liz could only see the distant sea with the Peñon de Ifach rising out of it.

Marriage, she thought, still dazed. Marriage. Why should he offer me, of all people, the thing that he has never offered to any of those other women?

Or maybe he has, and the one he wanted refused him. Could that be the reason he has played the field so intensively? Because someone has broken his heart?

She looked at his long straight back, the taut backside and the set of his head on his neck. Physically, everything about him was attractive. But what was he like inside?

Presently Cam came back. 'Have you worked it out?'

She nodded. 'I think so. She needs to know that he's kind, that he has a sense of humour, and that he won't bore her.' There was a fourth essential—that he was a considerate lover—but it wasn't something she could discuss with him.

'And how do I rate?'

'You rate well…as far as I can tell. But I think it takes time to be sure…more time than we've known each other.'

The younger of the two women came out with a basket of bread, a bowl of olives and a dish of mussels, their black shells piped with what looked like fine squiggles of icing sugar but what turned out to be a corraline trail left on them by some other sea creature.

'Do you like mussels?' Cam asked. They had not been offered a choice of starters, only the option to have lamb chops or paella for their main course.

'I don't know. I've never tried them before. They're a beautiful colour.' Before she ate, she added, 'This is all pretty basic compared with the restaurants you took me to. But my friend said it was a glimpse of the way Spain used to be, before it was colonised by northerners. But of course you were here as a schoolboy so you know what it was like then.'

He said, 'But now I am a man who has missed a lot of the best things life has to offer, and who wants to make up for lost time. Liz, I don't want to seem intrusive, but were you and your husband childless by choice or chance?'

'Certainly not by choice. We both wanted children, but it wasn't possible. Duncan had had orchitis in his teens. His family doctor didn't warn him that, occasionally, it leaves men infertile.' Though she had always suspected that Duncan's possessive mother had known it was a possibility. 'Not that it would have made any difference if we had known. I loved him. I would have married him regardless.'

'"Love is not love which alters when it alteration finds…O, no! it is an ever-fixed mark"',' Cam quoted.

For a moment she was tempted to confide in him. Instead she said, 'There's no guarantee that I can have children now. I passed all the tests at the time, but it was a long time ago and the chances don't get better as women get older.'

'You're not that old,' he said, smiling. 'Lots of women don't start their families until forty is on the horizon. The pattern of life has changed since our parents' time. I know a number of couples who've decided not to have children. They feel procreation should be an option, not a convention. I agree with that point of view. But, for myself, I'd like to have a crack at parenthood.'

'Is that your main reason for deciding to marry?'

'Certainly not. If I arranged my reasons in order, it would be well down the list.'

'What would come first?'

He drank some wine before he answered. 'Two things: companionship and sex. Someone to share my thoughts and my bed.'

'Rumour says there's never been any shortage of bed partners.'

'Rumour tends to exaggerate. I'm not denying that my past has not been monastic, but that doesn't mean I'm incapable of fidelity in a permanent relationship.'

'Don't you think you might get bored in a permanent relationship?'

'No, I don't. I'm not bored by my favourite books, my favourite music, my favourite paintings. While I hope to go on making new friends for the rest of my life, I don't expect to lose interest in my first close friends.' He paused. 'To be blunt about it, freewheeling girls like Fiona were a pleasant expedient while I was footloose, with a good chance of being blown to bits. You may think that reprehensible, but making love is a fundamental human need. You married young. If you hadn't, are you sure you wouldn't have had some pleasant but temporary relationships while you waited for a permanent partner to show up?'

'I expect I might have,' she agreed. 'Though I can't imagine ever going to bed with anyone unless I had *some* feelings for them…unless I had hopes that it would last. But, I suppose, if you're in a job that involves serious risks you probably look at it differently…the way people do in wartime. Live for today in case there is no tomorrow.'

'Well, as you know better than most, tomorrow is never a sure thing for anyone. But I'm certain that your husband, if he could have foreseen the premature ending of his life, would not have wanted you to spend the rest of yours in mourning for him.' Cam said quietly. 'Romantic love isn't the only basis for a successful marriage, you know. In a lot of cultures it starts as a practical arrangement and affection grows on the way along.'

'But not in our culture.'

'Our culture is in the melting pot. Who can say where it's heading? I think we are all on the threshold of enormous, exciting changes. I also think you and I would enjoy them more if we faced them together.'

At this point the restaurant's owner came out to collect their plates and the dish of empty shells and squeezed halves of lemon.

'*Bien?*' she enquired.

'*Muy bien, señora.*' Cam chatted to her as easily as if the conversation she had interrupted had been of no special consequence.

Did he take it for granted that she would accept his proposal? Liz wondered. But really why should he not? He had a great deal to offer. There must be any number of women who, given the chance, would jump at becoming Mrs Cameron Fielding, wife of a well-known man who was also exceptionally attractive. He was everything most women dreamed of, except that he didn't believe in love and perhaps was incapable of feeling it.

'Have you never been in love?' she asked, when they were alone again.

'Yes…in my youth…of course,' he said, looking amused. 'Between seventeen and twenty-three I fell in love several times, but fortunately the girls didn't feel the same way or their parents intervened.'

'Fortunately?'

He shrugged. 'I didn't see it as fortunate at the time, but I do now. Generally speaking people in their teens and early twenties are far too immature to embark on a serious relationship. They need to find out who they are before they can tell who will suit them for the rest of their lives. You may have known who you were when you got married, but most people don't till much later.'

'I'm not sure I know who I am even now,' she said, in a

wry tone. 'Life seems to happen to me. I don't feel I'm in control.'

'You made the decision to come here, to make a fresh start.'

'It was more of an impulse than a considered decision…something that happened by chance rather than by design. I didn't decide in advance that I wanted to live abroad.'

'Well, now there is a decision to make and I think we should fix a time limit. I'll give you until the mimosa in my garden comes out. What could be more romantic?' he said, with a teasing smile.

'When does that happen?' She had heard there were seven varieties of mimosa growing in Spain, some flowering earlier than others.

'Depends…usually in March, but sometimes earlier if the winter has been particularly mild. Meantime we can spend a lot of time together and do an in-depth check for incompatibilities.'

'I can spot one big one already. You take the idea of marriage a lot less seriously than I do,' she retorted, rather brusquely.

The *paella* was brought in a large shallow metal pan and set on the end of the table. The yellow rice, coloured with saffron, glistened in the sunlight. Half a dozen prawns were arranged round the edge of the dish and there were chunks of chicken and possibly rabbit half hidden in the rice.

'I'll serve it, shall I?' said Cam, and he performed this task as expertly as a Spanish waiter.

As was customary in small Spanish restaurants, the plates had not been heated, so they concentrated on eating and did not talk. Fortunately the *paella* in the pan stayed hot. They both had second helpings and Cam finished up what was left.

'Mmm…very good,' he said, patting his flat midriff in a gesture of appreciation. 'Why does food always taste better out of doors, I wonder?'

Considering that he had probably eaten at some of the

world's best restaurants, Liz felt his comments owed more to politeness than truth.

A car arrived and parked near hers under the pine trees. Two middle-aged couples got out and came to the table next to the one where Cam and Liz were sitting. The newcomers greeted them in Spanish, then continued their conversation in a language she didn't recognise and thought must be something Scandinavian.

The already large and still expanding expatriate community included many nationalities from all parts of Europe and also from North America. There had also been an influx of people from North Africa and South America, but they were mostly to be seen working on the land or selling goods in the street markets and *rastros*. Some were illegal immigrants, striving to make a better life for themselves. Many of the comfortably off expats disapproved of them, but Liz felt sorry for anyone forced, by poverty, to uproot themselves from their homelands.

'Shall we go for a stroll and have our fruit and coffee a little later?' Cam suggested.

'Won't the *señora* mind if we walk off without paying? Perhaps I should pay her first?'

'She won't mind if I explain. She's not a worrier like you are,' he said, before going inside the building.

Am I a worrier? Liz wondered. If I am, why does he want me in his life instead of some carefree butterfly like Fiona?

Cam reappeared. 'Let's go that way.' He indicated a rough track on the opposite side of the road passing the restaurant.

'You didn't pay her yourself, did you?' asked Liz, prepared to be angry if he had.

'You said you wanted to pick up the bill today.'

'Yes, but I know what men are. They like to be in charge.'

'Sometimes…not always,' he said mildly. 'There's a hawk.' He pointed at a bird hovering in the bright air.

They walked as far as a small deserted stone building that might once have been a dwelling in the time when all the terraces in this area were still under cultivation.

'It's hard for us to imagine spending our whole lives, from birth to death, in one small corner of the world,' said Cam, as they looked through what had once been the doorway to a single room. 'I don't think I could have stood it…day after day, year after year of relentless labour to scrape a living. I'd have had to go off and find out what was on the other side of the *sierra*—' waving his arm at the mountainside looming above them. 'But perhaps, having seen it, I would have come back and settled. There's a peacefulness here that you never find in a city or even a town.'

He turned to her. 'You've gone very quiet. What are you thinking about?'

'About your bombshell, of course. What else would I be thinking of?'

He came to where she was standing, putting his hands lightly on her shoulders.

'"Bombshell" implies something unpleasant. I can understand you being surprised, if you took me for a dedicated loner. But is the idea of being my wife so completely unacceptable that you can't believe I've suggested it?'

Then, before she could form her reply, he bent his head and kissed her mouth.

It was the lightest and most fleeting of kisses but, in an instant, it reactivated the feelings she had experienced in his garden after their first lunch together. Powerful sensations surged through her. In that moment she recognised the truth that her brain had been trying to deny. She had fallen in love with him.

As if that were not enough to cope with, Cam took his hands from her shoulders, but not to leave her free to step back if she wanted to. Instead he slipped his arms round her, gathered her close and kissed her again, this time with less restraint.

Some immeasurable time later—it might have been seconds or minutes, she only knew it was too brief to satisfy her body and far too long for her peace of mind—he brought the kiss to an end.

Still holding her, he said, 'I liked that. How about you?'

Stumped for a suitable answer, Liz freed herself. 'I think we should go back.'

It amazed her that her voice was steady when the rest of her felt like jelly. With a single kiss he had made her want him so badly that she couldn't believe the strength of the urges aroused in her.

'Whatever you say. It's your party.' He gestured for her to go ahead of him.

In a daze of conflicting emotions, she set out along the path.

Following her, Cam was pretty sure he knew what was going on in her mind. The kiss had made her understand what she hadn't taken in before: that her physical needs hadn't atrophied in the years she had been on her own but had merely been dormant and were now back in action and clamouring for satisfaction.

He noticed she was treading on stones that she would have avoided if she had been concentrating on the path instead of thinking about, and probably regretting, her response to his kiss.

Deliberately, he had not turned up the heat as high as it could have gone if he hadn't kept control. It would take time and patience to get her to the point when she wouldn't feel uneasy about the attraction between them.

He looked at her narrow waist and the feminine shape of her backside and he wished he could take her home and go to bed with her. But he was not going to do that—not today, not yet. It was too soon. She wasn't ready. He would have to be patient.

Back at the restaurant, they finished their meal with fresh fruit and coffee before driving back to Valdecarrasca. On the way, Cam suggested a detour to a *planterista* as he wanted some pots of geraniums for the sill of his street-side kitchen window.

'I thought geraniums needed sun, but there's a house near the bakery where they seem to thrive on a north-facing window ledge,' he said.

'Perhaps the owner has a sunny patio and swops them around,' said Liz.

He was the tallest, broadest passenger she had ever had in her small car and she was uneasily conscious of the long hard thighs on the other side of the gearstick and the rock-like chest that, not long ago, she had felt against her breasts.

'Perhaps.'

He had pushed the passenger seat as far back as it would go so that his backrest was several inches further back than hers. She knew he was watching her.

She forced herself to concentrate on driving, keeping an eye out for cars that, visible half a mile downhill, might vanish behind a bend just before the point when they met.

'Do you like driving?' Cam asked.

'I like country driving, but even that can be scary occasionally. I passed a van the other day whose driver was holding a mobile in one hand and making gestures with the other. He was on a straight stretch of road, but even so…'

'Maniac!' was Cam's comment. After a pause, he added, 'It makes a nice change to be driven…lets me look at the scenery in a way I can't at the wheel.'

The *planterista* they stopped at was not well-organised and some of the plants and shrubs on sale were in less than first-class condition. Cam decided to look for geraniums at one of the larger establishments catering to the thousands of villa-owners in the coastal belt.

'We could do that tomorrow,' he suggested, as they returned to the car. 'Also I wouldn't mind looking round the shops in Gata. I've been asked to a house-warming and I need to find a suitable present.'

Gata de Gorgos was a small town that straddled the main

coast road and was famous for its cane furniture and basket-work shops. As well as going to the cinema there, Liz had browsed in the shops. She would have liked to go again, but she felt it was wiser to say, 'I really need to work tomorrow.'

'And you're still in shock and want time to recover…yes?'

She knew without glancing at him that there would be the hint of a smile at the corners of his mouth.

'Yes, that too,' she admitted.

The car was not locked and he opened the driver's door for her. 'OK, I'll give you a breathing space. How about going to Gata on Friday? I really would be glad of your advice on this house-warming gift…and we do need to spend more time together to help you come to a decision.'

'All right…Friday,' she agreed.

Next morning she had a call from Leonora Dryden.

'Liz, do you have an hour to spare this afternoon? I'd like to make a start on the portrait.'

At three o'clock, taking the party dress in a carrier, Liz walked round to the Drydens' house to be met by Leonora wearing one of her husband's cast-off shirts and a pair of paint-stained cotton trousers.

'It's good of you to come at short notice.' Leonora took her upstairs to her bedroom where Liz changed into the dress.

For the first half an hour of the sitting they chatted about general subjects until, suddenly, the older woman said, 'There's tension about you that wasn't there the other night. Is there something on your mind today?'

Liz hesitated and then, on impulse, said, 'Yes, there is, but I didn't know it showed.'

Leonora, who had been looking from her subject to the canvas at fifteen-second intervals ever since, satisfied with the pose, she had started work, now gave her sitter a longer look.

'Is it something you can discuss? A problem shared is a problem halved, as the saying goes.'

Again Liz hesitated before deciding to confide her dilemma. 'Cam has asked me to marry him.'

Much to her surprise, Leonora showed no sign of being startled by this information.

'I could see he was very taken with you at the party. I discussed it with Todd afterwards. He thought I was being over-imaginative, but men are less sensitive to nuances than women. But he did agree it was high time Cam took a wife and that you seemed an ideal person to take on that role. Why are you hesitating? Because you haven't known him long?'

'That's one of the reasons,' said Liz. 'How long did you and Todd know each other before you decided to marry?'

'We've known each other since we were children, so although we married very young it wasn't as rash a step for me as it would have been for most girls of twenty. Generally speaking I think women need to be twenty-five and men around thirty before they're sufficiently mature to commit themselves to a lifelong partnership. You and Cam know who you are and what you want from life.'

'He does...but I'm not sure that I do...except that I'd like to have children. But is that a good enough reason to marry someone?'

'Does Cam want children?'

'He says so.'

Leonora lapsed into a thoughtful silence. Eventually, she said, 'The question you have to ask yourself is, How will this man enhance my life and how can I enhance his? The feminists would have my guts for garters if they heard me but, generally speaking, I think being a wife—given that one's husband isn't a brute or a slob—is always preferable to being single. Men are so useful. If I didn't have Todd, I should have to read the bank statements and paint the seats in the garden and recharge the car's battery when, occasionally, it goes flat. I could do all those things if I had to, but I'd rather not, just as Todd doesn't want to be bothered with

Christmas cards and duty letters to distant relations and choosing the fabric for new slipcovers.'

'But surely a marriage should be more than a matter of mutual convenience?' said Liz.

'Absolutely—but the day-to-day practicalities are an important part of life so it's crucial to be sure that you see eye to eye on the mundane matters. An obsessively neat person is unlikely to be happy with an untidy partner, and so on. Given roughly the same sort of personal habits, the next thing to consider is mind-sets. A free-thinker is never going to get along with someone extremely conventional. Todd and I have vigorous arguments on all sorts of topics, but in the important areas we're pretty much in agreement.'

'What do you see as the important areas?' Liz asked.

'Money, religion, politics and sex. Neither of us is extravagant, but nor are we mean. We're both atheists, but enjoy church architecture and music. We're both apolitical—despising all politicians impartially. We both take the view that fidelity is one of the keystones of marriage and affairs on the side are strictly off-limits. Have you discussed those areas with Cam?'

'Not yet. There hasn't been time to discuss anything much.'

Leonora took two steps backward and studied her canvas through narrowed eyes. 'I'd recommend thrashing them out as soon as possible. Cam's not the sort of man who will mind if you ask him point-blank what he thinks. What's more he'll tell you the truth and not just what he thinks you want to hear. He has one of the best-organised minds of anyone I know. There are not many subjects he doesn't have a point of view on.'

It was clear that she meant this comment to be encouraging, but Liz found it daunting, knowing that her own mind was far from well organised and there were lots of subjects about which she knew too little to have any firm opinions.

'I think that's enough for today. Time for a cup of tea,' said Leonora. 'I'll make it while you are changing. Would you mind leaving the dress here? I'd like to study that lovely shimmery effect.'

When Liz returned to her house, she opened her front door to find a bunch of flowers wrapped in florist's paper on the table inside it. There was only one person who could have left them there. Cam must have called while she was out and used the key she had given him to unlock the door.

Swathed in stiff dark green paper, the bunch of pale pink roses, cream carnations and various types of greenery that she didn't know the name of had a small envelope attached to it. Inside was a card on which he had written—

Thank you for yesterday.
Looking forward to tomorrow. C

Liz took the flowers to the kitchen. The only thing she had to put them in was a earthenware wine jug that was too rustic for the sophisticated flowers. As she snipped the tapes holding the stalks together, she wondered how much the flowers had cost. Probably a lot more than the price of yesterday's lunch. The envelope bore the name and address of the *floristería*. It was not the shop in the next village up the valley, but a florist in one of the coastal resorts. She wondered what other errand had taken him there. He would not have gone all that way just to buy flowers for her.

When the flowers were arranged, she went upstairs and sent him an e-mail.

Cam—I found your flowers when I got home from the first portrait session with Leonora. They are gorgeous. How kind of you—Liz

All evening she mulled over Leonora's advice. She had half expected the older woman to ask her about her marriage

and wondered why she hadn't. Not that Liz would have
wanted to talk about it. The past was better left undisturbed.

When, soon after ten, they set out for Gata, there were still
long streamers of mist lying over parts of the valley, waiting
to be dispersed by the sun. Most of the village streets were
still in shade, and the people they saw were warmly wrapped
up. One woman, returning from the *panadería* with bread in
a cotton bag with *pan* embroidered on it, was wearing a
quilted dressing gown, a garment often seen about the village
during the morning.

Guessing that it might be cold inside the shops in Gata,
Liz had taken the precaution of wearing a quilted gilet over
a sweater over a shirt.

'What sort of house are you looking for a present for?'
she asked, as they left the outskirts of the village.

'A converted farmhouse about ten miles further inland. It
should be habitable by Easter, possibly sooner. As soon as it
is, they'll be throwing a party. I suspect they'll be inundated
with stuff they don't really want and I don't want to add to
the junk.'

'Ornaments are the worst things to give,' said Liz, remembering a couple of horrors among her wedding presents. 'Not
that you would, but some people can't believe that what they
think is beautiful might be seen as hideous by someone else.'

She was looking at him as she spoke. When he laughed,
it deepened the line down his cheek and gave her a momentary glimpse of his teeth. She had never thought of teeth as
being sexy, but his were. Seeing them made her insides turn
over. His hands had a similar effect. Out of the corner of her
eye she watched the easy way he changed gear and his light
handling of the wheel. Yet she had the feeling that, should
an emergency occur, his reaction would be instantaneous and
exactly right for the circumstances.

There were two ways to get to Gata and he chose the back
road that followed the meandering course of a dry riverbed.
Ahead, in the distance, they could see the massive outline of

the mountain she had driven over with Deborah. Presently, a
bend in the road opened the view of the impressive modern
viaduct carrying the coastal *autopista* that Cam had mentioned when he was driving her to Alicante.

How incredulous she would have been, then, if someone
had suggested that, within a few weeks, he would ask her to
marry him.

As this seemed a good opportunity to broach the subjects
Leonora had mentioned yesterday, she said, 'I read an article
somewhere that said people contemplating marriage should
make sure their minds are in tune on four subjects.'

'Which are?'

'Money, religion, politics…and sex.' She hesitated slightly
before adding the fourth subject, the most difficult one for
her to discuss with him.

'Having eye-witnessed some of worst excesses committed
in the name of religion and politics, I don't have much time
for zealots or politicians,' he answered. 'If the world is ever
going to be a peaceful place, it will probably be the result of
scientists finding ways to correct genetic problems. I'm very
excited by the latest research into the human genome. I think
that's where our best hopes lie.'

'That's exactly my view.' During a sleepless night she had
worked out where she stood on three of the issues raised by
Leonora.

'Good…then no problems there. Where do you stand on
money?'

'As I've never had much, I don't really stand anywhere. I
don't like people who are stingy, but I'm certainly not a
member of the ''buy now, pay later'' brigade.'

'How do you feel about pre-nuptial settlements?'

'I don't approve of them *at all*,' she said, with vehement
emphasis. 'But then I don't see the point of getting married
if you think it might not be permanent.'

'But sometimes, despite both parties' good intentions, it
isn't permanent and there are children to be provided for.'

'The moral of that is not to have children by a man unless

you are certain he will stand by his obligations,' Liz said briskly.

'That's an idealist's view…sounds good in theory but often doesn't work out in practice.'

'I know…but I still think a pre-nuptial agreement makes it clear that there's no real love or trust in the marriage, that it's actually a cold-hearted exchange of assets, usually youth and beauty for fame and fortune.'

'You're thinking of showbiz alliances, I imagine. Like anyone who works in front of the TV cameras, I have a small amount of fame and some modest assets in a trust that was set up by my grandparents when I was a small boy. They were more prudent than my parents who are both incurably extravagant. Is your mother comfortably off?'

'She has a nice bungalow and enough to live on. I don't have to help her,' said Liz, in case he had been wondering whether her mother would be a liability he would have to shoulder. 'But I don't think my mother and yours would have anything in common. My background is very ordinary.'

'Are you an inverted snob, Liz?' He gave her a quizzical glance. 'One thing that any journalist learns early on is that a person's worth has nothing to do with their place in the pecking order. I once spent time with a man who cleaned London's sewers. In all the ways that really matter, he was a far better person than a man with a seat on several boards whom I interviewed shortly afterwards.'

'So he may have been, but that isn't to say they would have been comfortable in each other's company,' she pointed out.

'Possibly not. Although if they had been holed up together in some tricky situation they'd have probably got along fine…with the sewer man taking command and the boardroom guy glad to let him, I shouldn't wonder. But that's beside the point. All that matters in our case is that you and I are on the same wavelength. Whether our family members like each other is their problem, not ours.'

By this time they were on the outskirts of Gata. The streets behind the main thoroughfare had been built when traffic consisted of mule-drawn carts and Cam needed to give his full attention to passing lines of closely parked cars and turning tight corners.

He was able to find a parking spot not far from the main through road and soon they were in one of the many shops selling cane and basketware and glass and pottery. Here, and in other shops they visited, there was usually a middle-aged or elderly woman who emerged from the rear of the premises to keep an eye on them. When they found Cam spoke fluent Spanish, they seemed glad to gossip with him while Liz roamed the aisles between the crowded displays.

It was in the fourth shop that she noticed a set of sturdy wine goblets made from glass with a greenish tinge and bubbles of air in the stems that she thought would be perfect for the house he had described. Cam agreed with her and bought twenty of them and two matching jugs.

While they were being wrapped in newspaper and packed in a carton, Liz saw a square glass vase that was perfect for the flowers he had given her.

As he stowed their shopping in the back to the car, Cam said, 'Time for coffee…if you don't mind having it in a bar. I don't think Gata runs to anything smarter.'

'A bar is fine by me.'

On days out with Deborah, she had been into places they wouldn't have used back in England but found acceptable here, where small-town and village bars were mainly men's places, lacking the refinements of cafés and tea rooms designed to suit a feminine clientele.

The first bar they came to was empty apart from the barman who was sweeping up the litter of sugar wrappers and cigarette ends on the floor beneath the bar stools. The television was on and two fruit machines were flashing their lights, but the noise level wasn't intolerable as it sometimes could be in bars.

Liz chose a table away from the fruit machines and watched Cam's back view as he leaned against the bar while the man behind it dealt with his order. If she had needed any confirmation of her feelings about him, this moment would have been proof. Because he was with her, she would rather be here, in this scruffy Spanish bar, than anywhere on earth.

He carried two cups of coffee to the plastic-imitating-wood table with its ashtray, plastic pot of toothpicks and plastic container for the squares of paper napkin that, in Liz's experience, were never very absorbent.

'Not the most glamorous ambience, I'm afraid,' he said dryly, before turning away to fetch two glasses of white wine.

'You're used to more glamorous places than I am,' said Liz, when he came back.

'Sometimes...not always.' He pulled out a chair and sat down. 'Anyway it's the company that counts.' He smiled at her.

If only it counted for him as much as it did for her, she thought, with a pang. If only there was a chance that he might come to love her.

Cam drank some coffee. 'Now, where had we got to with your list of things to discuss? We've done religion and politics. As far as money is concerned, my view is that when people marry they should pool their resources, allocate themselves some spending money and confer about all their other expenses. Does that seems sensible?'

'Perfectly,' Liz agreed, aware that her pulse-rate had quickened with anticipated nervousness.

'Right, so that leaves only one more item on the agenda,' said Cam. 'But perhaps the most key of them all.' He paused, and there was a gleam in the steel-grey eyes that made her pulse beat even faster. 'Sex. What aspects of it are we supposed to discuss?'

CHAPTER SIX

Donde no hay amor, no hay dolor

Where there is no love, there is no pain

'I THINK fidelity is the big issue. I know I couldn't cope with an ''open'' marriage. But is fidelity possible for someone like yourself who's been used to…to variety?'

'Not only possible, but preferable. It was asking someone to marry me when I was a nomad, and there was always a chance I wouldn't come back, that was impossible.'

'But don't you think you might get bored with only one partner? A lot of men do.'

'A lot of men have unsatisfactory sex lives. They don't understand women's needs so they don't get the response they need and start looking elsewhere. They don't realise the problem lies with them.'

She wanted to ask, How come *you* understand? But this wasn't a subject she was comfortable with. Her unease was a hangover from her childhood when sex had never been discussed. Even when her father was not present, her mother had dealt with Liz's questions awkwardly, making her realise that, if she wanted satisfactory answers, she would have to find another source of information.

In the end, most of what she had learnt had come from books and magazines. But knowing the theory and putting it into practice were two different things, she had discovered.

From the other side of the table Cam watched Liz apparently studying the imitation wood grain of the tabletop. There was a slight frown between her eyebrows. He guessed that she wasn't seeing the pattern on the plastic but had retreated into a private part of her mind which he might never penetrate.

He said quietly, 'If you decide to marry me, I will be faithful to you. That's a promise. I'm not in favour of open marriages either.'

She looked up at him. He could read the uncertainty verging on disbelief in her eyes and he cursed the fact that, the first time they met, he had had Fiona with him. Obviously meeting one of his former girlfriends had confirmed all the gossip Liz had picked up about him. If she hadn't met Fiona, she might have taken it less seriously.

'My grandmother used to quote a saying about reformed rakes making the best husbands,' he told her. 'You wouldn't expect me, at my age, not to have had any relationships, would you?'

'No…but it does sound as if you've had rather a lot of them.'

It wasn't often that he found himself lost for words. Words were his stock in trade. But explaining his past life to Liz was a great deal harder than explaining the complexities of the Middle East or African politics to several million television viewers.

'You must have seen films or read about World War Two,' he said. 'When men didn't know if they were going to come back from their next bombing mission, or their next Atlantic convoy, they grabbed life with both hands while they had the chance. Women did too, even in those days when normal codes of behaviour were a great deal stricter than they are now.'

She nodded, listening intently.

'Reporters who cover war zones tend to feel the same way,' he went on. 'It's a high-risk occupation so they live for the present. Tomorrow may never happen. But now, unless I'm very unlucky, I can expect to live as long as my grandparents did. I can plan for the future.' He reached across the table and put his hand over hers. 'I'm hoping to spend it with you…raising a family and enjoying life together.'

He had hoped that she might react by turning her hand palm upwards and curling her fingers round his. But her hand remained motionless.

She said, 'Nowadays most people have a trial run before they marry. Don't you think that might be wiser than rushing into matrimony straight away?'

'Did you have a trial run with your husband?'

As he had noticed before, any mention of her husband lit a flicker of pain in her eyes.

Liz knew it was natural for Cam to be curious about her marriage and perhaps, one day, she would tell him the whole story, but not now, not yet.

She shook her head. 'Our families were very conventional. We both lived at home till we married. A trial run wasn't an option. I was never a rebel and neither was Duncan.'

'What was his job?'

'He was an accountant with an insurance company.' To Cam, she felt sure, such an occupation would seem the nadir of dullness.

'Was it what he wanted to do?'

'He wasn't unhappy doing it. I think he accepted that most people don't find their work exciting. Somebody has to do the dull jobs. He did enjoy his hobby—coin-collecting. He belonged to several collectors' clubs and wrote articles on numismatics.' That probably made Duncan sound even duller, she thought.

Rather to her surprise, Cam said, 'That's a fascinating field. I know next to nothing about it, but I can understand its appeal. My grandfather collected stamps but he didn't attempt to interest me in them. He believed that a passion for collecting couldn't be instilled but had to spring up naturally. However, getting back to the question of trial runs, I think, in a village like this, there's no point in inviting critical comment. In London and New York, no one gives a damn what anyone does. But here they have different values.'

Liz had no doubt he was right as far as the older women

were concerned. Most of them would have been virgin brides. But, according to what Alicia had told her, Spanish girls were rapidly catching up with their peers in northern Europe, even to the extent of setting up house with their boyfriends.

Alicia had also confided that, for her own generation, sexual relations ended with the menopause—and a good thing too, she had added, suggesting that her own experience of physical love had been a tiresome duty rather than the delight it was supposed to be.

In her still far from fluent Spanish, Liz had ventured to ask what their husbands thought about that. Alicia had shrugged her plump shoulders, at the same time pulling down the corners of her mouth and rolling her eyes. 'Men are men and will find their pleasures where they can,' she had said dismissively.

Deborah, when Liz had relayed this comment to her, had said, 'Haven't you noticed the ''clubs'' all along the main coast road? Club is a euphemism for brothel. I expect that's where they go. Don't look so shocked. Men are like that. If your husband wasn't, you were lucky.'

And, in that respect, she had been, Liz knew. There was no doubt in her mind that Duncan had always been faithful to her. He had disapproved of promiscuity and avoided colleagues who went boozing together or played the field. He would not have got on with Cam. They were poles apart.

Cam had withdrawn his hand and was drinking his wine and watching her with a faintly amused expression.

'It's not so long since you were warning me not to step out of line. Now you're the one suggesting we go to bed together, and you haven't made the decision to marry me yet—or have you?'

She felt herself flushing. 'No, I haven't. I still think the idea is mad.'

'On the contrary…eminently sane. But we won't argue about it. Bring me up to date with your online life.'

*   *   *

They didn't get back to the village until late afternoon, after looking round some more of Gata's shops and then having a late lunch during which Cam steered the conversation away from personal matters and made Liz laugh more often than she could ever remember laughing at a meal table.

When he dropped her outside her house, he got out to open the boot and give her the vase she had bought.

'Thank you for lunch,' she said, as he handed it over.

'Thank you for being my shopping adviser. Are you going to Benissa tomorrow?'

Benissa was a cathedral town where, on Saturdays, a picturesque street market supplied Spaniards, expats and tourists with excellent produce.

'Probably.'

'Why don't we go together and free a car parking space for someone else to use?'

Against her better judgement, she said, 'All right. What time?'

'Is half past nine too early?'

'No, that would be fine.'

'Hasta mañana.' Seeing that a heavy lorry was coming down the narrow street and would not be able to pass his car, he quickly returned to the wheel.

Presently, as she was rearranging his flowers in the new vase, Liz knew it would have been wiser to avoid his company for a few days and give herself time to think more clearly than she could when she was with him.

That evening, intending to do some work, she could not resist looking at the photo of him she had saved from the TV channel website. By using a photographic program, she was able to enlarge it and print it on a small colour printer she had bought at a special offer price. When used with special paper that was more expensive than ordinary paper, the printer produced prints of a quality as good as regular photographs.

Later, lying in bed, she spent a long time studying every detail of Cam's physiognomy, from the way his hair sprang from his broad, high forehead in an almost straight line with the hint of a peak in the centre, to the exact shape of his incisors.

She found that, if she covered his left eye with her hand, the right eye looked curiously stern. When she covered his right eye, the left had the sexy glint that she found so disturbing. With both eyes exposed it was less noticeable, as was the sternness.

She got out of bed for a hand mirror and studied her own eyes. Their expression seemed identical. Perhaps a difference was only noticeable in a photograph, but the only portrait photograph she had was in her passport and it was too small to be studied in the same way.

What worried her was that she remembered studying a picture of Duncan in just this way when she was in her late teens. Was she any wiser than she had been then? Older, yes—but not necessarily any more sensible.

She remembered some lines read at school. *Friendship is a disinterested commerce between equals; love, an abject intercourse between tyrants and slaves.*

Duncan, mildest of men, had not been a tyrant. Nevertheless her marriage had been a kind of slavery, a bondage from which there had seemed to be no escape until, suddenly, she was free—and sick with shame because the price of her freedom had been his life.

At midnight, unable to sleep, she went up to the flat roof for the first time since the night Cam had brought Fiona to La Higuera and she had seen them embracing by the guest room window.

Now the only room alight was the sitting room, but its occupant wasn't visible. Perhaps he was sitting on the sofa that had its back to the windows. If the television had been on, she would have seen the blue glow of its screen. But it wasn't so he must be reading.

At least they had that in common. They were both insatiable readers. But was it enough to build a marriage on?

*   *   *

Benissa market was already bustling when they arrived at the
street where it took place. On either side was a row of terraced houses, some tall, some smaller, but all with black-
painted iron *rejas* protecting the ground-floor windows,
narrow balconies at the windows above, and black or well-
polished brass knockers on the doors. Each terrace had a
narrow pavement and a roadway. One road was at a slightly
lower level than the other and between them was a narrow
railinged garden with palm trees towering above shrubs and
daisy bushes.

Today the two roadways were occupied by stalls display-
ing piles of shiny purple aubergines, ruby-red and dark green
peppers, garlic, mushrooms, strawberries, artichokes, oranges
and many other fruit and vegetables. Crowding the fronts of
the stalls were local housewives, some pulling shopping trol-
leys and others with small dummy-sucking children in push-
chairs. The air was loud with voices, most of them speaking Valenciano, the language of the region. But foreigners
speaking German, Dutch, French, English and various
Scandinavian languages added to the babel. Several children
were eating *churros* from a stall at one end of the market,
and a teenage girl was managing to navigate through the
crowd on Rollerblades.

Many curious and interested glances were directed at Cam,
Liz noticed, for not only was he taller than most of the shoppers, but he had the air of being someone special. She wondered if he would be recognised, though this was not the kind
of place where people would expect to find someone well-
known on TV. Despite its superior climate, the Costa Blanca
had never had the once fashionable and now somewhat dis-
reputable image of the Costa del Sol in the south of Spain.

'These *piel de sapo* melons are good—if you like melon,'
she said, picking up one shaped like a rugby ball, its name
deriving from the fact that the green rind with darker blotches
did resemble the skin of a toad.

Cam bought one and insisted on putting them both in the
rucksack he had slung over one broad shoulder. Though the

local people were always well-mannered, once or twice, on previous visits to the market, Liz had been jostled or elbowed aside by the kind of foreigner who felt he or she had the right to be served before other shoppers.

With Cam beside her, she knew this would not happen. His presence was like a shield. She felt an atavistic pleasure in being with someone larger and stronger who, in the unlikely event of an affray breaking out, would see it as his duty to protect her. Being a man's equal was good in many ways, but there were still circumstances in which any sensible woman would welcome a strong male arm around her, or a tough masculine body stepping in front of her to ward off whatever the threat was.

Just as she was thinking this, Cam, now standing behind her, leaned forward to pick out a grapefruit, the movement bringing his chest into contact with the back of her shoulder. At the same time she caught an aroma of soap, or shaving cream, or shower gel, that was more subtle than the fragrance of aftershave.

In that instant she knew that, however misguided it might be, she was going to accept his proposal of marriage. She was as incapable of resisting her feelings for him as she had been helpless to resist her girlish love for Duncan. All she could do was pray that, this time, it would turn out differently.

'Sorry, am I crowding you?' said Cam, looking down at the same moment that she looked up at him.

'Everyone's crowding everyone,' Liz said, with attempted lightness. But her heart was thudding against her ribs and her voice came out husky instead of cool. How was it possible to feel these intensely private and personal sensations in such a public place?

Still holding the grapefruit out towards the stall-holder, Cam bent his head towards hers. In a low voice, speaking close to her ear, he said, 'But these well-padded *amas de casa* and *hausfraus* don't have the same effect on me that you do. I'm controlling a strong desire to kiss you.'

She repressed an impulse to say, Why don't you? knowing he wasn't a man to resist a challenge, however inappropriate the setting.

Before she could think of another answer, his teasing expression changed and he said quietly, 'You've made up your mind, haven't you?'

His discernment stunned her. How could he read her mind so quickly and clearly? It was only moments since she had made the decision.

Then the stall-holder took the grapefruit from his hand and asked, *'Algo más, señor?'*

'Nada mas.' Cam handed over some coins and was given change. Turning to Liz, he said, 'Why don't I take our shopping back to the car while you have a browse round the other street? I'll join you there and then we'll go for a coffee.'

Taking her assent for granted, he took charge of the plastic carrier she was holding and turned away.

She watched him till he disappeared from view, and then she made her way slowly to a street at right angles to the market, where clothing and shoes were sold. There were also stalls selling cheap watches and jewellery or colourful rugs. The vendors of these were usually Africans or North Africans, their ebony or lighter brown skins adding a cosmopolitan touch to the small town atmosphere.

Usually Liz enjoyed browsing, but today her mind was focused on the shift about to take place in her relationship with Cam. Only yesterday she had told him a marriage between them was madness and now, as soon as he came back, she would have to admit she was ready to go ahead. Not only ready but eager—although she wouldn't tell him that.

When Cam rejoined her she was watching, with a couple of small children, a wind-up toy frog swimming around in a blue plastic bowl.

'Hi,' he said, putting a hand on her shoulder. 'If you'd like one of those for your bath, I'm in a spending mood.' Before she could stop him, he had asked the stall-holder, in Spanish, to wrap one up for her.

'Cam, you're crazy,' she protested.

'No, just happy,' he answered, smiling. 'How would it be if we put a jacuzzi in the courtyard and took outdoor tubs…you and me and the frog? I saw one advertised in the *Costa Blanca News*, or it may have been that freebie paper the *Entertainer*.'

'A jacuzzi would ruin the courtyard. It would be an eyesore. How can you even suggest such a thing?'

'For the pleasure of seeing you look horrified.' He presented her with the frog, now wrapped in gift paper. 'He's a place-holder until I can enjoy the privilege of sharing your bath.'

Place-holder was a computing term she had already explained to him. She said, 'You don't know for sure that I've decided to marry you. You're only assuming that.'

'Am I wrong?'

'No,' she admitted.

'Then let's find a secluded corner and start making plans.' He took her free hand in his and led the way through the crowd.

The bar most popular with the expats who shopped in Benissa was on the main square, near the fountain. But it was a noisy establishment where the tables often had to be shared. Cam took her to a quieter place where they could sit by themselves.

Having ordered coffee and *cava*, he said, 'I bought something else in the market. Another place-holder.' He felt in his trouser pocket and brought out something wrapped in coloured tissue paper fastened with sticky tape.

'A place-holder for what?' she asked, as he handed it to her.

'For something I need to discuss with you.'

Normally Liz was a person who unwrapped parcels carefully, patiently unfastening knots and trying not to tear the paper. This time she unwrapped the package quickly and, when she saw what was in it, gave a gasp of surprise.

Apart from the frog, the only thing in the market that had caught her eye for more than a moment had been an inexpensive bracelet of transparent blue and green beads. It was the sort of thing that looked pretty on the suntanned wrist of a teenage girl but she had felt was too young for her. It seemed extraordinary that Cam should have spotted the one thing she had liked.

He took it and put it on for her. 'It's a place-holder for an engagement ring. I don't know what kind of jewellery you like so we'll need to choose that together. Meanwhile you can wear this nonsense.' He lifted her hand to his lips and brushed a kiss on her knuckles. 'And that is also a place-holder until we can seal our bond in the traditional way.'

At this point the bar waiter brought their coffee, two glasses of champagne and some little dishes of nibbles. He released her hand and leaned back in his chair. But, as the waiter arranged the things on the table, Liz was aware that Cam was continuing to watch her.

She put her hands in her lap and looked down at the delicate web of beads. They were the colour of sea water.

'To us,' said Cam, raising his glass.

'To us,' she echoed. 'But, Cam, I don't need an engagement ring. I'm perfectly happy with this pretty bracelet.'

For a second or two, he frowned. Then the hint of displeasure vanished and he said easily, 'As you wish. How soon can we be married? From my point of view, the sooner the better. I'd prefer the quietest possible civil marriage. But you may have other ideas.'

'No, that would suit me too. I expect we can find out what the formalities are on the Web. But won't your parents expect to be present?'

'They may expect to be invited but I don't particularly want them there. Had my grandparents been alive, that would have been different.' He paused. 'I'm not suggesting you shouldn't invite your mother if you would like to have her there.'

'I couldn't invite her without asking my aunt and she'd want my cousins included. I think it would be much better not to have anyone. I can always put the blame on you.

They'll be too excited at having you in the family to stay in a huff for long,' said Liz.

'We had better fix a trip to the UK and break the news in person to both our families,' he said. 'What I particularly want to avoid is any press coverage. As far as I'm concerned my private life is private.'

'My friend Deborah takes *Hola!*, the Spanish version of *Hello*, and I admit to reading the copies she passes on, but I wouldn't want to be in it, however huge a fee was offered me.'

'Good, because there is no possibility that La Higuera will ever be featured in it,' said Cam. 'Working on the assumption that you were going to say yes, I was thinking last night that—unless you want to sell your house and invest the capital—it might be a good idea to have a door in the wall connecting the two courtyards and use your house as a visitors' cottage. That way you could use one of the present guest bedrooms as your studio and the other one, hopefully, we shall need as a nursery.'

'Cam, what if I can't give you children? Have you considered that possibility?'

'Having children is always the luck of the draw. If we can't, we can't,' he said shrugging.

'But children are one of your reasons for getting married,' she reminded him. 'When people are in love it's different. If their plans go awry, they have their love to fall back on. Ours is a practical marriage…a matter of mutual convenience.'

'And that means that, unlike couples who marry with their heads in a cloud of illusion, we aren't expecting perfection. If it doesn't pan out exactly as we hope, we'll adjust to that more easily than people who feel they're entitled to everything life has to offer. Maybe my experiences in Africa and other third world countries have made me overly impatient with some aspects of first world culture. I haven't a lot of time for the woman so obsessed with her right to motherhood that she spends thousands of pounds trying to get pregnant— money that would spare hundreds of African women the drudgery of walking miles to fetch water, or restore the sight of thousands of blind people in India.'

It was the first time Liz had heard this note of passionate intensity in his voice.

'I think it's hard for a man to understand how deeply some women long for children,' she answered. 'I wouldn't go to those lengths myself. Like you, I feel that if getting pregnant doesn't happen easily, then one should just accept it and get on with other things. But it has to be said,' she added, 'that a lot of people would be more supportive of the kinds of good causes you've mentioned if they didn't have an uneasy feeling that their donations were being siphoned off by corrupt officials rather than benefiting the people they would like to help.'

'I'm afraid you're right about that…and, from what I've seen, their fears are often justified. It's a mad world we live in…which is all the more reason for establishing our own pocket of sanity. We have a lifetime to discuss and argue the serious issues. Today let's just enjoy ourselves. To celebrate, I thought we'd drive into the mountains and have lunch at a hotel that I'm told has a spectacular view. We can drop off our shopping on the way through Valdecarrasca.'

As they drove back to the village, Liz was conscious of a huge sense of relief that her indecision was over and the die was cast.

'Rather than going to both houses, let's put all the stuff in my fridge and you can retrieve yours when we come back,' Cam suggested.

'OK…whatever you say.'

He gave her a smiling glance. 'I wonder if you'll say that to all my suggestions? Somehow I suspect not.'

'You don't want a doormat wife, do you?'

'Absolutely not. But when we cross swords, I'd rather we did it in private, not like some couples I know who fire broadsides at each other across other people's dinner tables.'

'I've known people like that too. It's always horribly embarrassing for the onlookers. Hopefully we won't need to cross swords.'

'I think we're bound to occasionally. No two people ever see eye to eye on everything.'

While he unloaded their shopping, Liz pulled down the passenger's sun-screen and found, as she had expected, that it had a mirror attached to it. Quickly she retouched her lipstick, remembering what he had said, at the market, about wanting to kiss her. When *would* he kiss her? she wondered. Perhaps this afternoon, when they returned from their outing.

She remembered his previous kisses and their effect on her. Even the memory set up a tremor inside her. She forced herself to think about something else.

They had left the village behind them and were driving west towards the far end of the valley and the more isolated valleys beyond it when Cam said, 'Do you mind if I play some music?'

'Not at all.' She wondered what kind of music he liked to listen to while driving. Her guess would be classical orchestral stuff, or jazz.

Moments later, to her complete surprise, she recognised the voice of Michael Crawford singing 'The Music of the Night' from *Phantom of the Opera*. This was followed by the beautiful duet 'All I Ask of You', a song that expressed her deepest beliefs about the nature of love.

Liz leaned her head against the backrest, closed her eyes and let Crawford's magical tenor and the equally lovely soprano voice of his leading lady sweep her away into a romantic dreamworld.

As usual, the tender lyrics brought a lump to her throat and the prickle of tears to her eyes.

Expecting to have the rest of the disc to recover herself, she was startled when, as the last notes of the song died away, there was a click and she felt the brakes being applied.

Opening eyes that were bright with emotion, she saw they were now on a straight stretch of road where stopping would not impede any other vehicles that might come along.

'Liz, I'm sorry if that music brings back painful memories. It's one of my favourite shows and I should have realised you probably saw it with your husband.'

'Actually I didn't. I saw it with a girlfriend,' she said, blinking, her voice husky.

'But you're upset,' he said, frowning.

'Not for the reason you thought. I'm afraid I'm just a sucker for schmaltz,' she admitted.

'Are you? I wouldn't have guessed it.'

'It's not something people advertise. Please…do play the rest. It's one of my favourite shows too.'

'All right…if you're sure.'

She smiled at him. 'I'm sure.'

Although it was not yet the height of the almond blossom season and some trees still had bare branches, in the more sheltered folds of the foothills there were almond groves where all the trees had their branches clustered with white and pink blossoms. The pink flowers came in two shades, one darker than the other. Here and there, bends in the road brought orange groves into view, the bright fruit hanging among the glossy dark foliage like baubles on Christmas trees. Always, when Liz saw oranges growing, her spirits lifted and she felt privileged to be here instead of trapped in the rat race.

The hotel that was their destination was built close to the crest of a hill, not far from a deep ravine and facing towards the distant coastal plain. The main building was faced with stone to blend into the landscape and all around it had been planted the thyme and lavender that thrived in this type of terrain.

They had a drink in the bar before being shown to their table in a dining room with many brick-edged arches.

'This area is supposed to have been the last stronghold of the Moors, who fought to stay here after the decree expelling them,' said Cam, as they waited for their first course. 'One can imagine how they felt. They had been in Spain for seven hundred years. They'd worked miracles making it fertile, and suddenly—out!' He made a sweeping gesture with his hand

They discussed the expulsion of the Jews and Moors, who had done so much to enrich Spain's culture, through most of lunch. Liz enjoyed the meal, but Cam was critical of the food and the service.

'I make allowances for the shortcomings of small country restaurants,' he said. 'But this place is setting out to be first class and has to be judged by more exacting standards. We won't be coming here for our honeymoon.'

She had not thought that far ahead, but evidently he had.

'We'll have to pick out a *parador*...unless you would rather we spent the time outside Spain. If there's somewhere you'd like to go, you have only to say so.'

Guessing that travelling abroad would be no treat for him, she said, 'A *parador* sounds fine to me. Have you stayed at a lot of them?'

'Only three. The modern one by the sea in Jávea, the one near the top of the Sierra Nevada, which is also modern and mostly used by skiers, and one in the restored castle at Tortosa on the river Ebro. I stayed there with my grandparents when they drove me back to school in England after a summer holiday with them. There are plenty of others to choose from.'

When they left the hotel, Liz assumed they would go home the way they had come. But Cam said there was another route he wanted to show her. It turned out to be a narrow byroad, with many twists and turns, and views that were some of the loveliest she had ever seen. Here, in wilder country than they had passed through on the way, the slopes surrounding the road were bright with yellow gorse.

'Could we stop for a minute?' she asked. For, though Cam was driving very slowly, she longed to get out and gaze at the colours and shapes of the mountains on the far side of the valley.

He stopped the car and they got out and stood at the edge of the track in companionable silence.

'I wish I'd brought the camera,' she said. 'I'd love to have a shot of this on my website...though I think it would take a professional photographer to do it justice.'

When Cam didn't answer, she glanced at him. He was standing with folded arms. As she looked at him, he unfolded them and beckoned her to him with both hands.

Her insides leaping about like a parcel of frogs, Liz moved towards him. A yard away she stopped.

'I think it's time I kissed you,' he said.

'You already have.'

'But in different circumstances. Now we are an item, as they say.'

He reached out and, placing his hands on the sides of her waist, drew her closer until there were only inches between them. Liz put her hands on his chest, feeling its warmth and solidity against her palms.

She wanted to say, I love you, but knew that she couldn't. Love, unless it was mutual, could only be a burden to the person who did not feel the same way. All she could do was to close her eyes and tilt her face up to him.

The touch of his lips sent the frogs into a frenzy. He gathered her into his arms and held her possessively close, his mouth persuading hers to open.

The kiss might have gone on indefinitely but for the sound of a tractor on the track above them. Cam did not let her go, but he lifted his head and relaxed his hold so that, though still embraced, they were no longer locked together when the tractor driver came by and shouted a greeting above the noise of the motor.

As the tractor trundled downhill, Cam said, 'If this were a hot afternoon in England, we could find a grassy spot and make love in the sun. But in Spain the ground doesn't lend itself to such pleasures.'

By 'making love' did he mean kissing, or more? she wondered. Had he changed his mind about not going to bed with her until they were married?

'Let's move on,' said Cam, keeping his right arm round her until he had opened the passenger door.

At the bottom of the hill they had to rumble and bounce over a dry riverbed and then up a short stony slope that brought them back to a road. On the way back he played the lovely 'Concierto de Aranjuez', a concerto for guitar and orchestra by the famous Spanish composer Joaquin Rodrigo.

She had heard part of the concerto on her first visit to Spain and later discovered the romantic story behind it. Rodrigo, who had died at the age of ninety-seven in 1999, had been seriously ill with diphtheria as a child of three. It had left him almost totally blind, but he had trained as a musician and, aided by Braille and his Turkish wife, also a professional musician, had become a successful composer, his most famous work—the one they were listening to now— being known all over the world

Back in Valdecarrasca, Cam didn't drive to his house as she'd expected but stopped the car outside hers. 'I'll bring your stuff down in a few minutes,' he said.

Liz wondered if that meant he was planning to stay with her for the rest of the day and where that might lead. Was she ready for it? For more kisses, yes. But the rest...? She wasn't sure.

It was half an hour before Cam reappeared with her shopping.

'Sorry to keep you waiting. As I was unlocking the door, the phone started ringing. I've only just got off the line.'

Although she was still very nervous of what he might have in mind—the effect of the wine with lunch had long since worn off—she felt she had to offer him a cup of tea.

'Tea would be great.'

'Was your phone call something interesting?' she asked, thinking it might have to do with his work.

'Not very. It was from a guy who needs a shrink to sort out his problems but doesn't want to pay the fees so he unloads them on me. He's his own worst enemy, and a bore, but I don't like to be too short with him. We go back a long way. Do you have girlfriends like that?'

'I knew one unloader in London, but we aren't in touch any more. What used to irritate me was that she talked for hours about her life but never showed the smallest interest in mine. Not that I had anything to unload—' or nothing that

I would talk about, was her thought '—but I think, if I had, she would have switched off.'

'Most people are pretty self-centred,' said Cam. 'From a journalist's point of view, that's good. On a personal level it's a turn-off.'

At her suggestion, they had tea on her flat roof. As they chatted and had second cups, there was nothing in the least amorous in his manner. She began to think she had panicked unnecessarily. Well, not panicked precisely, she corrected herself. But she had been in more of a flap than most women of thirty-six confronted with the possibility that, before the day was out, they might find themselves in bed with a highly desirable man whom they loved and were going to marry.

In England alone, not counting the rest of the world, there must be thousands of thirty-something singletons who would count themselves lucky to have sex with someone like Cam—even without marriage being on the agenda.

It was just that—

Cam interrupted her train of thought. 'What I must get down to, before long, is some intensive work on the stuff for my website.'

He discussed some more thoughts he had had since their last conversation on the subject. Then he rose from his deck-chair. 'No time like the present. I'll go and do some work now. Let me carry this down—' replacing his cup on the tray. 'You stay here and relax.'

On impulse, Liz said, 'After a large lunch, we won't need much supper. Would you like to come back about seven and share a pomegranate salad?'

'Sounds good. See you later.' He picked up the tray and went down the outside staircase, leaving Liz to wonder if she needed her brains tested.

Wouldn't any man, invited to supper, assume that it was an invitation to stay the night?

CHAPTER SEVEN

Amor, tos y dinero llevan cencerro

Love, a cough and money cannot be kept secret

LIZ stayed on the roof for some time after he had gone. She had only to close her eyes to be back among the golden gorse of the mountainside with Cam's strong arms around her and her lips parting under his. She could remember the taste of his mouth, the pleasant male smell of his skin and the warm rock-like feel of his shoulders as she slid her hands higher. Before the tractor came by, she had been on the point of slipping her arms round his neck.

The memory of those moments made her long to repeat the experience. If only it could stop at kisses...hours of rapturous kissing that was an end in itself without leading on to...

Her mind flinched from thoughts she did not want to recall. If only she could be certain that this time it would be different.

From the window of his workroom Cam saw her stand up, take a long look round at the sunlit vineyards, and then go slowly down the stairs.

She would never know how difficult it had been for him to force their conversation into a businesslike channel that would give him a pretext for leaving instead of staying on the roof and resuming the embrace interrupted by the tractor.

Surrounded by a waist-high wall, the roof was not totally private, although a sunbather lying on cushions on the tiled floor would not be seen. But the chances of anyone observing them, had he kissed her, were slight. It had not been that possibility that had restrained him—their relationship was probably the subject of speculation already—but rather an instinctive sense that making love to Liz was not going to be as straightforward and uncomplicated as his previous relationships with women.

For one thing it was four years since she had made love. For another she had only been to bed with one person in her life. And thirdly she was not in love with him which normally, for a woman like Liz, would be essential before she could let her hair down.

All told, getting it right was going to be extremely tricky. Getting it wrong disastrous.

He had no experience of women who were not experienced. Or of women who had been through the trauma of shock and grief she had suffered. He wanted her; had wanted her for some time. But, if they were going to spend the rest of their lives together, it was important, at this stage, to keep his own feelings under control and put her needs before his.

Whether he would be able to do that tonight was an open question. She was beginning to arouse him merely by smiling at him, or crossing her long slim legs, or making some gesture with her hand that made him want to reach out and catch it and hold it against him. Which, of course, would immediately undo all his efforts to make her relax with him. There was a chasteness about her that he found both refreshing and exciting.

He remembered a conversation with his grandmother relating to her favourite musical *My Fair Lady*. She had been at the opening night of the original stage production in 1956. At the end of her life she had taken her mind off her illness by replaying the video of the film version. More than once Cam had watched it with her, and the line that had prompted their subsequent conversation was Professor Higgins's complaint, 'Why can't a woman be more like a man?'

'The trouble is that nowadays girls *are* more like men,' his grandmother had said, with a sigh. 'Too much like them, in my view. Young men have always sown wild oats, but I don't think girls should.' She had been worried about one of her great-nieces who, not yet twenty, had already had several affairs.

When Cam had pointed out that sowing wild oats could not be done without female co-operation, Mrs Fielding, her perspective typical of her age group, had replied, 'They should do it with older women, not the sort of girls they might marry.'

Despite her out-of-date views, Cam had been influenced by his grandmother. Apart from anything else, she and his grandfather had embodied the kind of lasting happiness that was a universal ideal.

In many ways, Liz reminded Cam of his grandmother. He knew they would have liked each other. What his parents would make of Liz he couldn't tell. Not that their opinion mattered to him, but it might matter to her if she sensed they were hostile.

While Cam was thinking about her, Liz was relaxing in a scented bath. At least her body was relaxed and she was attempting, not altogether successfully, to think calming thoughts.

After her bath she did her nails and then used an expensive revitalising facial mask her aunt had given her at Christmas. These were things she usually did every Sunday but they helped to fill the time until seven.

It was a few minutes past the hour when she heard the rap of the knocker and went to let Cam in. He had changed into pale whipcord trousers and a cotton shirt finely checked in navy and white with a navy sweater slung round his shoulders, the sleeves casually tied across his chest.

'Hi.' He greeted her with a light kiss on the cheek. 'You look very nice.'

'Thank you.' Because there was a significant drop in the temperature after dark, she had lit the fire and put on a long dark brown wool skirt—the colour of black chocolate—and a short-waisted clingy sweater of lambswool mixed with angora in pale blue.

'What would you like to drink? Wine…gin…beer?' She gestured for him to take the large wing chair by the fire that, like most of the furniture, she had bought from Beatrice Maybury.

'Wine, please…red if you have it.'

Guessing he would like red wine to drink with their meal, she had already opened a bottle. He was still on his feet, looking at the print she had hung on the chimneybreast, when she brought him a glass. He remained standing until she sat down.

'How do you cope with the firewood problem?'

'You mean when it's dumped in a pile in the street and has to be carried through the house to the back yard? Mrs Maybury didn't mention that…and I didn't think to ask her. I'd never lived in a house with no rear access before.' Liz laughed. '*Caveat emptor*…let the buyer beware. I guess I was lucky that was the only hidden snag. It could have been something much worse. It's hard work getting the wood through, but a two thousand kilo load lasts me a long time.'

'You won't have to do it any more,' he reminded her. 'When we're married, I'll be stacking the logs and laying the fires.'

'I assumed you paid someone to do the stacking for you.'

He shook his head. 'It's a job I enjoy. There's something satisfying about a well-stacked log store, and it's good exercise. I like laying fires too. There's an art in it.'

'It seems an unlikely art for you to practise.'

'There's a streak of the boy scout in most men. Not that I ever was a scout. Were you a guide?'

'No, I went to dancing classes run by a retired chorus girl. In her teens my mother had dreamed of becoming a dancer. She projected that frustrated ambition onto me. She wanted me to be picked for the school's troupe who danced at charity shows. But, to her disappointment, I wasn't. I quite liked tap, but I wasn't much good at it.'

'Can you remember the steps? Give me a demo.'

Liz hesitated. Then she got up, lifted her skirt to mid-calf and, on a patch of tiled floor between the rugs, did a short routine she remembered and sometimes danced in the kitchen while waiting for the kettle to boil.

'I'd like to see you do that in black fishnet tights,' said Cam. 'Can you do high kicks and splits?'

'I could when I was twelve. I shouldn't care to risk it now. I might do myself an injury,' she said, laughing and letting down her skirt. 'Excuse me a minute. I need to put something in the oven.'

'I thought we were only going to have some fruit salad,' he said, as she turned towards the kitchen.

'We are, but I thought a small hot starter might be a good idea. It won't take long.'

When she came back she asked him to help her move a small table, that normally lived against the wall that blocked off the staircase, to a position in the centre of the room.

Without being asked, Cam fetched the two upright chairs from where they stood when not in use. With two other chairs from upstairs, Liz could seat four people for dinner.

She had everything ready on a tray in the kitchen. It didn't take long to lay the table.

'Right: if you'll sit there, I'll bring in the starter,' she said, hoping he wasn't expecting anything spectacular.

She had to use oven mitts to handle the earthenware dish from the oven. 'This is a poor man's version of angels-on-horseback,' she explained, setting it in front of him.

'I like anything wrapped in hot bacon. What have you used instead of oysters?'

'Pieces of banana…and I've also done anchovies on toast with a dab of alioli on them.'

Considering how many top-class restaurants he must have dined at, Cam was gratifyingly enthusiastic about her efforts. He couldn't have been nicer had he been in love with her, she thought. But that was wishful thinking and she must not indulge in it.

It was important to keep her feet firmly on the ground and remind herself at regular intervals that it was only good manners, not affection, that made him such an agreeable companion.

The fruit salad did look rather special. She had mixed some strawberries and Chinese gooseberries with the glistening red seeds from the pomegranate and, in place of cream, she served *queso fresco*, the Spanish equivalent of *fromage frais*.

'Did you know that the pomegranate is the symbol of Spain?' she asked, while she was serving it. 'A crowned pomegranate was Catherine of Aragon's personal badge.'

'How did you find that out?'

'When I was studying historical needlework at college. Stylised pomegranates appear on all sorts of period textiles. There are pomegranates in that copy of Elizabethan blackwork that I worked for one of my exams. But most people wouldn't recognise them as such.'

Cam rose from the table and went to look at the framed piece of embroidery she had indicated. When he came back, he said, 'You're a woman of many parts...tap dancer... expert embroiderer...what else am I going to discover about you?'

A sudden shiver of apprehension ran through her. What if she turned out to be a disaster in bed? What if, despite the excitement induced by his kisses, there came a point when...?

'Not nearly as many discoveries as I'm going to make about you, I expect,' she said, trying to sound carefree. 'Your life has been far more exciting than mine. I've never been outside Europe.'

'That reminds me, after supper why don't we take a look at the Spanish Tourist Board website and pick out a *parador* for our honeymoon?' he suggested. 'By the way, I've looked into the question of our getting married in Spain and I don't think it's going to be possible. There are no facilities for civil weddings at any of the British consulates. They suggest going

down to Gibraltar as an alternative. But I think it would be
easier to do it in London by special licence.'

'Might the fact that I'm now a Spanish resident be a com-
plication, do you think?'

'Possibly. I'll check. Up to now, I've never been here long
enough to become a resident. That's something else I must
look into.'

Unlike Cam, Liz did not have a dishwasher. After supper,
he insisted on washing up for her. Then they took their coffee
and what was left of the wine upstairs to her workroom.

From force of habit she had left her bedroom door open.
As she mounted the stairs ahead of him, she wondered what
construction Cam would put on the sight of her double bed
with its old-fashioned white cotton quilt and brass head and
foot rails. Might he think she had left the door wide open
deliberately?

The last time they had sat side by side at a computer she
had felt uneasy and made an excuse to move away. This time
she was still intensely aware of his nearness, but there was
no way to avoid it. Nor, to be honest, did she want to.

'Try keying in *parador* dot, e for España, s for Spain,'
Cam suggested, when she was online.

His guesswork proved correct. A moment later they were
at the Paradores Website, where a map marked the locations
of more than eighty *paradores*.

'I'll show you the ones I've stayed at.' Cam put his hand
over hers where it rested on the mouse and moved the cursor
to a point near the north-east coast. Without removing his
hand, he said, 'Click there.'

The feel of his palm on the back of her hand did crazy
things to her pulse-rate. 'Why don't we change places and
you do the clicking?' she suggested.

'I like it the way we are. Don't you?'

She could tell by the tone of his voice he was looking at
her, not the screen, and that he was smiling.

Then he put his free hand on her shoulder, the one farthest

from him, and moved the tips of his fingers over the softness of her sweater. 'This looks and feels very strokable.'

'We're supposed to be doing a tour of the *paradores*,' Liz said, her voice suddenly hoarse.

'I'd rather be doing a tour of you,' he said softly, and his hand moved down her back and moved slowly round her midriff till it lay over her ribs just below her left breast.

She stopped breathing. Or that was how it felt. As if she had gone into freeze mode, the way a computer sometimes did when its circuits became overloaded. The strange thing was that although all her normal responses had suddenly ceased to operate, others, normally dormant, were behaving like Geiger counters reacting to radiation.

There was nothing she could do but wait, staring blindly at the screen, for whatever was going to happen next. What happened was that Cam bent towards her and kissed the part of her neck just under her ear while, at the same time, his hand moved upwards to caress her breast.

'Mmm…your skin smells delicious,' he murmured, as his right hand stopped covering hers and came up to cradle her cheek and turn her face towards his.

There were moments, while he was kissing her mouth and gently fondling her breast, when Liz thought she could not contain the feelings he aroused, that he would be sure to guess the sensations he was inducing. But then, when the tension had built to the point when it had become almost unbearable, he took his mouth and his hand away.

'You're right…this won't do,' he said. 'If we're going to reserve these pleasures for our honeymoon, we had better get on with deciding where to spend it…and the sooner the better, don't you think?'

Later, when they were downstairs, saying goodnight, Liz had a wild impulse to say, Don't go. Stay with me tonight.

If he had kissed her, she might have done. But instead he bent over her hand in the most formal way, as if they were barely acquainted, not two people planning to marry.

After he had gone, knowing that she couldn't sleep, she got ready for bed but then went back to the computer and retraced the route they had followed. Jarandella de la Vera…Sigüenza…Ciudad Rodrigo…Chinchon…all of them well worth a visit but none, in Cam's view, the perfect place to start married life.

To her it was immaterial where they went. All she could think about was their wedding night and how it might turn out.

Tonight's experience should have allayed her misgivings. As it had…until she remembered that long, long ago she had felt similar sensations. Kissing and touching was one thing. Full intercourse was another. Just because she had come close to ecstasy tonight did not mean she could take it for granted that all would be well when he finally took her to bed.

They flew to England from Valencia, an airport that, unlike Alicante, was not seething with expats and holidaymakers but catered mainly to Spaniards, most of them well-dressed people flying around Europe on business.

They also flew business class which to Liz, used to the cramped conditions in economy, was unaccustomed luxury. Also, she soon discovered, travelling with Cam was like travelling with a prince. Even when he wasn't recognised, there was something about him that made people helpful and deferential. As his companion, she shared this special treatment.

At Heathrow, a driver was waiting to take them to Cam's apartment in central London where, that evening, his close family were coming to a dinner party organised by a catering firm he had used before.

Cam's flat was in a block overlooking the Thames and the view of the river from the large living room made it seem less citified than she had expected it to be.

'On my grandfather's advice, I bought a place to live as soon as I could afford to apply for a mortgage,' he told her, while showing her round. 'The way property prices have risen in London—or any big city—it hasn't been difficult to keep upgrading, especially for a bachelor without any of the usual family overheads. If you like the flat, we'll keep it. If you don't, we'll find somewhere else.'

He opened the door of a comfortable twin-bedded room. 'You'll be in here for the time being. My room overlooks the river and the third bedroom is an office with a sofa-bed for when my sisters and their children make use of the flat. I told them there wouldn't be room for them here tonight.'

'Won't they think that strange? I mean usually...'

'...people about to be married share a room,' he finished for her. 'Our sleeping arrangements are no one else's business, and after three or four hours of their company you'll be glad to see the back of them. Other people's relations can be heavy going, though I think you'll find Miranda on your wavelength. I have some phone calls to make and you'll want to get unpacked.'

Left on her own in his guest room, Liz surveyed her surroundings. The decor had the hallmarks of a professional designer's work and, though tasteful, lacked the personal feel of his house in Spain. She guessed that he didn't regard this place as a home so much as a necessary pied-à-terre and an investment.

A little while later Cam knocked on the door. When she opened it, he said, 'I have to go out for about an hour. The catering people won't show up much before seven. But in case you should be in the bath, or having a nap, I'll tell the hall porter to let them in. See you later.'

He didn't kiss her goodbye as a normal husband-to-be would have done, she noticed. Since the night he had come to supper, his behaviour towards her had been as circumspect as if they were living in a more conventional era. Was that because the waiting time was putting a strain on his will-power? Or was there some other reason?

It crossed her mind that he might have arranged to visit one of his former girlfriends with a view to releasing the controls he was exerting in his relationship with Liz. For a moment the thought made her steam with anger. Then she forced herself to dismiss it. If she thought Cam capable of that sort of behaviour, what was she doing committing her future to him?

Liz didn't emerge from her room till half an hour before the guests were due to arrive. She was wearing the dress she had worn to the Drydens' party, but with her hair in a French pleat instead of loose.

Cam was nowhere to be seen, but the catering team was in action. A long table, probably a board on trestles concealed by a long cloth, had been set up and laid for twelve. A lot of well-organised activity was taking place in the kitchen. Sophisticated flower arrangements that had not been there earlier had been placed around the living room.

'Would you like some champagne, madam?' asked one of the caterers, coming out of the kitchen. She was wearing a discreet little black dress and looked in her early twenties.

The 'madam' made Liz feel ancient. 'Yes, thank you, I would.'

She had taken her first sip when Cam appeared. He was wearing a dark grey suit with a lighter grey shirt and mimosa-coloured silk tie. His hair was damp from the shower as it had been the first time they met.

His gaze swept over her. 'Do you think a market bracelet is right for that dress?' he asked, raising an eyebrow.

She looked at the beads encircling her left wrist. 'I think it's perfect.' Something impelled her to add, 'Far more romantic than diamonds.'

'Diamonds are for queens or trophy wives. I think these are more your style.' He took from his pocket a long slim leather-covered box containing a string of stones that gleamed like crystallised sea water. Taking the bracelet from its satin bed, he put the box aside and came towards her.

'Hold this a moment while I take that thing off.' Having removed the beads, he tossed them into a nearby wastepaper basket. Then he took the aquamarines from her and fastened the clasp and safety clasp.

'Thank you. It's beautiful,' said Liz. 'But I still want to keep the beads. They were your first present to me. We might at least go through the motions of being a normal couple, don't you think?' She went to look in the basket, which was empty apart from the Spanish bracelet. 'I'll put this in my room.'

As she walked away from him, the doorbell rang.

She disliked his mother on sight, and she thought it was probably mutual. Mrs Nightingale, as she was now, was a tall woman with a discontented mouth and critical eyes.

'We have been *most* curious to meet you,' she said, as they shook hands after Cam had introduced them. 'Cameron has eluded matrimony for so long, we thought he would never settle down. I hope you know what you're letting yourself in for. Journalists make even worse husbands than diplomats. You will never enjoy any sense of permanence.'

To her own surprise, Liz found herself smiling. 'But I shall never be bored which I think is much more important,' she said cheerfully.

Mr Fielding was more tactful than his former wife. He congratulated his son and was complimentary to Liz but, again, she could see hardly any family resemblance except that he too was tall. Clearly most of Cam's genes had skipped a generation and came from his grandparents.

When, later, they sat down to dinner, she realised his seating plan was carefully thought out. He had placed his parents at opposite ends of the table with their new partners beside them. He and Liz sat opposite each other in the centre of the table, she flanked by two of his brothers-in-law and he by two of his sisters, with his third sister next to their mother and a brother-in-law next to his father. So Liz was two places removed from her formidable mother-in-law and within easy speaking distance of Miranda, the sister closest to him in age and temperament.

Even so, the feeling of being scrutinised by so many strangers made it a stressful occasion. And although Cam gave a masterly imitation of a man who has found the perfect woman for him, he could not deceive her.

It was long past midnight before Miranda and her husband were the last to leave.

'I expect you are thankful that's over,' said Cam, when he came back from seeing them into their taxi, as he had with all his departing guests.

'Not at all. They were charming to me,' she said, not entirely truthfully, 'and the dinner was delicious.'

'Yes, the food was excellent,' he agreed. 'Now I think we had better turn in. Tomorrow it's my turn for ordeal-by-in-law. Off you go. I'll put the lights out.' He gave her a chaste kiss on the cheek and then moved away to start switching off the room's many linen-shaded lamps.

When she was in bed, Liz tried to continue reading the second-hand book she had bought for the journey. But the story failed to stop her doing a mental postmortem on the evening, and then thinking about Cam and the reasons why they were sleeping apart in a world where other people hopped into bed together within hours of meeting.

She wondered what would happen if she went to his room and told him she couldn't sleep. But she knew she didn't have the courage to do that, much as she longed to end the suspense of waiting for their wedding night.

In his bedroom, Cam, who hadn't worn pyjamas since he left school, was sitting up in bed with the duvet drawn up to his waist and his laptop resting on his thighs.

He was reading an article in a bi-monthly magazine whose print edition was distributed to more than thirty thousand senior business executives in the US. The purpose of the publication was to explore business methods in a world transformed by technology, and to suggest ways to profit from the new business landscape.

The magazine's website was one he visited regularly, but tonight it failed to hold his attention and he soon moved on to another of his sources of information. He was reading a piece about the so-called gender wars when he came to a sentence relating to women and fundamental values of twenty-first-century western society.

'If you live in a distillery, maybe non-alcoholic lager is an exciting and refreshing sensation,' the columnist, a man, had written.

The analogy reminded Cam of some thoughts he had had a few days ago about why Liz appealed to him and why, when he wasn't actually fighting down arousal, he was glad that she didn't have a long line of lovers in her past or the brash sexual confidence that characterised many of today's women.

It was typical of her that she had retrieved the cheap bracelet from the wastepaper basket and insisted on keeping it, and equally typical that she had chosen to wear it tonight despite its unsuitability with her expensive dress.

'We might at least go through the motions of being a normal couple, don't you think?'

There had been a sparkle of anger in her eyes that had made him want to grab her and kiss the daylights out of her. But with his family due to show up at any second, it hadn't been the moment to wreck her lipstick and give himself a hard-on.

Even thinking about holding her could do that to him. She was like the mysterious and exciting parcels his grandparents had put under the tree when he spent Christmas with them; parcels he could hardly wait to unwrap. But none of them had contained anything he wanted as much as he wanted Liz.

The only fly in the ointment was that for her it was going to be a second wedding and a second honeymoon. Inevitably, everything was going to remind her of the first time and the husband she had loved with all her heart and probably still did.

'Sleep well?' Cam asked, rising, when Liz went to the kitchen and found him having breakfast.

'Yes, thank you,' she lied. 'Did you?'

'Always do. Would you like tea or coffee?'

'Tea, please…but there's no need for you to disturb yourself. I can deal with it. I'm sorry I overslept. You should have banged on my door.'

'I thought a lie-in would do you good. How about some scrambled eggs? They're my speciality.'

'Can I try them another time? As we're going out to lunch, toast and marmalade will be enough for me.'

Sharing a breakfast table with Cam for the first time, she remembered the hundreds of breakfasts she had cooked for Duncan who had eaten them in silence, reading a tabloid newspaper popular with Middle England. They had never talked much at meals. They had never talked much, period, she thought regretfully.

Cam kept up an easy flow of conversation about the news and feature stories he had read in the online editions of the broadsheets before he got up. He had printed out an obituary notice of a famous embroiderer that he thought would interest her.

'That was kind of you,' she said, as he handed the stapled pages to her.

'My pleasure.'

Even at this early hour, his smile activated butterflies in her stomach.

It wasn't until they were ready to leave for the suburbs that she discovered he had brought with him from Spain two expensive presentation boxes of *turrón*, the sugary confection made at Jijona, in the province where they lived, and eaten at all times of year but especially at Christmas.

'You told me your mother and aunt both had a sweet tooth,' he reminded her.

'But I didn't expect you to remember it.'

'I want them to warm to me. I ordered some flowers as

well. The hall porter has them. We'll pick them up on our way down to the garage.'

Liz hadn't realised the block had an underground garage and Cam kept a car in it. She had assumed that in London he used taxis or chauffeur-driven cars like the one that had met them yesterday.

When she said as much, he said, 'Did you think I never went into the country…never stayed with friends in other parts of England?'

'I suppose I thought you were almost always abroad.'

'I was…but there were gaps when I managed to get to the weddings and christenings of friends who took to matrimony and domesticity long before I did. I should be a godfather many times over if my views hadn't disqualified me.'

Liz knew that it was a flaw in her character to be embarrassed by the kitsch ornaments her father had bought for her parents' garden, and the style of the net curtains her mother had chosen for the bungalow's two bay windows. Even the ornamental name plate hanging on chains from the roof of the porch, and the name itself, made her uncomfortable. She despised herself for the feeling, but she couldn't help it.

He had scarcely parked the car before the front door opened and her mother and aunt surged down the path to meet them, a mixture of excitement and shyness visible in their faces.

The lunch, at a hotel, a few miles away, that Cam had organised by e-mail was more relaxed and enjoyable than Liz would have believed possible. It made her realise what an extraordinary gift he had for getting on with people and drawing them out.

It was in the middle of the main course, when apéritifs in the bar and white wine with the potted shrimps starter had already brought a flush to the two ladies' powdered cheeks, that he said, 'Mrs Bailey…or may I call you Maureen and Sue?'—with a smiling glance at her sister.

'Of course you can, dear.' As the endearment slipped out, Mrs Bailey looked uncertain for a second, then laughed and patted his hand which was resting on the table. 'It won't be long before we're all family, will it? Have you set the date yet? June is a lovely month for weddings.'

'That's what I wanted to talk to you about. We'd like to get married very quickly and quietly by special licence. The problem is that if we ask you and Sue, we shall have to ask members of my family. That's something I want to avoid. We'd like it to be as private as possible. Later on we may give a big party for everyone we know. But I feel—and Liz agrees—that, at our age and in our circumstances, just the two of us and a couple of witnesses is the best way to do it. I know this may disappoint you. But I hope, when you've thought it over, you'll agree it's the right decision.'

The sisters looked at each other, disappointment writ large on their chubby faces. It looked to Liz as if, even in the short time since her last visit, they had both put on several pounds.

On impulse, she said, 'But we'd like to arrange a treat for you to make up for the disappointment. What we thought would be fun, while we're on our honeymoon, is for you two to spend a week at one of those swish health farms. You've always said you'd like to go, Mum, and this is your chance.'

She knew it would cost a lot and might empty her bank account, but she felt it would be worth it.

'Ooh…that would lovely, wouldn't it, Sue?' said her mother, her expression brightening.

It was just as well that Cam was more abstemious than his guests. By the end of the lunch, the sisters were as animated and giggly as Liz had ever seen them. She felt sure that Mrs Nightingale, had she been present, would have been horrified that her son was forging a relationship with people she would have found unacceptable.

It was after three when they left the hotel and returned to the bungalow.

'What about a nice cup of tea?' said Mrs Bailey.

'Why don't we let Liz and Sue take care of that? I'd like to see your back garden,' said Cam.

'He's a lovely bloke, Liz,' said her aunt, when they were alone in the kitchen. 'You're a very fortunate girl, my love. It's not easy for someone of your age to marry again. What a lucky thing you moved to Spain. Who would have thought there'd be someone as nice as Cam living next door?'

In the garden, Maureen was telling Cam about the prizes her neighbour had won at the local flower show.

'Was your son-in-law keen on gardening?'

'Duncan? No, not at all. Liz looked after their garden. Duncan's interests were coin-collecting and sport—football and cricket. Hours he spent watching matches. Liz didn't mind. She liked reading better than TV. Not like her mum. A telly addict, she calls me—' with a giggle. Then her face clouded. 'Such a tragedy…him being drowned like that. She was devastated, poor kid. We wouldn't have been surprised if she'd had a nervous breakdown. They'd meant the world to each other since they were in their teens. Never looked at anyone else, either of them. But that's all behind her now. You can't live in the past, especially not at her age.'

'No, you can't,' Cam agreed. 'I hope, when we get back from our honeymoon, you and Sue will come and stay with us.'

'We'd love that. I feel a bit guilty I've never been down to see Liz's house, but the fact is I'm scared of flying. I know it's silly, but I am. But I've got to get over it.'

'Lots of people don't like flying. Someone you probably know by sight—' he named a well-known TV presenter '—has flown more than a million miles and still doesn't like it.'

'Really? I think he's lovely…he's one of my favourites.'

Looking out of the picture window at the rear of the lounge, Liz wondered what they were talking about.

Later, on the way back to the apartment, she asked him.

'Oh…this and that,' he said vaguely. 'I've invited them to stay with us in Spain. By the way, it was a brainwave on your part to suggest we send them off to a health farm to make up for not being present at the wedding.'

'There's absolutely no need for you to involve yourself, Cam. I can afford whatever it costs.'

'Those places are pretty expensive,' he said. 'I'd like to pay my share. What's mine is yours, and what's yours is mine. That's how I see our financial future. Do you disagree?'

'No…not in principle…but in practice it's going to be heavily weighted in my favour, your income being so much larger than mine.'

'Up to now, but not necessarily for ever. If your website business takes off and my career declines, you could find yourself supporting me,' he said, turning his head to smile at her.

On the morning of her wedding day, Liz was woken by the alarm she had set the night before. The register office ceremony was taking place early in order for them to fly to Madrid and then drive the rest of the way to the *parador* they had chosen for their honeymoon.

For a while she lay thinking about that other day, seventeen years ago, when there had been a billowing white taffeta bridal gown hanging on the front of her wardrobe, and a garland of white silk flowers for her hair on the dressing table. Her mother had wanted a big wedding, and Liz herself had not been averse to making the day as special as possible.

A tap at the door interrupted her thoughts.

'Come in.'

'Breakfast in bed for the bride,' said Cam, coming in with a tray. He was dressed in jeans and a tight white T-shirt that showed off his muscular build.

'Good morning. What luxury.' Liz sat up in bed. She was wearing an Indian cotton nightdress with white embroidery round the neck and down the front. A less modest garment was packed in her case for tonight.

The tray had a woven cane edge and short legs. He placed it across her lap.

'No last-minute doubts? No eleventh-hour jitters?' he asked, sitting down near her feet.

'Not for me. How about you?'

'I can't wait to call you my wife...and to make you my wife.'

The burning look, so early in the morning, startled her. He looked as if, for two pins, he would make love to her now.

While she stared at him, startled, he rose. 'I have things to do. See you later. *Buen provecho.*'

This was an expression the Spanish used before people started to eat. She had used it herself to the men who worked on the vines if she passed while they were sitting on a drystone wall, having a snack before continuing their labours.

When the door had closed behind him, Liz moved the tray and hopped out of bed to brush her teeth. To her surprise she had slept well.

My last night in a bed by myself, she thought: the same thought she had had on that other wedding morning. Except that then she had been impatient to surrender her virginity, eager to find out what it was all about, the mysterious act of union so often described but only fully understood by those who had experienced it.

Remembering her first experience, she did feel a moment of panic. Then she reminded herself that Duncan had also been a virgin and Cam was a man of experience who knew what he was about. At least she hoped he did.

He was not around when she took the tray to the kitchen and washed up the few things on it. Then she had a leisurely bath before starting to do her face. Her hair had been cut and blown dry yesterday morning. She was going to wear it loose.

Her wedding outfit was a cornflower-blue suit of classic design, the jacket buttoning high enough to be worn without a top under it. The colour emphasised her eyes and was also an excellent foil for the aquamarine bracelet. She had found a long chiffon scarf of exactly those two colours to twist round her neck with one end floating in front and the other behind.

She had finished dressing when she heard Cam speaking on the telephone in the living room and went to join him. Still in conversation, he looked her up and down. Was he disappointed? Had he expected something more high-key and glamorous?

'Thanks...goodbye.' He replaced the receiver and came towards her. 'You look beautiful. I was just about to bring these into you, but you don't have to wear them now if you'd rather keep them for later.'

He opened his closed hand, palm upwards, and she saw that he had been holding a pair of aquamarine earrings that matched the bracelet.

'They're lovely...but, Cam, I don't have anything for you.'

'You are giving me yourself. That's all I want.'

He said it with such unexpected tenderness that she felt a lump in her throat. 'Would you put them on for me, please?'

'Sure. Hold this.' He gave her one of the earrings and removed the butterfly fastening from the other. Deftly he threaded the pin through the tiny hole in her ear and fitted the fastening.

She hadn't realised the touch of his fingertips against the sensitive skin at the back of her lobes would send such a strong frisson through her.

When he had dealt with the other, he said softly, 'And tonight I will take them off for you.'

His voice held the promise of other intimacies that quickened her pulse and brought a flush to her cheeks. She wanted to say, I can't wait, but it was only half true.

It had gone so badly wrong before…not just once but many, many times. Would it go right this time? Or had part of the fault been hers? Was there something wrong with her?

Would tonight be a new beginning, or another disaster?

CHAPTER EIGHT

Tanto es amar sin ser amado como responder sin ser preguntado

To love without being loved is like answering without being asked

IT WAS a two-hour drive from Madrid's airport at nearby Barajas to the thirteenth-century castle where they were going to stay.

'I'm glad to be back in Spain,' said Liz, when they had skirted the outskirts of the capital and the landscape was becoming increasingly rural. 'Even though this part of the country is different from our *provincia*, it still feels more like home than London. I don't mean I didn't enjoy staying at your apartment—'

'I know exactly what you mean,' Cam cut in.

Like her, he was still in his wedding clothes but had removed his jacket, taken off his tie and unfastened the collar of his shirt.

'London is fine for short spells, but it isn't what I define as "real life". No big city is—at any rate not for me. I guess, at heart, I'm a country bumpkin.'

'Anyone less like a bumpkin is impossible to imagine,' Liz said, laughing. 'A grandee of Spain is what I should take you for, if you were a stranger. You look the way I imagine Spanish grandees...though the ones I've seen in the papers have been disappointingly short and ordinary-looking. The only one who came up to my expectations was the Duke who married the Infanta Elena...and even he isn't as good-looking as you are.'

He shot her an amused look. Then, the *autopista* being clear, he reached for her hand and lifted it to his lips. The car being left-hand drive, it was her left hand, the third finger now adorned by the beautiful and unusual combination engagement and wedding ring he had chosen for her. A wide band of matt gold set at intervals with lozenge-shaped sapphires and aquamarines, it looked modern but also reminiscent of the jewels worn by merchant princes' wives and mistresses during the Renaissance.

'Thank you, Mrs Fielding. I think you allow partiality to colour your judgement, but why not? It is our wedding day. If we don't see each other through rose-coloured glasses today, we're unlikely to do so in twenty years' time.' He returned her hand to her lap.

Although, on the flight, he had confined himself to a glass of champagne before lunch and another with it, Liz had drunk several glasses, which perhaps accounted for her outspokenness and her relaxed mood as the car Cam had rented cruised smoothly along the motorway taking them south.

But after they branched off the main highway, and once they were more than halfway to their destination, her misgivings kicked in again. Outwardly this trip had all the makings of an idyllic honeymoon. But, beneath the surface, the problem had not gone away. It was still there, like an anti-personnel mine embedded in a seemingly peaceful field. And like a mine it was capable, if detonated, of causing horrendous emotional damage from which their marriage might never recover.

When the *parador* came into view, it looked like an illustration in a fairy tale, a fortress built on the crest of a hill, its towers and battlements outlined against the blue sky. The approach road wound its way up by a series of hairpin bends until it bridged a ravine and they entered the castle by way of an arch and found themselves in a large courtyard now converted to the *parador's* car park.

'Not many people here,' said Cam, parking alongside a car

with a 'D' badge indicating German ownership, and another with the Swiss 'CH' badge. 'But perhaps some people staying here have gone out for the day, and I expect there'll be night-stoppers turning up later.'

Their arrival must have been noticed by someone inside the castle. As he was unlocking the boot, a young man still in his teens came out to help with the luggage.

The interior of the castle had a baronial atmosphere combined with the *ambiente* of a luxurious hotel. Cam signed the register and handed over his passport. Then they were taken by lift to a higher floor, along a corridor and up a stone staircase to their suite.

This had a spacious lobby leading into a sitting room which in turn led into a bedroom, dominated by a massive four-poster bed, with a bathroom leading off it. While Cam was talking to the porter, her attention was caught by the views from the sitting room windows.

The suite, she realised, was in one of the castle's square towers with one window overlooking a formal Spanish garden and the other looking down on a large swimming-pool that shimmered invitingly in the afternoon sun.

'Great for cooling off in the summer, but too cold for comfort now, I should think,' said Cam, looking over her shoulder.

The porter had gone. They were alone.

'I've asked them to send up some tea. Meanwhile...'

He turned her to face him, took her face between his hands, and bent his head to kiss her, first on one side of her mouth, then on the other, and then with his lips matched to hers. But it was a gentle rather than passionate kiss and, after a moment he straightened to smile at her before pulling her into his arms and holding her close in a bear hug.

'This is one of life's perfect moments,' he said. 'The right place...the right person...nothing to do but relax and enjoy ourselves.' She felt him kissing her hair. Then he gave a soft laugh and added, 'But I suppose, being a woman, you want to unpack your case and get all those drop-dead outfits hung up.'

In fact Liz was disappointed when he slackened his hold. Her clothes were the last thing on her mind.

She leaned back in his arms and said, 'The new things I bought are all rather simple. I didn't expect there to be much dressing up.'

'The foreigners probably won't cut much of a dash, but if Spanish people from the nearest town come to eat here they will dress up. If they're spending money, they like to make an occasion of it. Whatever you wear will be right. You have excellent taste. Come on: let's get our kit sorted, then we can really relax.'

'This bathroom is gorgeous,' said Liz, a few minutes later, when she was putting her toilet bag on the marble counter surrounding the twin basins.

He came to stand in the doorway and look at the peach and white decor she was admiring. Then a buzzer sounded and he went to answer it. Moments later, Liz heard a young female voice speaking Spanish and Cam replying. Somehow the language accentuated the sexiness of his voice.

She returned to the sitting room to find a plump girl in a black skirt and white blouse arranging tea things on the low table in front of the sofa. *'Buenas tardes, señora.'*

Liz smiled at her. *'Buenas tardes.'*

There were sandwiches and Spanish pastries to sustain them until the dining room opened at nine.

When the girl had gone, Cam said, 'The tea will be far too strong. Let's fish out some of the tea bags.' He extracted a couple from the pot.

They sat on the feather-cushioned sofa and had afternoon tea and discussed the appointments of the room until Cam said, 'It's a long time till dinner. Why don't we have a bath and then a *siesta*?'

By *siesta* did he mean a sleep? Liz wondered. Or the other kind of *siesta*?

'That sounds a good idea.'

'We can bath together. There's plenty of room. It's a large tub. I'll go and run the water.' He rose and disappeared.

A bath *together*! Liz remained where she was, paralysed with shyness. On her previous honeymoon, they had reached the hotel late, had dinner almost immediately and then gone for a walk along the promenade before going upstairs to their room. Everything had happened with the lights out. Now, all these years later, with her body no longer as taut as it had been at nineteen, she was going to have to climb into a tub with a man who, in terms of physical contact, was almost a stranger.

She heard the water starting to run and wondered if she ought to go into the bedroom and start undressing. The trouble was she had no idea how she was supposed to behave in this situation. It seemed best to sit tight and wait for Cam to call her or come for her.

The water seemed to run for a long time, but then, as he had said, it was an extra-large bath designed to accommodate Texans and Scandinavians and other men of Cam's height and build.

When he appeared in the doorway, he was naked except for a towel wrapped round his hips. Liz rose to her feet, trying to look less uncertain than she felt. They met at the halfway point between the sofa and the bedroom door. He took her hand in his and led her to the bathroom where he closed he door behind them. Then he started to undress her.

'I've been looking forward to this for a long time,' he told her, unfastening the buttons of her blue jacket. She had removed the scarf on the aeroplane.

Tongue-tied, she kept her eyes fixed on his hard brown chest. She had never in her life felt more self-conscious and awkward...or more tense. Her insides were in knots.

Cam opened the jacket and slipped it off her shoulders so that it slid down her arms. He hung it on one of the hooks on the back of the door, which was within his reach.

'This is pretty.' He was looking at her pale blue silk camisole edged and strapped with white satin.

He reached round behind her to unbutton the waistband of her skirt and pull down the zipper. He slid it down over her hips and let it drop to the floor so that she could step out of it. Then he picked it up and hung it with the jacket. The skirt being lined, this left Liz in her tights and panties. Quickly, she slipped off her shoes, reducing her height by two inches.

Though it seemly unlikely he knew the silk camisole was cut on the cross and therefore more elastic than straight-cut fabric, Cam took hold of the hem and drew it upwards so that she had to raise her arms to allow him to draw it over her head. She thought he would reach for the clip of her white embroidered net bra, but instead he put his fingers inside the waistband of her tights and drew them downwards over her hips and thighs. Then he put his hand behind her right knee and raised her leg in order to peel the nylon away from her calf and foot. Seconds later her tights were lying on the floor in a diaphanous swirl like the snake's sloughed-off skin she had seen on one of her rambles in the mountains.

Cam put his hands on either side of her bare waist, drew her towards him and gave her a lingering kiss. Now there was only the fragile texture of net between her breasts and his chest. Surely he must feel or hear the wild beating of her heart?

He reached behind her and she felt the band of her bra slacken. He pushed the straps off the ends of her shoulders and, his mouth still locked with hers, disposed of the bra, leaving no barrier between her soft yielding flesh and the warm solidity of his torso.

Slowly, caressingly, he eased the elastic at the top of her panties over the swell of her behind and pushed them downwards until she had only to part her knees for them to slither to her ankles.

Finally, he ended the kiss and drew back, taking in her nakedness with a look that felt like a sudden rush of hot air on her bare skin.

'You're even more beautiful without your clothes on,' he said huskily.

And then he shed his towel and, briefly, she had a glimpse of his own magnificent, aroused body before he turned away, stepped into the bath and sat down in it.

'Come on in. The water's great,' he said, smiling and holding out his arms in an invitation to join him.

There was no option but to obey. Turning her back to him, Liz stepped over the rim of the bath with one foot then the other. Conscious that he would be getting a head-on view of her backside—'in your face' took on a new meaning here—she bent to put her hands on the bath's sides while lowering herself to sit between his long brown thighs.

Cam's hands on her hips helped her, sliding round to her midriff as he sank back against the bath's sloping end and drew her against him. For the first time in her life she experienced the luxury of leaning against a man's body instead of the unyielding surface of enamelled steel.

It felt wonderful: the difference between the metal type of park bench and the comfort of a feather-cushioned armchair.

'This is where it begins to get really good, don't you think?' he murmured close to her ear.

Not trusting her voice to work normally, Liz nodded her head.

'And it gets better...much better.' One of his hands slid downwards to stroke her stomach and the other moved higher to gently explore her right breast, sending a lightning-flash of exquisite sensation through her.

Then he took the upper hand away. 'I forgot something...'

She felt his stomach muscles contract and harden as he used them to pull himself upwards, lifting her with him to reach for the water controls set in the centre of the long inner side of the bath.

It was only when the water began to bubble and swirl that she realised the bath was equipped with jets that now were sending gentle currents in several directions.

Behind her, Cam relaxed and resumed the gentle exploration of her breast, moving his palm lightly over the part that was reacting to his touch. His other thumb was caressing her navel which suddenly seemed to have become a previously undiscovered erogenous zone.

She heard herself give a long shuddering sigh and, seemingly of their own volition, her hands, which had been lying at the tops of her legs, moved to rest on his longer legs, her fingers spread on the tanned thighs raised at an angle on either side of her.

She heard him say, 'Close your eyes…don't think about anything but how good this is…for both of us.'

She did as he told her, discovering that it intensified her response to his touch. But her inhibitions revived when the hand on her belly suddenly moved down, his long fingers invading the tangle of wet curls at the apex of her thighs, startling her into an instinctive recoil.

'Relax…it's all right…it's fine.'

With that low, calm voice he might have been reassuring a nervous animal; and in a sense she was, she acknowledged. Though it wasn't him she was nervous of, but rather herself, of her own inability to—

The thought was cut short by a wave of intense sensation as his fingers began to explore.

The minutes passed. There was silence except for the murmurous sound of the churning water and her own increasingly laboured breathing. Soon she was lost, her neck arched, her hands gripping his legs, her body convulsed by spasm after delicious spasm against which there was no possible resistance.

When it was over, when his hands were no longer touching her most sensitive places but were merely fondling her shoulders, she became aware of what, overwhelmed by ecstasy, she had temporarily forgotten: the hard ridge of engorged male flesh she could feel pressing against the base of her spine. While she was relaxed, all her tensions released, he was not, or that part of him was not. Yet, despite his palpable lust for her, he wasn't sending out any signals of impatience. How strange! Her experience was that male urges had to be satisfied quickly, not kept waiting. Not that Cam's could be satisfied in a tub that, large though it was, was not *that* large. But he showed no inclination to bring their time in it to an end. He must have exceptional self-control, she thought.

'If you want to nod off, don't mind me,' he said. 'It's been a long action-packed day. Have a mini-*siesta*...do you good.'

She did feel extraordinarily drowsy. As he said, it must be the combined after-effect of this morning's wedding, the flight, the drive from Madrid, the apprehension about their first time in bed together followed by the soothing warmth of the water and the physical release he had given her.

'But what about you?' she murmured.

'Don't worry about me. My turn will come later. This is your time for unwinding...the more unwound you are, the better it will be for us both.'

It was tempting to do as he suggested and slip into a doze, and perhaps she did for a few minutes. Afterwards she wasn't sure whether she had been sleeping when he started caressing her again.

'Oh, Cam...no...please,' she protested.

But he ignored her. The slow build-up of pleasure began again and she let it happen, helpless against those skilful, commanding hands that understood exactly how to undermine her resistance. There was a part of her mind that didn't approve of her capitulation, but her mind wasn't in control, only her senses.

This time the pleasure grew even more intense. Her body tingled and throbbed and she could not stop herself making small ecstatic noises and, at the final moment, a louder sound that she tried to muffle with her hand.

'Anyone listening outside the bathroom door would think I was torturing you,' he said, with amusement in his voice.

In a way he was. She had kept her emotions under wraps for so long that now to abandon all control felt as horrendous as betraying secrets to the enemy.

'Nice as this is, I think we'd better transfer ourselves,' he said. 'If we stay in the bath too long, you'll be getting washerwoman's fingers.'

Pulling himself into a sitting position, and her with him, he gave her a swift kiss on the back of the neck before climbing out. A moment later he was holding a large bath sheet, ready to wrap it round her when she rose from the water and stepped onto the bath mat.

As soon as she was enveloped in the thick soft white pile of the towel, Cam leaned over the bath to turn off the jets and pull out the plug. He was obviously completely at ease with his own body and she envied him his freedom from self-consciousness. But how many other women had seen him like this? she wondered, with a pang, averting her eyes from the sight of his arousal. But not quickly enough to avoid being caught out as he turned and intercepted the direction of her gaze.

After shrugging on his bathrobe, he said, 'Let's go and try out the bed.'

'Shouldn't we dry our feet first?'

His response to this was to put his hands on her shoulders and steer her into a sitting position on the edge of the bath. Then, taking one of the smaller towels, he began to dry her feet for her.

She looked at the dark head bent over her foot and couldn't repress the impulse to stroke his thick glossy hair and let her fingers slide to the back of his brown neck. He didn't look up but she saw his mouth curve in a smile. It encouraged her to obey the urge to lean forward and put her lips to his cheek.

'You're being incredibly nice to me,' she murmured.

'It's not hard.' He kept his mouth straight, but his eyes were amused.

As soon as her other foot was dry, he tossed the towel aside and scooped her into his arms.

Liz had never been carried before, or not since she was small. Cam carried her to the bedroom as easily as if she were a child, not an adult female weighing one hundred and thirty pounds. She found it curiously exciting to be swept off her feet and supported by strong arms around her back and under her knees. It was also, she discovered, a turn-on. It made her feel fragile and helpless, and totally in his power, not a state of mind she would have expected to like—or would have liked with anyone else. But because it was Cam she did.

Earlier, when they had first entered the suite, the bed-clothes had been hidden by a spread that matched the curtains at the corners of the bed. Now the spread had vanished, presumably removed by Cam before he started running their bath.

At the side of the bed, he set her on her feet, removing the towel he had wrapped round her and letting it fall on the rug. Then, picking her up, he put her on the bed before walking round to the other side of it, at the same time shedding his robe. A moment later he was stretched out beside her, propped on one elbow while his other hand gently but firmly parted her legs. Stroking the sensitive skin on the insides of her thighs with his fingertips, slowly he bent his head till his mouth was only an inch from her breast and she was holding her breath, knowing that the touch of his lips was going to send a thousand watts of ecstasy shooting through every nerve in her body.

As it did.

It was a long time later, and Liz was lying with closed eyes, exhausted by wave after wave of mind-blowing pleasure, when suddenly Cam was above her and inside her. It happened so smoothly and easily, like a sword sliding into its scabbard, that it took her by surprise. It had never been like this before, but then nothing in her previous experience had been remotely like Cam's way of making love.

Swept by an overwhelming longing to return the heavenly sensations he had given her, she obeyed an instinct to slide her arms round his neck and embrace his hips with her legs. It must have been the right thing to do because, from deep inside his chest, came the same sort of sound he had forced from her in the bath. And then her mind switched off and instinct took over completely.

*   *   *

Before she was fully awake, Liz knew that something extraordinary and life-changing had happened. She opened her eyes and saw, with momentary puzzlement, not a ceiling but the roof of a tent that, seconds later, she recognised as the canopy of the four-poster bed.

Then everything else came back in a rush of vivid memory and, turning her head, she saw, lying beside her, her husband who was now also her lover.

As the details of what they had done together came back, she felt a powerful longing to repeat the experience.

But Cam was asleep, lying on his back with one hand under his head and the other spread on his midriff.

Slowly and carefully, so as not to disturb him, Liz raised herself on her elbow and began a leisurely study of him, starting with his unconscious face and moving slowly down his long relaxed body until she came to the place where the part of him that had fitted so perfectly inside her now lay lax and quiescent among his dark curls, like a slow-worm sleeping in a nest of heather.

There had been so little real intimacy in her previous marriage that she was intensely curious about the transformation from this state to the other. She wanted to see it happen…to make it happen…to give him the same intense long-drawn-out pleasure he had given her.

Impelled by an irresistible urge, she reached out and laid the flat of her hand very lightly on the warm skin below the small hollow of his navel. He did not stir. Encouraged, she slid her fingers across his flat stomach, feeling the underlying muscles that were slack now but could quickly harden as they had in the bath. He continued to sleep, his breathing so deep and slow that he scarcely seemed to be breathing at all.

She leaned over and put her lips to the place where her hand had been, tasting his skin with her tongue while her hand ventured further afield, exploring the foreign territory of a body that was the way a man's body ought to be, lean and powerful and compellingly male.

Who would have thought that a man like this could also

be so intuitive about a woman like her beset by so many hang-ups and inhibitions? Gratitude for his patience and understanding welled up inside her. In one day—even one hour—he had given her more pleasure than she would have thought possible in the light of her previous disillusioning experience.

For several minutes she explored, with soft kisses and gentle caresses, every part of his torso except the one she wanted to touch. Then she plucked up her courage and curled her hand lightly round him, ready to snatch it away if he showed signs of waking up. Not that he was likely to mind her exploration, but she hadn't yet reached the point of feeling no shyness with him. Hopefully that would happen as the honeymoon progressed, but this was only the first day.

Cam's body began to respond yet he still seemed soundly asleep. Her confidence growing, she watched the miraculous transformation that her touch was inducing. Why, until now, had she always thought of a man's wedding tackle as ugly, even grotesque, when in fact it was strangely beautiful in its colouring, shape and texture?

I suppose it's because I love him, she thought. Nothing about him disgusts me. Everything about him delights me. But I can never tell him that. This is the only way I can express my feelings.

'Are you trying to tell me something?'

The unexpected question made her jump.

Disconcerted, she said, 'I—I thought you were having a nap.'

His eyes gleamed through half-closed lids. 'I was, but you woke me up…in the nicest possible way.'

As she let go, he captured her hand and replaced it where it had been. 'Don't stop. I like it. I'd like to be woken this way from all my *siestas*.'

Then his shoulders came off the bed and his mouth found hers. Her last coherent thought was that he would never know how close his question had come to the truth.

* * *

Most of the *parador's* guests had already assembled in the bar when, a little before nine, Cam and Liz went down to dinner.

After a waiter brought their drinks, Cam lifted his glass to her. Leaning forward and looking into her eyes, he said, ' "To me in your arms and you in my room…a door that is locked and a key that is lost…and a night that's a thousand years long".'

His voice was never loud, but a woman sitting nearby, not listening to her elderly husband pontificating to another man, gave Cam a startled look that made Liz want to laugh.

'Is that from a poem?' she asked.

He nodded. 'An anonymous verse in a book of erotic poetry that we'll read together when we get home. Not that I feel we're much in need of inspiration.' He cast an eye round the room and dropped his voice to a level that only she would hear. 'Some of this lot look as if they've forgotten all the pleasures of the flesh except eating.'

'Perhaps they have,' she said, sympathising with them. Until this afternoon she had been in a similar predicament.

The dining room was a lofty mediaeval hall, its stone walls hung with colourful banners. The high-backed chairs were upholstered with crimson velvet and the lamps on the tables had red silk shades.

'If we're going to be here for a week, there's plenty of time to try all these regional specialities,' said Liz, after studying the menù. 'Would you mind if, tonight, I had something light? Having eaten on the plane, and had tea when we arrived, I'm not terribly hungry. But I don't want to stop you feasting.'

'I feel exactly the same,' said Cam. 'What about having some asparagus to start with and then *huevos en conchas*—eggs in scallop shells. They're very light.'

'That sounds perfect.'

After signalling to the head waiter and giving him their order, Cam said, 'Large meals late in the evening are not conducive to "nights a thousand years long"…or would you rather spend tonight sleeping? As you say, we have plenty of time.'

Whether it was deliberate she couldn't tell, but his tone and the caressing look he gave her made her long to be upstairs, alone with him, instead of down here surrounded by guests and staff.

'Perhaps we shall need to spend some of it sleeping, but not all of it,' she said demurely.

And then she began to laugh because, whatever was wrong with their marriage, there was a lot that was right with it, and here and now—which was what life was really about—she was happy. Very happy.

Cam put his hand over hers. 'A long time ago—I think it was the day you nearly stormed out of my garden because you were nervous that I was planning to seduce you—I wondered how you would look with your eyes sparkling. They're sparkling now.'

She turned her hand to clasp his. 'I think what you're seeing must be what one of my favourite poets called "the lineaments of gratified desire".'

She wondered if he would know which poet she meant and the context of the phrase she had quoted—'In a wife I would desire what in whores is always found—the lineaments of gratified desire'. Cam was a well-read man, but William Blake, the visionary poet and painter, unrecognised in his lifetime, was still not as widely known as she felt he deserved to be.

To her delight, Cam said, 'At school I thought poetry was boring waffle until I read Blake's "Tyger! Tyger! burning bright In the forests of the night, What immortal hand or eye Could frame thy fearful symmetry?"'

Discussing Blake's life and his strange, powerful paintings led them to other subjects that kept them talking until they had finished their meal.

'It's a mild night and there's a full moon. Shall we walk round the gardens?' Cam suggested, as they left the dining room.

Outside the building, he tucked her arm through his and they strolled along the gravel walks in companionable silence until he stopped and said, 'It's a little cooler than I thought. You'd better have my jacket. I don't want you getting chilled.'

He had been shedding his jacket while he was speaking. Now he wrapped it round her and then bent his head to kiss her.

'Maybe it would be a better idea to tour the garden tomorrow,' he said, against her lips. 'Stone seats look romantic but they're not that comfortable to sit on. Upstairs we have a sofa… What do you think?'

'I vote for the sofa,' said Liz, thinking it might not be long before the four-poster bed seemed an even better option.

They had been honeymooning for three days when a courier service delivered the photographs taken outside the register office by a photographer Cam knew who could be relied on to not sell any prints to the press.

Later, studying the pictures in greater detail while Cam was checking his e-mails, as he did once a day, Liz thought that no one would guess that it hadn't been a normal wedding. She was also surprised by how much she had changed since her first in-laws had taken some holidays snaps of her. The woman in the blue suit smiling up at Cam seemed a different person from the one she had been six or seven years ago when the previous snaps had been taken.

On their final morning at the *parador*, they shared the bath for the last time and then dried and went back to bed to make leisurely love.

Later, in the peaceful aftermath, when they were still locked in each other's arms but their hearts were beating at a normal rate, Cam said quietly, close to her ear, 'Have you enjoyed staying here?'

Liz raised her head just enough to press a kiss on the

muscular shoulder an inch or two from her mouth. 'Silly question…you know I have. The walks…the food…the views…having nothing to do but relax…it's been perfect.'

Not quite perfect, was her afterthought, but she dismissed it. She was here in his arms, wasn't she?

When, a little later, Cam rolled onto his back and stretched his long frame out beside her, he considered suggesting they should extend their visit. It was tempting to prolong this extraordinarily pleasurable hiatus between the past and the future. As Liz said, the setting was idyllic and the food superb.

One thing she hadn't listed was the great sex they had shared. But he knew that, physically at least, she had enjoyed it as much as he. He had never known anyone more desirable than the woman lying quietly beside him. To look at her was to want her, and it wasn't the kind of desire that quickly wore off because they had other things in common. He liked her mind as much as her lovely body.

But he couldn't forget that, after the first time he had made love to her, she had cried. Still imprisoned in his arms, she must have thought he was dozing, but he had been awake and had known what was happening. Maybe it would have been better to have talked about it. But at the time he had felt it was best to ignore it.

Perhaps that had been a mistake.

On the night they returned to Valdecarrasca, they had dinner with the Drydens.

Greeting Liz with a hug, Leonora said, 'It's a cliché but there's no other word for it…you look radiant, my dear. Cam, too, if radiant can be applied to a man. Was the *parador* wonderful? It's not one I've ever been to.'

'It's a good one,' said Cam. 'But it was my companion who made it special.' The look he gave Liz as he said it was so convincingly lover-like that it crossed her mind he might have been even more successful as an actor than as a TV reporter.

She gave him the sort of smile that was appropriate for a bride when her husband is being gallant. 'Yes, it was a lovely place. Although it was my first experience of a *parador*, I'm sure it has to be one of the best,' she told the Drydens.

The meal Leonora provided was an informal family supper starting with avocados and followed by an earthenware dish of sliced aubergines and peppers topped with cheese and baked in the oven. For pudding they had fresh fruit.

They stayed till about eleven and then walked home to La Higuera with Cam holding her hand as if she were the wife he had always longed for.

At night, in his bedroom, which it would take time to think of as their bedroom, it was easy to delude herself that it was only a matter of time before the illusion of a normal marriage developed into a reality. But downstairs, during the daylight hours, she had moments of acute doubt. Every day her longing to express her feelings in words increased. Sometimes when he touched her in a loving way, she had difficulty not recoiling from the caress because what she really wanted was for him to tell her he loved her.

But how could he tell her that, when it wasn't true? She was wishing for the moon and she knew it. Love wasn't part of their bargain. She knew she should be content with what she had: a beautiful home and an expert lover who had already given her hours of physical pleasure.

You can't have everything, she told herself. But, as much as living at La Higuera delighted her, she would have swapped it for a tumbledown *casita* on a mountainside, with water drawn from a well and primitive sanitation, to hear Cam say those three little words.

Cam was beginning to feel there was a ghost in his house: the spectre of a man who, although he had ended his life heroically, didn't sound as if he had been a ball of fun while he was alive. Neither of Liz's first husband's interests, coin-collecting and watching sport on TV, were activities that appealed to him. He found spectator sports boring and, at school, had never distinguished himself playing team games though he had enjoyed ski-ing and canoeing.

It had always been his impression that hogging the TV remote control, and spending hours glued to football and cricket matches, were minuses rather than pluses when women were rating male behaviour. But it seemed that Liz had accepted these shortcomings where Duncan was concerned.

Cam also suspected that she wasn't wholly comfortable with the excellence of their own sexual relationship. She enjoyed it while it was happening but, when they were not in bed together, he had the feeling she experienced powerful guilt feelings, as if she had betrayed a trust.

How long was Duncan's ghost going to haunt her…haunt them both? he wondered.

In theory, as long as their marriage was working according to the terms agreed, he should have been satisfied. But somehow he wasn't. He wanted her to be happy…happier than she was. He had no emotional baggage from the past, and it irked him that she had…might always have.

One afternoon when Cam was working on an article he had been commissioned to contribute to an influential magazine, Liz went down to her house to sort through her drawers and cupboards. She had more or less decided to put the house on the market and invest whatever price it fetched.

Among the things she came across was the album of photographs of her first wedding and another album of snapshots of herself and Duncan taken in their teens and twenties.

I don't need to keep these, she thought. They record a part of my life that is better laid to rest. Or perhaps I should send some of them to Duncan's parents. They have a duplicate of the wedding album but they may not have some of the other pictures of him.

Going through them, taking out the photographs she thought her first in-laws might not have copies of, she came to a studio portrait of Duncan that before their engagement had lived in the drawer of her bedside table and, afterwards, had been framed to stand on her dressing table. It showed him in the suit he had bought for job interviews, his hair cut in the style of the time, a slightly self-conscious smile on his face.

She thought of the hours she had spent gazing at features that had seemed to her then to embody every masculine virtue and charm. How different they looked to her now. Her eyes misted, her lips quivered, and tears brimmed over and trailed down her cheeks.

It was at that moment that the front door opened and Cam walked in. 'Hi…how are you getting on?' he asked, closing the door behind him. 'I've finished the draft of my piece. Later I'll get you to read it…see what you think.'

Then he saw her fumbling for a tissue and, when she couldn't find one, wiping her cheeks with her fingers.

'Liz…darling…what's wrong?'

He produced a man-sized tissue and gave it to her, his expression concerned. Even in her dismay at being caught having a foolish weep, she registered the 'darling'. He had never called her that before.

Cam noticed what she was holding and took it from her. 'Who's this? Need I ask? Duncan.'

As he studied his predecessor, she saw a range of reactions reflected in his face, the first unwilling curiosity being quickly replaced by a look of disdain, as if he could see at a glance what had taken her a long time to recognise.

Then, as he tossed the photograph on top of the pile of others, his face became a mask of anger she had never seen him wear before.

'For God's sake,' he blazed at her, 'are you going to spend the rest of your life in mourning? He's been dead for four years. Whatever you shared with him is over and done with. You're *my* wife now. It's not right to be down here, mooning over the past.'

'I wasn't mooning,' she protested. 'You don't understand.'

'No, I bloody well don't! It's time you snapped out of it. Life moves on and, if we have any sense, we move with it. We may not have married for the conventional reasons, but now that's all changed. I love you…and you could love me if you tried…if you put your mind to it…if you stopped mourning him.'

She sprang to her feet. 'What do you mean…you love me? You've never said so.'

'Well, I'm saying it now.' He sounded more enraged than loving. 'I didn't expect to fall in love with you, but I have…and I want you to love me…not him—' with a glare at the topmost photo.

'I never loved him.'

For the first time she said aloud the truth that for years she had chosen not to acknowledge because facing it had been more painful than living a lie.

'You never loved him?' Cam repeated. But now it was a question, not a statement.

'It was calf love…not the real thing. I realised that on our honeymoon,' she said, in a low voice. 'It was so different from ours…you can't begin to imagine. You are everything that he wasn't…tender…unselfish…imaginative. That first night at the *parador* was like being led into paradise after years in purgatory.' She gave a long uneven sigh. 'The only remaining torment was not being able to tell you I loved you. Do you *really* love me? Do you mean it?'

For answer he pulled her into his arms and gripped her so tightly she thought her ribs might crack. But after a moment or two he relaxed and adjusted his hold.

'I must be as thick as two planks,' he said, speaking into her hair. 'I've been falling in love with you for months, but I didn't recognise the symptoms. I knew that you were every-thing I wanted and needed in a woman, and I knew I was as jealous as hell of your first husband, but I didn't put two and two together. How stupid can a guy be?'

He drew back slightly and tilted her face up to his. 'Liz…sweet, lovely Liz…what a dumbo you've married.'

And then he kissed her with a tenderness that was both familiar and novel because now, at last, there were no secrets between them.

One kiss led to another and presently Cam picked her up and carried her up the stairs to her bedroom, where they tore off their clothes and made eager love on the unmade bed, their caresses accompanied by many whispers of 'I love you' and other passionate endearments.

Afterwards they both slept for a little while, waking at the same time to smile into each other's eyes, luxuriating in this new and wonderful harmony that flowed between them like an invisible current.

Presently, Liz said, 'Would you like a cup of tea?'

Cam burst out laughing. 'A houri and a housewife rolled into one. What more can any man ask for? Yes, I'd love a cup of tea, dearest girl, but let's go home and have it there.'

Later, when they were sitting in the sun near the fig tree, watching and listening to the bees at work in the lavender bushes, he said, 'If you were unhappy with Duncan, why didn't you leave him?'

It took her some moments to answer. Eventually, she said, 'I had promised to be his wife "for better or worse". If you make that commitment, I think you should try to stick to it…as long as there is no cruelty or infidelity involved, which there wasn't in our case. Anyway Duncan *was* happy. In his way, he loved me. He didn't deserve to be left in the lurch…and he couldn't keep up the mortgage without my contribution.' She sighed. 'It's a long story. Do you really want to hear it?'

'Very much…I want to know everything about you.'

'Duncan was the boy next door. I had a crush on him from about the age of fourteen. By the time I was seventeen I was fathoms deep in love…or thought I was. What did I know…what does anybody know about love at that age? If he hadn't been interested in me, or if either of us had left home and seen a bit of the world, it would have worn off—no harm done.'

'But he was interested in you?'

'Yes, and our parents encouraged us. Legally, of course, they couldn't have stopped us marrying when I was nineteen. But they could and should have done more to make us see sense and wait. I'm sure there are people who mature early and marry young and it works out. But we weren't among them.'

'You said earlier that you realised that on your honeymoon. You were a virgin, obviously. Was he?'

'I'm not certain about that. I asked him, but he was evasive. If he had had any previous experience, it hadn't taught him anything. He was like someone who's colour blind or has no ear for music. He had no instinctive understanding of what sexual love is about. I knew it might hurt the first time, but it went on hurting for weeks and months.'

'Wham, bam, thank you, ma'am?'

Cam's query brought a faint smile to her mouth. 'Exactly. I knew all the theory and I tried to get it across that he…we weren't going about things the right way.'

'But he resented any suggestion that he wasn't the world's best lover?'

'How did you guess?'

'The world is full of guys who can't take any criticism of their driving let alone their technique in bed. Did you try giving him a book on the subject?'

'Yes, but it didn't work. Duncan was strangely prudish in lots of ways…I think he got it from his mother. We always had sex on Wednesdays and Saturdays, and always in the dark.' For the first time she was able to laugh about it with genuine amusement and no tightening of the throat.

'*Dios mio!*' said Cam. 'What an idiot.' They had been sitting close but not actually touching. Now he put his arm round her and pulled her against him. 'I'm amazed you could stand it.'

'Sometimes I wondered that. It wasn't just our disastrous sex life…we had nothing in common. Different senses of humour. Different views about life. But I don't think that's so unusual. Every time you go to a restaurant you see couples with nothing to say to each other, lost in their separate thoughts instead of chatting and laughing.'

'So it wasn't grief you were feeling when I saw that look in your eyes that I took to be sadness?'

'I expect it was guilt because I wasn't able to grieve for him. Or it may have been worry because, for a long time, I thought I was in the grip of another infatuation—for you. I was worried that I was falling into the same trap again.' She snuggled against him, leaning her head on his shoulder. 'I had got it into my head that a man with such powerful sexual magnetism had to be a worthless person—or at least rather second-rate.'

'It was unfortunate that we met when I had a girlfriend in tow,' he said dryly. 'I could tell that put you off. There were strong vibes of disapproval.'

'The night you arrived I saw you kissing her through that window,' she said, pointing to it. 'I wasn't sure who you were then and I remember envying her because no one was ever going to hold me and kiss me like that.'

'You were wrong there. Someone is going to hold you and kiss you every day for the next forty years…longer with any luck. Shall I open a bottle of wine?'

'Why not?' she said happily.

'Sit tight. I won't be long.' He rose from the seat, then bent to drop a kiss on her forehead. Going up the steps to the upper terrace, he blew her some more kisses.

Liz returned them, wondering how long the impasse between them might have continued if he hadn't found her in tears and thought she was weeping for Duncan rather than over her own youthful folly.

How difficult it was to see into people's hearts if they had reasons for concealing their innermost feelings, she thought.

When he came back with glasses and an opened bottle of white wine in a plastic cooler, she said, 'When did you know you loved me?'

'I'd have to think about that. Men aren't continually analysing their emotions the way women seem to,' he said teasingly. Then, more seriously, 'Perhaps I knew from the beginning that you were someone special but I didn't want to acknowledge it. When you've been independent for years, it's hard to adjust to the fact that you've lost that autonomy…that someone else is in charge of your happiness.'

After a pause he added, 'After the first time I made love to you, you cried. You thought I was dozing, but I could feel your chest heaving. That worried me a lot.'

Remembering the tears she had fought to control, she said, 'If I'd had any sense I'd have had a big boo-hoo, and you'd have asked why, and I would have told you. It was only relief and happiness because, at long last, I'd felt all the things women are supposed to feel.'

'I thought you were probably crying from some kind of guilt about experiencing pleasure without any deep emotional engagement, or from a feeling that you had betrayed the memory of the man you had loved,' said Cam. 'I took it as read that your first marriage had been happy, and from that basic misconception drew a lot of other false conclusions.'

'What I didn't…still don't understand is why you held off from trying me out, bedwise, before taking me on as a wife,' said Liz. 'If you had been a shy man, awkward with women, it might have made sense. But for Valdecarrasca's notorious womaniser to hold back seemed very peculiar.'

'I guess the answer to that is that Valdecarrasca's notorious womaniser had found the woman he wanted for the rest of his life and was nervous of putting a foot wrong. I hadn't recognised my own condition. I thought you'd agreed to our marriage mainly to have some babies. Since getting it right in bed can sometimes take time, it seemed wise to postpone it until we were past the point of no return.'

A few days later, Liz returned from accompanying Leonora to choose a frame for the portrait to see, from the kitchen window, Cam sitting in the garden reading a letter, more mail on the seat beside him.

After filling two tall glasses with spring water they had collected from one of the many *fontanales* to be found in the countryside, she went out to join him.

'Anything for me?'

'Not today, babe.' He stood up to kiss her, then moved the pile of shrink-wrapped magazines and manila envelopes to make room for her to sit next to him. 'How did the session with the framer go?'

'Fine. We found something we both like and I'm sure you will too.' She could see that his thoughts were elsewhere. 'Anything exciting in your post?'

Cam gave her a look she found hard to interpret. For a moment it took her back to the time when neither of them had understood the other. But that was over: now they understood every nuance of each other's tones and expressions. Or so she had thought.

He said slowly, 'I've been asked to step into the shoes of one of Britain's top journalists in Washington DC. He died a couple of weeks ago after working there for twenty years. He was a giant among journalists. It's a huge compliment to be invited to take his place.'

Something his mother had said at the pre-wedding party echoed in her mind. *I hope you know what you're letting yourself in for… You will never enjoy any sense of permanence.*

She said, 'That's wonderful news. When do you have to start? If they want you immediately, I can close up the house and follow you later.'

He was visibly astonished. 'You can't be serious? You love it here. You don't want to leave.'

'I wouldn't want to go back where I came from, but the chance to live in America—that's different. Valdecarrasca won't go away. It will always be here for us.'

Cam swallowed the rest of the water and then sprang to his feet and started pacing back and forth. 'I don't know…it's not what we planned. Washington is a big city and I'd need to live in the centre.'

'If it's one of the pinnacles of a career in journalism, I think you should at least try it. If you don't, you'll always regret it.'

He came back to where she was sitting and crouched down in front of her, putting his hands over her knees. 'But what about you, darling girl? We're a partnership now. We have to consider what's right for us both. If, in a few months' time, you find that you're pregnant, wouldn't you rather be here in the village than in a capital city on the other side of the Atlantic?'

Liz was beginning to think that she might be pregnant already. Her period, normally punctual to the day, was three days overdue and none of her usual mild PM symptoms had materialised.

'I think for someone of my age, having a first baby, Washington might have advantages over provincial Spain. Medical care in the US is said to be second to none—as long as people can afford it. Here…I'm not really sure. I've heard some excellent reports and I've also heard horror stories. Anyway, that's not the crux of the matter. The crux is…if you want to go, I'll be happy to come with you.' Leaning forward, she rested her forearms on his broad shoulders. 'There are thousands of places in the world where I could enjoy living. But only one man I want to live with…and who wants to live with me.'

The most important decision was not the only one. There were many lesser decisions to make.

Later that day, Cam said, 'I don't much like the idea of other people living at La Higuera, but it doesn't make sense to leave it empty for several years, particularly as, under Spanish law, tax is payable on the theoretical letting value.'

'What about storing all your most personal possessions next door?' Liz suggested. 'It would be awful to come back and find that a tenant's obnoxious child had thrown a dart at the portrait of Captain Fielding, or ruined one of your rugs.' Throughout the house the floors were spread with rugs he had bought on his travels.

'*Our* rugs,' he corrected her. 'Hopefully the letting agency will make sure nobody with obnoxious children is allowed near the place. But that's a good idea. We can use your little house as a store.'

'*Our* little house,' she teased him.

He pulled her into his arms. 'Houses…possessions… they're all expendable,' he said, hugging her. 'That you are mine and I am yours is the only thing that really matters.'

On their last morning in Spain, Liz went to the bakery for bread. On the way home she made a detour, climbing the path that led up to the cemetery and passed behind it to join a flight of rough stone steps leading downwards.

At the top of the steps she paused to look down on the clustered rooftops of Valdecarrasca and, beyond them, the vineyards spreading across the floor of the valley. Between some of the rows of vines the coppery soil had been rotavated. Some were still green with the foliage of low-growing plants. Either way, from this height, the vines themselves looked like rows of cross-stitch worked with varying degrees of skill.

I am going to miss it, she thought. I wonder how long it will be before we come back?

She was certain now that she had started a baby. But she hadn't mentioned it to Cam yet and, observant as he was, he had been too preoccupied with the preparations for departure to register that they had been making love without any marked interruption since they were married.

Perhaps she would tell him on the flight from Madrid to Washington. Or perhaps she would wait until her instinctive feeling that there was a new life beginning inside her body had been confirmed by a doctor.

She began to descend the steps, wondering if Valdecarrasca would have changed by the time they saw it again. She hoped not. To her, it was perfect as it was, a backwater set apart from the turbulent mainstream of modern life.

Part of her longed to stay, to see the young leaves starting to sprout on the vines and, as the nights grew warmer, to have candlelit suppers for friends in the courtyard. There were also small improvements she wanted to make to the house and garden.

But she hadn't forgotten that on the day he had proposed to her Cam had said that a successful marriage was an intimate friendship between people prepared to make trade-offs.

For the amazing difference he had made to her life, she was more than willing to make this particular trade-off.

Cam must have seen her coming down the steps from the kitchen window. He was at the door to meet her. 'I was beginning to wonder what had happened to you.'

'What could happen to me here?' she said, smiling.

'Nothing, I guess.' He drew her into the house, took the bread bag from her and hung it from the curlicue at the end of the staircase handrail in order to have both hands free to draw her to him. 'I get a little jumpy when you're gone for longer than I expected. Hopefully it will wear off after we've been together twenty or thirty years.'

She wrapped her arms round him. 'I was saying goodbye to the village.'

He tipped up her chin. 'You're sad to be leaving it, aren't you?'

'Only a little…aren't you?'

'There'll be times when I'll miss it. We both will. But the village will always be here for us, and you're going to like America.'

His kiss dispelled her regret for all they were leaving. Since the beginning of history women had been following men to the ends of the earth, saying goodbye to the safe and familiar and setting out on adventures in faraway places.

She had done it before, on her own. If she hadn't, she wouldn't be in the arms of this man she loved and who loved her.

When the kiss ended, she said, 'You're right. It's going to be fun. So let's have breakfast and get on with closing down the house. I wonder how long it will be before someone rents it?'

* * * * *

HIS BROTHER'S SON

by

Jennifer Taylor

Jennifer Taylor lives in the north-west of England, in a small village surrounded by some really beautiful countryside. She has written for several different Mills & Boon® series in the past, but it wasn't until she read her first Medical™ romance that she truly found her niche. She was so captivated by these heart-warming stories that she set out to write them herself!

When not writing or doing research for her latest book, Jennifer's hobbies include reading, gardening, travel, and chatting to friends, both on- and off-line. She is always delighted to hear from readers, so do visit her website at www.jennifer-taylor.com

Don't miss Jennifer Taylor's exciting new novel, *The Surgeon's Fatherhood Surprise*, out in March 2008 from Mills & Boon® Medical™.

CHAPTER ONE

IT STILL wasn't too late to change her mind. All she had to do was ask the taxi-driver to take her back to the airport. She might be able to catch an earlier flight back to London and…

And what? The situation hadn't changed. She was in exactly the same position as she had been in that morning when she'd set out to Mallorca. No matter how much the idea terrified her she had to accept that she needed Felipe Valdez's help.

'*Señorita?*'

Rebecca Williams started when the taxi-driver turned to her. She looked up in surprise, feeling her stomach churn with nerves when she realised they had stopped. Her grey eyes widened as she looked out of the window and got her first glimpse of the Clinica Valdez.

It was so much bigger than she'd expected. Maybe it was the word 'clinic' that had misled her because she'd never imagined it would be so imposing. As her gaze swept over the elegant, whitewashed building set in the midst of several acres of manicured lawns she could feel her heart racing.

Antonio had told her that his brother had founded the clinic two years previously, but she hadn't realised before exactly what an achievement that had been. Just raising the finance for such a venture must have needed a great deal of determination, plus a ruthless will to succeed. Added to what she already knew about Felipe Valdez, it wasn't encouraging.

Was he really the kind of man who would be prepared to help her financially without expecting something in return?

Becky bit her lip as a wave of panic threatened to engulf her. She could be making a big mistake…a *huge* mistake…if she went in there and asked to see Valdez when she had no idea how he would react to what she had to tell him.

5

Announcing that his brother had had a son would be bound to come as a shock to him. Then there were the circumstances surrounding Josh's birth.

Whilst Felipe Valdez might accept that his brother had been right to protect his unborn child, would he approve of her role in the baby's life? What if he decided to use his money and influence to take Josh away from her?

It might not be enough that she was Josh's legal guardian. The courts would need to take account of all sorts of issues if there was a battle for custody. She barely earned enough to meet their bills, and the fact that she had needed to return to full-time work at St Leonard's Hospital might also go against her. What chance would she really have of keeping the little boy when she wasn't his natural mother…?

'Señorita! Por favor!'

Becky jumped when the taxi driver spoke sharply to her. It was obvious that he was impatient for her to get out so that he could find another fare. She quickly pulled some money out of her bag and paid him, thinking that she may as well get out now that she was here.

She just needed a little more time to think everything through properly. She couldn't afford to make a mistake. She had to be sure that she was making the right decision—for Josh's sake.

Felipe Valdez sighed as he got up from his desk. He'd spent the best part of the morning dealing with paperwork. It was an aspect of his job which he particularly loathed but there was no way to avoid it.

As director of the Clinica Valdez, his say-so was needed before any decisions could be taken. Oh, he had some excellent people working for him, but he preferred to keep his finger very firmly on the pulse. He knew that his staff considered him to be something of a control freak, but they didn't understand. The Clinica Valdez was not only his greatest achievement—it was the main focus of his life. He had worked too hard and made too many sacrifices to take a chance on anything going wrong.

A frown drew his thick, black brows together because that thought had caused him more than a little pain. He tried not to think about the mistakes he had made in his life, but sometimes it wasn't easy to block them out. Now, as he looked out of the window at the sunlit grounds of the private hospital, he felt a familiar ache settle in his heart as he thought about his brother Antonio.

If he hadn't been so busy opening the clinic, he might have realised that something was wrong with Antonio. Maybe he would have been able to make his brother understand that he had to continue to receive proper medical care. Antonio should *never* have been allowed to leave hospital when he'd been so ill. With the right kind of treatment he could have lived for another six months at least.

Not that he blamed Antonio, of course. He had been too ill to realise what he'd been doing, too ill and too much under the influence of that woman. No, if anyone was to blame for Antonio's premature death, it was Rebecca Williams!

Felipe's mouth thinned. With his austerely handsome features he looked even more forbidding as he stared out of the window. He tried not to think about Rebecca Williams very often because it was pointless getting upset. However, sometimes he found himself wishing that he'd gone to see her in London after Antonio's funeral and told her exactly what he thought about her.

Only close family and friends had attended the service in Mallorca. Rebecca Williams certainly hadn't been invited so they'd never met. He had seen a photograph of her, however, and even though he'd torn it up he could still recall every detail, from the long blonde hair falling softly around her oval face to those huge grey eyes. She had looked like every man's vision of a ministering angel, but he knew how misleading appearances could be. Was it any wonder that poor Antonio had been deceived?

A woman suddenly walked along the path beneath his window and Felipe blinked. Just for a moment he felt his mind spin as he stared at her. Her blonde hair was caught up into a knot on the top of her head and her face was in profile, but there was something strangely familiar about her…

His heart began to pound as he turned and strode to the door. He wrenched it open, startling his secretary who had been about to knock. Felipe shook his head when she opened her mouth to speak.

'Later!' he ordered in a tone that brooked no argument.

He hurried into the corridor, taking the stairs two at a time as he raced down to the ground floor. There was a queue of people in Reception but he didn't pause as he made his way to the entrance. His heart was pounding, the blood drumming painfully in his ears, the need to check if he'd been right urging him on. If it *had* been Rebecca Williams walking past his window just now then, by God, he didn't intend to let her escape!

She was sitting on a bench outside the main doors. Felipe ground to a halt, feeling his breath coming in laboured spurts. There was something almost tragic about the way she sat there so still, so alone. When a wisp of pale blonde hair blew across her face, he was shocked when he saw how her hand trembled as she tucked it behind her ear.

He was suddenly overwhelmed by a feeling of compassion that stunned him because it was the last thing he'd expected to feel if they ever met. She looked so sad, so lonely, so deeply unhappy that his heart was immediately touched before he forced himself to remember who and what she was.

This was the woman who had hastened Antonio's death because of her own greed for his money. Did he really have any sympathy to spare for someone like her?

He must have made some small sound of disgust because she suddenly glanced round and he saw the colour drain from her face. She rose to her feet and he could see the tremor that passed through her slender body and was pleased. He had no idea why she had come to see him but it didn't really matter. It was enough that he would have the chance to tell her what he thought of her at last.

'You're Antonio's brother, aren't you?'

Her voice was low and surprisingly sweet. He frowned because it surprised him that he should have noticed a thing like that.

'I am Felipe Valdez,' he said harshly, and saw her flinch. He took a few quick steps and stopped in front of her, surprised once again when he realised how tiny she was. For some reason he'd imagined that she would be much taller and far less fragile-looking, so it threw him off balance for a moment to realise that the image he'd formed of her hadn't been wholly accurate.

'You probably don't know who I am,' she began in that low, sweet voice, but he curtly interrupted her, irritated that his mind should start running off at tangents at a time like this.

'You're Rebecca Williams. My brother's girlfriend, for want of a better description.' He smiled thinly when he saw her surprise. 'Antonio sent me a photograph of you. He said that he wanted me to see the most important person in his life.'

'I didn't know… He never told me…' Her grey eyes filled with tears and she turned away while she hunted a tissue out of her bag.

Felipe's hands clenched because the urge to touch her then was so very strong. It shocked him to the depths of his being that he should feel such a need to comfort her, shocked and angered him because wasn't it an indication of her power? If he could be manipulated like this, how much easier must it have been for her to persuade Antonio to do what she'd wanted?

The thought was just what he needed. Placing his hand under her elbow, he briskly steered her away from the main entrance, ignoring her murmured protest as he led her along the path until they reached a sheltered spot well away from any prying eyes. He had no idea what she wanted but he preferred to keep their dealings private if possible.

He had never spoken of his feelings about this woman to anyone, and certainly hadn't shared the contempt he felt for her with any of his colleagues. He preferred to keep his own counsel when something affected him deeply. Only once in his life had he ever opened his heart to anyone, and look how badly that had turned out.

He was surprised when that thought crossed his mind because it had been years since he'd thought about his engagement to Teresa and how it had ended. He had no time to dwell on it, however, as Rebecca Williams wrenched her arm out of his grasp. There was a touch of colour in her face and a glint in her grey eyes that told him she was angry about the way he'd behaved towards her, but she had forfeited her right to be treated with courtesy after what she had done to Antonio.

'I don't know what you think you're doing—' she began hotly, but he brusquely interrupted her once more.

'What precisely do you want, Miss Williams?' He smiled sardonically when she fell silent and stared warily at him. 'You must have had a reason for coming here, so why don't you tell me what it is? What is that wonderful phrase you use in England? Ah, yes, beating about the bush. I can see no point in us beating about the bush. *Sí?*'

'Who said that I wanted anything?' She walked a little way across the grass then turned to face him. 'I might have come here purely and simply because I wanted to meet you.'

'You might, but I don't think so.' Felipe folded his arms and studied her closely, knowing that all the contempt he felt must be clear to see in his sherry-brown eyes.

She was beautiful, all right, with that silky, pale hair, those delicate features, that air of innocence, but he wasn't fool enough to be taken in. Rebecca Williams was a cold-hearted, mercenary gold-digger, and it broke his heart to know that his brother had fallen into her clutches when he'd been at his most vulnerable.

Anger burned hotly inside him but he'd learned a long time ago how to use it to its best effect. He continued to study her, watching the play of emotions that crossed her face before her head suddenly bowed. When she spoke this time her voice echoed with a pain that sounded almost real—if he'd been foolish enough to believe that a woman like her was capable of any genuine emotions.

'You hate me, don't you? I can hear it in your voice, see it in your eyes.'

She suddenly looked up and Felipe felt his stomach clench when he saw the bewilderment in her beautiful grey eyes. 'Why? I don't understand why you should feel like that. I've never done anything to hurt you. We hadn't even met until today. So why do you…you *loathe* me like this?'

'Why do you think, Miss Williams? The answer isn't all that difficult, surely?'

He closed his mind to the swift stab of guilt that had speared through him. Rebecca Williams was a consummate actress. She must be if she'd managed to fool Antonio for all that time. How long had it been that she and his brother had lived together?

He was rather hazy about the details because it had been a while before Antonio had written to tell him the address where he was staying in England, and even then all he'd said in the letter had been that he'd met someone and that they were living together in London. Felipe hadn't heard from him again for many months, not until after Antonio had signed himself out of hospital after refusing further treatment. By the time that letter had reached him, his brother had been dead.

'Because of Antonio, you mean? But why? I don't understand. I never did anything to harm your brother. All I ever wanted was to help him!'

He pushed the memory to the back of his mind because he couldn't deal with it right then. Rebecca Williams was staring at him, and if he'd been gullible enough he might have believed that she really was as shocked as she was making herself out to be.

'Really? How touching.' He treated her to a contemptuous smile and saw her flinch. 'So you had Antonio's welfare at heart, did you?'

'Of course! I don't know why you need to ask me that. Everything I did was aimed purely and simply at making his life more…more bearable.'

Her voice broke and she looked away. Felipe's hands

clenched because he wasn't sure if he wanted to shake her or hug her at that moment. She'd sounded so sincere and yet how could he believe a word she said when he had indisputable evidence to the contrary?

It shocked him that he should feel this strange mixture of emotions when the situation was so clear cut. He knew what she'd done so maybe it was time he let her know that rather than allow the situation to turn into a complete farce.

'And the fact that you managed to greatly improve the quality of your own life was your reward for making my brother's last few weeks on this earth bearable? Is that what you are saying, Miss Williams?'

'I don't know what you mean…' she began, then suddenly stopped. He saw her take a deep breath that made her small breasts rise and fall beneath the soft cotton of her blue dress, but her voice sounded strangely thin when she continued, as though the accusation had sucked all the strength out of her. Maybe it was difficult to be forced to admit the truth, even for a woman like her.

'You're talking about Antonio's will, aren't you? And the fact that he left me all that money?'

Becky could feel the tremor that was working its way through her body but she made herself stand rigidly still. Felipe Valdez was watching her and the contempt in his eyes should have hurt or angered her, but in a funny sort of way she suddenly felt detached from what was happening. It was as though she had stepped outside herself and was watching the scene that was being played out in the sunlit grounds of the hospital.

There she stood in her best dress—the one she had chosen especially because she'd hoped it would make the right impression—and there was Felipe standing so tall and straight, his mouth curled into that arrogant smile which a moment ago had seemed to chill her soul.

She found herself wondering what would happen if she blinked—if she would open her eyes and find herself back in the flat in London, waking to the sound of Josh's noisy shouts as he clamoured for her to lift him out of his cot…

She closed her eyes then opened them again, but the scene was just the same. The only difference was that Felipe was now speaking. It was an effort to make sense of what he was saying.

'I see we have made a breakthrough at last. This reluctance to talk about money is so very English. But why pretend that it means nothing when we both know that it is the driving force behind so much that people do?'

He shrugged, his broad shoulders moving lightly beneath the fine wool of his dark grey suit. It was obviously expensive, Becky thought inconsequentially, because it fitted him to perfection, the jacket tailored to accommodate the width of his shoulders and chest, the trimness of his waist.

Her gaze swept lower, taking stock of the long trouser-clad legs, the polished black shoes on his feet. They were hand-made, from the look of them, and cut from the softest leather—luxurious, costly. Felipe Valdez obviously saw no reason not to indulge himself and yet he'd seen fit to query what Antonio had done with his inheritance, to question whether his brother had had the right to spend it as he'd wished. Was that what all this antagonism was about—money?

Her eyes rose to his face and she made no attempt to hide her scorn. 'Your brother knew exactly what he wanted to do with his inheritance, Dr Valdez. It was his decision.'

'And you're prepared to swear that you didn't try to influence him in any way? That you didn't take advantage of the fact that he was sick? That you never, *ever,* thought to yourself how wonderful it would be to have all that money at your disposal?'

He laughed when she gasped, deliberately closing his mind to how shocked she looked because he didn't want to have to consider whether or not he was hurting her. 'Or that it would be so much better if Antonio died sooner rather than later so that you wouldn't have to wait quite so long to get your hands on it?'

'No! I can't believe you're saying such things. I *never*

wanted Antonio's money! I *never* tried to influence him to name me in his will. It was his decision, and his alone!'

Becky could feel the bile rushing into her throat and turned away when she realised that she was going to be sick. Stumbling to the flower-bed, she bent over and retched, but she'd had nothing to eat since the previous night so her stomach was mercifully empty.

'Here.'

A tanned hand suddenly appeared, offering her a clean white handkerchief, but she shook her head. She wanted nothing from this man, nothing at all. What a fool she'd been to consider asking him for help. Hadn't Antonio told her that everything had to be on Felipe's terms, that he always had to be in control? Was she really prepared to run the risk of him taking charge of Josh, taking Josh away from her?

The thought steadied her and she stood up straight. Felipe Valdez was watching her and she saw the oddest expression cross his face before the mask of indifference slid back into place.

'Are you feeling better?'

'I'm fine.' She turned and walked towards the path, but he stepped in front of her, putting out a detaining hand when she tried to step around him.

Becky shivered when she felt his cool fingers fastening around her wrist, but she refused to let him think she was afraid by snatching her hand away. She looked up at him with steady eyes and was surprised when she saw a thin line of colour run along his angular cheekbones.

'It would be better if you came into the clinic and rested for a while,' he said shortly.

'I'm fine,' she repeated. She tilted her head so that she could look him straight in the eyes. 'Thank you for the offer, but I have a plane to catch. I shall go straight to the airport. I apologise for disrupting your morning, Dr Valdez.'

She gently withdrew her arm and this time he made no attempt to stop her. Becky walked back along the path and she could feel him watching her every step of the way. She paused when she reached the corner, but the desire to look back was too strong to resist.

He was standing exactly where she'd left him and she felt her heart curl up when she saw the expression on his face. Even from that distance she could see the contempt in his eyes, the disdain.

Her eyes filled with tears but she refused to let him see that he'd upset her. She raised her hand in a mocking salute then carried on, waiting until she was out of sight before finding a tissue and wiping her eyes.

As luck would have it there was a taxi dropping off a fare outside the clinic. Becky flagged it down and asked the driver to take her to the airport. She caught a glimpse of Felipe Valdez as the taxi headed back down the drive, and quickly averted her eyes when he glanced her way.

This would be the first and the last time they ever met because she certainly wouldn't come here again after what had happened today. She was only grateful that she hadn't made the mistake of telling him why she'd come.

Becky sighed as she thought back to that dreadful day when Antonio had told her that his former girlfriend, Tara Lewis, was pregnant with his child and that she intended to get rid of it. It had been a shock for her as well as for him.

Antonio's affair with Tara had been over for some time by then, and he had made no secret of the fact that he regretted having got involved with her. Becky had been a little concerned that he might have been rushing into their own relationship too soon, and had insisted on them taking things slowly at first.

Antonio had had no such reservations, however. He had told Becky that he loved her and that he hoped one day that she might grow to love him in return. Becky had appreciated the fact that he hadn't tried to rush her. She had sensed that she'd been falling in love with him and that all it had needed was a little more time for her own feelings to become clear. Then, just six weeks after they'd started going out together, Antonio had discovered that he had cancer and everything had changed. Time had been the one thing they'd no longer had.

Becky had known from the outset that she wanted to be there for him and had never once wavered in her decision. Antonio had been the sweetest, gentlest man she'd ever known and she'd loved him dearly. When Tara had dropped her bombshell it couldn't have come at a worse time. Antonio had just been told that the treatment he'd needed so desperately would make him sterile, and there Tara had been, telling him that she wanted to abort his child.

He had been close to despair as he'd poured out the whole story to Becky, and that had been when she'd come up with the plan to pay Tara to have the baby. Antonio had inherited a large sum of money on his birthday, so she'd suggested that he use some of that. And then she'd told him that, no matter what happened, she would always take care of the child. It had been that which had convinced him to go ahead.

He and Tara had struck a deal. He would pay her fifty thousand pounds immediately with another fifty thousand when the baby was born, plus an allowance of five thousand pounds each month she was pregnant. If Tara had only stuck to their bargain there wouldn't have been a problem, but there had been constant demands for more money. Becky had hoped that once Tara had received her final payment, that would have been the end of it. But two weeks earlier Tara had turned up at her flat and demanded a further twenty thousand pounds.

Becky simply didn't have that kind of money and had told her so, but Tara had refused to believe her. She'd issued Becky with an ultimatum—either find the money or she would take her to court and claim that she'd been coerced into signing over custody of the baby.

Horrified by the thought of what might happen, Becky had tried to make her see sense. However, Tara had just laughed and told Becky that the courts would probably take Josh into care and then neither one of them would end up with custody of him. As Tara had pointed out, she didn't care what happened to him. She never had. She'd only agreed to give birth to him because Antonio had paid her not to have an abortion.

Becky took a deep breath. She had promised Antonio she

would take care of Josh and she wouldn't let him down. Some-how, some way she would find the money she needed without asking Felipe Valdez for help.

'Everything looks fine, Miss Prentice. There will be some ten-derness for a few days, but once the drainage tube has been removed I am confident that you won't have any further prob-ems.'

Felipe stepped back as a nurse drew the sheet over the young woman. Lisa Prentice had been rushed into the Clinica Valdez with a seriously inflamed appendix. Felipe's colleague, Silvia Ramirez, had performed the operation, and now he turned to her.

'An excellent job, Dr Ramirez, performed under very diffi-cult circumstances. I believe the appendix was ready to burst.'

'That's correct, sir,' Silvia replied, smiling with pleasure at the compliment. She was an attractive brunette in her thirties, engaged to be married to another doctor on the surgical team which Felipe headed. He appreciated the fact that neither of them had allowed their relationship to intrude into their work, although he would have had no hesitation in doing something about it if it had. The welfare of the patients they treated at the Clinica Valdez came first and foremost, and always would.

'Another half-hour and the outcome might not have been quite so fortunate. *Sí?*' He turned to the young woman in the bed once again and frowned.

'Did you have no indication that there might be something wrong before you set out on your holiday, Miss Prentice? I find it strange that you experienced no discomfort.'

Lisa flushed when she heard the scepticism in his voice. She was a pretty girl in her teens and had come on holiday to Mallorca with a group of her friends. Felipe couldn't fail to see how uncomfortable she looked about having to answer the question.

'I did have a few twinges the night before we were due to fly over here,' she muttered. 'I just hoped it was indigestion or something.'

'I see.' His black brows swooped upwards as he regarded her with cool, brown eyes. 'It never occurred to you that it might be something more serious and that perhaps you should visit your doctor before you set off on your holiday?'

'Not really. I mean, if Mum had found out that I wasn't feeling too good she might have stopped me going...' She tailed off uncertainly.

Felipe bit back a sigh. The young woman had preferred to run the risk of being seriously ill rather than cancel her holiday. It would take more than the promise of two weeks in the sun to get him on a plane if he were feeling under the weather.

That thought reminded him of what had happened earlier in the day, and he frowned. Had Rebecca Williams been feeling ill before she'd come to see him or had it been what he'd said that had had such disastrous consequences? Even the most consummate actress couldn't have faked that bout of sickness, and it troubled him to know that he might have been responsible for it, troubled him more than it should, too. Why should he care about the wretched woman after the way she had used his brother?

His brows drew even further together and he saw Silvia glance rather nervously at him. She was obviously wondering if she'd done something to cause his displeasure so he quickly smoothed his features into their customary bland mask.

'May I suggest that the next time you go on holiday you are a little more sensible, Miss Prentice? As it is you will not get to enjoy very much of your stay on the island, I'm afraid. We shall keep you here for the next two to three days then I shall recommend to your insurance company that you should be flown home immediately.'

'Oh! I didn't realise I would have to go home.' Tears filled the girl's eyes. 'I thought I would be able to join my friends. We've been saving up for this holiday for months, you see, and now I won't have a chance to enjoy any of it.'

Felipe sighed, although he couldn't help wondering why the sight of the girl's tears should have moved him. He wasn't uncaring about the people he treated, but he'd learned a long time ago to distance himself. It puzzled him that he didn't seem able to do so right then...

Unless it was that meeting with Rebecca Williams which had allowed his emotions to surface?

It was a deeply disquieting thought and he ruthlessly drove it out of his mind. 'I feel that it would be far more sensible if you returned home as soon as you are discharged from the clinic, Miss Prentice. However...' He held up his hand when Lisa started to say something and was unsurprised when she fell silent. Few people stood up to him, he'd found, although whether that was a good thing was open to question. Maybe he would be a better person if occasionally he had to bow to another person's will? He couldn't remember the last time anyone had contradicted him—apart from Rebecca Williams, of course.

It was an effort to hide his dismay as that thought slid into his mind, but hiding his feelings was something he was particularly good at. '*However*, I am prepared to review your case in a few days' time.'

He shrugged when he heard the young woman's gasp of delight, clamping down on the urge to smile at her because it wouldn't be right to let her think that his agreement was a foregone conclusion. 'If you continue making such excellent progress it might be possible to allow you to carry on with your holiday—with certain provisos, of course.'

'Oh, thank you, Dr Valdez, and you, too, Dr Ramirez. That's just brilliant news!'

Lisa was beaming when they moved away from her bed. Felipe sensed that Silvia was looking at him and glanced at her. 'You disagree with my decision, Dr Ramirez? Please, feel free to say so if you do.'

'Not at all,' she said quickly. He saw a little colour touch her cheeks and sighed when it struck him what was wrong. Silvia was surprised because he'd changed his mind. Frankly, it was unheard of for him to go back on a decision once he had made it.

It made him wonder what was wrong with him that day and

why he seemed to be acting so out of character. He had
changed his mind about sending Lisa home once she was discharged and now he found himself wishing that he'd discovered what Rebecca Williams had wanted. It had seemed enough
at the time that he'd been able to tell her what he thought of
her, but all of a sudden he was beset by curiosity.

Why *had* she come to see him? He'd heard her telling the
taxi-driver to take her to the airport so had it been a sudden
whim that had made her spend her last few hours on the island
visiting him, or had there been another reason behind it?

The question nagged at him for the rest of the day so that
by the time he left the hospital he was tired of thinking about
it. He made his way from the main building and followed the
path through the trees until he came to a pink-washed villa. It
was almost seven and the sun was sinking low in the sky
casting a burnished haze across the bay.

Felipe paused as he always did to admire the view, but that
evening it didn't soothe him. He felt too on edge and keyed
up, a feeling of tension making his nerves hum. It had been
years since he'd felt that way. The last time had been when
he'd found out that his fiancée had been cheating on him.

He'd solved that problem by ending the engagement and
hadn't made the mistake of getting involved with anyone ever
since. Any relationships he'd had in the intervening years had
meant little to him apart from physically. If only he could apply
the same objectivity to what had happened that day, but wondering what Rebecca Williams had wanted was eating away at
him.

He let himself into the villa, bypassing the dining-room
where his housekeeper had left his supper in the heated serving
trolley. Usually he enjoyed her cooking but that night the smell
of meat and vegetables made him feel sick, although not as
sick as Rebecca had been that morning.

'*Madre de Dios!*' He slammed his hand against the study
door, feeling pain shoot through his palm when it connected
with the ornately carved wood. It stunned him to feel it and

know that he was capable of such anger when he had always—*always*—been able to control his emotions before.

But this was different. This all had to do with Antonio, and there were too many emotions churning inside him. He felt guilt and anger, grief and pain, all laced with a deep contempt for the way that woman had used his brother when he had been so vulnerable.

Antonio hadn't deserved to be treated like that!

Tears stung Felipe's eyes but he blinked them away. In his heart he knew that he might be making a mistake, but he didn't have a choice. He had to sort this out once and for all, bring everything to its rightful conclusion. Rebecca Williams must be made to pay.

He went to his desk and picked up the phone, his hand was rock steady when he dialled the number. It was the usual push-button service but he obeyed each command without experiencing his usual irritation until, finally, he was connected to an operator.

'I wish to book a seat on the next flight to London. My name? Valdez, Dr Felipe Valdez.'

CHAPTER TWO

'YOU'VE not got much of a suntan, I must say. Don't tell me it was raining in Mallorca?'

Becky glanced round as her friend, Karen Hardy, came into the staffroom where she'd been making a cup of coffee. It had been a hectic morning on the paediatric intensive care unit of St Leonard's Hospital, where she worked, and it was the first opportunity she'd had to take a break. She automatically reached for the jar of coffee and made Karen a drink as well.

'It wasn't raining, but I didn't get much chance to enjoy the sun,' she explained, handing her friend the mug.

She picked up her own cup, hoping that the hot coffee would help to warm away the chill which seemed to have invaded her since the previous day. She'd felt cold ever since she had got back from Mallorca despite the fact that the weather in London was surprisingly warm for the time of year. But maybe the chill she felt owed itself less to the outside temperature than to the frosty reception she had received at the Clinica Valdez.

Her grey eyes clouded as she recalled what Felipe Valdez had said to her. She had spent the night going over and over every cruel word, but nothing seemed to take the sting out of them. He honestly believed that she had *used* Antonio for her own ends. The thought still made her feel ill.

'Hey, are you OK? You look as though you'd just swallowed something nasty.' Karen sniffed her coffee suspiciously. 'The milk isn't off again, is it?'

'No, it's fine. Don't worry, I'm not trying to poison you,' Becky quickly assured her. 'Here have one of these.'

She offered Karen the packet of chocolate biscuits which one of the doctors on the unit had given her in the hope that it would distract her from asking anything else. Karen was a good friend but Becky had deemed it wiser not to tell anyone too much since she'd taken the job at St Leonard's. People would have been bound to gossip if the truth had got out, and that was the last thing she wanted to happen.

She'd told everyone the story that she and Antonio had decided upon—that she was a single mother, bringing up her nine-month-old son on her own. Whenever anyone asked about Josh's father, she answered quite truthfully that he had died not long after the baby had been born.

Everyone had accepted it without question, and although she occasionally felt guilty about having to deceive them she felt she didn't have a choice. She wouldn't take any risks where Josh was concerned.

'Thanks.' Karen took a biscuit and carried on talking through a mouthful of crumbs. 'So why didn't you get much chance to enjoy the sun while you were in Mallorca?'

'Oh, it was just a flying visit. I was there and back within a day.'

'Really?' Karen made no attempt to hide her surprise. Her blue eyes gleamed with curiosity as she stared at Becky. 'You must have had a very good reason for not stopping. I mean, it's a long way to go just for a few hours, isn't it?'

Becky sighed as she realised her mistake. She shouldn't have said that because her friend wouldn't have been any the wiser if she'd let her believe that she had stayed in Mallorca. She'd had five days' leave owing to her and had planned the trip to coincide with them. Not for the first time she rued the fact that being deceitful didn't come naturally to her. Even when speaking to Felipe Valdez she had needed to watch every word she'd said.

'I had something to sort out,' she replied quickly, not wanting to dwell on the previous day's events. Recalling the contempt on Felipe's face still had the power to upset her, even though she didn't understand why his opinion should carry any weight. So long as Josh was safe, nothing else mattered. And once she found the money she needed to pay Tara, her biggest problem would have been solved.

'Something to do with Josh, do you mean?' Karen guessed astutely. 'You mentioned something about his father coming from Mallorca—did you go there to see his family?'

'That's right.' Becky shrugged. 'As I said, it was just a flying visit—that's why I didn't stay very long. Anyway, I wanted to get home to Josh.'

'You didn't take him with you?'

She groaned when she heard the surprise in Karen's voice. What was that saying about the tangled webs we weave? One lie seemed to lead to another and if she wasn't careful she would start tripping herself up.

'He had an ear infection so I didn't think it would be wise to take him on the plane. He stayed with the childminder so he was perfectly happy.'

She could tell that Karen was going to ask her something else so it was a relief when their new trainee nurse, Debbie Rothwell, put her head round the door.

'I'm awfully sorry, Becky, but can you come? Holly is crying and I've no idea what's wrong with her. All the monitor readings are fine. I've double-checked.'

Becky put her cup on the draining-board and smiled at the younger woman. Debbie was still very nervous about the responsibility involved with working in the IC unit and rarely trusted her instincts where the children were concerned. Whilst the monitoring equipment was invaluable it didn't supply all the answers.

'Have you tried asking her what's wrong?'

'Well, no, I haven't, actually,' Debbie admitted, looking even more flustered. 'I suppose I should have thought of that first.'

'Don't worry. It takes a while to slot into the routine here,' Becky said kindly, going to the door. 'Let's go and have a look at Holly and see if we can find out what's the matter with her. She's due to be transferred to a ward once Mr Watts has seen her, so there's no need to be overly concerned. She's well on the mend, I'm glad to say.'

They made their way into the IC unit and went straight to

Holly Benson's bed. The four year-old had been admitted the previous week after suffering a stroke. She had been gravely ill at the time and the prognosis hadn't been good. However, dedicated nursing care, plus the child's own will to survive, had pulled her through.

The good news was that young children were known to make an excellent recovery after they'd suffered a stroke. Nobody was exactly sure how it worked, but it had been proved that other parts of the brain took over the tasks performed by any damaged areas. With a bit of luck, little Holly would lead a full and active life.

'Now then, sweetheart, what's the matter? Does your head hurt or do you have a pain anywhere?' she asked gently, bending down beside the child's bed.

Although Holly had been removed from most of the monitoring equipment, she was still attached to the machine that was checking her blood pressure and heart rate. Becky saw the child pluck at the leads attached to her, and gently moved Holly's hand away so that she couldn't dislodge them.

'Want to get up,' the little girl said, her lower lip pouting. 'Want to play!'

'Oh, I see!'

She laughed as she kissed the little girl's cheek, thinking what a good sign that was. When a child was fretting because she wanted to get out of bed, she had to be on the mend.

'I'm afraid you can't get up just yet, poppet. The doctor has to see how you are first.'

She turned to Debbie and grinned when she saw the relief on the young nurse's face. 'Panic over. How do you fancy reading Holly a story while we wait for Mr Watts to make his appearance? I wouldn't like him to think that we don't keep our patients happy while they're with us.'

She moved away from the bed after both Holly and Debbie had agreed that it sounded like the perfect solution and made her way down the ward, automatically checking each child as she passed. There were ten beds in the paediatric intensive care unit and every one of them was in use. She had no doubt that the minute Holly was transferred to the medical ward, another young patient would arrive.

St Leonard's was the only paediatric intensive care unit in that area of London, and beds there were always at a premium. It meant that her role as a staff nurse was a demanding one, but she'd never regretted her decision to work there. The fact that she'd been able to choose to work permanent days had been a real bonus because she didn't know how she would have managed to look after Josh if she'd had to work shifts.

A smile softened her mouth as she thought about the little boy. Even though it was a huge responsibility, she had never regretted offering to take care of him. Josh was Antonio's son and doubly precious because of that. She couldn't have loved any child more than she loved him.

Becky left the ward and went to the office. Sister Reece was on holiday that week so Becky was in charge in her absence and there was a stack of paperwork to catch up with. She opened the office door then froze when she caught sight of the man standing by the window. For one horrible moment she thought she was going to faint as the floor seemed to rush up to meet her.

She saw him turn, saw the concern that crossed his face, saw him take a step towards her—and it was that which steadied her. The thought of Felipe Valdez actually touching her was more than she could bear.

'Don't!'

Felipe froze when he heard the total rejection in Rebecca's voice. Frankly, he wasn't sure what to do. She looked as though she was ready to keel over, yet the expression on her face dared him to go to her assistance.

He took a deep breath while he tried to think, but it was surprisingly difficult to assess the situation. Knowing that he was the object of all those waves of antipathy that were flowing across the room had thrown him off course. He could no longer take a rational view of what was happening and it shocked him to realise that he was in danger of acting instinctively and without thought.

'What do you want?'

Her voice sounded cold and sharp, as though all the warmth and sweetness had been drained from it, and he frowned because it was strangely distressing to know that he was responsible for the change. He found himself wondering if he should apologise for what he had done before common sense reasserted itself. If there was any apologising to be done, it needed to come from her, not him.

'I want to know why you came to see me yesterday.'

He saw her slender body stiffen but he refused to let himself be swayed by this act she was putting on. He had known that she was a nurse because Antonio had told him that in his last letter, but it had been a shock to discover that she worked in one of the most demanding departments in any hospital.

When he'd called at the house where she lived, a neighbour had told him that Rebecca worked in the paediatric intensive care unit of St Leonard's Hospital. He had taken a taxi there, trying to reconcile himself to the thought of her doing such a demanding job. Yet why should he have been so surprised? Who better than Rebecca Williams to deal with sick children when she was incapable of feeling any genuine emotion? The thought made his heart ache for some reason.

'You must have had a very good reason for coming to see me, Miss Williams, and I want to know what it was. Although maybe I could make an educated guess.'

'I don't know what you mean,' she said quickly, but he could see the fear that had darkened her eyes. 'I told you that I just wanted to meet you—'

'And it was a lie.'

He smiled sardonically when she fell silent, wondering why he couldn't seem to derive any pleasure from her discomfort. It felt on a par with pulling the wings off a butterfly to stand there and mock her, but he couldn't afford to weaken, wouldn't allow himself to forget what had driven him to come. He just had to think about Antonio and anything…*anything*…was justified!

'Please, don't insult my intelligence, Miss Williams. We

both know that you wanted something from me. Was it money that you were after, by any chance?'

He glanced around the room, fighting the feeling of sickness that was welling inside him because he knew his suspicions had been correct. She *had* come to see him to ask for money and the proof of that was the way she stood there without making any attempt to deny the accusation.

It was an effort to look at her again because he didn't think he had ever felt more angry than he did at that moment. 'Have you spent what Antonio left you already? Is that why you're working here when you should be living in the lap of luxury?'

He shook his head reprovingly, determined not to let her know how much it disturbed him to see her looking so shocked. Why should he care about her feelings when she'd cared so little about Antonio's? It didn't make sense.

'I'm not sure exactly how much my brother left you. Our parents put two hundred thousand pounds in a trust fund for Antonio, for when he reached the age of twenty-five. I doubt he had the time to spend very much of it before he died, so you must have received quite a considerable sum. Yet you have managed to spend it all in a few short months, apparently.'

He smiled thinly, wondering why she didn't try to justify her actions, although maybe she knew how pointless it would be to try and play on his sympathy. It might have worked in the past because he could understand that many men must have been taken in by her beauty. Even he was aware of it and could feel himself responding on a purely physical level.

No man could look at Rebecca Williams and not want her. Even though he despised everything she stood for, he could feel a stirring in his blood. Her delicate beauty and that air of vulnerability she projected was a potent mixture and he could understand how his brother had been fooled by it. However, that was where he and Antonio differed. *He* knew that beneath the beautiful outer shell was a woman who would stop at nothing to get what she wanted. And what she wanted most of all was money.

'I almost feel sorry for you, because I'm sure that working

for your living wasn't part of your plan.' His voice grated because the thought seemed to sear right through him. All she'd ever wanted from Antonio had been his money!

'Nevertheless, I'm very much afraid that I shall have to disappoint you even further because you won't get a penny out of me. I am not my brother. I am not as gullible as poor Antonio was!'

He brushed past her, feeling the tremor that coursed through his body when his arm brushed her shoulder. Revulsion, he told himself as he went to the door, simple revulsion—if anything to do with this woman could be classed as simple. He had no idea how she'd hoped to extract money from him, but he couldn't bear to question her further. Finding out more about Rebecca Williams's sordid life certainly wouldn't make him feel any better.

'Becky, can you come—? Oops, sorry. I didn't know you were busy.'

Felipe ground to a halt when a nurse suddenly appeared. He saw her look curiously at him before she turned to Rebecca and spoke more formally this time.

'Mr Watts is on his way. I thought I'd better warn you because he's in a rush. Something about having to go to Leeds to give a lecture this evening, or so Simon said.'

'Thank you, Karen. I'll be right there.'

Felipe flinched when she spoke, wondering what had caused that ripple to run through him. He shot her an uneasy glance over his shoulder but she wasn't looking at him. She took a stack of folders off the desk and went to the door, all the time avoiding eye contact with him.

She smiled as she handed the notes to the nurse, but Felipe could tell the effort it cost her to act as though nothing was wrong. All of a sudden, he wished that he hadn't come because he'd achieved nothing from his visit. He'd simply upset himself and upset Rebecca, too.

Oddly, that last thought was the most disturbing of all. Hurting Rebecca hadn't given him any satisfaction, as he'd hoped it would. It was an effort to hide his dismay when Rebecca addressed the other woman in a cool little voice that told him just how difficult she had found the past few minutes.

'Check that all the obs are up to date, will you, Karen? You know how Mr Watts hates it if everything isn't spot on.'

'Do I ever!' The nurse took the bundle then looked worriedly at Rebecca. 'You will be there when he arrives? I don't think I'm up to coping with one of his high-speed ward rounds.'

'Of course. Dr Valdez was just leaving so I won't be long.'

'*Valdez!* Oh, I didn't realise.' The young nurse laughed as she turned to him. 'What an idiot I am! I should have known the minute I saw you.'

She gave him a considering look. 'Yes, I can see the resemblance now, especially around the eyes. Josh has exactly the same colour eyes as you have. Isn't it amazing how something like eye colour can be passed on through a family?'

Felipe didn't know what to say. He knew that she was waiting for him to answer, but there was no way that he could have formed even the simplest sentence.

He turned to Rebecca and this time she was looking straight at him—staring at him, to be precise. Her eyes seemed to be riveted to his face and the expression in them made his heart race. He had never seen such fear in anyone's eyes before.

He heard the door close as the nurse hurriedly left, and almost laughed out loud. It was obvious that she was trying to be tactful because she'd sensed that she might have said something wrong, but it was far too late for that now. With a few unguarded words his life had been turned on its head.

'Who is Josh?'

He didn't realise the question had come from his lips at first because it hadn't sounded like his voice. It had sounded too strained, too raw, too full of emotion to be the voice of Felipe Valdez. He saw Rebecca swallow, watched her mouth open and struggled to concentrate because it was vitally important that he heard what she said.

'Josh is my son.'

She paused and he knew that he was holding his breath as he waited for her to continue. 'He's Antonio's son, too.'

Becky could feel her heart beating, but it felt as though time had suddenly come to a halt. Felipe was standing stock still and the expression of shock on his face would have made her laugh if there had been anything remotely funny about the situation.

She saw him swallow and tried to prepare herself for what he would ask her. He would be bound to have questions—dozens of them—and she needed to decide what to tell him. But it was hard to think when her brain felt as though it had seized up.

'My…my brother had a child…a son?'

Her heart ached with a sudden, fierce pain when she heard the bewilderment in his voice. For some reason she wanted to make this as easy as possible for him, even though she knew how dangerous it was to consider his feelings. One small slip, one unguarded word and the situation could spiral out of control.

'Yes. His name is Josh and he's nine months old,' she told him quietly. 'He looks very like Antonio and you, too, I suppose.'

She gave him a tentative smile, watching the rapid play of emotions that crossed his face as he struggled to make sense of what she was saying. 'He definitely has your colour eyes, as Karen just mentioned. Antonio's eyes were a lot darker.'

'Antonio took after our mother,' he said roughly. 'I favour my father's side of the family.'

'But there's still a strong resemblance between you both.' She felt her heart catch because until then she really hadn't been aware of the similarities between the two brothers. Now it scared her to realise how alike they were. The last thing she could afford was to look at Felipe and see Antonio. She had to remember that they were two very different people.

It was a relief when there was a knock on the door because she desperately needed some time to think about what had happened. She hurried to answer it, shaking her head when Debbie apologised for the interruption.

'It's fine, really. Don't worry. Has Mr Watts arrived?'

'Yes. Karen sent me to tell you.' Debbie shot a curious glance at Felipe then lowered her voice. 'He's none too pleased because you weren't there to meet him, I'm afraid, Becky.'

'I'll be straight there,' she assured her.

She closed the door then felt her heart skip a beat when she turned and found Felipe standing right behind her. He was so close that she could smell the tangy scent of his aftershave, feel the heat of his body, and all of a sudden it felt as though her senses were being swamped by him.

'I have to go,' she explained, quickly moving away. She went to the desk and picked up a pen, trying her best not to let him see how nervous she was all of a sudden. She had never felt like this around Antonio, never once felt so deeply aware of him as she was of his brother. The idea worried her for a moment until it struck her that it was because Antonio had never presented a threat to her, like Felipe did.

'I have to get back to work,' she said more calmly, relieved to have found such a simple explanation.

'But we need to talk, Rebecca. That is obvious. *Sí?*'

He had phrased it as a question, but Becky knew there wasn't the slightest chance that he would let her refuse. He wanted to know all about Josh, and who could blame him?

Finding out that he was an uncle had come as a shock to him, but it was what happened from here on that frightened her most. She was under no illusions as to how Felipe felt about her. He might be struggling to come to terms with what had happened at the moment, but it wouldn't be long before the implications of it hit him.

How would he feel about her being Josh's mother? Maybe he would have to accept it while he believed that Josh really was her child, but if the truth ever emerged it would be a very different story. There wasn't a doubt in her mind that Felipe would waste no time trying to remove her from his nephew's life.

She bit her lip as the irony of the situation struck her. A few days ago she had seen Felipe Valdez as her only hope to stop

Josh being taken away from her. Now he presented as big a threat as Tara did.

It was an effort to contain her panic, but she couldn't afford to give in to it. She carefully wiped all expression from her face when Felipe spoke.

'This is the address and telephone number of the hotel where I am staying. I shall expect you to call me as soon as you are free.' He took a notebook from his jacket pocket and wrote down the details then tore off the sheet and handed it to her. 'We need to arrange a time this evening when we can meet.'

'But I don't finish work until six,' she protested, knowing that she needed more time to work out what she should tell him.

'Six o'clock will be fine. I shall expect you to call me then. To be perfectly blunt, Miss Williams, I am not prepared to wait while you choose a time that is more convenient for you.'

He didn't say anything else before he left. Becky heard his footsteps echoing along the corridor and shuddered as reaction set in. She took a deep breath, but the feeling of panic was getting worse.

Maybe it was understandable that he should want to know all about his brother's child, but she didn't dare think about how difficult it was going to be, explaining everything to him. How much could she really afford to tell him?

It was an effort to put that thought out of her mind as she hurried into the ward. James Watts, the consultant in charge of the IC unit, was waiting by the door with his party, and he greeted her with noticeable coolness.

'Ah, there you are, Staff. Good of you to join us. If we're all here at last, shall we get started? I have to be in Sheffield by five, and the last thing I need are any more delays.'

Becky hastily apologised, feeling suitably rebuked. They went straight to Danny Epstein's bed and she handed James the boy's notes. Danny had been admitted a few days earlier with severe endocarditis—inflammation of the internal lining of the heart—and he was still giving them cause for concern. She waited by the bed while James read through the night staff's report in his usual thorough fashion. Although the consultant had brought several students with him that morning, as well as his two registrars, it was very quiet. Nobody dared to interrupt him or they would suffer the consequences.

Becky found her thoughts drifting back to what had happened in the office as the silence lengthened. What would be the best way to handle this coming meeting with Felipe? He was bound to have a lot of questions and she had to find a way to answer them without arousing his suspicions—

'We'll continue the high-dose antibiotics and hope that they'll clear things up eventually... Staff?'

She blinked as James Watts paused and peered at her over the top of his spectacles. A wash of colour ran up her face when she saw Simon Montague, the senior registrar, treat her to a conspiratorial grin. It must have been obvious to everyone that she hadn't been paying attention, and it alarmed her that she had allowed her own problems to intrude on her work.

'I'll mark that down on Danny's card,' she said, hurriedly thinking back over what the consultant had said. 'Is the cardio team planning on replacing the damaged heart valves soon?'

'Once we have the infection under control,' James replied shortly, making sure she knew that he didn't appreciate it when members of his staff failed to give him their undivided attention.

Becky breathed a sigh of relief when James turned to the students and began to outline the boy's case history. She'd got off pretty lightly, bearing in mind that she'd already provoked the consultant's wrath once that day.

'This young fellow caught an infection whilst having a tooth extracted,' James explained. He paused, the students hanging on his every word. 'Lo and behold, a few days later he came down with endocarditis. We know for certain that two of the valves have been damaged, but we shall have to wait and see how badly the rest have been affected.'

Becky gathered together the notes as the students exclaimed in amazement. They were in their first year at medical school and it was obvious they'd never realised that having a tooth out could be such a risky procedure. James had played up the dangers for dramatic effect, but at least it had helped to restore his good humour when his audience had responded as he'd hoped.

'OK, so what's wrong? You look as though you've got the weight of the world on your shoulders.' Simon hung back to talk to her as the others moved to the next bed.

Becky sighed inwardly when she saw the concern on his face. Simon was really nice and if it had been anything else worrying her she might have been tempted to unburden herself. However, there was no way that she could tell him what was wrong that day.

'Nothing's wrong. I'm fine,' she began, then looked round when James coughed. She flushed again when he treated her to another frosty stare.

'I *would* like to finish this round some time today, Staff. So if you and Dr Montague would be kind enough to join us, I shall be eternally grateful.'

'I'm sorry, sir,' she said, hurrying over to join him. She could tell that Simon hadn't believed her, but she decided that it would be simpler to let the subject drop. Although she wouldn't like to offend Simon, he really wasn't her priority at the moment.

She purposely drove all thoughts of Felipe Valdez out of her head while they completed the round then hurried to the office and busied herself with phoning through an order to the supplies department so that she could avoid having to speak to Simon again. He poked his head round the door and mouthed that he would catch her later then hurried away.

Becky sighed as she hung up. What *was* she going to do? Felipe now knew about Josh even though he wasn't in possession of all the facts. But exactly how much should she tell him?

It was impossible to answer that question because so much depended on what Felipe intended to do. However, it did make her see how foolish it would be not to phone him as soon as she got home from work. Felipe Valdez wasn't the kind of man who would simply disappear from her life because she wanted him to.

She frowned. Was that really what she wanted, though? Did she honestly wish that she would never have to see him again?

The answer should have been a resounding *yes*. Felipe was undoubtedly a threat to her and Josh, but her feelings towards him weren't as clear-cut as they should have been.

Felipe couldn't relax. For the past three hours he'd done nothing but pace his hotel room. Everything he'd learned kept whirling around inside his head and he couldn't make sense of it.

Antonio had had a child with Rebecca Williams. A son. Was it true? Or was it another one of her schemes, another lie to add to the web of deceit that surrounded her?

He sank onto a chair and picked up the phone then sat and stared at it. He knew the number of the hospital by heart, but should he phone her or wait until she phoned him? He had to decide what he intended to ask her first. If she still maintained that the child—Josh, she'd called him—was Antonio's son, surely he needed proof. Who knew how many men Rebecca Williams might have slept with? Any one of them could be the child's father...

Only he had a gut feeling that wasn't the case. Rebecca's son was also his brother's child, the only thing left on this earth that could provide a tangible link to Antonio. By heaven, he wasn't going to sit there and phone her or wait for her to contact him. He was going to see her again, and this time he intended to find out exactly what was going on.

A thin smile curved his mouth. He only hoped that Rebecca wouldn't try to lie to him because it would be a mistake.

Becky was late leaving the hospital because there had been a crisis when Danny Epstein had arrested. It had taken the combined efforts of the whole team to stabilise him and he had now been sent to Theatre to have two badly damaged heart valves replaced.

Whether he would survive the operation in his weakened state was in the lap of the gods, but it was his only chance and she applauded his parents' decision to take it. It wasn't easy being a parent, as she had discovered.

A smile tilted her lips as she hurried out of the main doors. She loved collecting Josh at the end of the day because he was always so happy to see her. The little boy had a wonderfully sunny nature, which had made him rather a pet of the child-minder who looked after him while she was at work. It was reassuring to know that he was being well cared for when she couldn't be with him.

'Miss Williams.'

She stopped dead when she recognised the voice that had called her name. She'd known that Felipe wouldn't rest until he'd got to the bottom of this situation, but she'd hoped to have a little more time before she spoke to him again. Now, when she turned and saw the uncompromising expression on his face, she felt her heart start to race.

Would she be able to stop him finding out that she wasn't Josh's real mother? Everything hinged on her doing that.

CHAPTER THREE

'I NEED to speak to you, Miss Williams. There's a bar across the road—maybe we can go there.'

'I can't.'

Felipe frowned when he heard the anxiety in Rebecca's voice. Although he understood how stressful this situation must be for her he couldn't understand why she sounded so scared.

Once again the idea that she might have been telling him a pack of lies about the child being Antonio's son filled his mind. After all, why hadn't Antonio written and told him that he'd become a father? Despite that row they'd had before Antonio had left Mallorca, his brother had never been the kind of person to harbour a grudge. There was something about this situation which didn't add up.

'Can't or won't?' he said tersely. 'I'm having a great deal of difficulty understanding what is going on, Miss Williams. A few hours ago you told me that you and my brother had had a son and now you refuse to talk to me about the child.'

Her lids lowered, effectively hiding her eyes from view. 'I'm not refusing to talk to you, Dr Valdez.' She shrugged, but he wasn't blind to the strain that was etched on her face when she glanced up. 'However, I thought we'd agreed that I would telephone you and arrange a time when we could meet.'

'We did, but I can see no reason why we cannot talk now and get this all sorted out.' He went to slide his hand under her elbow, but she stepped smartly out of reach.

'I've just told you that I can't talk to you now. I have to collect Josh. I'm late as it is because we had an emergency and the childminder will be wondering where I am.'

She started hurrying down the path, but if she thought that he was prepared to let her walk away, she was mistaken. Who knew what she might be planning? She claimed that she'd intended to phone him, but could he trust her? What if she took Josh and disappeared? How would he feel if his brother's only child was left in the care of a woman like her?

He strode after her, his long legs swiftly bringing him level with her. He saw her glance round, saw her pretty mouth compress, but she didn't say a word. They walked in silence down the path and across the busy London street. It was the middle of the rush hour and the traffic was horrendous, car after car belching out fumes.

He suddenly wished that he was back home in Mallorca, breathing in the fresh, salt-laden air as it blew in from the bay. Had Antonio really preferred to exchange all that beauty for this?

'Antonio used to love the rush hour. He spent a lot of time looking out of the window when…when he became too weak to go out.'

He heard the catch in her voice and felt his heart ache. He had tried many times to imagine how his brother must have felt, knowing that he was dying. Suddenly, he needed to know how Antonio had dealt with it.

'How was he toward the end?' He heard the roughness in his voice and knew that she had heard it, too, but, oddly, he didn't feel embarrassed. He cleared his throat, deeply disturbed by the thought. 'It must have been difficult for him to come to terms with the fact that he was dying.'

'I think by that time he had come to accept what was going to happen.' She smiled gently. 'He told me that he didn't want to waste his last few weeks on earth by feeling bitter. And, of course, having Josh helped tremendously. Knowing that a little bit of him would live on after his death gave him strength.'

'Did he see the child, then?' Felipe asked, keeping his gaze averted because he was deeply moved by what she had said. He wasn't embarrassed, but he was too private a person to feel completely comfortable about exposing his feelings.

The problem was that it was so hard to think about Antonio at the end of his life; he kept having flashbacks to when he'd been born. Felipe had been fifteen when his brother had arrived in the world. His parents had been shocked at first when they'd discovered they were having another child and delighted later when the baby had been born.

Antonio had brought great joy to his parent's lives, great joy to his own life as well. After their parents had been killed in a car accident when Antonio was ten, Felipe had willingly taken over the task of raising him.

He had done his best to guide Antonio, but maybe he'd been too strict. If he hadn't been so set on making Antonio do as he'd wanted him to, his brother might never have left Mallorca and certainly wouldn't have ended up having a child with Rebecca Williams. How strange it was the way everything had worked out.

'Oh, yes. Josh was born a few weeks before…well, before Antonio died. He was in a lot of pain by then and his medication had been increased because of it. He used to sleep most of the time, but once I brought Josh home from hospital Antonio refused to take more than the barest minimum of pain relief.'

He saw her dash her hand across her eyes and could hear how her voice had thickened with tears. 'He said that he didn't want to miss a single minute he had left with Josh. He used to hold him all day long. My one abiding memory of Antonio is seeing him sitting by the window, cradling his son in his arms.'

Her voice broke on a sob and it seemed the most natural thing in the world to take her in his arms and hold her while she cried. In his heart, Felipe knew that he was probably making a mistake, but he couldn't stop himself wanting to comfort her.

He drew her closer, amazed by the sense of helplessness he felt. He couldn't assuage her grief and for some reason it hurt to know that she was crying for his brother and that there wasn't a thing he could do about it.

He smoothed his hand over her hair, feeling the silky strands snagging against his palm. Her hair felt like gossamer, so light, so soft, so sensuous. He found himself staring at it in wonderment, watching the play of light and shadow as the pale gold strands rippled beneath his fingers. All of a sudden he wished that this moment could last for ever, that he could keep her here in his arms and never let her go. She would be safe then, because he would be able to protect her from any more pain.

A shiver ran through him and he stiffened, shocked that he should be thinking thoughts like that. This was Rebecca Williams in his arms, not some woman with whom he was thinking of having an affair. It was a relief when she abruptly stepped back so that he was forced to release her.

'I'm sorry. I didn't mean to do that,' she said softly, her voice quavering, although whether it was from embarrassment or pleasure at him having held her he couldn't decide.

He took a deep breath and deliberately rid himself of that foolish notion before it had a chance to take hold. Rebecca was wiping her eyes with a tissue and there was a strangely touching dignity about the way she stood up straighter once she had finished.

All of a sudden it struck him that she possessed certain qualities he had never expected, and it worried him to realise that he might have misjudged her when he'd been so sure that he knew everything that he needed to know. Was Rebecca really the scheming, self-serving woman he'd believed her to be? Or had he been wrong about her?

Suddenly, it seemed equally important that he find out the answer to those questions, too.

Becky took a deep breath, but she felt such a fool for breaking down. She shot a wary glance at Felipe but, surprisingly, there was no sign of the contempt which she had expected to see on his face.

Her heart gave a painful lurch as she recalled how good it had felt when he'd held her in his arms. His body had felt so strong as he'd cradled her against him. She'd had an overwhelming urge to lean on him and keep on leaning. The past year had been so hard and it would be wonderful to be able to share this burden...

But dangerous.

What would Felipe do if he found out the truth about Josh? Antonio had signed a document appointing her as the child's legal guardian, and had got Tara to sign it, too, but would it hold up in a court of law?

That had been her fear all along, that her claim on Josh might be overruled. Antonio's solicitor had warned them that there was always a chance of that happening, that nothing—not even a legal document—was guaranteed in this kind of a situation.

That was why she'd panicked when Tara had threatened her, yet the thought that, unwittingly, she might have put herself and Josh in even more danger filled her with dread. No matter how wonderful it had felt to have him comfort her, she had to remember that Felipe was her enemy.

'I don't usually go to pieces like that,' she said stiffly. She didn't want to think of him as her enemy, although she wasn't sure why. She felt a ripple of alarm scurry through her when she saw his eyes suddenly narrow.

'I don't imagine that you usually find yourself in a position like this, Miss Williams, so, please, don't apologise. Unfortunately, we cannot always predict how we will react.'

She wasn't sure what he had meant by that, and frowned. Was Felipe admitting that he had reacted strangely by taking her in his arms and trying to comfort her perhaps?

Now she thought about it, it was a strange thing for him to have done. Maybe she had difficulty thinking of him as her enemy, but surely he didn't have any problems with the idea? And yet he had held her with such tenderness, such gentleness that it hadn't felt as though he hated her.

The thought bothered her probably more than it should have done. She tried to put it out of her head as she started walking again, trying to quell the noisy beating of her heart when he immediately followed her. It was obvious that he didn't intend to let her out of his sight, so she decided that it would be best if she accepted that. There was no point trying to fight the inevitable when she might need her strength for more important battles.

The traffic congestion eased after a little while. This part of

London was in a state of limbo, she always thought, not quite fashionable but not totally run-down. However, from the look of disdain on Felipe's handsome face as he studied the long row of Victorian terraced houses, it could have been a slum.

He frowned when she stopped outside one of the houses and rang the bell. 'This is where my brother's son spends his days? Surely you could have found somewhere more suitable, a nursery where he would be properly cared for?'

'Josh is very happy here,' she said shortly, stung by the criticism. 'Doreen—that's the childminder—is marvellous with all the children; she loves them as if they were her own. Anyway, I can't afford a nursery place for him. It costs a fortune in London to put a child into a private nursery.'

She realised her mistake the moment she saw his mouth thin into that tight line she was starting to recognise only too well. She was already preparing herself for the next onslaught before he spoke, but nothing could stem the quiver that ran through her when she heard the biting contempt in his voice.

'But my brother left you a considerable sum, didn't he? You were named in his will as the sole beneficiary of his estate. *Sí?*'

'Yes.' She rang the bell a second time, praying that Doreen would answer it soon. She didn't know how she could explain what had happened to the money Antonio had left without giving everything away.

Tara had received most of it as her final payment for having Josh. The little bit that had been left over had been swallowed up by bills in the first few months when she'd been unable to work because she had been looking after the baby. She could account for every single penny if she had to, but it would mean her admitting that she wasn't Josh's real mother and that was something she desperately wanted to avoid.

'So was it too much to expect that you might spend some of that money on making sure that Antonio's son was properly cared for? Did it never cross your mind that you had no right to spend it all on yourself?'

She could hear the anger in his voice and her heart ran wild

as she struggled to explain without telling him the truth. 'There
were expenses—'

'Expenses? Come, Miss Williams, you must have been enjoying a very lavish lifestyle if you managed to spend all that
money in less than a year!' he shot back, glaring at her.

'It wasn't like that. You don't understand,' she said desperately, hurt beyond belief by the way he was looking at her. 'I
didn't spend—'

The door suddenly opened and she stopped when Doreen
appeared, holding Josh. Becky automatically reached out and
took the child as he lunged towards her. She snuggled him
close, breathing in his wonderful baby smell while she tried to
calm down.

If Doreen hadn't opened the door then she would have
blurted it all out and told him that nearly every penny of
Antonio's inheritance had gone on buying his son. How would
Felipe feel about that? Would he blame her for what had happened because it had been her idea?

Felipe felt his anger disappear the moment he looked at the
baby in Rebecca's arms.

The little boy was the image of Antonio!

From his shiny black curls to his chubby little feet, he was
a miniature replica of his father. In that instant any doubts he'd
had about the child's parentage disappeared. This was
Antonio's son, his own flesh and blood.

He wasn't aware of what he was doing as he held out his
arms. The little boy gurgled happily as Rebecca silently handed
him over. He could feel the weight of the child's sturdy little
body in his arms and had to make a conscious effort not to
hold him too tightly.

He wanted to press him to his heart and keep him there,
pretend, even if it was only for a moment, that he had Antonio
back and that he could keep him safe from harm. It was all he
had ever wanted to do and he had failed, but he wouldn't fail
this child, his brother's son.

It was a moment which Felipe knew he would remember all
his life, a moment of such pain and such joy that he found it

hard to comprehend what he was feeling. It was as though all of a sudden a key had turned and the door to his heart had been flung wide open. It was a relief when the baby suddenly grabbed a handful of his hair and tugged it hard, because he wasn't used to dealing with so much emotion.

A smile tugged at the corners of Felipe's mouth as he gently unfurled the baby's fingers. 'I shall have no hair left if you keep that up, young man,' he told him in Spanish. 'Your uncle will be bald.'

'He's a devil for pulling your hair,' Becky said softly. 'It's a wonder I'm not bald as well the way he tugs my hair.'

Felipe's black brows rose in surprise. 'You speak Spanish?'

'Yes. I'm not very fluent, but I can get by.' She gave him a sad little smile that made his heart ache all over again. 'Antonio offered to give me Spanish lessons in exchange for a favour I did him. That's how we became friends.'

She looked at the baby and sighed. 'I've tried to keep it up so that I can teach Josh when he's old enough. It seemed important that he should be able to speak his father's language.'

Felipe was deeply moved, so much so that he didn't dare show how much it had affected him. He passed the baby back to her, trying to put what he had learned into context. It was probably just some wonderful story that she had dreamed up to impress him...

Only he didn't believe that.

He went back down the steps while she had a final word with the childminder. It was obvious that the woman was asking who he was, but he didn't feel inclined to join in the conversation. He needed to clear his mind so that he could focus on what he intended to do.

Josh was Antonio's son. There wasn't any doubt in his mind about that. Obviously, he would need to take that into account before he made any decisions.

He took a deep breath but the tension that had been building inside him all day was suddenly worse than ever. Rebecca was the child's mother. He would need to take account of that as well.

Doreen had been intrigued to learn that Felipe was Josh's uncle. Becky kept trying to edge away but the woman kept asking her more questions. Becky glanced over her shoulder and sighed when she saw Felipe standing by the kerb.

It was obvious that he was impatient to leave, even though he was making an effort not to show it. However, the number of times Felipe had needed to wait for anyone had to be few and far between. He was the kind of man who was accustomed to people jumping to obey his every command.

The thought was a little disquieting, but Becky refused to let him see how on edge she felt as she finally took her leave of the childminder. Josh was gurgling away, trying to tell her what he had done during the day. They usually played a game on the way home: she asked him questions about his day and pretended she understood what he was saying to her. However, that day she felt far too self-conscious with Felipe being there. It would hardly improve his opinion of her to know that she held in-depth conversations with a nine-month-old baby!

'What happens now? Do you usually take Josh straight home?'

She jumped when he spoke, wondering why she should be the least bit worried about what he thought of her. Felipe's views on her as a person had been expounded in graphic detail the day before and she doubted if anything would improve his opinion.

It was a painful thought so she focused on the question instead because it was easier. 'Yes. He's had his supper at Doreen's so he just needs a bath and a cuddle, then it will be time for him to go to bed.'

'It appears that you spend very little time with him. Surely it can't be good for a child this young to spend so much time away from his mother?'

She shrugged, not wanting him to guess that the thought had troubled her often during the past few months. 'He seems perfectly happy. And I need to work.'

'Because of the money?'

'Yes,' she snapped, disliking his tone. It hurt to know that he believed she was capable of such massive self-indulgence but, short of telling him the truth about the money, there was nothing she could do.

She quickened her pace, not bothering to check if he was keeping up as they made their way along the street. She lived just a short walk away from the childminder's house so it took them barely five minutes to reach her flat. She stopped on the step, juggling a wriggling Josh in her arms while she hunted her key out of her bag.

'I'll take him.'

Felipe lifted the baby out of her arms without giving her a chance to reply. Becky's mouth thinned because it seemed yet another example of his high-handed attitude. What made it worse was the fact that Josh was obviously delighted to have his uncle holding him.

The baby's chuckles accompanied them as they made their way up the three flights of stairs to the top floor. She rented the attic flat and had always felt quite proud of the fact that she'd transformed a rather dingy space into a place of colour and light. Now, as she slid her key into the lock, she found herself wondering what Felipe would think of her home. Recalling the elegance of the Clinica Valdez, she doubted if his opinion would be all that favourable.

'Put Josh in his play-pen,' she instructed as she let them into the tiny hall. She tossed her bag onto the small table she'd spent so much time lovingly restoring and slipped off her coat. 'It's through there, in the sitting-room.'

Felipe didn't say anything as he carried the child into the adjoining room. Becky hung her coat on a peg then followed him. She paused in the doorway and watched him looking around, wondering what he would think of the place.

She'd worked so hard scraping the walls to get rid of the hideous paper the previous tenants had hung, but she'd been really pleased with the results. At this time of the day, when the evening sun was streaming in through the skylight, the whole room seemed to glow, the rich, golden yellow paint she had chosen for the walls reflecting the light.

The furniture was a mismatched assortment bought from the local flea market, but she'd spent hours polishing the scratches out of the coffee-table and sewing new mossy-green covers for the old sofa.

An area rug in faded green and gold—another flea-market find—made a small oasis in the centre of the floor and set off the richness of the polished wooden floorboards. She had done everything she could to make a pleasant home for herself and Josh, but would Felipe realise how much effort and love she'd put into it?

'This is charming. The colour of the walls, the sun-light…everything.' He smiled and she felt instantly warmed when she saw the approval in his eyes.

'Thank you,' she said softly, looking around. 'I wanted it to be a real home for Josh, so it seemed worth it.'

'Ah, I see. You had someone to decorate for you?' He shot another assessing look around the room. 'I should have realised. No wonder you have managed to spend so much money. It is extremely costly, hiring a good interior designer. *Sí?*'

'No! I didn't hire anyone. I did it all myself. I meant that it had been worth all the effort!'

She took a deep breath when she saw Josh's lower lip start to wobble when he heard her raised voice. It wasn't fair to upset him because Felipe was set on believing the worst about her. 'I suggest we stick to what needs to be said, Dr Valdez. Trying to be polite to one another is pointless.'

'Of course. I am in full agreement with you, Rebecca.'

He carefully put Josh into the play-pen and handed him some soft plastic blocks before he looked at her again. 'I hope you don't mind if I call you Rebecca. After all, we are virtually family so it seems silly to continue being so formal. And you must call me Felipe, of course.'

'My friends call me Becky,' she said automatically. She looked up when he laughed, feeling her stomach churn when she saw the disdain on his face.

'I doubt if you and I will ever be friends, Rebecca. I think that is asking too much of both of us.'

He pinned her with a cool stare that seemed to draw out what little warmth she had in her body. 'I am prepared to tolerate you purely and simply because you are the mother of my brother's child. And for Antonio's sake I am also prepared to treat you with a degree of civility. However, given the choice, I would have nothing whatsoever to do with you. Is that clear?'

'Perfectly clear, Felipe,' she replied, praying that he couldn't hear the hurt in her voice.

Becky turned away, fighting to control the rush of tears that threatened her. She wouldn't break down again. She wouldn't give him the satisfaction of knowing that he'd hurt her. And yet there was something in his voice when he continued that told her he had guessed and that it wasn't satisfaction he was feeling, oddly enough. It threw her into total confusion to hear that note of regret in his voice so that it was a moment before she realised what he had said.

'When *we* go to Mallorca? What do you mean?' she demanded incredulously.

'It is quite simple, Rebecca. Antonio's son should be brought up in the country of his father's birth. He deserves better than the life you can give him here. That is why you and Josh will be moving to Mallorca as soon as I can make all the necessary arrangements.'

He smiled sardonically when she gasped. 'And as an inducement, which I know you won't be able to resist, I am prepared to give you however much money you want. How much were you planning on asking me for when you came to see me yesterday?'

'Twenty thousand pounds,' she murmured, unable to lie because she was so shocked. He couldn't honestly believe that she would agree to uproot herself and Josh and move to another country to live. It was ridiculous.

'So little?' His black brows rose steeply. 'I expected you to demand a much larger sum than that, but if you are happy with that amount then so be it. However, I must warn you, Rebecca, that this will be the one and only time that I shall give you any money. From now on you will need to earn your living.'

'Earn my living,' she repeated dully. She took a deep breath, hoping it would clear her head. Everything seemed to be whirling around so that it was difficult to think. 'I do that already. I earn my living by working at the hospital.'

'*Claro que sí!* Of course, and how fortunate that you have such marketable skills at your disposal.' Felipe smiled and she shivered when she saw the chill in his brown eyes.

'There will be a job waiting for you at the Clinica Valdez as soon as you move to Mallorca. How well everything is working out for you, Rebecca. *Sí?*'

CHAPTER FOUR

FELIPE held his smile but it was an effort. Rebecca was staring at him and it was obvious how shocked she was. It didn't make him feel good to know that he was responsible for that expression of horror on her face so that it was a relief when Josh suddenly started to wail.

Bending, he lifted the child out of the play-pen and handed him to her. 'Perhaps he is tired.'

'Yes.'

Her voice was so low that he had difficulty hearing the single word, but he refused to let himself dwell on how upset she appeared to be. He had to remember that this woman was capable of anything if it meant that she could get her own way. Hadn't she deceived Antonio, tricked him into leaving her all that money, hastened his death by encouraging him to refuse further treatment?

Anger rose swiftly inside him, but he managed to curb it in case he frightened the child. The baby was the innocent victim of Rebecca's scheming and he wouldn't do anything to harm Josh, although that didn't mean he wouldn't get to the bottom of what had gone on. Something told him that there was still a lot about this situation that he hadn't been told.

Felipe sat down on the sofa as Rebecca carried the baby from the room. The sun was streaming through the skylight and he closed his eyes as he settled back against the cushions. He could hear the murmur of her voice as she spoke to the baby, the sound of water running as she filled the bath. They were such ordinary, everyday sounds and yet they filled him with a sense of unreality. He had never imagined when he had got on the plane that morning that this would happen.

He got up, suddenly too on edge to sit still. He prowled

around the room, picking up a book from the coffee-table and putting it down again, taking an ornament off the shelf then replacing it. His hand brushed against a photograph which had been propped against a small glass vase, and he sighed when it fell to the floor.

He picked it up and felt his heart ache when he realised that it was a picture of Antonio holding Josh. If Rebecca hadn't told him that story about how his brother had loved to sit holding the baby, he might not have recognised Antonio. He was a doctor and he'd seen the devastation that cancer could cause many times, but it was hard to believe that this gaunt-faced man was the brother whom he had loved and cared for most of his adult life.

'That was taken two days before he died.'

He looked round when he realised that Rebecca had come back into the room. He felt so choked with emotion that it was impossible to reply, and she seemed to understand that. A frisson raced through him because he had never imagined that a woman like her would be capable of such sensitivity.

'I always think Antonio looks so peaceful in that photo. That's why I like to keep it where I can see it.'

She came and stood beside him and he could smell the scent of baby soap and talc that clung to her skin. Reaching out, she ran her finger over the picture and there was something almost heartbreakingly sad about the way she let it linger on his brother's smiling face.

'It's his smile, I think. He looks like a man who's been given the one thing he wanted most.'

Felipe cleared his throat but it was an effort to rid his voice of all the emotion he could feel welling inside him. 'You mean Josh?'

'Yes. Having Josh was the most important thing that could have happened to Antonio. It made everything else bearable.'

He heard the fervour in her voice and frowned. It was obviously important to her that he should believe that, and he couldn't understand why. He'd accepted that the thought of the baby had helped Antonio through those last, difficult days so why did Rebecca feel it was necessary to stress that to him?

Once again he had the feeling that there was a lot he didn't understand, but he also knew that he would have to bide his time. She would only tell him what she wanted him to know. Maybe it would help if he tried to win her confidence, although the thought wasn't wholly a comfortable one. Becoming the confidant of this woman wasn't a role he'd planned on playing.

'Did you look after Antonio or did he have someone else to take care of him?' he said, deliberately keeping his tone free from any hint of criticism.

It was something which had bothered him many times; he had lain awake wondering if Antonio had been well cared for after he'd left hospital.

'Both. I took care of his day-to-day needs—washing, feeding and so on—and the hospital arranged for the Macmillan nurses to visit him each day. They were absolutely marvellous. They are specialist nurses who deal with the care of the terminally ill and they were able to adjust Antonio's drugs regime as and when necessary.'

She moved away and sat on the sofa, tilting back her head and closing her eyes just as Felipe had done a short time before. The comparison made his skin prickle, as though it had forged a bond between them.

He cleared his throat again, deeply disturbed by the idea that he and Rebecca might have anything in common. 'If Antonio had been persuaded to stay in hospital, he would not have needed to be treated by them.'

'No, he wouldn't.' A smile curled her mouth, although she didn't open her eyes. 'I lost count of the number of times I tried explaining that to him, but he wouldn't listen. And in the end he was proved right.'

'Right? How can you say that?' Anger flowed through him and he glared at her even though she couldn't see his expression. 'My brother might have lived another six months if he'd remained in hospital!'

'Yes, he might have done. But you're a doctor and you must

have some experience of dealing with patients with terminal cancer. There comes a point when the decision has to be made either to prolong life or to try and improve its quality.'

Her eyes suddenly opened and Felipe was surprised when he saw the assurance they held. 'Antonio refused to undergo any more treatment because it made him feel so ill. He thought it all through and weighed up what he was doing. His consultant had told him that there was no possibility of them curing him— they were simply trying to buy him extra time. He decided that he preferred quality to quantity.'

It made sense. In the logical part of his mind, Felipe knew that, but he couldn't and wouldn't accept that *she* hadn't been the one to influence his brother for her own ends.

'And the fact that Antonio's decision fitted in so perfectly with your plans was just a bonus?' he said acidly.

'I didn't try to influence Antonio in any way,' she stated, and there was something about her calmness and lack of emotion that made it impossible to dispute what she had said.

Felipe felt his head whirl as once again he was forced to reassess his opinion of her. Rebecca hadn't persuaded Antonio to refuse treatment. The decision had been his brother's. Was it the shock of realising that which filled him with such relief?

He pushed that thought to the back of his mind as Rebecca got up and went to the old-fashioned bureau by the door. Opening one of the drawers, she took out a wad of photographs and handed them to him.

'These are all of Antonio, taken shortly after he found out about Josh right up till the week he died.' She gave a husky laugh. 'He used to groan every time I appeared with the camera, but it seemed important that Josh should have some idea what his father looked like in years to come.'

Felipe sat down because his legs suddenly felt too weak to hold him. He flicked through the pictures then went back to the beginning and studied them more slowly. He could see the deterioration in his brother's appearance as the months had passed, and yet the one thing that struck him was that even though his health had been failing, Antonio had looked increasingly serene.

'Did he not feel bitter about what was happening?' he asked, staring at the pictures one after the other.

'Oh, yes, at first he did. He was very bitter—and angry, too. Who wouldn't be? He was twenty-five and going to die.' She sighed. 'We spent night after night talking it all through, trying to make sense of it, but you can't rationalise something like that, can you? In the end, Antonio realised that himself.'

'Was he working at the time—when he found out that he was ill, I mean?' he asked, wondering if he would have had the strength of mind to cope. It shook him that his brother— the brother he had always taken care of—had dealt with his illness with such equanimity because Felipe himself wasn't sure if he could have managed that.

'Yes, and he continued working right up until a couple of months before he died.'

She came and sat beside him on the sofa and he felt a tremor run through his body when she leant over to look at the photographs. All of a sudden he was so deeply aware of her that he could barely breathe. He could feel the warmth of her arm next to his, the slight pressure of her hip as she settled herself more comfortably on the seat. He had to make a conscious effort to drag some air into his lungs, yet he still felt strangely breathless after he had done so.

'He worked as a session musician at one of the clubs not far from here. He played guitar, as you know, and a couple of nights they gave him a solo spot when Tara wasn't singing.'

'Tara?' he queried automatically, forcing himself to concentrate when she carried on speaking. He felt a sharp stab of pain spear him. It grieved him to realise how far apart he and Antonio had drifted. He'd had no idea that his brother had been earning his living through his music. It had been Antonio's dream, of course, the only thing he had ever wanted to do and the cause of that dreadful argument they'd had.

Antonio had wanted to be a musician and he had tried to persuade him to choose a different career, something that would be more lucrative and stable. How very pointless it all seemed now.

Felipe looked up when he realised that Rebecca hadn't answered, and felt his heart turn over when he saw the expression on her face. He couldn't recall ever seeing anyone who looked as stricken as she did at that moment.

He took another deep breath but his voice sounded strained when it emerged. Maybe he was mistaken, but he had a gut feeling that her answer might hold the key to what had really gone on.

'Who is Tara? And what was her relationship to my brother?'

Becky could feel her pulse racing. She couldn't believe she had allowed Tara's name to slip out!

She summoned a smile but she knew how difficult it was going to be to extricate herself from this mess. Felipe was obviously suspicious and she had to be extremely careful what she said.

'Tara Lewis. She sings at the club where Antonio worked. Antonio went out with her for a time when he first arrived in London.' She shrugged. 'We met after he and Tara had split up so that's all I can tell you, I'm afraid.'

She stood up, gathering together the photographs to give herself a breathing space, but her heart was racing. Had Felipe believed her?

She shot him a wary glance and bit her lip when she saw the frown on his handsome face. Although there was a strong resemblance between him and Antonio, it was far more difficult to tell what Felipe was thinking. She took rapid stock of the thin-lipped, oddly sensual mouth, the long straight nose with its slightly flaring nostrils and the angular cheekbones in the hope that it might help if she took note of the similarities between the two men.

There definitely was a strong family likeness, although Felipe's features were more austere than Antonio's. His hair was just as thick and black as Antonio's had been when she'd met him, but whereas Antonio had worn his long, Felipe's was cut very short, the crisp strands lying neatly against his well-shaped head.

Once again that day he was wearing a suit, and again the fine black cloth was tailored to perfection. His white shirt looked as fresh as when he must have put it on that morning and his burgundy silk tie was perfectly knotted.

Antonio hadn't even possessed a suit to her knowledge. She certainly hadn't seen him wearing one. Jeans and a shirt had been his usual attire and she couldn't remember him ever wearing anything else.

His style had been casual, easygoing, a world removed from the sophisticated face Felipe presented to the world. Maybe she should take that as a warning. It would be a mistake to underestimate what Felipe was capable of by comparing him to his brother.

'How long exactly were you and my brother together?'

Becky started nervously when he spoke and some of the photographs shot out of her hands and fell onto the floor. Bending, she scooped them into a pile then jumped again when Felipe handed her one that had slid under the sofa.

'Thank you,' she said quietly, walking to the bureau. She placed the photos back in the drawer then turned to face him, praying that he couldn't tell how difficult this was for her. It would be so easy to make another slip. The last thing she wanted was for him to start adding everything up and working out that she couldn't possibly be Josh's mother.

'I really can't see where this is leading. What difference does it make how long Antonio and I were together? We had Josh, didn't we?'

'So you did, and that should tell me everything I need to know.'

He stood up abruptly and she had to physically stop herself backing away when he came towards her. 'After all, it's the child who is my main concern now, my brother's son. It is his future I intend to focus on.'

'Of course. But what you said about us moving to Mallorca…well, you do realise that it is out of the question?'

She summoned a smile but the way he was looking at her wasn't reassuring. 'My life is here in England and I have no intention of uprooting myself and Josh.'

'I don't see that you have any choice, Rebecca, not if you want to keep your son.'

'What do you mean?' she demanded, feeling the blood starting to drum in her temples again.

'Simply that I'm sure, with the right lawyers at my disposal, I could make a very good case if I decided to sue for custody of the child.'

He smiled but there wasn't a hint of warmth in his eyes as they skimmed her face. 'Once I point out to the judge that you only had the baby so that it would give you a certain…*leverage* over my brother then I'm sure he would find in my favour.

'You had Josh purely and simply for the money, didn't you, Rebecca? It's taken a little time for everything to slot into place, but I know that I'm right. Antonio bought himself a son. It's as simple as that.'

Felipe watched the guilty colour sweep up her face and knew that he was right. Rebecca had had the baby as a means to extract money from his brother.

It was an effort to hide his disgust but he knew that it would be giving her an advantage if he let her see how much it had upset him to finally learn the truth. He had to pretend that it made no difference, but he knew in his heart that it did.

He felt deeply and bitterly disappointed, and the fact that he could feel such an emotion about this woman dismayed him. He'd known all along what she was like, so why should he feel upset because he had been proved right?

Suddenly, he knew that he couldn't take any more. He turned and strode to the door, barely pausing when she called out 'Wait!' in a quavery little voice. He turned to look at her, steeling himself when he saw the total absence of colour in her face.

'Yes?'

'What do you intend to do…about Josh, I mean?'

'That depends on what you decide to do, Rebecca.' He

shrugged, striving for a nonchalance he wished he felt. 'I am not prepared to leave my brother's son here in England with you. It's as simple as that.'

'But I have a job here, a home, friends,' she protested.

'You will have a job and a home in Mallorca. As for friends—well, that will be up to you, of course. Although, naturally, I would take a poor view of you becoming involved with anyone unsuitable. It might be best if you concentrated on being a mother for a while and forgot about your love life.'

He saw her open her mouth then shut it again, and found himself wondering what she'd been going to say before she had thought better of it. Had she been about to claim to him that her only concern *was* her child?

Felipe felt a bitter laugh welling inside him and turned so that Rebecca couldn't see his expression. Women like her were magnets to men, and it wouldn't be long before she found someone else to take Antonio's place, if she hadn't already done so, of course.

The thought stung far more than it should, but he gave no sign of it as he walked along the hall. He let himself out of the flat and in deference to the sleeping child didn't slam the door behind him as he felt like doing. The encounter had left a sour taste in his mouth, a feeling of heaviness in his heart. As he strode down the stairs Felipe inwardly cursed.

Damn Rebecca Williams and her scheming and conniving, her trickery and treachery. Damn her for being everything he had thought she would be, and worse!

Becky heard the door closing and only then did she let herself breathe. Her lungs were burning from the lack of oxygen but Felipe's accusation had stolen her ability to perform such a rudimentary task. He had been right in a way and yet so horribly wrong that it was the bitterest kind of irony. It hadn't been her who had sold her baby but Tara!

She made herself take another deep breath in the hope that it would ease the pain she felt. Maybe it was silly to get upset, but it hurt to know that he believed her capable of such a dreadful thing. However, Felipe's views on her really weren't the most pressing issue at the moment. She had to decide what she intended to do.

The choice appeared to be perfectly simple—she could agree to Felipe's demands and move to Mallorca with Josh, and by so doing she had would obtain the money she needed to pay Tara, or she could refuse and end up with nothing. She didn't doubt that Tara would carry out her threat to take her to court—and even if she didn't, Felipe would.

A bitter smile curled her mouth. It didn't seem like much of a choice after all.

'What did you say?'

'I said that I'm moving to Mallorca at the end of the month.' Becky summoned a smile but it was hard to maintain an outward show of happiness when her heart felt like lead.

She had spent a sleepless night, trying to find another solution to her problems, but the answer kept coming out the same no matter which way she approached it. If she moved to Mallorca she would be able to pay off Tara. It would also mean that she could get Josh out of London because she wasn't foolish enough to believe that Tara wouldn't demand more money at some point in the future. Moving to Mallorca would solve that problem, although it was bound to create others.

Her heart lurched at the thought of what Felipe might do if he found out the truth—that she wasn't Josh's real mother—but she couldn't worry about that now. She had to deal with this a step at a time, and the first step was to inform her colleagues of her decision, as she was in the process of doing.

'I don't know what to say… I mean it's all rather sudden, isn't it, Becky?' Simon Montague's pleasant face filled with concern. They were in the staff canteen, having their lunch, and he leant forward so that the people at the next table couldn't hear him. 'You're not in any kind of trouble, are you?'

'Of course not! Why on earth do you think that?' She tried to laugh but it sounded too forced to be convincing and she saw Simon frown.

'Because nobody makes a rush decision like this about their

future.' He shook his head when she went to speak. 'No, don't, Becky. I can tell you're going to deny it, but I know I'm right. Karen told me about Josh's uncle turning up yesterday and how upset you appeared to be. Has this anything to do with him?'

'No, of course not,' she began, then sighed when she saw the look he gave her. 'Well, yes, I suppose it has. Felipe told me that he would like to spend more time with Josh,' she explained, skating over the facts to make them more palatable. 'It was his idea that we should move to Mallorca and I just thought it would be good for all of us.'

'He could fly over here and see him,' Simon said bluntly. 'It only takes three hours so it's not as though he would need to travel from one side of the globe to the other. It takes me longer when I go up to Scotland to visit my family.'

'I know,' she agreed, wishing that she'd given a bit more thought to what she intended to tell everyone. 'But it wouldn't be the same as seeing Josh on a daily basis, would it? You know how fast children grow up and—'

'And I've never heard such a cock-and-bull story in my life!' Simon's face was almost as red as his hair as he leant across the table and gripped her hand. 'This guy, Valdez, is putting pressure on you, isn't he, Becky? What's he threatening to do, try and get custody of Josh? He sounds very possessive.'

Becky shivered. She couldn't help wondering if Simon was right. Did Felipe feel possessive about Josh? The fact that the baby was his nephew was bound to create a tie between them, but might he feel that it was his duty to take over the role Antonio would have played in the little boy's life? Did Felipe see himself as a substitute father perhaps?

The thought was deeply disquieting because it made her see just how tenuous her position was. If Felipe ever found out that she wasn't Josh's real mother, he could order her out of the child's life. The thought of the little boy growing up without her was more than she could bear and tears filled her eyes.

'Oh, hell! I didn't mean to scare you, Becky. Take no notice of me. There isn't a court in the world who would take a child away from its mother and hand him over to a total stranger.'

Simon grimaced as he gave her fingers a reassuring squeeze. 'I'm just letting my imagination run away with me because it was such a shock to hear that you'll be leaving. I'm really going to miss you, you know?'

'And I'm going to miss you, too, Simon, really I am.' She dashed the tears from her eyes and summoned a smile. The urge to tell him the whole sorry story was very strong, but she knew in her heart that she couldn't burden him with it. Simon was a good friend, but it wouldn't be fair to expect him to solve her problems.

'Who's going to make sure I get my daily ration of chocolate biscuits?' she teased, with an attempt at levity.

'Cupboard love! So that's it. Here I was thinking that you found me irresistible and all you're really after is the bickies I keep bringing you.' He rolled his eyes comically, but she wasn't blind to the disappointment they held. 'It's the story of my life!'

'I can't help it if I have a sweet tooth.'

Becky swallowed a sigh because she couldn't help wishing that her life was less complicated. If it had been, there would be nothing to stop her going out with Simon. He had asked her often enough, but she had always found some excuse to turn him down. She was fond of him but not really attracted to him. She had always been more attracted to dark-haired men like Antonio...

She bit her lip as an image sprang to mind, because it wasn't Antonio's face she had conjured up but Felipe's. It was as though Felipe had suddenly supplanted Antonio in her thoughts. The idea made her tremble and she saw Simon look at her in alarm.

'Are you OK?'

'Fine. Just a bit worn out with everything that's been happening recently.'

'It can't have been an easy decision to make, Becky. I don't think I'd fancy just upping and leaving as you're planning on doing, but, then, I don't have a child to consider.' He gave her a quick smile. 'You're doing this for Josh, aren't you?'

'Yes.' She took a steadying breath. It would serve no purpose to worry about why she had thought of Felipe instead of Antonio when there were more important matters to consider.

'I believe this is the right thing for Josh,' she said firmly, trying to inject a degree of certainty into her voice. It obviously worked because Simon nodded in agreement.

'Then I hope it works out for you, Becky, really I do.'

'Thank you,' she said, touched by his obvious sincerity.

They changed the subject after that, but it had helped her put everything into perspective. Even though she didn't like the idea of moving to Mallorca and being forced to live in such close to proximity to Felipe, it would mean that Josh would be safe. Tara wouldn't be able to find them there and she would no longer have to worry about her threats.

Simon had to leave shortly afterwards so Becky finished her lunch and went out onto the terrace for a few minutes before she returned to the ward. It was a particularly clear day and the view over the city was superb. She could see Big Ben and the Houses of Parliament, and the silvery curve of the London Eye shimmering in the sunshine.

She had lived in London for most of her adult life and was used to the sights, but that day she saw them with a fresh eye. Soon there would be new sights to see, a new way of life to get used to. It would be a big change when she moved to Mallorca but she would cope. She really would. For Josh's sake she would make the adjustment.

Maybe Felipe believed that he had forced her hand but it no longer felt that way. The decision was hers, not his, and as long as she stopped him finding out the truth about Josh, she could continue making decisions about the child's future. Felipe Valdez was the baby's uncle, not his father. As long as he understood what his role was, they should get along fine.

The view suddenly swam before her eyes. *Should*, not would, because there weren't any guarantees.

CHAPTER FIVE

FELIPE was feeling decidedly out of sorts by the time lunchtime arrived. He phoned room service and ordered a plate of sandwiches and a pot of coffee because he knew that he should eat something. He'd spent a sleepless night going over everything that had happened, examining each and every word Rebecca had said, but he still couldn't rid himself of the nagging feeling that he was missing something.

He went to the window, resting his head tiredly against the glass as he looked out. His room overlooked one of the parks and he could see dozens of people taking advantage of the fine weather. The triple glazing meant that there was no sound coming into the room from outside and it added a sense of unreality to the scene to be able to watch people talking and not hear what they were saying.

He turned away from the view, suddenly impatient with himself. He should be thinking about what Rebecca intended to do instead of worrying about the conversations of a bunch of strangers. Would she agree to his demands to move to Mallorca, or would she refuse?

It would be marvellous to think that he had the power to make her do what he wanted, but the truth was that he didn't. It was the uncertainty that was causing him such anguish, the fear that he might not be able to do anything for Antonio's son after all. He didn't think he could bear it if he failed in this, as he had failed to look after his brother.

The phone suddenly rang and he hurried towards it then cursed when at the same moment there was a knock on the door. Snatching the receiver from its rest, he rapped out, *'Un momento, por favor!'* Then went to let in the waiter who had brought his lunch.

Felipe tipped the man, and probably too generously from the expression of delight on his face, as he hurriedly left. But money was the least of his concerns even though it could be the deciding factor for Rebecca. If her need for money was great enough, surely she would do as he wanted?

His mouth thinned as he picked up the receiver again. She had used Antonio's child as a commercial venture and it sickened him to know that she was capable of such a thing. It was little wonder that he felt his stomach churn when he recognised her voice on the other end of the line, he told himself. It certainly couldn't be pleasure that had caused it to react like that.

'It's Rebecca. I wonder if I could have a word with you tonight after work?'

'Of course,' he agreed, deliberately removing any trace of emotion from his voice because he didn't want her to guess there was anything wrong. He couldn't explain it, but he felt that it would give her an advantage to know that she possessed this power to upset him. 'What time would be convenient for you?'

'Straight after I leave work would be best. I should finish around six so maybe I could meet you in that bar you mentioned yesterday.'

He heard her take a quick breath and had a sudden, vivid image of her at the other end of the phone line. There would be a tiny frown on her face as she waited to hear what he would say, a hint of uncertainty in her huge grey eyes as she stood there, wondering if he would agree...

He drove the image from his mind, but it unnerved him just how quickly he had managed to conjure up a picture of her. 'That will be fine. Six o'clock it is.'

'Thank you. I...I promise that I won't keep you very long.'

She put down the phone without saying anything else, and after a moment Felipe hung up as well. He went and poured himself a cup of coffee, but all the time he was doing so he kept hearing her voice inside his head, and the hairs on his arms pricked as he recalled its sweetness. All of a sudden, he knew that he couldn't wait for the allotted time to arrive when he would see her again, and the thought scared him because he couldn't afford to feel like this where she was concerned.

Rebecca Williams was a scheming, mercenary gold-digger. He made himself repeat the litany, but it seemed to have lost its power for some reason. They were just words now, words that didn't seem to mean very much.

'Let's drop the head of the bed and see if we can get her pressure back up.'

Becky glanced round, immediately taking note of the panic on Debbie Rothwell's face. It was obvious that the trainee wasn't coping well with this latest emergency so she decided that it would be best if she got her out of the way.

'Debbie, go to the office and ask the switchboard to page James Watts. I don't like the look of what's happening and I think we need him here stat.'

Debbie made no attempt to hide her relief as she hurried away. Becky sighed as she turned back to the patient. It was becoming increasingly obvious that Debbie didn't have what it took to work in the IC unit. It wasn't always easy to maintain one's composure, but it was vital when faced with an emergency such as the one they had to deal with at the moment.

The patient, an eight-year-old girl called Rosie Stokes, had been transferred to the unit from a hospital in their catchment area a short time before. Rosie had been involved in a car crash on her way to school that morning and had suffered a serious head injury. She'd needed an operation to relieve the pressure on her brain but, according to the notes that accompanied her, everything had gone according to plan.

Now, however, she was showing signs of shock and acute kidney failure, and Becky couldn't understand what had gone wrong. The child should have been closely monitored from the time she'd left Theatre to prevent something like this happening.

There had been no bed available in the IC unit that morning, which was why Rosie had been kept at the other hospital until one had become free that afternoon. But even without IC care, there were basic procedures that should have been carried out.

'How many mils of urine has she passed since she was admitted?' she asked, glancing at Karen.

Karen checked the plastic bag at the end of the child's bed and shook her head. 'Zero. The bag's empty.'

'This can't just have happened!' Becky exclaimed, checking the monitor readings. Rosie's blood pressure was still falling so she quickly adjusted the drip. 'Even with acute kidney failure there are warning signs, so why weren't they picked up before? How long has she been here now?'

Karen checked the admission notes. 'Less than an hour. She was logged in at ten minutes past four. She had been catheterised prior to her op. I checked her bag and assumed they must have changed it before they transferred her to us. It's only a ten-minute drive from St Ada's after all. But now I'm wondering if that really was the case.'

'From the look of things I'd say that there's been no urine output for some time,' Becky observed worriedly. 'I'll order a blood test to check her levels of urea and creatinine. That will tell us if her kidneys have completely shut down. Heaven knows what's caused it to happen because everything was going smoothly, according to her notes.'

'Could it be internal bleeding?' Karen suggested. 'Something they didn't pick up on earlier.'

'It could, but they should have given her a full examination when she was admitted,' she said bluntly.

'I've heard rumours about St Ada's,' Karen said darkly. 'The word is that the standards there have dropped dramatically of late.'

'It used to be a marvellous hospital, too.' Becky sighed as she set about drawing off the small sample of blood. It saddened her to think that the child's life might have been put at risk because of inadequate nursing care. She couldn't help wondering how she would feel if it were Josh lying in the bed. She would want him to have the very best treatment possible, and resolved to do all she could to help poor Rosie through thi crisis.

She quickly sealed the vial and labelled it with the patient' details, checking the child's notes to make sure that she ha her date of birth correct. Her eye was caught by a note on th top of the page stating that Rosie's blood group was A-positiv and her heart sank in dismay.

'Here, grab hold of this.' She thrust the vial into Karen' hands and hurried around the bed to check the unit of bloo that was being drip-fed into the girl's arm. It was clearly la belled as B-positive, not A.

'She's been given the wrong blood,' she said, quickly clos ing the valve in the line. 'That's why her kidneys have faile and she's in shock.'

'Hell's teeth!' Karen exclaimed. 'How on earth did a thin like that happen?'

'Heaven knows,' Becky replied, rapidly detaching the ba from the cannula in the child's arm. She glanced round whe she heard footsteps and grimaced when she saw that Jame Watts had arrived. 'But somehow I don't think that answer i going to satisfy the boss when he finds out. He's going to b furious.'

'Furious and determined to get to the bottom of this.' Kare sighed as she looked at the clock. 'And to think I was hopin that we might get away on time tonight for once. Fat chanc of that happening now!'

Neither of them said anything else because James Watts ha reached them by then. As Becky drew the consultant aside an explained what had happened, she couldn't help wonderin what Felipe would think when she didn't turn up for their mee ing. One thing was certain: it wouldn't be anything favourabl So far as Felipe was concerned there was absolutely nothin about her that met with his approval.

It was odd how much that thought hurt.

Felipe checked his watch again. He'd arrived a good te minutes before the time they had arranged to meet, but it wa now almost seven and there was still no sign of Rebecca. He had just made up his mind to leave if she didn't show up in the next five minutes when she came rushing through the door.

'I'm *so* sorry!' she apologised, hurrying to his table. 'We had an emergency and Mr Watts wanted to hear all the ins and outs, and he can be so pedantic at times! I must have told him a hundred times that it had nothing whatsoever to do with us and that it was the staff at St Ada's he needed to speak to, but he's the sort of person who needs everything written out in triplicate...'

She suddenly stopped and he was intrigued to see a wash of colour flow up her face. 'You really don't want to hear all this, do you? I'm sorry that you had to wait, but it was unavoidable, I'm afraid.'

Felipe smiled, wondering why he felt a need to reassure her. Just for a moment Rebecca had forgotten that he was her enemy and had spoken to him without her usual reserve. It had been an intriguing insight into her as a person and he had to admit that his curiosity had been piqued.

'There is nothing to apologise for. I know only too well the pitfalls involved with the career we have chosen.'

He shrugged, watching the rapid play of emotions that crossed her face. She was obviously trying to decide if she could take what he'd said at face value, and he realised how much he wanted her to believe him. He didn't want her to think of him purely as her enemy, funnily enough.

The thought slid into his mind too quickly to stop it so he chose to ignore it instead. Standing, he politely drew out a chair for her to sit down and frowned when she shook her head.

'Look, I'm sorry to be a nuisance but I really can't stay,' she explained. 'I have to collect Josh because he'll be wondering where I am.' She half turned to leave then paused, and he saw her take a quick breath. He knew that she was steeling herself to say something else and the muscles in his stomach clenched in anticipation.

'Would you like to come with me? I know I suggested that

we meet here and it would have been easier if we'd been able to talk on our own, but…'

'Yes.'

He pushed back his chair, seeing her start of surprise at his easy acquiescence. Frankly, he was rather surprised himself because it wasn't like him to change his plans.

He suddenly found himself thinking that he must try to be a little more flexible in the future. He had to learn how to adapt to this situation, although perhaps that wasn't the most reassuring of thoughts in relation to Rebecca Williams. Exactly how adaptable did he intend to be?

'Of course I would like to come with you,' he said politely, refusing to think too hard about such a facile question.

'Oh, well, good. That solves that problem, then,' she said brightly, but he could see that the flush in her cheeks had deepened.

Felipe allowed himself a small smile as he followed her to the door. It was obvious that Rebecca was surprised by the way he'd acted and it was encouraging to know that he was still able to disconcert her. In the past few hours, he'd had the uncomfortable feeling that the balance of power had shifted in her favour and it was a relief to see that he'd been wrong. He needed to control this area of his life as much as the rest of it.

They had just reached the door when a red-haired man came into the bar. Felipe saw Rebecca stiffen as they all stopped. Instinctively, he put his hand under her elbow and he saw the man look at him before he turned to Rebecca and smiled.

'Fancy seeing you here, Becky. I didn't realise this was one of your haunts.'

'It isn't. I'd arranged to meet Felipe here, but it ended up with me being late,' she said quickly.

Felipe saw her glance nervously at him and frowned. It was obvious that Rebecca was uncomfortable about the encounter, but why? Who was this man?

'Aren't you going to introduce me, Rebecca?' he said smoothly.

'Yes, of course.' She sounded flustered as she set about mak-

ing the introductions. 'Felipe, this is Simon Montague, the senior registrar on the IC unit. Simon, this is Josh's uncle, Dr
Felipe Valdez.'

'Oh, I see. That explains it.' Montague smiled but Felipe
could see the hostility in his eyes. 'You're the guy who's trying
to persuade Becky to move to Mallorca. Do you really believe
that it's in her best interests to leave everything she knows and
move to a place where she has no friends?'

'I imagine that is for Rebecca to decide,' Felipe said calmly,
trying not to let the younger man see that he was annoyed.

No wonder she was on edge! She had obviously discussed
her plans with Montague but it was the reason why she had
done so that infuriated him. Had she sounded him out to see
if he could come up with a better idea perhaps? After all, if
Montague could come up with the money she needed, what
reason was there to uproot herself? The truth was that there
were always options for a woman like her, always another man
gullible enough to help her.

The thought angered him even more but he refused to let
either of them see how he felt. He turned to Rebecca and
smiled, but maybe he wasn't as adept at hiding his feelings as
he'd thought, he realised when he saw her frown. It was obvious that she had sensed something was wrong and it bothered
him to know that she'd picked up on his mood so easily.

'We should go. Josh will be wondering where you are,' he
told her, deliberately blanking out that thought because it
wouldn't help.

'Of course.' She gave him the ghost of a smile before she
turned to Simon Montague, and Felipe had to steel himself not
to react when he heard the entreaty in her voice. 'I'll catch up
with you tomorrow, Simon. Promise. Take care, now.'

'You, too, my sweet.'

Montague gave him another hard stare before they left, but
Felipe ignored him. He still had hold of Rebecca's arm but he
released her as soon as they were outside. The meeting had left
him with a bad taste in his mouth and a feeling of dissatisfac-
tion which he knew was a dangerous indulgence.

So what if Rebecca *was* looking for ways and means to avoid having to do as he wanted her to? What if she *was* trying to keep Montague sweet in the hope that he would help her? Surely it was only what he would have expected of her?

'All right, you may as well tell me what's wrong.' She stopped and glared at him, giving him no choice but to stop as well.

Felipe glanced round, feeling uncomfortable when he saw people staring at them. Rebecca had both hands placed on her slender hips and it must have been obvious to anyone who was passing that she was furiously angry.

'I have no idea what you are talking about,' he said shortly.

'Rubbish! That's just a cop-out because you either don't want to or can't answer the question.'

Her grey eyes shot sparks at him. 'You might be able to fool most people with that ice-man routine, but you don't fool me! Something has upset you and I want to know what it is, although why I am even asking is beyond me. Just the fact that I'm still breathing is probably your worst nightmare, isn't it?'

He saw tears well into her eyes as she turned and began hurrying along the street. He went after her, his long legs quickly making up the distance. He put his hand on her arm to stop her, feeling a ripple of raw awareness shoot through him. It was as though he could suddenly *feel* her pain. He had an overwhelming urge to take her in his arms and comfort her, promise that he would never do anything else to hurt her. Maybe they could find some way to compromise. He didn't want to keep fighting with her...

He took a deep breath as Rebecca shrugged off his hand and carried on walking. He felt quite sick as he realised how foolish he was being. How could he ever compromise? How could he ever forget what she'd done? She deserved everything that happened to her because she had brought it all on herself!

Oddly enough, it didn't make him feel better to realise that. By the time they'd collected Josh and arrived at her flat, he was beginning to feel like the lowest form of pond life.

Rebecca hadn't said a word to him all the way home. She'd totally ignored him as she'd chatted to the baby.

Felipe wasn't used to being ignored and it irked him that she seemed able to blank him out like that. He stood to one side while she juggled the baby and the key before opening the front door. It was clear that any offer of help would be rejected.

He followed her up the three flights of stairs and went into the sitting-room when she disappeared into the bathroom with Josh. What made him feel even worse was that it was all done in a silence that said far more than any amount of angry words.

He sank onto the sofa and closed his eyes. He had known all along that Rebecca had the power to manipulate men. He just hadn't realised that he would be as susceptible as all the rest.

'And here comes another bubble... Pop!'

Becky smiled when Josh chortled with laughter. He was obviously enjoying the fact that she'd let him stay in the bath far longer than normal. He was usually tucked up in his cot by now, but the extra playtime had given her a chance to calm down.

It was silly to get upset but it had been obvious what Felipe had been thinking when they'd met Simon. He believed that Simon was the latest in a long string of men who had come and gone in her life. He wouldn't believe her if she told him the truth, that there were no men in her life, so why get upset? She needed a clear head when she laid down the rules that would have to be met before she agreed to move to Mallorca.

'You will both be waterlogged soon. Do you usually let him play for so long?'

She felt her heart bounce against her ribs when she looked round and saw Felipe standing in the doorway. There was a faint smile on his mouth and a softness about his eyes which she hadn't seen before. She found herself thinking how wonderful it would be to have him look at her that way all the time before common sense reasserted itself. Any softening in his attitude was because of Josh, not because of anything she had done.

'Not usually,' she said coolly, trying her best not to let him see how much that thought had upset her. 'I thought he deserved a little treat tonight—didn't you, poppet?'

She went to kiss the top of Josh's damp head and gasped when he suddenly slammed both chubby little fists into the water. A wave of soap suds lapped over the side of the bath and landed in her lap.

Felipe laughed throatily when he saw what had happened. 'It is truly amazing how much mess one small child can make, *sí?*'

'It is.' Becky grabbed a towel from the rack and mopped at her skirt, but the water had soaked right through it. Tossing the towel aside, she pulled a face at the little boy.

'You're a monster, Joshua Valdez! I'm going to splash you back for doing that.'

She gently patted the water and sent a soapy wave cascading over the baby's tummy, much to his delight. He rapidly beat his hands up and down in the water to show his appreciation. Becky groaned as another little tidal wave slopped over the side of the bath and once again landed on her. 'Well, I've only got myself to blame, I suppose.'

'Would you like me to stay here and watch him while you change into some dry clothes?'

She stared at him. 'You?'

A little colour ran up Felipe's cheeks when he heard the surprise in her voice. 'I think I am capable of looking after him for a short while. I assure you that I know all about the dangers of leaving a young child unattended in the bath, so you can trust me not to wander off.'

'I didn't mean that you weren't capable. I just meant that it doesn't really seem your sort of thing.' She shrugged, wishing that she'd simply refused the offer rather than try to explain how she felt about it. 'I mean, how often have you ever bathed a baby?'

'Ah, now, let me see.' He stared at the ceiling and there was an expression of such intense concentration on his face that she found herself holding her breath.

'Twice, I think. Yes, that's right, although I have to confess that one time it wasn't a real baby.'

'Not a real baby?' she parroted, feeling her heart perform the most peculiar manoeuvre when he suddenly smiled at her. It felt as though it had performed a full three-hundred-and-sixty-degree turn, which was a physiological impossibility. However, even knowing that didn't negate the effect it had had so it was an effort to concentrate when he continued.

'No. It was a doll, you see, a very ugly, very pink, rubber doll called Esmeralda.'

His lips twitched when he saw her eyes widen but his voice remained perfectly composed. 'I grew very fond of that doll, in fact. I was quite sad when the time came for us to go our separate ways.'

Becky opened her mouth then shut it again because she wasn't sure what to say in response to such an admission. The thought of Felipe 'growing fond' of a pink, rubber doll was rather too much to take in.

She stared at him, hoping that he would tell her more, wondering why she should want to hear it. Why on earth should she be interested in a crazy story like this? And yet she knew that she was.

He gave her another one of those highly unsettling smiles but this time she was prepared and her heart only managed half a turn not a full one.

'My first job after I qualified was in a maternity unit. I do not wish to be unkind but the sister there was an absolute dragon—there is no other word I can think of to describe her.'

Felipe laughed softly when her mouth twitched. 'I can tell that you understand what I mean, Rebecca. Everything had to be done according to her rules and heaven help any member of staff—nurses or doctors—who failed to meet her exacting standards.'

'I've worked with a few like that over the years,' she admitted. 'So go on, tell me about the doll.'

He leant against the side of the bath, smiling as he watched Josh happily splashing. 'It was one of Sister's strictest rules that everyone who worked in her ward must know how to bathe and dress a baby as well as feed and change it. She didn't trust us with any of her precious babies, of course, so she had purchased the doll especially for this purpose. I shall never forget the sight of grown men sweating as they struggled to put a nappy onto that bundle of pink plastic.'

Becky burst out laughing. 'Oh, I can just picture it! What a wonderful story, Felipe. It's one of those tales that gets better every time you tell it, isn't it?'

'I wouldn't know. It is the first time I have ever told anyone the story.' He shrugged but she saw the uncertainty that had clouded his beautiful eyes. 'I am not sure why I told you just now, to be honest.'

'To convince me that you are capable of looking after Josh for a few minutes,' she said quickly, because she didn't want him to start regretting what he had done.

She stood up, trying to hide how touched she felt because he had chosen to tell her that tale when he had told nobody else. Had he been afraid that people would laugh *at* him and not *with* him if he had told them? she wondered.

She sensed it was so and it just served to make her feel even more confused that he should have confided in her when he'd made no secret of the fact that he didn't like her.

'Right, now that I know you're fully qualified to care for babies, I'll leave you in charge while I find something dry to wear,' she said, adopting a deliberately bright tone because she didn't want him to suspect anything was wrong. 'Just don't blame me if you end up regretting your impulsive offer. This little horror is a dab hand with the water!'

'So I can see.' He smiled, but she could tell that he was still rather puzzled by what he'd done.

Becky headed for the door, knowing that it was pointless dwelling on it. She was just about to leave him to it when a thought suddenly occurred to her and she paused to look back. 'You said that you'd bathed two babies. You've explained about Esmeralda, but what about the other baby? Was it a real one?'

'Oh, yes, it was real.'

He took off his jacket and rolled up his shirtsleeves before he crouched beside the bath. Becky saw him scoop up a handful of water and watched as he let it dribble through his fingers onto Josh's tummy. She wasn't sure how she knew what he was going to say, but all of a sudden her heart began to ache.

'I helped my mother bath Antonio when she brought him home from hospital. He was just three days old and like most fifteen-year-old boys I had never touched a child so small before.'

He looked up and there was a world of pain in his eyes when he looked at her. 'I made a promise on that day that I would always take care of him, but I failed. I wasn't there when he needed me most.'

Becky didn't know what to say. Anything sounded trite in the face of his grief. All the anger she'd felt about the way he had behaved towards her suddenly seemed self-indulgent. Felipe was tormenting himself because he hadn't been able to do anything to help his brother, and yet he had nothing to blame himself for.

She took a deep breath but there was only one thing she could say that might comfort him. 'You're here now and that's what matters. Antonio would be so pleased to know that you're going to take care of his son.'

She didn't wait to hear what he might say as she quickly left the room. She went into her bedroom and sat on the bed, feeling the fear uncoiling inside her. She had just given Felipe permission to play a central role in Josh's life. Although she knew it had been the right thing to do, it still scared her. The more she involved him in Josh's life, the greater the risk that the truth would slip out.

She bit her lip but the facts had to be faced. She could end up losing this precious child if she cared too much about his uncle's feelings.

CHAPTER SIX

JOSH was getting restless so Felipe pulled out the plug and let the water drain away. Reaching for a towel, he swaddled the baby in it and lifted him out of the bath. There was a changing table against one wall so he laid him down on it.

Josh regarded him with big solemn eyes while his uncle carefully dried him. He didn't seem at all alarmed about being looked after by a stranger, but maybe he had grown used to being handled by different people. Maybe Rebecca had entrusted him to the care of other men who had accompanied her home?

Felipe shut off that thought because it felt wrong to think it. She had been both kind and generous in what she'd said to him, and it didn't feel right to repay her by allowing such thoughts into his head. There was a stack of disposable nappies on a nearby shelf so he helped himself to one and placed it on the table. However, it proved to be incredibly difficult to get the baby into it when he kept squirming about.

Bending, he gave the little boy a mock-ferocious stare. 'We can do this the easy way or the hard way, young man, so which is it to be?'

Josh chortled as he grabbed hold of Felipe's nose and tugged it hard. Felipe winced as he gently unfurled the tiny fingers. 'Mmm, I see. You prefer the hard way, do you?'

Gently grasping the baby's ankles in one hand, he cautiously raised Josh's bottom a fraction so that he could slide the nappy under him. It had been a long time since those lessons with Esmeralda but it worked a treat. He smiled victoriously as he lowered the wriggling baby into position.

'See. All it takes is a little co-operation, *pequeño*.'

He quickly folded over the sections of the nappy and stuck

down the tapes to hold it in place. There was a pile of clean baby clothes on the shelf as well so he selected a pale blue sleepsuit and set about getting Josh into it.

He couldn't help thinking how organised everything was—nappies and clean clothes readily to hand, baby wipes and talcum powder placed where they could easily be reached. It surprised him that Rebecca was so methodical because it didn't jell with the image he had of her. He found himself looking for some small anomaly, something missing, but as far as he could tell she had thought of everything. The only slightly odd thing was that none of the baby things looked really new.

Felipe frowned as he took another look around. He hadn't noticed it before, but all of a sudden he realised that everything, from the changing mat the baby was lying on to the sleepsuit he was wearing, looked as though it had been purchased second-hand. Although everything was spotlessly clean, the signs of wear and tear were clear to see now that he was looking for them. The pattern on the mat was faded in places and the sleepsuit had a neat little darn in its heel.

He felt a wave of anger suddenly surface. What the hell was going on? Why was his nephew wearing second-hand clothes when Antonio had left all that money?

'Oh, you didn't need to dress him. That was kind of you.'

He spun round when he heard Rebecca's voice. In a fast sweep his eyes skimmed over her, searching for evidence of her perfidy. If she hadn't spent the money on Josh, she must have spent it on herself.

It was the only logical explanation but, try as he may, he couldn't find anything to back it up. Nothing she was wearing looked new or expensive, from the worn denim jeans with their frayed hems to the faded lemon sweatshirt with its baggy neckline.

His gaze moved to her feet in the hope that she might be wearing designer shoes because at least that would help to solve the puzzle. But her feet were bare, the pale skin so translucent that he could see her veins showing through it.

His heart gave the oddest little lurch before he made himself remember that he was supposed to be finding some clue as to what she had done with the money, not letting himself get sidetracked by the sight of her small feet. He deliberately let his eyes track back up her body, but not even a second, more thorough viewing solved the problem.

Her skin was bare of make-up so he could rule out costly cosmetics, and her blonde hair was too natural-looking to be the product of frequent visits to an expensive salon. Even her jewellery was nothing more than a schoolgirlish wristwatch with a worn leather strap. Everything about her appearance hinted at someone who was frugal with money, and it didn't make sense.

If Rebecca hadn't spent Antonio's money on the baby or herself, what had she spent it on?

'Want me to take him? He just needs his bottle then I can put him down for the night…'

Becky trailed off as she became aware of the silence. She felt a shiver work its way down her spine when she saw the way Felipe was staring at her. She wet her lips but it was an effort to ask the question when she knew in her heart that she wasn't going to like the answer.

'Is something wrong?'

'You tell me.' He gave her a slow smile, a world removed from the one he'd given her when he had related that story about the doll.

Becky felt her heart shrivel as though he had just stamped on it, but she tried not to let him see how much it had hurt that he could treat her this way again. Maybe it was foolish, but she'd hoped that they might have got past the point where they each needed to keep scoring points off each other.

'It's a little difficult when I don't know what's going on,' she said stiffly.

'Then maybe it would help if I explained the problem I am having understanding this situation.' He looked pointedly around the bathroom. 'Antonio left you a lot of money—'

'Not that again! For heaven's sake, how many more times do I need to tell you that I never asked him to leave it to me?'

She cuddled Josh to her when she felt him stiffen. He'd sensed she was angry and she didn't want to upset him. However, it was hard not to react when Felipe had seen fit to raise the subject of the money again.

'It was Antonio's decision,' she said more quietly. 'It had nothing whatsoever to do with me.'

'I am not disputing that,' he said calmly, matching his tone to hers. 'My problem is understanding what you spent it on. You mentioned expenses when I asked you the last time, so I can only assume you meant things like clothes and equipment for the baby, maybe some things for yourself, *sí*?'

'Um…yes, that's right.'

She edged towards the door, suddenly uneasy about the direction in which the conversation was heading. She needed some time to work out what she should say, only Felipe obviously didn't intend to wait for an answer. He stepped in front of the door, effectively barring her exit.

'So where are all these expensive things that you bought, Rebecca? Do you have them tucked away in a cupboard somewhere? Do you just get them out on special occasions?'

He flicked a dismissive glance at the changing table with its faded mat, the pile of clean baby clothes, her own outfit, and she willed herself not to give in to the panic she could feel building inside her.

'Nothing I can see in here looks expensive. If I'm not mistaken, most of it has been bought second-hand. So tell me what you spent all that money on, Rebecca, because I want to know.'

Becky took a deep breath but her heart was racing. How on earth could she explain without telling him the truth, that it had all gone to Tara?

Tara's demands had started the moment she'd agreed not to have an abortion. As well as the initial payment of fifty thousand pounds and the monthly allowance she had received, there had been credit-card bills to be paid, plus payments on a flashy little sports car that Tara had bought. And, as if all that wasn't enough, she had visited Antonio on a number of occasions and asked him for more money to buy baby clothes and equipment.

Tara had claimed that even though she wasn't going to keep the baby, she felt it was only right that she should get everything ready for its arrival.

Becky had had her suspicions that very little of it would be spent on the child, although she hadn't said anything to Antonio. He had been far too ill to deal with Tara's lies. It had only been after Josh's birth that she'd discovered that Tara hadn't spent a penny on the child. There had been no clothes, no cot, no pram—nothing. Instead, Becky had been forced to withdraw the last of her savings to buy what was needed.

By that time all that had been left in Antonio's bank account had been Tara's final payment, and she hadn't dared dip into that. Antonio had given Becky power of attorney over his finances and affairs once he became too ill to manage them himself. He'd never realised how much money Tara had taken, and Becky had been careful not to tell him. It would have upset him too much to know that there would be nothing left for her and Josh when he died.

She hadn't been able to afford to buy anything new for the baby so she'd bought everything second-hand and had spent hours washing and scrubbing to make sure it was all fit for Antonio's precious son.

Antonio had never noticed that, but Felipe had. Now she had to think up an explanation that would satisfy him, even if it meant that his opinion of her ended up worse than before.

'It's very expensive, living in London,' she said, deliberately blanking out that last thought because it was the one that hurt most of all. 'Rent is extortionate even in an area like this. Don't forget there were many months when I couldn't work.'

'So Antonio supported you? Fine, but I still cannot understand how in the months since Josh was born you managed to spend so much money and yet have so little to show for it.'

'There were other bills to be paid as well as rent,' she protested. 'Gas, electric, food...'

'*Claro que sí!* Of course! But you must have been living a very lavish lifestyle if you spent all those thousands of pounds on food and heating.'

Becky bit her lip. It was obvious that he didn't believe her and who could blame him? The figures simply didn't add up. But the thought of him digging deeper and uncovering the truth was more than she could bear. There wasn't a doubt in her mind that Felipe would find some way to dispense with her if he discovered that she wasn't Josh's real mother.

'I...I had debts,' she whispered, hating the fact that she was going to have to lie to him. How ironic it was that not only had she taken over Tara's role as Josh's mother but she would have to assume the other woman's lifestyle as well.

'Debts?' He frowned, his black brows drawing together as he stared at her. 'Do you mean that you had bought things that you could not pay for?'

'Yes. It's not easy to manage on a nurse's salary and things...well, things got out of hand. There were credit-card bills to pay and loan payments on a car... All sorts of things.'

She swallowed the knot in her throat, wondering if he would believe her. Surely he must realise that she wasn't the kind of person who bought herself luxuries that she couldn't afford?

'I see. That explains it, then,' he said flatly, and she felt her heart ache when she heard the disdain in his voice. He *had* believed her and even though she knew that she should feel relieved, it hurt to know what kind of an opinion he had of her.

Felipe stepped aside without another word and Becky hurried to the kitchen. She took a bottle of baby milk from the fridge and quickly warmed it. Josh was starting to grizzle because he was tired, but he soon settled down when she took him into the bedroom and sat on the low nursing chair to feed him.

She watched his eyelids droop as he greedily drank the milk, one small hand rhythmically patting the bottle. He was content and happy, secure in his little world with people who loved him.

She would do everything it took to keep him safe, but she wished with all her heart that she could have done things differently. If she'd had a choice she wouldn't have lied to Felipe and be sitting here now, feeling so wretched. Instead, she would have told him the truth about Tara and Josh, and Antonio and the money.

She knew what she would have liked to have done, but it was too risky. Felipe might not understand that she had only ever wanted to help.

Felipe could feel his head starting to ache as he waited for Rebecca to come back. He massaged his temples, praying that he wasn't about to have one of his infrequent migraine attacks. The past two days had been a strain and his body was reacting to the pressure he had been under. However, the flashpoint had been Rebecca's confession and how it had made him feel.

He didn't believe her. It was as simple as that. Rebecca had claimed that she'd spent the money Antonio had left her, paying off her debts, but she'd lied. Why had she chosen to make herself look even worse in his eyes rather than tell him the truth? Was it because the truth would be even more unacceptable?

He swore softly, giving vent to his frustration in a rare outburst which would have shocked his colleagues had they witnessed it. He knew that the people he worked with considered him to be a very cold fish and that his reputation was well deserved. Nevertheless, it was hard to keep his emotions in check right then.

His opinion of Rebecca had improved dramatically after the compassionate way she'd spoken to him earlier, but now he didn't know what to think. Why had she lied to him? What dreadful secret was she keeping? Why did it scare him to death to realise that it had to be something really bad?

An aura of colour suddenly started to shimmer at the outer edges of his vision and he groaned when he realised that it was a migraine attack starting. It had been years since he'd had the last one and he couldn't believe his bad luck that it should happen now. He glanced round as Rebecca came back into the room, but it was difficult to focus on her.

'Josh is asleep,' she said quietly, coming into the room and witching on the lamps. She shot him an uncertain look when e put his hand over his eyes to protect them from the light. Are you all right?'

'Fine,' he snapped, hating to show any sign of weakness in ont of her when he already felt so vulnerable.

His feelings towards Rebecca had shifted and he was no onger sure that he could be totally dispassionate about this tuation. He knew that he should focus solely on doing what as right for Josh, but he couldn't ignore Rebecca's feelings. mattered to him if she was hurt or scared and afraid. If only e would tell him the truth, maybe there was something he ould do to help her...

'You don't look it,' she said bluntly, bending to turn off the mp nearest to him.

'Do not concern yourself about me, Rebecca,' he said rusquely, struggling to deal with that idea. Why did he want help her when he should be trying to make her tell him the uth?

It was almost a relief when whirling circles of colour started inning before his eyes and drove the question from his head. he migraine attack was rapidly getting worse and he groaned hen he felt his stomach churn in an all-too-familiar prelude the next stage. He rose awkwardly to his feet, deeply emarrassed about what was happening, although there was nothg he could do. The attack had to run its course before he ould feel any better.

'Here. Let me help you.' She put her arm around his waist nd helped him to the bathroom, lifting the lid on the lavatory nce she'd propped him against the wall.

'Give me a shout if you need me. I'll just be outside,' she iid, briskly making her exit and sparing him the indignity of aving her watch him throwing up.

Felipe sluiced his face afterwards, feeling a little better deite his embarrassment. He had been fortunate in the past and ad always had a few minutes' warning before an attack had ruck, but this one had come out of the blue. It didn't make im feel good to know that Rebecca had witnessed it, but there

was nothing more than kindly concern on her face when h
finally left the bathroom.

'How do you feel now? A bit better, I hope?'

She slid her arm around his waist again, ignoring his mu
mured protest that he could manage. Felipe held himself rig
as she helped him back to the living-room. She was so peti
that he was afraid of hurting her if he leant too heavily on he
yet when he tried to set some distance between them she tigh
ened her hold on him.

A shiver ran through him when he felt her fingers grippin
his waist. He hadn't put his jacket back on after bathing Jos
and he could feel the warmth of her hand through the thinne
of his shirt. Her hand was so small, yet her fingers were su
prisingly strong as they held onto him, strong and determine
too. He had the strangest feeling that, no matter what happene
Rebecca would do everything she could to help him, that noth
ing and nobody would get in her way once she had made u
her mind.

Was that how she'd felt about Antonio? he wondered. Ha
she been determined to do all she could for his brother and ha
that determination stretched as far as having his child?

He'd believed her when she'd told him that having Josh ha
given Antonio the will to keep fighting his illness. Somehov
it just seemed to fit. Maybe Rebecca hadn't had the baby f
monetary gain after all, but to help his brother. The thoug
made his head spin all over again.

Rebecca helped him to the sofa and got him settled. Drawir
over a footstool, she lifted his feet onto it then quickly turne
off the lamps so that the room was in darkness.

'Just rest there for a few minutes. I'll make you a cup
herb tea. It's feverfew. I don't know if you've tried it, but it
marvellous for headaches and migraine attacks.'

'Thank you.' Felipe closed his eyes as she hurried awa
wondering if he was behaving like a fool. There was no pro
that Rebecca had had the baby for Antonio's sake. Everythir
he'd learned so far was against it, in fact. Even the conce
she'd shown him that night might have been nothing more tha

means to improve his opinion of her. Yet no matter how he tried to rationalise it, the feeling that he might have misjudged her wouldn't go away.

She came back a few minutes later with a steaming cup of liquid which she placed on the table next to him. 'It's too hot to drink at the moment so let it cool down.'

Felipe didn't open his eyes because it was easier to keep them shut. The darkness always helped when he had a migraine attack and he really didn't want her seeing how confused he felt…

He jumped when he felt something cool touch his forehead. His eyes flew open and a ripple ran through him when he found her bending over him. 'What are you doing?' he demanded, putting up a restraining hand.

She gently moved his hand out of the way. 'I'm going to massage your head. It's a technique we use with the children sometimes. Most headaches, even some migraines, are triggered by tension and it helps the muscles to relax.'

'There is no need,' he said shortly, wondering why the thought of her touching him had caused such a violent reaction. His heart was hammering far too fast and his veins felt as though they might burst as the blood pounded through them.

'I know there isn't. But why suffer if there's a chance that can help you?'

Her voice was so quiet, so uncontentious that he found it difficult to argue. He closed his eyes again, feeling every nerve in his body tense when he felt her hands moving over his forehead. His nose wrinkled when an unfamiliar scent assailed his nostrils.

'What are you using?'

'A few drops of lavender oil, mixed with some almond oil to act as a carrier for it,' she replied softly, gently stroking his temples.

'And do you believe these oils help?' he asked, although it was difficult to keep his mind on the conversation when her hands were having such a marvellous effect. He was already

starting to feel a lot more relaxed and his head wasn't hurtin
nearly as much as it had been doing.

'Oh, yes. Aromotherapy has been proved to help in man
cases. There have been studies done which prove how muc
benefit people can derive from the use of essential oils.'

Felipe frowned because he couldn't help feeling sceptic:
about that claim. 'In what way can they help?'

'Well, take my own department—Intensive Care—for i
stance. There was a French study carried out a few years ag
which proved that tea tree oil can have beneficial effects i
treating MRSA. Highly resistant bacterial infections like th:
are a nightmare in any IC unit. They inhabit the artificial ver
tilators and cause real problems for post-operative patient:
Most essential oils are antiseptic, as you probably know, an
we use tea tree oil quite a lot at St Leonard's. We've foun
that it makes a big difference.'

'Really?' Despite himself, Felipe was intrigued.

'Yes, really. You just have to put aside all your preconceive
ideas about it being a lot of mumbo-jumbo. People have use
the oils from plants for thousands of years to help cure then
so why should modern-day patients be any different?'

'It sounds as though you have studied this,' he said softly
sighing when he felt her fingers gently massaging his sku
The effect was so wonderfully soothing that he almost groane
out loud, but he managed to stop himself at the very last m
ment.

'I did a course after I left my previous post. I'd been workin
in an IC unit but it was closed down as part of a cost-cuttin
exercise. I'd always been interested in the use of oils and herb:
medicines so I decided to get a grounding in the basics.'

She moved her fingers across his scalp in a gentle, circul:
motion. 'I was working for an agency at the time. It was mainl
night work so I was able to study during the day.'

Felipe frowned. He couldn't help thinking that it had neede
a great deal of dedication to study whilst holding down a jo
It jarred to think of Rebecca doing that. It didn't fit in with th
image of a woman who'd claimed to have squandered a fortun

on luxuries. Suddenly he was more convinced than ever that she'd lied to him about the money, but how could he make her tell him the truth?

'How does that feel now? Any easier?'

He jumped when she spoke, only then realising that she'd finished the massage. He cautiously opened his eyes, but his headache was nowhere near as bad as it had been.

'Much better. Thank you,' he said formally.

'Good.' She came around the sofa and smiled at him. 'Now, drink that tea and you'll feel even better, I guarantee it.'

He picked up the cup, grimacing as he took a tentative sip of the hot liquid. Rebecca laughed softly, a musical sound which for some reason made his stomach muscles clench.

'You look just like Josh does when I try to introduce some new food to his diet. Be brave and drink it all up. I promise that it won't poison you.'

'Even though it would solve a lot of your problems if you managed to get rid of me from your life?' he suggested drily, taking another sip of the tea.

'We can't always have everything we want, can we? We all have to compromise at times.'

He put down the cup and looked at her because there had been something in her voice that told him it hadn't been an idle statement. It was dark in the room with just the light from the skylight to chase away the shadows. Rebecca was wiping the oil from her hands on an old towel and she didn't look at him even though she must have known he was looking at her.

Felipe found himself wishing that he could tell what she was thinking, but her face was little more than a blur, her soft, blonde hair falling around it. Maybe it was the fact that she looked so young and vulnerable at that moment which made him oddly hesitant about demanding an explanation. Or maybe the truth was that he didn't want another confrontation that night. Whatever, his tone was gentler than it might otherwise have been.

'Meaning that I will need to compromise as well as you?'

'Yes.' She shrugged but there was an air of tension about

her all of a sudden which made his skin prickle. 'We shall both
have to compromise if this is going to work. You want me to
go to Mallorca to live and I've decided that's what I shall do,
but there are conditions.'

'What kind of conditions?' he asked flatly, because he refused to let her see how that statement had worried him.

'That I have the final say where Josh is concerned. I know
how easy it would be for you to take over, Felipe. You're used
to doing things your way, but you have to accept that I know
what's best for Josh. I'm happy for you to play a role in his
life, but it has to be on my terms.'

He heard Rebecca take a deep breath and he felt his stomach
muscles tighten as he waited to hear what else she had to say.

'You have to remember that you're his uncle, not his father.
I know what Antonio wanted for Josh and I intend to see that
his wishes are respected.'

'And you believe that I would try to override my brother's
wishes?' It was impossible to keep the hurt out of his voice
and he heard her sigh.

'I don't believe that you would do it intentionally, Felipe. I
know how much you loved Antonio and how upset you've
been because you believe that you let him down. But trying to
compensate by using Josh as a substitute for your brother
would be wrong. Josh is Josh. He's a person in his own right.'

He didn't know what to say. Was she right? Had he been
hoping to ease his grief over his brother's death by taking control of his nephew's future? He couldn't dispute it but didn't
want to agree with it either, and it was his own inability to
know how he felt which worried him most. It simply wasn't
like him to be so indecisive.

He stood up, knowing that he needed some time on his own
to think about everything that had happened that night. Rebecca
didn't try to stop him as he left the room. She followed him
into the hall and opened the front door.

'I'll speak to you tomorrow to finalise the arrangements,'
she said quietly, and he nodded because he didn't trust himself
to speak.

She suddenly reached up on tiptoe and he felt shock score through him when she brushed his cheek with her lips. It was the first time that she'd touched him of her own volition and it felt like a turning point, as though from that moment their relationship would be on a different footing. The idea worried him and it must have shown.

'Don't look so worried, Felipe. Everything will work out if we really want it to.'

He heard the plea in her voice but exactly what did she want him to believe? That the situation would work out as she'd said it would? Or that she really *cared* how he felt after everything that had been said between them, all the insults and harsh words?

He left the flat and made his way downstairs. The streetlights were on and he wondered if it was the light from them which had made his vision blur again until he realised it was the tears in his eyes. In his heart he knew that he might be making a mistake but he couldn't help it. He *wanted* to believe that Rebecca cared about his feelings, wanted it so much that it scared him to acknowledge the depth of his need.

What did it mean? Surely he couldn't be falling under her spell the same way Antonio had?

CHAPTER SEVEN

'THERE will need to be an inquest, of course. Highly regret
table, but one can understand the parents' distress. One minute
they're told that their daughter should make a full recovery and
the next they're being told that she's died because of some
dreadful blunder.'

Becky sighed as she looked around the office at all the
gloomy faces. Little Rosie Stokes had died during the night
despite all their efforts to redress the damage caused by the
wrong blood transfusion. As if that wasn't bad enough, the staff
from St Ada's were claiming that she'd been given the wrong
transfusion on admission to St Leonard's and that they weren't
to blame for what had happened. It meant that everyone in
volved would need to give a statement.

'Just what we need, I don't think,' Karen declared as they
left the office.

Sister Reece was back on duty that day so Becky had left
her to deal with an irate James Watts. The consultant was fu
rious that even a hint of blame might be attached to him and
his staff, and intended to get to the bottom of the affair. Simon
was in the office with them and he rolled his eyes at her as
she passed the window.

She gave him a quick smile and hurried into the ward. Simon
had been trying to get her on her own all morning but so far
she'd managed to avoid him. He obviously wanted to talk about
what had happened when she'd introduced him to Felipe but
frankly, she didn't want to discuss it. She had enough problems
without adding any more.

A frown pleated her brows as for the hundredth time she
found herself wondering why she'd kissed Felipe. At the time
it had seemed the most natural thing to do. It was only after

shutting the front door that she'd started wondering what had prompted her to do such a thing. Had it been simply a way to comfort him because he'd been upset?

She'd tried to tell herself that all night long, but she knew in her heart that it hadn't been the only reason. There was something about Felipe that drew her to him, and it scared her to have to admit that it wasn't just because he bore a striking resemblance to Antonio.

'You don't believe what Ada's lot are saying, do you, Becky?'

Becky looked up, realising that she'd missed what Karen had said. 'Sorry, what was that?'

'I asked you if you believed what the staff from St Ada's are saying—about it being our fault, not theirs.' Karen frowned. 'What *is* the matter with you today? You've been miles away. There's nothing wrong with Josh, is there?'

'No, he's fine. I'm just a bit distracted, I suppose.' She took a quick breath, realising this was the perfect opportunity to break the news of her departure. 'I'm handing in my notice today. I've decided to move to Mallorca at the end of the month.'

'So it is true? Simon mentioned something about it yesterday but I thought he was having me on because you hadn't said anything to me.'

Becky bit back a sigh when she heard the hurt note in Karen's voice. 'I never had a chance because we were so busy all day long. I only told Simon because we happened to be sitting together at lunchtime.'

'Oh, that explains it, then. I was a bit miffed that you'd told him and not me. Mind you, I did wonder if you'd told him that to sort of gee him up,' Karen said cheerfully, taking Danny Epstein's notes from the end of his bed and quickly writing down his obs.

The boy had come through the operation to replace his damaged heart valves far better than anyone had dared to hope and was starting to show signs of improvement. His parents had been so encouraged by his progress, in fact, that they'd taken a break that morning, having spent the whole week at his bedside.

Becky smiled as she checked the readings as Karen jotted them down. 'He's doing really well, isn't he?'

'He is, but stop trying to change the subject. We were talking about you and Simon.' Karen hung the clipboard back in its place and looked at her. 'So?'

'So what?' She sighed when her friend rolled her eyes in exasperation. 'There is no me and Simon, and I wasn't trying to "gee him up", as you so eloquently put it. We're just friends, that's all.'

'Maybe that's how you feel, but I have the distinct impression that Simon was hoping to be rather more than just a friend,' Karen retorted.

'I don't have time for a relationship,' she said bluntly. 'I have my work cut out trying to hold down a full-time job and take care of Josh.'

'But you'll have a bit more time when you move to Mallorca?' Karen suggested. 'I can see why you've decided it might be a good idea. I expect Josh's uncle will help you look after him so you'll have some time for yourself. Families come in very handy at times, don't they?'

'They do,' Becky murmured, not wanting to be drawn into a discussion about the extent of Felipe's involvement.

Would he accept what she'd said about her being in charge of any decisions concerning Josh's future? she wondered as they moved to the next bed. Or would he try to usurp her authority once she was living in Mallorca?

It was impossible to guess, but it was unsettling to think that she might have a fight on her hands. Becky tried to put it out of her mind while she concentrated on her work, but it was an unsettling day all round.

James Watts got in touch with the consultant at St Ada's and it appeared that the blood that had been given to Rosie hadn't come from them. Each 500 ml unit of blood was bar-coded so it could be traced back to its source, and their records showed that it had come from St Leonard's supplies.

Becky was called into the office to explain what had gone on from the minute the child had been admitted to the IC unit. Although she hadn't dealt with the transfer herself, she had been in overall charge at the time. Karen had been responsible for settling the little girl and she'd had Debbie to help her. When Karen had been called away, the trainee had been left on her own.

Debbie was interviewed, but she categorically denied having changed the transfusion. As she pointed out, Rosie had arrived with a transfusion already set up and there had been no need to fetch a fresh unit of blood when more than half of it had been left. How the child had ended up with blood that had come from St Leonard's was a mystery, but Becky knew that there needed to be an investigation.

It left everyone feeling very edgy so it was a relief when it was time to go home. She had a word with Debbie and tried to reassure her that she wasn't being blamed for what had happened, but it was obvious that the trainee was upset about being under suspicion.

Becky left the hospital at a little after six, half expecting to find Felipe waiting for her. There was no sign of him so she collected Josh and took him home. They went through their usual night-time routine and all the while she kept waiting for the phone to ring. However, by the time she'd settled Josh for the night, Felipe still hadn't contacted her. She was making herself some supper when there was a knock on the door.

Her heart was hammering as she hurried to answer it because she had no idea what she would say if Felipe raised the matter of that kiss. How could she explain if he demanded to know why she'd done it? Telling him that it had felt like the right thing to do sounded a very lame excuse. It was a relief to discover that it wasn't Felipe after all, but a neighbour from the flat downstairs with a package for her.

She went back to the kitchen and opened it, staring in bewilderment at the two plane tickets. There was one for her and one for Josh, first-class seats for a one-way trip to Mallorca at the end of the month. There was an envelope as well and inside it there was a cheque for twenty thousand pounds.

Becky ripped open the package but there was nothing else, not even a note. Felipe had simply sent her everything she needed. A few kindly words of reassurance that she was doing the right thing obviously hadn't featured on his list of essentials. It hurt to realise that he could ignore her feelings when she cared so much about his.

She felt her breath catch as that thought sank in. When had she stopped seeing him as a threat and started worrying about him as a person? Had it been last night when she'd kissed him? She wasn't sure, but she knew in her heart that her feelings towards him had changed in the past three days.

It worried her because she couldn't afford to start having doubts at this stage. She had to think about Josh and making sure that he was safe.

Josh needed her. She had to hold onto that thought and know in her heart that everything she'd done had been justified. And yet she couldn't help wondering how Felipe would feel if he found out the truth, if he would be hurt as well as angry because she had lied to him.

She cared how he felt, she realised. She cared a great deal.

'Dr Valdez! This is a surprise.'

Felipe smiled thinly when he heard the shock in Domingo Santiago's voice. It was obvious that the younger doctor hadn't been expecting him to turn up at the Clinica Valdez at that time of the night. It was a little after eleven and it was rare for him to arrive so late unless there was an emergency. However, he'd felt a deep reluctance to go home after the taxi had brought him back from the airport. He had been too on edge to sit in the villa with only his thoughts for company.

'I thought I would check to see if there have been any problems in my absence, Dr Santiago. Have we had many new admissions while I was away?'

He followed the younger man across the foyer, deliberately cleansing his mind of any thoughts except what might have happened at the clinic in his absence. He had spent hours going over what had happened the night before, recalling time after time how Rebecca had kissed him. Even now he could taste the sweetness of her lips, remember with an alarming clarity just how soft they'd felt. If he'd allowed himself to he could have conjured up her image as well, seen in his mind's eye her beautiful face, her soft grey eyes, the sweetness of her smile...

'Sadly, yes. It has been extremely busy.'

He blinked when he realised that Domingo was speaking. He felt a shudder run through him as he realised how easily his thoughts had returned to Rebecca even though he'd been determined not to think about her. It was an effort to respond with an outward show of calm when his heart was racing.

'Indeed? And has anything serious happened?'

'This morning there was a particularly nasty accident in the bay. A man overturned one of those jet-skis which are so popular with the tourists at the moment.' Domingo sighed. 'He suffered a broken collar-bone and some cuts and bruises, but his son was far more seriously injured. The child has a fractured skull and I needed to operate on him.'

Felipe's mouth thinned. There had been several bad accidents involving jet-skis in the past year.

'People do not seem to understand the risks they take,' he said shortly, pressing the button to summon the lift. 'If one hits water whilst travelling at speed the impact is every bit as great as crashing into a brick wall and can have equally devastating consequences.'

'I know.' Domingo sounded a little nervous as they got into the lift and sent it on its way to the children's department.

Felipe bit back a sigh when he realised that the younger doctor had picked up on his tension and was afraid that he'd done something to upset him. It wasn't true, of course. He was just feeling out of sorts because of everything that had happened of late. Why *had* Rebecca kissed him?

The thought slid into his mind again and he groaned then hurriedly covered it with a cough when he saw Domingo's alarmed expression. 'I would like to take a look at the child if you don't mind, Dr Santiago. Not that I am in any doubt that you have done everything possible to help him.'

'*Claro que sí!* Of course.' Domingo looked pleased as they left the lift and made their way to the child's room.

Felipe smiled to himself because he couldn't help thinking how odd it was that a few words could soothe someone's fears. He knew that the younger man was somewhat in awe of him and resolved to be more aware of that in his dealings with Domingo in future.

It was an idea that would never have crossed his mind a few days earlier and he frowned when he realised it. Was it Rebecca's influence again? he found himself wondering as they made their way into the room where the child lay unconscious. Maybe. It was disturbing to realise the effect she was having on his life.

The boy's parents were sitting with their son so Felipe put aside his own problems while he spoke to them. They were hollow-eyed with grief and he was shocked when he found his own emotions welling to the surface. There was actually a lump in his throat when he saw the mother's distress and tears in his own eyes when the father broke down and cried.

What was happening to him? he wondered. Why did he feel things so acutely all of a sudden? Was this *all* due to Rebecca? Did her influence extend to this area of his life as well?

It was an effort to hide his dismay as he assured the worried parents that everything possible was being done for their child. They looked a little better when he took his leave of them and Domingo remarked on it as they left the room.

'It helped to have a word with you, sir. Silvia and I have done our best to reassure them, but it's a very worrying time for them. At least you have managed to set their minds at rest.'

Felipe nodded, appreciating the fact that the younger man had seen fit to say anything. 'Thank you, Domingo, but if there is any credit due, it must go to you. You did an excellent job on the child. If he recovers—which I am in no doubt that he will—it will be thanks to your skill.'

'*Gracias!*' Domingo sounded stunned. He was obviously

overcome at being complimented twice in one night and looked relieved when his beeper sounded. He hurried off to A and E to deal with a new casualty while Felipe took himself to his office.

He closed the door then looked around the room. Everything was exactly as he'd left it, his desk still neatly stacked with papers, his white coat hanging on the coat-stand, and yet it all looked different, strange, as though the few days he had been away had made him see it through new eyes. This had been his world for so many years yet all of a sudden he found himself wondering if it was all he wanted from life. Surely there should be more than this rather sterile existence?

Unbidden, an image of Rebecca slid into his mind once again and he sighed because it was pointless trying to shut it out. He may as well think about her rather than fight it, remember how she'd looked last night with her feet bare and her blonde hair falling around her face, remember once again how sweetly sensual her lips had felt when they'd brushed his cheek.

A pulse started beating low in his stomach and he shifted uncomfortably, but it didn't ease. It just grew stronger, turned into the throbbing ache which he hadn't felt for so long that it stunned him to feel it then. To feel his body growing hot with desire and know it was for the woman whom he had always believed had used his brother shocked him, but he couldn't stop what was happening any more than he could have stopped breathing.

He wanted Rebecca, wanted her as a man wanted a woman, wanted her in the basest yet the most wonderful of ways, and nothing he could do would stop this hunger growing inside him.

Felipe took a deep breath, let it out slowly, did it all over again a dozen more times, and after a while the feeling began to recede. Moving around the desk, he sat in the big leather chair and thought about what had happened and what it might mean.

Maybe he was sexually frustrated because it had been a while since he had slept with a woman, but he couldn't in all honesty claim that as the explanation. He had encountered other beautiful women in the past but they hadn't stirred him the way Rebecca did.

That was the reason why he'd not gone to see her before he'd left London. He'd been afraid that she would guess how mixed up he felt about that kiss, afraid that she might use it to her advantage and his detriment. He might respond to Rebecca on many levels but he didn't trust her, not yet, not until he'd found out why she had lied to him about the money. And it was the fear of what he might uncover that now caused him such anguish.

He didn't want to find a reason to hate her.

The phone suddenly rang and he quickly reached for the receiver. He listened intently while Domingo outlined the new casualty's injuries then brusquely interrupted him. 'I shall be straight there. Get the patient ready for Theatre.'

He stood up and if he felt a sense of relief at being spared any more soul-searching he made no apologies for it. He would be able to deal with Rebecca and the effect she had on him so much better if he got himself back on track.

Josh had grizzled steadily throughout the flight. He was normally such a good baby that it was a surprise how fretful he had been that day. Becky had done her best but nothing had seemed to soothe him.

Maybe he'd picked up on her own mood, she thought as the plane began its descent into Palma airport. She had been on edge for the past three weeks, waiting for this day to come, dreading its arrival. Considering this was the first step on the way to a new life for them both, she couldn't claim that she felt happy about it.

The plane finally landed and by that time Josh was screaming in earnest. Becky smiled her thanks when the man in the next seat helpfully carried her flight bag while she struggled to hang onto Josh.

She made her way to the baggage reclaim area while Josh roared his disapproval. Fortunately, another person lifted her case off the carousel and put it on a trolley for her. She pushed it through customs, hoping there would be someone at the airport to meet her.

She had sent a fax to the clinic, confirming that she would be on the flight, so hopefully Felipe would have arranged for a taxi to collect her. However, it wasn't until she spotted him standing on the fringes of the crowd that she realised he'd decided to come himself.

Becky felt her heart give the most peculiar jolt as she watched him striding towards her. He was wearing a light grey suit that day and he stood out from the crowd of casually dressed holidaymakers. She saw two young women turn and look at him as he passed, but he ignored them as he made his way straight to her.

'Is there something wrong with Josh? I could hear him screaming while you were collecting your luggage.'

'He's probably upset because of the change to his routine,' she replied, trying not to let him see how aware of him she was. It was three weeks since she had seen him and now she was struck by how tall he was, how imposing, how very handsome. It was hard not to stare at him but not for the life of her would she let him guess what was going through her mind.

'Are you sure he isn't sick?' he asked worriedly, laying a gentle hand on Josh's forehead. 'He feels very hot.'

'That's because he's got himself into a real tizz,' she replied, shifting the baby onto her other hip. He was getting heavy now and it was quite tiring, having to carry him.

'A tizz?' Felipe repeated uncertainly.

'Grumpy, angry, fretful, all sort of mixed up together,' she explained, then looked at him in surprise when he laughed.

'Ah, I understand exactly how he feels, *pobrecito*.'

Becky frowned because she wasn't sure what he'd meant by that. She looked at him questioningly and was surprised when she saw a little colour darken his cheeks before he briskly took charge of the trolley.

'This way. I managed to park near the entrance so it isn't far to walk.'

She followed him in silence, wondering why her heart seemed to be playing hopscotch across her ribs all of a sudden. Had that been a reference to the fact that Felipe himself had been feeling grumpy and mixed up, perhaps?

She sensed it was so and also guessed that the reason for his mood owed itself to something she had done. Had it been that kiss? Had it caused him as many sleepless nights as it had caused her? Frankly, she couldn't believe how one chaste kiss could have caused such havoc, for him as well as her.

The sun was brilliant when they stepped outside. Josh let out a shriek as the bright light assailed his eyes and Becky hastily shook off the moment of introspection. He buried his face in her shoulder, screaming harder than ever when she tried to console him.

Felipe shot the baby a worried look as he unlocked the car. 'Does he want a drink, perhaps, or something to eat?'

'Probably both. He wouldn't have anything on the plane, but maybe he'll have some juice now. It's worth a try.'

She tried to retrieve the bottle of fruit juice from her shoulder-bag, but it was hard to unzip it with the baby clinging to her. Felipe quickly stepped forward and took Josh from her, jiggling him up and down in his arms while she found the bottle.

Becky smiled when she heard him talking to the child, telling him that he would soon be home and that there was no need to cry. It was doubtful if Josh was listening to a word he said as he roared his displeasure, but that didn't seem to deter Felipe from trying. Frankly, she was touched by his obvious concern for the little boy. There would be few men who would willingly try to calm a screaming infant the way he was doing.

'Get into the car and I'll pass him to you,' he instructed when she had found the bottle. 'I've had a baby-seat fitted into the back and he will be safer in that than on your knee.'

'Thanks,' she replied, grateful for his thoughtfulness.

She took Josh from him and quickly strapped him into the comfy little seat. Taking the top off the bottle, she let a few drops of the juice dribble onto the baby's lips. He stopped crying immediately and reached for the bottle.

She let him hold it, keeping a careful watch on him while Felipe got into the car and started the engine. He turned on the air-conditioning so that within minutes the interior of the car felt blissfully cool. She sighed in relief.

'That's better! Even Josh is starting to feel a bit better now, aren't you, sweetheart?'

She buzzed the baby's downy cheek with a kiss then looked up and found that Felipe was watching her in the rear-view mirror. She felt herself blush because she couldn't help thinking about the way she'd kissed *his* cheek. What made it worse was that she knew he was remembering it as well.

It was a relief when he looked away and busied himself with pulling out of the parking space. They left the airport and he turned onto a busy main road. It was midday and a lot of holiday flights had landed. The road was crowded with taxis and coaches ferrying people to their hotels and apartments.

Becky stared out of the window, thinking about the last time she'd travelled this route on her way back from the Clinica Valdez after that first unhappy meeting with Felipe. She had never imagined that she would be making a return trip, certainly hadn't expected to be living on the island a few weeks later. Had she done the right thing by coming here?

Just for a moment she was assailed by panic before she forced herself to calm down and consider the facts. She would never have got hold of the money to pay Tara if she hadn't agreed to come to Mallorca. She had deposited a cheque for twenty thousand pounds in the woman's bank account, and as far as she was concerned that was the end of the matter, although she doubted if Tara saw it that way.

Tara would, no doubt, make more demands at some point, but now she wouldn't know where to find her and Josh. Becky had taken care not to leave a forwarding address at the flat and had told nobody, apart from the people she worked with, where she was going. Of course, there was always a chance that Tara would go to the hospital and ask for her new address, but she would deal with that problem if it arose. For a few months, at least, Josh would be safe.

'He seems to have settled down now.'

She looked up when Felipe spoke, once again feeling her heart surge when she saw him watching her in the mirror. 'Um…yes. He's worn out, poor little scrap.'

'It will take a few days for him to adjust to his new surroundings,' he said levelly, returning his attention to the road. 'He is bound to be a little fractious at first.'

'Probably. I suppose I've been spoilt really,' she said, gently easing the bottle out of Josh's hand. His eyelids were drooping and it was obvious that he was about to doze.

'Why do you say that?' Felipe asked, his deep voice filled with curiosity.

'Because Josh has been such a good baby right from the start. He rarely cried even when he was just a few days old, and especially not when Antonio was looking after him.'

She smiled as she brushed a wispy curl off the baby's flushed little cheek. 'I think he sensed that his daddy was ill and he wanted to help him.'

'Do you think a child is capable of sensing things like that?' he asked, and she frowned when she heard how gruff his voice had sounded. Did he think she was crazy to suggest such a thing? she wondered, shooting him a wary glance.

It came as a surprise when she realised that there wasn't a trace of scepticism on his face. It was only when his eyes met hers in the mirror that she could see the emotion they held and realised that he'd been deeply moved by the idea.

'Yes, I do. Babies are very receptive to mood. Everyone knows that they react to anger and laughter so why shouldn't they respond to other emotions? It's only as we grow older that we develop a need to hide our feelings.'

'Maybe we come to realise that it can be dangerous to show how we feel, Rebecca. There are always people who are ready to take advantage of our weakness.'

'I don't think it's a sign of weakness to show one's feelings,' she protested.

She frowned because she sensed that the comment had been a personal one rather than a general statement. Had something happened to Felipe in the past that had taught him not to show his emotions?

It might be the key to understanding Felipe better if she found out the answer. Without stopping to think about what she was doing, she leant forward in the seat.

'Did somebody take advantage of you, Felipe? Is that why you try to distance yourself from people?'

CHAPTER EIGHT

FELIPE felt a nerve start to tick in his jaw. He knew that Rebecca was waiting for him to answer, but for the life of him he didn't know what to say.

He had never spoken about his hurt when he'd found out how Teresa had deceived him all those years ago and would have denied that it had influenced his behaviour in the intervening years. But suddenly he could see the effect it had had on him.

Discovering that his fiancée had been having an affair with his best friend had been a shock, even though he'd realised eventually that he had been partly to blame. He had been so busy with his work and looking after Antonio that Teresa had grown tired of being ignored and had sought consolation elsewhere.

He had learned a valuable lesson from the experience, though, and had made up his mind never again to mix love with the demands of his job. The breakdown of his relationship with Teresa had affected everything he did. It was the reason why he needed to be in control all the time and the motivation for choosing the kind of life he led. If he hadn't let it affect him, surely he would have had more in his life by now than just his work at the clinic?

'I'm sorry. I really shouldn't have asked you a question like that. I didn't mean to be rude.'

He heard the apology in her voice but it didn't disguise the concern he could hear in it as well. The nerve in his jaw beat all the harder. Rebecca cared—really *cared*—about what had happened to him, and it touched his heart to realise it.

It was on the tip of his tongue to pour out the whole story when a taxi suddenly cut in front of him, causing him to swerve

sharply to avoid a collision. He heard Rebecca gasp with fright
and little Josh give a great wail as he was jolted awake.

Drawing in to the side of the road, he turned to look at them
both, and felt his heart swell with tenderness when he saw how
Rebecca was fussing over the baby and ignoring the fright
she'd had. She was such a good mother, kind and loving, always putting the child's welfare before her own. The thought
shocked him to the core so that it was an effort to respond
when she looked up.

'He's OK. He just had a bit of fright, didn't you, poppet?'
She kissed the baby's chubby little fist then blew a raspberry
on his palm, smiling when Josh gave a reluctant chuckle.
Lifting the hem of his blue T-shirt, she blew another raspberry
on the child's tummy and laughed when Josh gurgled with
delight.

'See, you're fine now, aren't you, darling? And it won't be
long before your Uncle Felipe shows you his beautiful clinic.
Won't that be fun?'

Felipe found himself smiling as he listened to her. Josh
couldn't possibly understand what she was saying, but the child
responded to the tone of her voice. She *was* a good mother and
there was no denying that, even though it caused him some
anguish to admit it.

If Rebecca was such a good mother and such a caring person,
why had she felt it necessary to lie to him about the money?
What was she trying to cover up?

The thought had plagued him for the past three weeks but
all of a sudden he knew that he had to find out the answer. If
there was anything he could do to help her, he would.

His heart jolted as he started the car, but there was no way
that he could lie to himself. He wanted to help Rebecca because
he cared about her. If someone had told him a few short weeks
ago that he would be in this situation, he would have laughed.
However, he didn't feel like laughing now. Finding out the
truth about Rebecca was even more important now than it had
been in the beginning.

It didn't take them very long to reach the clinic after that.
Felipe drove straight to his house and drew up outside. He got

out and helped Rebecca from the car, automatically taking Josh from her.

'Is this where you live?' she asked, taking a long look around.

She raised her hand to shade her eyes as she stared across the bay, and he felt his stomach clench when he saw how the action had made her small breasts press against the soft cotton of her white T-shirt. She wasn't wearing a bra and he could see the outline of her nipples through the thin fabric. His mouth suddenly went dry so that it was an effort to act as though nothing was wrong when she turned to him.

'It's absolutely beautiful, Felipe! The view is superb. Are Josh and I staying near here? I do hope so because it would be marvellous to wake up each morning to a view like that.'

'Then you will be pleased to hear that you and Josh will be living right here in the villa.'

He summoned a smile but it alarmed him to know how quickly he'd responded to her. He could have had his pick of women over the years but, apart from a few brief liaisons, he'd preferred not to complicate his life. Yet he only had to look at Rebecca and his blood started racing, his heart started pounding and his head began to fill with all kinds of crazy ideas.

'Come, I shall show you to your rooms.'

He slid his hand under her elbow to lead her towards the house, praying that she couldn't tell that he was in such turmoil. He had to find a way to stop himself thinking about her all the time, but it wasn't going to be easy. All of a sudden he found himself wondering if he'd made a mistake by bringing her to Mallorca.

How long would he be able to keep his distance from her when she would be living in his house?

Becky felt her heart give one great bounding leap as Felipe put his hand under her elbow. She quickly jerked away and stared at him in dismay.

'What do you mean—Josh and I will be living here? You made no mention of that when I agreed to come here.'

'We never discussed where you would be living, as I recall,' he said calmly, although she could see the impatience in his sherry-brown eyes. It was obvious that he wasn't pleased that she'd seen fit to question his arrangements, but hard luck. Living with Felipe definitely hadn't been part of their bargain.

She opened her mouth to tell him in no uncertain terms that she wouldn't be staying at the villa when an elderly woman suddenly appeared. She rushed down the steps towards them, exclaiming in rapid Spanish when she saw Josh. Holding out her arms, she took the baby from Felipe and hugged him to her.

Josh responded with one of his most angelic smiles as the woman carried him indoors. Becky had no option but to follow and found herself in a huge black-and-white tiled hall. Although the villa was obviously new, the decor was traditional and very Spanish, with lots of dark carved woodwork offset by starkly white walls on which several beautiful watercolours in ornate gilt frames were hung.

She automatically stopped to look around then realised that she was in danger of getting sidetracked. She turned to Felipe, who had followed with her luggage. 'You should have told me that you expected us to stay with you.'

'I realise that and I apologise. It simply never occurred to me that it would create a problem.'

He smiled at the elderly woman, who had hesitantly come forward to be introduced. 'This is my housekeeper, Maria. As you can see, she adores babies. She was my parents' house-keeper for many years and she loved Antonio. She looked after him when he was a child.'

Becky summoned a smile as she shook the woman's hand, not wanting her to think that she was annoyed with her. It was Felipe she was angry with for not having explained the situation.

'I'm delighted to meet you, Maria,' she said in her careful Spanish. The woman said something to her but she spoke so fast that Becky couldn't catch what she'd said.

'She said that she will be delighted to help you take care of Antonio's son if you will let her,' Felipe explained.

'*Gracias*, Maria,' she replied, feeling a little dizzy from the speed with which everything seemed to be happening.

When Maria suggested taking Josh into the kitchen to find him something to eat, she found herself agreeing because it was easier than arguing. Obviously, this would need sorting out because she couldn't stay at the villa, but right at that moment she didn't have the strength for a full-blown argument.

'I can tell that you are upset, Rebecca, and that was never my intention.'

She turned when he spoke, feeling a shiver run down her spine when she saw the regret in his eyes. It made her feel very strange to realise that he cared about her feelings so it was an effort to focus when he continued.

'I hope that you will bear with me until I can make other arrangements for you and Josh. However, at this time of the year, when the holiday season is under way, it can be difficult to find suitable accommodation, you understand.'

'So long as it doesn't take too long,' she said quickly, not wanting there to be any misunderstanding. Maybe he hadn't meant to upset her, but it would be far too difficult to live in the villa with him for any length of time.

Her heart gave a small hiccup at the thought of them sharing the intimacies that came with living under the same roof, and she hurried on. It wouldn't help to dwell on how it would feel to wake each morning and see Felipe over the breakfast table, to go to bed each night and know that he was sleeping close by. Thoughts like that only confused her.

'I would prefer it if we had a place of our own. And I'm sure that you must enjoy your privacy as much as I do.'

His face closed up and she frowned when she heard the biting note in his voice. 'Rest assured that you are free to do whatever you wish while you are living here. I have no intention of curtailing your social life because you are living under my roof.'

'That wasn't what I meant!' she exploded, her face flaming as she realised what he was suggesting. 'Let's get this straight, Felipe. I am not looking for a social life, as you put it so delicately. My only interest is in making sure that Josh is safe and happy.'

'Then there should be no problem about you staying here

for a short while. Josh's welfare is my only concern, too,' he said smoothly.

Picking up her case, he led the way across the hall and down a wide passageway. Becky followed him because there wasn't much else she could do. He stopped and opened a door, moving aside so that she could enter the room.

'I thought this room would be the most suitable. There is a small dressing room leading off it which I've had converted into a nursery. You will be close at hand if Josh should need you during the night.'

'It's beautiful,' she said simply, looking around.

Once again the style was very Spanish in character, with dark oak furniture, white walls and a tiled floor. The bed was enormous, with an intricately carved headboard and covered with a finely woven spread in shades of cream and gold. There were shutters over the window, which had been closed to keep out the sun, and she gasped in delight when she opened them and saw that she had a stunning view over the bay.

Turning, she hurried across the room and peeked inside the *en suite* bathroom, admiring its buttery-coloured marble walls and floor, then checked out Josh's room, shaking her head in amazement when she saw the cot and the toys, the shelves stacked high with baby things.

'You've thought of everything. I don't know what to say, really I don't.'

She opened one of the cupboards, feeling herself choke up when she saw the rows of beautiful little garments for Josh to wear. How many times had she wished that she could afford to buy him things like these?

'I'm pleased that you are satisfied,' he said calmly, and she laughed shakily.

'I'm amazed! I never expected any of this.'

She glanced round and felt her heart lurch when she saw the way he was watching her with such tenderness in his eyes. It stunned her to have him look at her that way, and it was a relief when Maria appeared, carrying a sleepy-looking Josh.

Becky took the baby from the housekeeper and looked at Felipe. 'I'll put him down for a nap, if you don't mind.'

'Of course.' He glanced at his watch and frowned. 'I need to return to the clinic. Perhaps you would join me there once Josh is asleep? Maria will be happy to look after him so it will be the perfect opportunity to acquaint you with the layout of the building before you start work.'

Was that a reminder that she was expected to earn her keep while she was there? Felipe might have been happy to fill the nursery with luxuries for Josh but she couldn't expect such treatment for herself. The only reason she was there was because of Josh and if Felipe found a good enough reason to get rid of her, he wouldn't hesitate to do so.

Becky felt fear rise sharply inside her so that it was an effort to appear calm. 'Of course. I'll be there as soon as I can.'

'*Gracias.*' He inclined his head but she saw a faint puzzlement in his eyes, as though he had picked up on her fear and was wondering what had caused it.

She drove that thought from her head because it was pointless worrying about it. Her main concern had to be to make sure that Felipe never found out that she wasn't Josh's real mother. The thought of his anger was scary enough, but it was the thought that his opinion of her would plummet even further which hurt the most.

She didn't want Felipe to think too badly of her, even though she refused to go into the reasons why. Something told her that her life might become even more difficult if she found out the answer.

'This next patient was admitted yesterday. He dived into the shallow end of the swimming pool and broke his neck. There is extensive swelling in the area so the X-rays aren't very clear. However, we are hopeful that the spinal cord hasn't been damaged.'

Felipe led the way into the room, smiling calmly at the young man lying in the bed. There was a metal fame supporting his head and neck and a specially adapted mattress to hold his body still and stop him turning.

'Good afternoon, Mr Jeffries. How are you feeling today?'

'About how you'd expect to feel with a broken neck,' the young man replied laconically.

Felipe heard Rebecca laugh and tensed when she moved nearer to the bed. He was far too aware of her and unable to do anything about it. Now he found his hands clenching when he saw her smile at the young man.

'Bit of a silly thing to do, wasn't it?' she teased. 'It might have been better to check how much water was in there first.'

'Now she tells me!' Richard rolled his eyes. He was a good-looking young man in his twenties, one of a party of ten friends who had come on holiday to the island from Scotland.

Felipe had been impressed by his positive attitude. However, he was less impressed when he saw the appreciation in the young man's eyes as he looked at Rebecca. It was obvious that Richard found her attractive and for some reason he bitterly resented it.

'Why weren't you there when I needed you? I wouldn't have been diving into any rotten old swimming pool if I'd had you to keep me company!'

'Are you sure you didn't kiss the Blarney stone instead of the bottom of the pool?' Rebecca retorted, chuckling.

'I'm gutted,' Richard replied. 'You don't really believe that was a line, do you?'

'I most certainly do. And on a score of one to ten I'd rate it as a five, so my advice is to keep practising.'

Felipe shifted abruptly, trying to curb his growing impatience. The pair were carrying on as though he were invisible, and he didn't appreciate being ignored. Rebecca shot him a questioning look then turned when Richard spoke. Felipe saw her face fill with compassion when she heard the fear that underpinned the young man's voice.

'I might not need to practise if I've damaged my spinal cord. I'm not going to have much pulling power if I end up flat on my back in a hospital bed for the rest of my days.'

'You mustn't think like that,' she said quickly, squeezing his hand. 'Dr Valdez has just told me that he's hopeful that it's only bruising which is causing you not to be able to move your limbs.'

'I didn't know if that was just a way to keep me quiet,' Richard confessed, his eyes welling with tears.

'I told you the truth, Mr Jeffries. The X-rays aren't clear because of the swelling in the affected area, but I am as confident as I can be in the circumstances that your spinal cord hasn't been severed.'

Felipe smiled reassuringly at the young man, wondering how he had let himself be hoodwinked into believing that Richard was coping so well with his accident. If Rebecca hadn't drawn him out, the poor soul might have lain there, worrying himself to death.

It was an unsettling thought and he resolved never to let it happen again as they left the room. He would be more sensitive in future, look past the façade people put up and try to gain a better understanding of how they were feeling.

He sighed because it would never have occurred to him to do that a few weeks ago. It seemed to highlight all the changes that had happened to him of late. He didn't need to search too hard to understand who had brought them about. Having Rebecca in his life had changed everything.

'Where to now?'

He jumped when she spoke, and felt himself tense when her arm brushed his. He could feel the silky blonde hairs on her arm tickling his skin and he swallowed as a surge of awareness rushed through his system.

They had reached the end of the corridor and there was just a set of glass doors ahead leading to the theatres. Domingo and Silvia had a list of routine operations that day. He hadn't been needed because they were perfectly capable of managing without him. However, he suddenly found himself wishing that he could immerse himself in some sort of complex surgery which wouldn't allow him to think about anything else. He knew where he was when it involved his work. It was only in other areas of his life that he seemed to have difficulty coping at the moment.

'Felipe?'

He fixed a smile to his mouth when she prompted him, wishing that he felt anywhere near as calm inside where it mattered

'The children's department is next. That is where you will be working.'

He led the way through the doors and down the stairs to the floor below, struggling to get himself in check. Life was going to be extremely difficult if he couldn't learn to deal with these feelings Rebecca aroused inside him.

'Do you have an IC unit here?' she asked as they made their way down. They reached the landing and he heard her gasp as her feet skidded on the marble floor when she hurried to keep up with him.

Instinctively, he reached out to steady her, feeling the surge of heat that ran through his palm when his hand closed around her arm. Her skin felt so soft and smooth, he thought wonderingly. He could feel those tiny, golden hairs clinging to his fingers now and had the craziest urge to run his hand over them...

'Oops! That was clumsy of me. I should have worn sensible shoes instead of these sandals.'

He heard the breathy note in her voice and only then realised that he still had hold of her. He let her go abruptly and carried on walking, praying that Rebecca hadn't noticed anything amiss. The thought that she might have guessed how sexually aware he was of her was more than he could bear.

He tried reminding himself who she was as they made their way along the corridor, but it no longer worked because he no longer believed it. He couldn't look at Rebecca and see her as a grasping, mercenary gold-digger any more. His feelings about her were far more complex than that. But even if his mind was having difficulty working out how he felt about her, his body had no such compunctions!

Becky took a deep breath as she followed Felipe into the room. She wasn't sure what had happened, but she was aware of the tension that emanated from him.

She rubbed her arm to ease the odd tingling sensation on her skin, but it refused to go away. She could feel it spreading up her arm until it felt as though every inch of her was tingling. And all because Felipe had touched her? It didn't make sense.

'There's still no change, Dr Valdez. Do you think he'll ever wake up?'

She blinked and it felt as though she were awakening from a trance as the room and its occupants suddenly rushed into focus. Becky felt her heart ache when she saw the worried faces of the two people sitting beside the bed. Their expressions were ones she'd seen far too many times over the years. Fear, guilt, grief—the usual reaction of parents faced with a child's illness.

'Unfortunately, there is no way of knowing when Ryan will recover consciousness,' Felipe was saying quietly. He turned to draw her forward and introduce her.

'This is Staff Nurse Williams. She will be looking after your son in the coming weeks. Miss Williams worked in the paediatric intensive care unit at St Leonard's Hospital in London before she decided to join us at the clinic. We are delighted to have her. She has a great deal of experience in dealing with very sick children.'

Becky hid her surprise at the wonderful build-up. Maybe Felipe had wanted to impress upon the parents that their son was receiving the best possible care, but she had to admit that it was good to have her skills recognised.

'Please, call me Rebecca,' she said, shaking hands with Diane and Tim Palmer. She waved Tim back to his chair when he stood up, pulling up another chair so that she could sit with them. She had found that it helped enormously to be on the same level when talking to people.

'What happened to Ryan?' she asked gently. She knew that she could get all the details from the child's notes, but she also knew that the parents often found it cathartic to talk through what had gone on. It also helped them come to terms with what had happened. Most parents found it difficult to accept when their child was gravely ill and often entered a period of denial. It was better if they could face the facts.

She nodded as Tim Palmer explained how his son had been thrown from the jet-ski and had fractured his skull. Tears streamed down his face while he was telling her the story, but it was better than him bottling up his grief.

Becky turned to Diane while Tim composed himself. 'Has there been any sign that Tim knows you're here?'

'None. I've tried talking to him, tried playing him his favourite music, even telling him about his favourite football team, but he doesn't respond.' Diane wiped her own eyes with a tissue as she looked at her six-year-old son. 'It's as though he's not in his body any longer.'

Becky sighed, wondering if she might be stepping on anyone's toes if she gave her opinion. She glanced at Felipe for guidance but he was standing with his arms folded and a completely neutral expression on his face. She took a deep breath. In for a penny, in for a pound!

'In my experience of dealing with children who are in comas, it's best not to try to stimulate them too soon. The brain needs time to recover from the shock of the accident, a bit like a cut needs time to scab over before it will heal,' she explained gently. 'Don't bombard Ryan with too many different experiences. Just understand that it's going to take time and go slowly.'

'And you think that will help him?' Diane asked uncertainly. 'I mean, you read all these articles in the newspapers about people suddenly recovering from a coma because they've been played a favourite bit of music or something.'

'And things like that do happen.' Becky squeezed the woman's hands. 'Don't give up hope that it will happen in Ryan's case, but give him time. Sit here and hold his hand. Maybe you can talk to him for a little while, but don't over-stimulate his brain while it's going through this healing process.'

'What do you think, Dr Valdez?' Tim asked doubtfully. 'Is Rebecca right?'

Becky held her breath because she knew that some doctors didn't agree with the theory even though it had been proved to have positive effects. Would Felipe take the opposite view to the one she had expounded?

'I think there is a lot of truth in what Rebecca said. Many neurologists believe that the brain needs to go through a healing period and now opt for a treatment designed not to over-stimulate the patient.' He shrugged. 'Of course, there are still many specialists who prefer the older methods and can produce evidence to back them up.'

Becky let out a sigh of relief that he hadn't seen fit to contradict her. Maybe it was silly, but she would have felt dreadful if he had. If Felipe didn't value her as a person, at least he could value her as a nurse.

It was an effort to hide how much that thought had hurt as Diane and Tim eagerly agreed to try the new system. They left them discussing it and carried on with their tour of the clinic, but Becky couldn't shake off the heaviness that had settled in her heart.

She wanted Felipe to see her as the person she really was, but there was no chance of that happening unless she told him the truth. Even then it might not improve his opinion of her to learn that they had paid Tara for Josh. He might think that Josh should have stayed with Tara and that with a bit of encouragement and support the woman would have come to love him in time.

She had no doubt that would never have happened, but would Felipe believe her if she told him everything Tara had done? It seemed inconceivable that anyone would behave so callously so she could understand if he had difficulty accepting it. After all, she had lied to him once so he might think that she was lying to him again. And she was afraid of what might happen if he didn't believe her.

She could end up losing Josh if Felipe didn't think that she was fit to look after him.

CHAPTER NINE

A WEEK passed and Felipe was pleased to see how easily Rebecca had fitted in at the clinic. She was calm and competent, never getting stressed or upset despite the amount of pressure she was under.

It was one of the busiest periods he could remember since the clinic had opened, and many of the patients they admitted were children. However, she coped with it all in the same professional manner that he couldn't help but admire. It was yet another facet of her character, another query to add to the growing list—could she be the woman he had once believed her to be and still hold down an exacting job like this?

He found himself thinking about that question far too many times throughout the day and it worried him that it should be on his mind so much. However, it was at night when he found the situation most difficult to deal with. Although Rebecca was never intrusive, he couldn't ignore her presence in the villa.

He would hear her talking to Maria when he got home from work, hear her singing to Josh while she bathed him, simply *feel* that she was there. His home no longer felt as though it truly belonged to him because he was so aware of her and, frankly, it was a strain.

He resolved to find her alternative accommodation as soon as possible but, as he'd predicted, there wasn't anything available. It appeared that he would have to wait until the main holiday period was over, and the thought of having her around for all those weeks wasn't a comforting one.

He arrived home very late one evening because they'd had an emergency admission as he'd been about to leave. The patient, an elderly man in his seventies, had had a heart attack on the flight to Palma. He'd been rushed straight to the clinic but, despite all their efforts, had died a short time later.

It had been a distressing incident for everyone involved, and he sighed as he let himself into the villa. What he needed most at that moment was a drink and a couple of hours on his own, but there was dinner to get through first—a dinner with Rebecca while he carefully masked his feelings in case she realised how mixed up he felt. When he heard her footsteps crossing the hall he steeled himself before he turned then felt his heart sink when he saw the grave expression on her face.

'What's happened?' he demanded, hurrying towards her. 'Is it Josh?'

'No, Josh is fine.' She gave him a rather abstracted smile then turned when Maria appeared. It was obvious that the housekeeper had been crying and Felipe watched as Rebecca put her arm around her. She looked up and he saw the worry in her soft grey eyes.

'Maria's son has had an accident. I've phoned for a taxi to take her to the airport but I'd like to go with her if you don't mind. She's never flown before and she's a bit scared by the thought of going on a plane.'

'*Claro que sí!*' He frowned, dredging his mind to recall something about Maria's son. He had an idea that José had moved to mainland Spain to work, but he might be mistaken.

He glanced at Rebecca as the housekeeper hurried away to fetch her overnight case. 'Is José still living on the mainland?'

'Yes. He was due to come home a couple of weeks ago, but he stayed on to help finish the new hotel he's been working on,' she explained. 'He works on construction sites at the big Spanish resorts during the winter then comes back to Mallorca for the summer season and works as a waiter at one of the hotels in Alcudia. Maria has been so looking forward to him coming home and now this has to happen.'

Felipe shook his head, wondering how she'd found out so much in such a short time. Maria had been his housekeeper for years yet he'd had no idea that was how her son earned his living. It made him feel rather uncomfortable to realise how little interest he had taken in the past.

'Is everything arranged?' he asked abruptly, hating the fact that he felt at a disadvantage. 'What about the plane ticket? I shall pay for it, of course.'

'No, it's all sorted out,' she said quickly as Maria came back. She linked her arm through the housekeeper's and helped her to the door as the taxi arrived and beeped its horn. 'Josh has had his bath and I've put him down for the night, but he seems a bit restless. If you could keep an eye on him until I get back…'

'Of course,' he said quickly, following them to the door. He patted Maria's shoulder, seeing how she clung to Rebecca. It was obvious they had formed a close bond and he could barely hide his surprise. Maria was normally very reserved with strangers, but not with Rebecca, it seemed.

Felipe waved the two women off then went back indoors, still thinking about it. It was yet another indication that he'd misjudged Rebecca in the beginning. She was kind and caring, and the proof of that was the way she had helped Maria that night. How many people would have done what she had, gone out of their way to make the arrangements for the flight then insisted on going to the airport with the old lady?

It made him even more impatient to get to the bottom of what was going on, but until Rebecca opened up to him there was little he could do. If he could make her trust him then she might, finally, tell him the truth. If she did that, they could move on…

He sighed because he knew how dangerous it was to indulge in thoughts like that. Letting himself dream that he and Rebecca might one day have more than just Josh in common was inviting trouble.

He tried to put it from his mind as he made his way to the nursery, stopping off *en route* to shed his jacket and tie as he passed his bedroom. Josh was singing to himself when he went to check on him, burbling away in baby-talk.

Felipe crept into the nursery but the moment the child saw

him he held up his arms to be picked up. He lifted him out of
the cot, tossing him gently into the air and smiling when he
heard the baby chortling with delight. He didn't look the least
bit sleepy so Felipe took him to the kitchen while he found
himself something to eat.

He balanced Josh on his knees while he wolfed down a piece
of cold chicken, laughing when the child opened his mouth,
obviously hoping for a taste. 'I don't think your mama would
want you to have any of this, *pequeño*. Let's see if we can find
you something else.'

Lifting Josh onto his shoulder, he investigated the contents
of the refrigerator and found a punnet of strawberries in the
cooler. He took out a handful, grinning when Josh made a grab
for them.

'Ah, so you like these, do you? Come along, then, let's go
into the sitting-room and relax while you have your snack.' He
placed a plump red berry into the baby's hand and smiled at
him again. 'But don't tell your mama or she might tell me off
for spoiling you.'

He carried the baby into the sitting-room and sat down on
the sofa, using his handkerchief as a makeshift bib as Josh
munched his way through the fruit. It was rather a messy process and both of them were spattered with juice by the time
the last strawberry had disappeared. Josh was starting to look
sleepy by that point, but he cried when Felipe got up to take
him back to his room.

He sat down again, settling the child on his knee in the hope
that he would doze off. It was very quiet in the villa. Felipe
felt his own eyelids drooping and blinked himself awake.
However, it had been a long day and within minutes both he
and Josh were fast asleep.

Becky let herself into the villa and quietly closed the front door.
She paused for a moment but there was no sound coming from
the nursery so she could only assume that Josh was asleep.
Where Felipe had got to she had no idea, but he was probably
in his study. He spent a lot of time in there of an evening,

although she suspected it was less out of a desire to work than a means to escape her. Maybe he found it as difficult having her staying there as she found it being a guest in his house. She was always too aware of him to relax.

She went to the kitchen and cut herself a hunk of cheese then ate it standing at the counter. Maria had been too upset to worry about making dinner and she found herself suddenly wondering how Felipe had fared. She sighed because her conscience wouldn't allow her to let him go hungry.

She left the kitchen and went to see if he wanted her to make him an omelette, but there was no sign of him in the study when she tapped on the door. She backtracked across the hall to the sitting-room and gasped at the sight that met her.

Felipe and Josh were sprawled out on the sofa, fast asleep. Josh's clean sleepsuit was now covered in red juice and Felipe's shirt looked little better. There were red stains all down the front and it was very creased. Frankly, Becky didn't know whether to laugh or scold them because it was obvious that the pair had been up to mischief. She was still trying to decide what to do when Felipe opened one eye a crack and saw her.

He came awake with a rush, sitting up and blinking. 'I must have dozed off,' he said, his deep voice sounding even deeper with sleep.

Becky felt her stomach coil into a tight little bud and had to make a conscious effort not to react. Did he have any idea how sexy he looked, she wondered, with his black hair all rumpled and his beautiful brown eyes heavy-lidded with sleep?

'So I can see. What interests me is what you two were up to before you fell asleep.' She regarded him levelly, praying that she could keep up the pretence long enough to convince him that all she felt was annoyance because of the state Josh was in.

'Why should you think that we were up to anything?' He shot the baby a quick look and she saw a wash of colour run up his cheeks. It gave him the appearance of a small boy who had been caught doing something naughty. It was such a contrast to his usual air of being totally in control that she couldn't help staring at him.

'Ah, I see. It seems that I shall have to confess my sins, Rebecca.'

'I don't think you need to confess,' she observed with mock severity, struggling to get a grip on herself. 'The evidence speaks for itself. You two have had a strawberry feast, haven't you?'

'Guilty.' He gave her a slow smile that made his mouth curl delectably at the corners. 'But you must blame your son, not me. He is the one who ate all the strawberries. I was just his willing accomplice. Is that the right word for someone who aids and abets a criminal?'

'Criminal?' Her brows rose, although it was hard not to laugh at such nonsense. 'How can you claim that a ten-month-old baby is a criminal? He needed help to *commit* his crime!'

'Maybe he is very advanced for his age,' he suggested, completely deadpan.

'He would need to be. You're saying that he managed to get out of his cot and make his way to the kitchen. And then he opened the refrigerator door all by himself…'

'I just admitted that I was his accomplice,' he said, with a grin that made her heart melt. 'I just never realised how quick he is to learn new skills.'

'Especially when there's someone around who can teach them to him,' she shot back. 'You might be leading him down the road to ruin, Felipe, you realise?'

'Oh, I doubt if I could be blamed for doing that.'

'But I could?' Suddenly it was an effort to hold her smile. Maybe she was being overly sensitive but that comment had seemed rather too pointed. 'After all, I'm the one who teaches Josh the things he needs to know. If he doesn't turn out as you hope he will, you can lay the blame at my door, can't you, Felipe?'

'No! I never meant to imply any such thing—'

'Forget it,' she snapped, not wanting to hear any more because there was no point. She knew how he felt about her and she'd be a fool to hope that his opinion might have improved.

'Rebecca, please—'

'I told you that it doesn't matter.'

She took Josh from him, cradling the baby to her as she hurried from the room. It took only a few minutes to wash his hands and change him. Josh gave her a sleepy smile and immediately dropped off to sleep again when she laid him in his cot.

Becky moved about the room, clearing up the odds and ends she'd used, and it was only when she caught sight of herself in the mirror over the dresser that she realised she was crying.

Felipe hated her! He must do. He obviously believed that she was a bad influence on Josh and she didn't think she could bear it.

'Oh, *querida*, don't cry. Please. There is no need. This is all a silly misunderstanding.'

She hadn't heard him coming into the room and she froze when she heard his voice. When she felt his hands on her shoulders as he turned her to face him she closed her eyes because she didn't want him to see how upset she was. If Felipe knew that he had the power to hurt her, he might use it again and again…

'I am so sorry, Rebecca. Truly I am.' He drew her to him and she could feel his hands moving gently up and down her back as he tried to soothe her. 'I can't bear to see you upset like this.'

Once again his hands slid down her back and she shivered when they gently followed the curve of her spine. Felipe must have felt her tremble because his hands stilled for a moment before they moved on, only this time it felt more like he was trying to caress her than comfort her.

Becky's eyes flew open and she felt a spasm run through her when she saw the expression on his face. To see him looking at her with such hunger, such need should have shocked or scared her, but oddly enough it did neither. In some strange, inexplicable way it felt as though she had been waiting for this moment to happen all her life.

'Rebecca.'

Her name was just a whisper as it came from his lips, but it felt to her as though he had shouted it out loud. Every nerve in her body pulsed with the sound of it, trembled because of the way he had said it. When he bent towards her she was already moving towards him so that their mouths met with a small jolt.

Becky clung to him as her head spun, feeling the solidness of his body beneath her hands. He was still wearing the rumpled shirt and she could feel the heat of his skin flowing through her palms. The delicate scent of crushed strawberries mingled with the scent of his body to create a musky perfume that stirred her unbearably so that her senses seemed to be far more acute than normal.

She could hear the rasp of his breathing, the whisper of hers, feel his heart beating and hers trying to match its rhythm; she could taste the heady flavour of him when he opened his mouth and let his tongue slide inside hers…

Becky gave a sharp, little moan, unable to hold back when she felt his tongue tracing the outline of her lips. Their mouths were barely touching yet it was the most sensually stirring experience she'd ever had. She could feel Felipe's tongue following the curve of her upper lip, feel her breath catch when it paused while he enjoyed its shape and taste a moment longer, feel the ripple that ran through her when it moved on. By the time he reached her lower lip and gently drew it into his mouth she was trembling. It seemed the most natural thing in the world when he slowly backed her up against the wall and let his weight settle against her so that she could feel the hard evidence of his desire.

'Feel what you do to me, *querida*?' he whispered, his breath warm on her skin as his mouth glided over her jaw and down her throat.

Becky moaned when she felt little pools of heat collecting beneath her skin wherever his lips had touched. 'Yes,' she whispered huskily, unable to manage more than the single word.

His lips glided back up her throat, found her mouth again, treated her to another drugging kiss. And all the time desire was building inside her, growing stronger with each second that passed. Each touch of his hands made her tremble, each kiss made her burn, each beat of her heart and his made their passion for each other grow stronger.

What was happening was unlike anything she'd experienced with Antonio. She had loved Antonio very much, but her feelings for Felipe were far more complex. Felipe had the power to hurt her on so many different levels if she wasn't careful.

He must have felt her tense because his hands and mouth suddenly stilled. Becky heard him draw in a rasping breath before he pulled away from her. Just for a moment there was a blaze of passion in his eyes that made her ache to have him take her back in his arms. Then it was gone and she saw the bitter self-reproach that had replaced it.

'I apologise, Rebecca. That should never have happened.'

He turned and strode out of the room and she heard his bedroom door close a moment later. Becky stood where she was, feeling desire growing cold inside her. She had seen the regret in Felipe's eyes and knew that he would never forgive himself for what had happened. Maybe he wouldn't forgive her for causing it either. After all, he had come within a hairsbreadth of making love to her, the woman he despised.

Her eyes filled with tears again. If the situation had been bad before, it could only get worse.

He couldn't believe he had done that!

Felipe paced his room, but there was no way he could ease the agony he felt. He had almost made love to Rebecca…

Hell, he *had* made love to her! Why should he spare himself when the truth had to be faced? He had kissed and caressed her in the most intimate way, and even though technically they hadn't made love it had felt as though they had. He'd felt more while he'd been kissing her than he'd felt after spending a whole night in bed with another woman.

The thought brought him up short. Kissing Rebecca had felt more wonderful than making love even to Teresa. With Rebecca he hadn't been able to keep any part of him separate. His whole being—everything he was—had been caught up by the need to love her. If he hadn't felt her withdrawal, who knew what might have happened? But it was the reason why she had drawn back that caused him such pain.

Had Rebecca suddenly thought about Antonio? And had she been ashamed of what they'd been doing?

He swore softly. He was too experienced not to know that she'd been with him every step of the way, that her desire had been just as great as his. But had it been right to make her feel like that? Was it right to want her this way? She was the mother of his brother's son, the woman Antonio had loved, and he had been making love to her.

He doubted if he could have felt more wretched as he was assailed by guilt. What made it even worse was knowing that Rebecca was probably in her room at that very moment, torturing herself with the thought of how she had betrayed Antonio.

She had no need to blame herself, though. She was still a young woman with her whole life ahead of her. Even though she had loved Antonio, she couldn't live on her memories for ever. Antonio wouldn't have wanted her to—he knew that without the shadow of a doubt. Antonio would have wanted Rebecca to be happy.

The thought seemed to wash away his guilt and it no longer felt as though he needed to reproach himself. Antonio would have wanted only the best for Rebecca and Josh, that they would be loved and cared for, cherished. Maybe he was being presumptuous, but all of a sudden Felipe knew that he wanted to be the one to care for them. The question was, would Rebecca let him? Would she trust him to help her, tell him why she was afraid?

She might if he was honest with her, a small voice inside his head suggested, and he laughed.

Why on earth hadn't he thought of doing that before? He knew in his heart that she hadn't used Antonio for his money, that everything she had done had been with the very best of intentions, so maybe it was time he told *her* that.

His heart lifted. He would talk to Rebecca in the morning, tell her how he felt then ask her to tell him the truth. No matter what this secret was that she was keeping from him, it couldn't be *that* bad. They would find a way to work it out, he and Rebecca.

Together.

Becky was up before six and had Josh washed and dressed a short time later. She took him into the kitchen and let him crawl around the floor while she made him some breakfast.

He was still a little unsteady and kept going backwards instead of forwards, but he would soon get the hang of it. In another few weeks he would be walking and talking, growing from a baby into an inquisitive little boy. She only hoped that she would be around to watch him growing up, but there were no guarantees. Not after last night and what had happened. Felipe might use it as the perfect excuse to get rid of her.

A sob caught in her throat but she refused to cry. Tears weren't going to help. She had to face what she had done and deal with the repercussions it was bound to cause.

She picked up Josh and put him in his high chair then helped him spoon cereal into his mouth. He was at the stage of wanting to do everything himself so mealtimes were rather messy affairs. She was just wiping up a dollop of cereal that had ended up on the floor when she looked up and saw Felipe standing in the doorway, watching her.

'Buenos dias,' he said politely, coming into the room and pausing beside Josh's chair to ruffle his hair.

'Good morning,' she replied, praying that he couldn't hear the strain in her voice. She finished cleaning up the mess then went to the sink to rinse out the cloth, glancing round when Felipe reached for the coffee-pot on the counter beside her.

'Would you like coffee, Rebecca?' he asked in the same perfectly polite tone, which was starting to grate on her nerves.

'If you're having some,' she said equally politely, then felt herself flush when she caught the amused look he gave her.

Turning, she took a towel off the rack, dried her hands then went to get Josh a banana. She sliced it up and put it in a dish, taking her time because she wasn't sure how to handle the situation. Should she mention what had happened last night, or wait and see if Felipe brought it up?

'I'm making toast—would you like some as well?'

She jumped when he spoke, casting an uncertain glance over her shoulder at him. He was slicing bread to go in the toaster and he smiled calmly at her. 'You really should eat something, Rebecca. You didn't have any dinner last night and you must be hungry.'

'I'll have a slice if you're making some,' she said quickly, afraid that mention of dinner would lead to other topics.

She took a deep breath as he turned to put the bread in the toaster, trying to blot out the images that filled her mind. It would serve no purpose recalling how his mouth had felt when he'd kissed her, how his hands had caressed her, how his skin had smelled...

Josh knocked his dish onto the floor and Becky jumped. She bent to pick it up, but her hands were trembling so much that it was an effort to make them obey her. Slippery bits of banana slid through her fingers and she bit her lip in dismay.

'Let me do that.'

Felipe gently grasped her shoulders and helped her to her feet, and she was shocked by the tenderness in his eyes. He quickly cleared up the mess and wiped Josh's sticky fingers then lifted him out of his chair and put him on the floor.

Becky looked round uncertainly, feeling at a loss to know what to do. Felipe seemed to have taken charge, making her superfluous. When he placed a cup of coffee on the breakfast bar, along with a plate of buttered toast, she automatically sat down.

He poured himself a cup of coffee and sat beside her, and she flinched when his arm brushed hers. All of a sudden the tension in the kitchen was palpable. She could feel it and knew that he could, too.

'What happened last night wasn't planned, Rebecca.'

His voice was perfectly level so that for a moment she didn't realise what he meant. She felt a wash of colour run up her face when it sank in. She doubted if she could have sounded so matter-of-fact, but maybe he found it easier to deal with the thought of them making love than she did. It was an effort to keep her mind focused when he continued in the same even tone.

'Nevertheless, I do not regret that it happened. In fact, I'm glad that it did because it has helped me see this situation far more clearly.'

She looked at him, unable to hide her surprise. 'What do you mean?'

'That I've been wrong about you, Rebecca.' He shrugged but she could see a nerve beating in his jaw and realised that he was nowhere near as calm as he was pretending to be. 'You aren't who I thought you were.'

'I don't know what you expect me to say,' she said hoarsely. The statement had come like a bolt from the blue and she had no idea how to react. 'You had formed your own opinion of me before we even met.'

'I know. And now I realise that I was completely wrong about you.'

His voice was so gentle that she couldn't find it in her to resist when he turned her to face him. 'I know in my heart that you aren't the scheming, mercenary woman I thought you to be. I apologise for having thought that of you in the first place.'

His fingers brushed the soft skin under her jaw and she shivered because it had triggered memories of the night before. It was an effort to focus on what he was saying when he continued in the same butter-soft tone.

'You are a kind and caring woman, a loving mother to Josh and a skilled nurse. I know all that now, Rebecca, and I admit that I was wrong. What I don't understand is why you let me believe the worst when you could have told me the truth. What are you hiding from me?'

Felipe held his breath. Would Rebecca find the courage to tell him? Would she open her heart and share this dreadful secret with him so that he could help her?

He had barely slept with worrying about it, but he didn't dare let her see how important it was to him. He had to make her trust him, had to make her understand that he wouldn't do anything to hurt her. All of a sudden that seemed more important than anything. She had suffered enough and she shouldn't be allowed to endure any more.

'I…I don't know what you mean,' she began, then stopped and swallowed.

He heard the dry click of her throat and his heart ached because of what she must be going through. It was obvious how afraid she was and he wished with all his heart that he could think of a way to make this easier for her, but there was nothing he could do. He had taken the first step and she had to take the next all by herself.

'I'm glad you realise that I never deceived Antonio,' she said at last with a catch in her voice. 'I loved him too much to hurt him.'

Felipe's heart contracted on a spasm of pain. Even though it made him feel awful to admit it, it hurt to hear her say how much she had loved his brother. It was an effort to keep the ache out of his voice, but he couldn't and wouldn't put her under any more pressure.

'And I know how much Antonio loved you because he told me in his last letter.' He sighed when he saw the sadness in her beautiful eyes. 'I chose to ignore that and believe only what I wanted to believe, but now I want to know the truth. What haven't you told me? Has it something to do with Josh?'

He knew he was right the moment he saw panic flare in her eyes. This secret Rebecca was keeping concerned his nephew, but for the life of him he couldn't imagine what it was. The boy was obviously Antonio's son so that couldn't be the problem...

She suddenly pushed back her chair and stood up. Bending, she scooped Josh up into her arms. Her face was set into tight lines that hinted at the strain she was under, but she faced him squarely.

'You're imagining things, Felipe.' She shrugged but he'd seen the tremor that had raced through her slender body and knew that she was lying. 'I'm not keeping anything from you.'

He stood up abruptly, knowing that it was pointless trying to press her at the moment. She was too afraid to tell him the truth even after what had happened between them last night...

Maybe *because* of what had happened, a small voice inside him whispered. Maybe she regretted those minutes she had spent in his arms, and it was that which was causing her such distress now.

Felipe felt a knifing pain run through him at the thought. The last thing he wanted was to cause her any more distress, but there was little he could do about it. Rebecca had to deal with her feelings for Antonio in her own time—if she ever learned to deal with them, of course.

It was an effort not to show how much that idea upset him, but there was no way that he would add to her anguish. 'Then there is nothing more to be said on the subject, is there?'

He gave her a gentle smile but his heart felt like lead. Had he been a fool to imagine that she'd responded to *him* last night? Maybe the true explanation was that he had been merely a substitute for his brother. Had Rebecca pretended that it had been Antonio holding her in his arms, Antonio who'd been kissing her?

'It will not be possible for you to work with Maria not being here to look after Josh,' he told her, amazed that his voice sounded so normal when it felt as though he had been dealt the most horrendous blow. 'I shall inform your colleagues not to expect you today.'

She shook her head. 'No, don't do that. I'll take Josh to the crèche. He will enjoy being with the other children for a change.'

'If that is what you wish to do. The staff who work in the crèche are all highly trained.'

'I know. Like everyone else who works at the Clinica Valdez.'

'I wanted only the best when I opened the clinic,' he said flatly. 'The best staff, the best facilities, the best of everything.'

'And you've achieved all that. It's a wonderful place, Felipe. You must have worked very hard to set it up,' she said softly

'Sí.' He shrugged but he couldn't deny the hollow feeling it gave him to realise how much of his life had been spent achieving his dream. Would he do the same again if he was given the same choices? Once he would have said yes, of course he would, but now he was no longer certain.

It scared him to have to face that fact. If he didn't have his work, what did he have that meant anything to him? Maybe it was that thought which made him open his heart when it should have been the last thing he did right then.

'It was my dream to one day open my own hospital, but it came at a price. It left me with very little time for a personal life.'

'And you regret that?' she asked, as though his answer really mattered to her.

'Yes. By now I might have had a wife and family if I hadn't devoted so much of my time to the Clinica Valdez.'

'At least you have Josh,' she said with a catch in her voice which made his heart ache even more. Even now she was worried about him, cared how he felt. It was both a pleasure and a pain to realise it, to know once again how wrong he had been about her in the beginning.

'Only for as long as you choose to remain here.' He took a deep breath but there was no way that he could lie to her now. 'If you decide to leave, I can't stop you, Rebecca. After all, you are the child's mother.'

'Yes,' she said hollowly. 'I'm his mother.'

She turned to leave but he'd seen the fear that had flared in her eyes once again. Felipe frowned as he heard her footsteps crossing the hall. He was convinced that whatever she was hiding from him had to do with Josh, but what was it? What was this dreadful secret that she was too scared to tell him?

He knew that he wouldn't rest until he'd found out the truth. Maybe Rebecca could never be anything more to him than the mother of his brother's child, but he needed to solve this last piece of the puzzle.

CHAPTER TEN

'HE JUST opened his eyes and said, "I'm thirsty, Mum." I couldn't believe it!'

'I'm so pleased for you both!' Becky hugged Diane and Tim Palmer then laughed as she wiped a tear from her eyes. 'I don't know why we're crying when we should be celebrating!'

Ryan had suddenly awoken from his coma that morning. Felipe was with him at the moment, running some tests. Silvia Ramirez had told her that a neurologist was flying out from Madrid that afternoon to carry out more tests, but so far the signs were encouraging.

'Does this mean that we'll be able to take Ryan home soon?' Diane demanded eagerly.

'Hopefully, although you might need to stay a while longer just to make sure that he's stable,' Becky warned, sitting down beside Diane on the sofa.

They were using the relatives' suite—a comfortable little apartment attached to the children's department. Diane and Tim had been staying there ever since Ryan had been admitted to the hospital. Becky found herself thinking that Felipe had thought of everything when he'd had the plans drawn up for the Clinica Valdez.

The thought naturally reminded her of what had happened that morning and she sighed because it was hard to recall the sadness in his voice when he'd spoken about the emptiness of his life. She'd never imagined that she would feel such sympathy for him, although sympathy wasn't the only thing she felt.

Heat rushed through her as she recalled the way he'd kissed her. Even though he'd appeared to regret it afterwards, it didn't change what had happened. It had made it even more difficult

136

to deal with his searching questions that morning. She longed to tell him the truth, but how could she take that risk?

Felipe had told her he'd revised his opinion of her, but how would he feel if he found out that she wasn't Josh's real mother? His views could change again and the fear that he might try to take Josh away from her couldn't be quietened.

It was an effort to put aside such worrying thoughts when Tim asked her about the tests that were being carried out on his son. Becky explained that Ryan's responses to various stimuli would be tested to ascertain that his brain was functioning properly. The child's basic responses such as breathing, yawning, coughing and swallowing had been fine all along, so there was obviously no damage to his brain stem. However, there might be damage to other areas.

Diane and Tim listened intently, asking questions whenever they didn't understand. Becky didn't go into too much detail about the problems they might face in the future because it would be best if the neurologist completed his assessment first. Physical and mental disability couldn't be ruled out at this stage, but there was no point worrying them unnecessarily. However, by the time Felipe arrived, they were beginning to realise that Ryan wasn't completely out of the woods yet.

He smiled as he sat down. 'Ryan is asking for you, but before you go back to see him I just wanted to say that the signs are very encouraging. Obviously, my colleague, Dr Menendez, is the expert in this field, but we're hopeful that there is no serious brain damage.'

Becky heaved a sigh of relief as Diane and Tim left, looking a lot happier. 'Thank heavens for that! It's been such a worrying time for them.'

'It has.' He smiled and she felt heat ripple along her veins when she saw the warmth in his eyes. When had he started looking at her like that? she wondered. Since last night? She'd thought he'd regretted what had happened but maybe—just maybe—she'd been wrong.

'Silvia told me that you offered to give up your break and

talk to them while we carried out the tests on Ryan,' he said quietly. 'Thank you.'

'It's what I'm paid to do,' she replied, quickly standing up. She couldn't afford to let herself be distracted by the thought. She had to remember what a dangerous situation she was in. It would take very little to uncover her secret.

'No, you are paid to care for the children we treat here. Giving support to the parents is something you do out of the goodness of your heart, Rebecca.'

There was a grating note in his voice when he said that, and she sighed. 'I didn't think you believed that I had a heart.'

He looked at her with a searching light in his eyes. 'I told you this morning that I knew I was wrong about you.'

She half expected him to say something else, maybe bring up the subject of why she had allowed him to continue thinking so badly of her, but surprisingly he didn't pursue it. 'So how was Josh when you left him at the crèche?'

'Fine. He was very excited because he could see all the other children.' She summoned a smile, not wanting him to see how relieved she felt because it would only arouse his curiosity. 'He barely spared me a glance when I left, in fact.'

'He is a credit to you, Rebecca. The fact that he is happy to be left with strangers proves how secure he feels.'

'Thank you.' She was deeply touched by the comment. 'All I ever wanted was for him to be safe and happy.'

'I realise that. Everything you have done has been for his sake. And for Antonio's sake, of course. It must mean a lot to you to take care of his son.'

'Do you really believe that?' she said urgently. If she could believe what he'd said then maybe she could risk telling him the truth after all?

'*Claro que sí*. Of course,' he said flatly, and her heart sank when she heard the reservation in his voice.

'But? There was a definite *but* tagged onto the end of that, Felipe, wasn't there?'

'Perhaps.' He sighed. 'Sometimes people do things in good faith and end up causing themselves a great many problems. I only hope that your desire to look after Josh hasn't caused you to do something you now regret.'

'I did what had to be done and I would do exactly the same thing all over again,' she said flatly, because it was true. No matter how difficult the situation was or how much anguish it caused her personally, she didn't regret the decisions she'd made.

'Then I hope that one day you will trust me enough to tell me the truth, Rebecca. Like you, my only concern is Josh's welfare.'

Becky sensed that he was hurt by her refusal to tell him the whole story, but she still wasn't sure that he would understand. She heard Felipe sigh when she remained silent.

'It would be best if we left this conversation until another time. Work isn't the place to discuss it.' He turned to leave then paused and glanced back. 'Before I forget, I shall be out this evening so you will have the villa to yourself. Dr Menendez and I are old friends and I have invited him out for dinner. It will give us a chance to catch up on what has been happening.'

'Oh, right. Thank you for letting me know.' She shrugged when he looked quizzically at her. 'I was going to make dinner for us both, but I won't need to bother now.'

'I do not expect you to cook for me because you are living under my roof, Rebecca.'

'I never imagined that you did. However, with Maria being away, it seemed more sensible to make a meal for us both.'

She could feel the colour rushing up her face and turned to plump up the cushions on the sofa. Did Felipe think that she was trying to ingratiate herself even further by offering to cook him a meal?

'I'm sorry. I did not mean that the way it sounded.' He sighed when she shot him a startled look. 'I am not used to having to think before I speak, I'm afraid. There has never been anyone to question me before.'

'Before me, you mean?' She gave a light laugh, hoping it didn't sound as strained to him as it did to her. 'You must be sorry you met me, Felipe. I've done nothing but disrupt your life, have I?'

'You have turned everything on its head, Rebecca, although I am not sorry about it.'

'What do you mean?' she demanded, startled.

'That maybe my life needed to be disrupted before I could see what was missing from it. I don't regret meeting you, Rebecca. If there is anything I regret, it's that we didn't meet before.'

Before Antonio.

The words hung between them, unspoken yet clear all the same. Becky felt her heart pound when she looked into his eyes and saw the expression they held. There was regret in them but it was mingled with another emotion which made her body burn with a sudden intense heat. To know that Felipe still wanted her that morning as he had wanted her the night before made her feel as though the bottom had just dropped out of her world.

It was a relief when he abruptly left the room because she had no idea what she might have said. Her head seemed to be whirling. Felipe had admitted that his opinion of her had undergone a complete reversal, but so, too, had her opinion of him. The idea terrified her.

If he was no longer her enemy, how much more difficult was it going to be to keep her secret from him? Could you love someone and keep a part of yourself separate?

The thought slid into her mind and she gasped. Was she falling in love with Felipe? Was it possible? She wanted to deny it, but it wasn't possible to do that.

Not after last night.

Why on earth had he said that?

Felipe bit back a groan as he went into his office. He sat down behind his desk, automatically reaching for the pile of letters his secretary had left for him to sign. He stared at the beautifully printed pages without seeing a word that was written on them. He kept hearing himself telling Rebecca that he regretted not having met her *before* she'd met Antonio.

He pushed back his chair and paced the room, too on edge to sit still. She had understood what he'd meant even though he'd managed to stop himself saying his brother's name. He'd seen the shock in her eyes and the awareness that had followed it. And yet she hadn't looked as though the idea had sickened her. He'd had the definite impression that she wished the same thing, in fact. But if that was the case, why was she so reluctant to tell him the truth? Just how bad was this secret she was keeping?

He groaned again. The harder he tried to understand the situation, the more difficult it became. Frankly, there was a danger that it would drive him insane if he didn't find out the truth soon. Maybe it was time he did just that. It didn't feel right to go behind Rebecca's back, but he had no choice. If she wouldn't tell him, someone else would!

Picking up the phone, he dialled the London office of the firm of solicitors his brother had used. He'd had little contact with them since the funeral, but maybe it was time he started asking some questions. The solicitor who had handled Antonio's affairs was in court that day so Felipe left a message asking the man to get back to him and hung up.

Picking up the letters, he tried to concentrate, but it was impossible to keep his mind on the task. Finding out the truth about Rebecca seemed far more important than the smooth running of the Clinica Valdez. It scared him to death to have to admit it.

All of a sudden it felt as though there were no longer any guidelines in his life. He was drifting through time and space with no idea what would happen next. All he could do was hope that he wouldn't regret discovering Rebecca's secret. It could prove to be a big mistake, but it was a risk he had to take.

Until he knew what Rebecca was hiding, he couldn't make any plans for their future. Whether he liked the idea or not, the two were intrinsically linked.

*　　*　　*

It was a busy afternoon. They had several new admissions to the children's ward so Becky was kept busy dealing with them. One child in particular was giving cause for concern.

Four-year-old Christopher Thomas was suffering from hyperpyrexia, a severe form of heatstroke. He had been playing in the sun and had suffered quite extensive sunburn to his back and shoulders. Becky got him settled then went to have a word with his parents.

'Christopher's temperature is coming down but he's still quite poorly,' she explained. 'The staff in Casualty managed to cool him by wrapping him in a wet sheet and using a fan. However, we shall need to keep him on a drip overnight to replace all the fluids he's lost.'

'He will be all right, won't he?' Elaine Thomas demanded. 'We had no idea he was ill until one of the reps from the hotel came to fetch us.'

'He wasn't with you?' Becky asked in surprise.

'No, we left him at the children's club. I mean, that's the whole point of going on holiday, isn't it?' Michael Thomas, the child's father, put in belligerently. 'You can offload the kids and have some time to yourself. Elaine and I were in the bar when that girl who runs the club came to find us.'

'So have you any idea how long Christopher was out in the sun?' Becky asked.

'A couple of hours, I suppose. He was at the kids' club all morning then we told him to stay by the pool after that. Elaine and I always go to the bar at lunchtime and he's such a nuisance if we take him with us, all the time asking if he can go and play,' Michael told her. 'Of course, I blame the staff for what's happened. They should have been keeping an eye on him, shouldn't they? That's what they're paid to do. I wouldn't mind but I'd just ordered a round of drinks and we had to leave them to bring him here because that rep insisted.'

Becky managed to hide her dismay. It was hard to imagine how any father could be more concerned about a drink than his child's welfare. 'It's a good job you did bring him straight to the clinic, Mr Thomas. Christopher was very ill when he was admitted. Not to put too fine a point on it, he could have died.'

She gave the parents a moment to digest that, hoping it would stop them being so careless in the future. Heatstroke was far more serious than people realised. Once the body lost its ability to cool itself, its core temperature rose dramatically. It wasn't unknown for people to die from severe heatstroke, especially a child of Christopher's age.

'Anyway, I'll take you in to see him now. He's been sick and he might be a little disorientated, but by tomorrow he should be feeling much better. We'll keep him in overnight to monitor his condition.'

'We won't have to stay, will we?' Michael demanded. 'I mean, this is a proper hospital, isn't it? There'll be nurses here to look after him?'

'Of course. The Clinica Valdez is one of the biggest hospitals on the island,' she assured him. 'But I'm sure Christopher would prefer it if you were to stay with him. It really isn't a problem as far as we're concerned, I assure you. There's a family suite that you can use.'

'Maybe it's not a problem for you, but it's a problem for us. We've booked to go on a trip tonight and they won't refund our money if we cancel at the last minute.' Michael turned to his wife. 'There's not much point in us staying here, is there, Elaine?'

'Well, I suppose not,' she agreed hesitantly. She gave Becky a watery smile. 'So long as you're sure Christopher will be properly looked after, of course.'

'Christopher will receive the very best care,' she said shortly, not trusting herself to say too much.

She led the couple into the room and left them there. How long they would stay was anyone's guess. Frankly, she found it hard to believe that people could be so callous, although she could easily imagine Tara leaving Josh in a hospital on his own while she went off to enjoy herself.

The thought made her see that she'd been right to come to Mallorca. Making sure that Josh was safe was the only thing that mattered. It would be marvellous if she could tell Felipe the truth, of course, but it was too dangerous.

She couldn't afford to let her feelings for him overrule common sense. Deep down she knew that Felipe would have a hard time accepting that she had lied to him about being Josh's mother. He might never be able to forgive her for deceiving him. She might not only lose Josh but Felipe's support as well.

Her heart ached at the thought.

Becky collected Josh from the crèche at the end of the day and took him back to the villa. It felt strange, letting herself in to the empty house. Normally Maria would have come bustling out to meet her, telling her all about the things Josh had done while she'd been at work.

She took him into the kitchen and gave him some wooden spoons to play with while she made them something to eat. They both had scrambled eggs, with toast soldiers for Josh, and strawberries to follow. She wiped his hands and face then lifted him out of his high chair and kissed him.

'Not as much fun as when your Uncle Felipe gave you those strawberries last night, was it, poppet?'

Josh bounced up and down in her arms, seeming to react to the name, or maybe it was she who had reacted to it. Just saying Felipe's name out loud had sent a thrill coursing through her, made her skin tingle and her breath catch. It made her realise just how difficult it was going to be, living under the same roof as this man without letting him see how she felt.

It was a sobering thought and it stayed with her the whole time she was getting Josh ready for bed. He was worn out after his day in the crèche and could hardly keep his eyes open while she was bathing him. She laid him in his cot and wound up the clockwork mobile that hung from the ceiling so that he could watch the plastic fishes and dolphins bobbing around while he fell asleep.

It had just gone seven when she went into the sitting room and found herself wondering how to fill in the hours until it was time for bed. Although Felipe rarely spent any time with her once they'd finished dinner, she had never felt lonely. Just knowing that he was in the house had always seemed to be enough.

Becky sighed because that thought simply reinforced all her earlier ones about her feelings for him. It was worrying to think that she was falling in love with him when there was no future for them. Unless she told him the truth about Josh there was no chance of their relationship developing.

Her heart felt unusually heavy as she wandered out onto the terrace and stared across the bay. The sun was riding low in the sky, turning the sea blood-red where the last dying rays touched it. It had been extremely hot all day and the temperature hadn't dropped very much. She would have loved a dip in the pool, but she didn't like to stray too far from the house in case Josh woke up. She was just about to go back inside when she heard footsteps coming along the path and gasped when Felipe appeared.

'What are you doing here? I thought you were going out to dinner with your friend?'

'I was, but Ramon decided to catch the early flight back to Madrid. He has a busy day tomorrow and needed time to prepare for it.' Felipe summoned a smile, hoping that Rebecca wouldn't question him about his change of plans. Did he really want her to find out that it had been *he* who had cut short the evening and not Ramon Menendez?

He knew that Ramon had been looking forward to the evening, but as the afternoon had passed he'd found himself growing increasingly reluctant about their proposed dinner. In the end he'd cancelled their arrangements, using the excuse that something urgent had cropped up at the clinic.

Ramon had accepted it without question, used to having his own plans disrupted by the demands of the job. However, Felipe wasn't as confident that Rebecca would believe him, and it was the thought of her guessing that he hadn't been able to stand being apart from her for a whole evening that made him feel so uncomfortable.

'What a shame!' she exclaimed. 'You were looking forward to it, too.'

'I was. But these things happen so there is no point worrying about them,' he said, feeling worse because she was obviously disappointed for him.

'I suppose so. Anyway, are you hungry? You must be if you've missed out on dinner,' she continued, and he felt himself relax when he realised that she'd accepted his story.

'Not really,' he replied truthfully. 'It's so hot tonight that I think I would prefer a swim rather than a meal.'

'I was just wishing I could go for a swim,' she said wistfully. She shrugged when he looked quizzically at her. 'I didn't want to miss hearing Josh if he woke up so I thought it best not to go as far as the pool.'

'You could move the baby alarm onto the patio,' he suggested, thinking how typical it was of her to put the baby's welfare first. He felt a little flurry of pleasure run through him because it was proof that he had no need to worry what the solicitor might tell him. How could there be anything bad to say about Rebecca when he could see for himself what kind of a woman she was?

'Why didn't I think of that?' she exclaimed, laughing. 'I suppose I'm not used to having a baby alarm. There wasn't much need for one when Josh and I were sharing a bedroom, but it's the perfect solution.'

'Good. I'm glad that is settled.'

Felipe smiled back because her delight was so contagious. He followed her back inside while they got changed, parting company in the hall to go to their respective bedrooms. Rebecca's door was closed when he passed it a few minutes later so he didn't wait for her. He didn't want her to think that he was too eager to spend the evening with her.

He sighed as he made his way down to the pool. He couldn't lie to himself, though. Just the thought of having a few hours alone with her was making his blood heat, but he had to control himself. Until he'd cleared up the last little question about what she was hiding from him he had to keep his emotions in check.

It was something he'd never had any difficulty doing in the past, but as he slid into the water he knew it was going to be a struggle. It was hard to resist temptation when it came in the form of Rebecca.

Felipe was already in the pool by the time Becky arrived. He had switched on the perimeter lights and the water was the most glorious shade of azure blue. He swam over to the side and smiled up at her.

'The water is wonderful. Not too hot and not too cool.'

'Oh, good.'

She summoned a smile but it wasn't easy to control the surge her pulse gave. It was the first time she had seen him wearing swimming trunks and he was an arresting sight. His body was firm and well muscled, the thick dark hair that covered his chest arrowing down and disappearing into the waistband of his black trunks.

She felt incredibly self-conscious as she pulled her T-shirt over her head and dropped it on the grass. She could feel him watching her as she sat on the side of the pool, and wished that she had something more glamorous to wear than the modest blue swimsuit which she had bought from a local charity shop. It was a relief to slide into the water and hide herself from view, although the coolness of it took her breath away.

'I thought you said it wasn't cold!'

'It isn't. It only feels that way because you are so hot.' He smiled at her, his eyes playing over her face before they dropped to her body.

Becky felt a shiver run through her that owed itself less to the chilly water than to the intent scrutiny he was subjecting her to. And yet when his eyes came back to her face they were so full of warmth that she was instantly flooded with heat again. There wasn't a doubt in her mind that he'd liked what he'd seen, unglamorous swimsuit notwithstanding.

She ducked under the water, afraid that he would guess how that made her feel. It helped to cool her down, probably too much, because she was shivering when she surfaced.

Felipe frowned when he saw her shiver. 'You really are cold. Come, I shall race you to the other end of the pool. That will help you to warm up.'

'You're on,' she agreed, and swam as fast as she could to the other end. She was halfway there when she realised that Felipe was swimming alongside her, although he made no attempt to overtake her. She caught hold of the handrail, dragging in a lungful of air because she was so out of breath although Felipe wasn't even breathing hard.

'You let me win. You could easily have beaten me if you'd tried.'

'Perhaps. But at least it helped you to warm up, didn't it, Rebecca?' He gave her a quick smile then dived under the water and swam to the opposite end of the pool.

Becky sighed as she set off at a more sedate pace. There was no doubt that his attitude towards her had undergone a massive change, but could she be sure that he would understand if she told him the truth about Josh? She was tempted, very tempted, but she needed to be sure that she was doing the right thing.

The thought stayed with her as she swam up and down the pool. She wasn't a strong swimmer so she turned onto her back after a couple of lengths and let herself drift. Night was drawing in and the sky was turning black. The garden was secluded and there was little noise beyond the faint drone of traffic passing along the main road.

It was soothing to float in the water and she gradually felt herself relax. Maybe she was making things too difficult. Maybe she should stop looking for problems and trust her instincts...

'Come, Rebecca, we have been in the water quite long enough. I would not like you to catch a chill.'

She jumped when Felipe appeared beside her, beating at the water in sudden panic when she felt herself starting to sink. He put his arms around her and drew her against him, supporting her while she got her breath back.

'I'm sorry,' he said contritely. 'I didn't mean to scare you.'

'I didn't realise I was in the deep end,' she murmured, because it was impossible to form the words any more clearly.

She took another breath as the water lapped around them but it did very little to help. Felipe needed to kick his legs to keep them both afloat, and each time she felt his muscular thighs touching hers a little more air escaped from her body instead of entering it.

'You were daydreaming,' he said softly, his deep voice sounding oddly strained. He kicked once again and she stiffened when she felt his hips brushing hers this time, felt the way his body responded immediately to the contact. Her eyes rose to his face and she knew that he could see the awareness they held.

'Felipe...'

'No. Don't say anything. There is no need because I understand how you feel. Or I hope I do.' His smile was tender and oddly hesitant, as though he was no longer sure about anything any more.

It touched her to know that this proud, confident man could have doubts. At that moment all she wanted to do was reassure him, make him understand that she had never set out to hurt him, yet there wasn't any way to do that unless she told him the truth, and that was the one thing she couldn't do. Not yet. It was that last thought which prompted her to do what she did next.

She slid her arms around his neck and pulled his head down so that she could kiss him. There was a moment when she felt him tense, when she wondered if he would resist, and then he was bending towards her. Their mouths met softly then drew apart. Becky could feel her heart drumming and knew that he could feel it, too, but there was nothing she could do about it.

The water lapped around them, pushing them together then drawing them apart, and it was the sweetest kind of torment to feel his body, so hard and strong, brushing against hers. When Felipe removed one hand from her waist and placed it gently at the side of her neck so that he could tilt her face up, she shuddered and felt the answering ripple that ran through him.

She gave a sharp little moan when she felt his lips closing over hers and tasted their sweetness, their coolness. And yet beneath the chill caused by the water there was heat, such heat that it seemed to flare along her veins and burn her up until it felt as though her whole body was consumed by it.

He dragged his mouth away from hers and his eyes were filled with such passion that she started shivering uncontrollably despite the heat that was flowing through her limbs. 'I want you so much, Rebecca, but I will not do anything you don't want me to do. Tell me to stop if that is what you want.'

'It…it isn't.' Her voice barely carried above the sound of the water slapping against the sides of the pool. She swallowed hard, feeling the knot of tension and desire clogging her throat. 'I don't want you to stop, Felipe. Please.'

He gave a rough little laugh as he pulled her to him, his hands firm on her hips as he held her against him and let her feel his desire for her. 'Then your wish shall be granted, *querida*.'

Becky clung to him as passion rose and swelled inside her again just as the water swelled around them. When she felt his hands sliding up her body she bit her lip then gasped when she felt his fingers move inside the cups of her swimsuit and brush her nipples. When he suddenly lifted her up in the water and placed his mouth to the taut little buds she closed her eyes.

Every bit of her seemed to be consumed by what was happening as wave after wave of sensation flowed through her, weakening her limbs, making her tremble. When he let her slide back down into the water and into his arms, she couldn't have kept herself afloat if he hadn't been holding her. It took her a moment before she realised that he was speaking.

'I'm sorry….?'

'Josh is crying. Listen.'

Becky took a deep breath as she heard the thin little wail coming from the speaker she had set up on the patio. 'I…I'd better go and see if he's all right.'

'*Sí.*' Felipe kept his arms around her waist and his eyes were very dark as he looked at her, full of tenderness. 'Do you need help to swim to the steps, Rebecca?'

'I… No. Thank you. I can manage.'

She summoned a smile but the speed with which everything had happened had shocked her. How could she have let it happen again after last night? How could Felipe, because he had been just as willing a participant in what had gone on. His passion had been equally great as hers had been.

The thought sent a tremor coursing through her. It took every scrap of strength she possessed to swim to the steps and climb out of the pool. Dragging on her T-shirt, she hurried into the villa and went to check on Josh.

He was hot and thirsty so she sponged him down and changed him, then gave him a drink of water. He was still a little fretful so she took him into her room and laid him on her bed while she changed out of the wet swimsuit into her nightdress.

Picking him up again, she carried him to the window and looked out across the darkened gardens. The pool lights were still on and as she watched she saw Felipe getting out of the water. For a moment he was caught in the glow from the lights and she felt her heart catch as she looked at him standing there, so tall and strong, so handsome and desirable.

She wanted him so much that it was like a fever in her blood. She wanted to run outside and pour out the whole story, trust that he would understand so that they could find the happiness she knew could be theirs. She'd seen how he'd looked at her, felt how he'd wanted her, *knew* that they could have something so wonderful, so magical that it would last the whole of their lives and beyond.

She wanted to tell him the truth, but she didn't dare.

CHAPTER ELEVEN

'AND there was a phone call from the Clinica Rosada, Dr Valdez. The director was expecting you to call him yesterday to finalise the arrangements for the conference next month.'

'I'm afraid I forgot.' Felipe saw the surprise in his secretary's eyes and bit back a sigh. It simply wasn't like him to forget anything that concerned his work so it was no wonder she was shocked.

He picked up his diary, not wanting to dwell on the reason he had overlooked the call. It wouldn't help to admit that his mind was so full of thoughts of Rebecca that he found it difficult to concentrate on anything else.

'Contact his secretary and ask her to schedule a call for this afternoon around three. I should be finished in Theatre by then. And, please, make sure that letters of confirmation are sent to everyone who has expressed an interest in attending the conference.'

'I have done that already, Dr Valdez. I left them on your desk yesterday for you to sign,' his secretary reminded him primly.

'So you did. Thank you. That will be all for now.'

Felipe managed to hide his dismay until the woman had left, but it worried him that he had forgotten about signing the letters. It just proved how abstracted he had been of late.

He got up and went to the window, thinking about what had happened last night in the pool. He knew that if Josh hadn't woken, he and Rebecca would have ended up in bed together. But would that have been the right thing to do?

He smiled thinly. Right or wrong hadn't entered into it. The moment he'd taken her in his arms he hadn't been able to think of anything apart from making love to her. He ached to hold her even now, and that was why he'd left the villa early that morning before she'd got up. He hadn't trusted himself not to try to carry on where they'd left off, but he had to be sensible until he had spoken to the solicitor in London. Once everything was cleared up, he could do what he wanted most and make her a permanent part of his life.

He could no longer deny that was what he desired more than anything so he didn't try. He had fallen head over heels in love with Rebecca and he wanted her in his life from now till eternity. He hadn't planned on it happening, certainly hadn't expected it to, but it was a fact. He loved her and he sensed that she felt the same about him.

Felipe went back to his desk when the phone rang, feeling his heart lift when his secretary informed him that there was a call for him from London. He found himself smiling as he told her to put it through because it seemed propitious that it should have happened then.

Maybe he would be able to solve the last bit of the puzzle sooner than he'd expected, although it couldn't be soon enough as far as he was concerned. He had a future to plan, a future with Rebecca and Josh.

How very right it felt to know that he would be able to take care of his brother's child.

'You will need to pop up to the administration department and fill in the insurance claim forms. Once that's done you can take Christopher back to the hotel.'

Becky smiled at the little boy. 'You feel a lot better today, don't you, sweetheart?'

Christopher gave her a shy little smile although he didn't say anything. Becky guessed that he'd been a bit scared about having to stay in the hospital on his own, despite the fact that the nurses on duty had lavished attention on him. To be honest, she didn't have much time to spare for his parents after the callous way they'd treated the child, but she tried not to let her feelings show when Michael Thomas drew her aside.

'I thought all this treatment was free because we're in the EU,' he demanded.

'There is a reciprocal arrangement between EU countries for basic health care, but it doesn't cover everything,' she explained politely. 'The administration department will sort it all out if you have a word with them. You'll need to take a copy of your insurance certificate with you. The tour company should have issued you with one before you left England.'

'We didn't buy insurance off the holiday company. It was too expensive.'

Michael was starting to look very uneasy. Becky frowned because she couldn't understand why he had a problem with what should have been a routine matter. 'So you took out a separate policy? That isn't a problem…'

'We didn't buy *any* insurance,' he snapped, glaring at her. 'I couldn't see any point in wasting money when there was no need.'

She bit back a sigh. 'Then I'm afraid that you'll have to pay the bill for any treatment outside of the basics yourself, Mr Thomas. Do you have a credit card with you?' She carried on when he nodded, not giving him the chance to say anything else. 'You will be able to pay the bill with that, then.'

She left him standing there, glaring after her. If it had been anyone else she might have felt a certain sympathy, but not after the way he'd treated his son. She made her way to the nurses' room and poured herself a cup of coffee. It was time for the morning break and there were several other nurses already in there.

She exchanged a few words with them then decided to take her drink onto the terrace. Frankly, she felt as though she needed a bit of breathing space to think about what had happened the night before. Not that it would help her decide what to do, of course. She wanted to tell Felipe the truth but she was afraid. End of story.

She found a sheltered spot on the terrace and sat on a bench to drink her coffee. She'd been surprised when she'd discovered that Felipe had already left the villa by the time she and

Josh had got up. Maybe he'd had an urgent call, although she hadn't heard the telephone ringing. She was just wondering what had happened to him when he appeared, and she laughed.

'I was just thinking about you!'

'Indeed? I wonder what you were plotting this time, Rebecca.'

'Plotting?' she echoed. She looked at him in confusion and felt her heart sink when she saw the expression on his face. He was looking at her as though she were a stranger, someone he barely knew.

She rose unsteadily to her feet, feeling her legs trembling. 'What's happened, Felipe? Why are you looking at me like that after…?' She bit her lip. Did she really want to remind him of last night and the way he'd held her, kissed her, loved her?

Her mind stalled on that word because nobody could look at another person this way and feel love for them.

'After what we did last night? Come, Rebecca, why are you shy to talk about it? You certainly weren't shy at the time as I recall. You were only too willing to let me enjoy your beautiful body, and it didn't happen just the once either. Was the first time to whet my appetite and the second to get me completely under your spell? I really am interested to hear the answer, *querida*.'

'I have no idea what this is all about, but I don't intend to stand here and let you insult me.' She spun on her heel but he was too fast for her. She stopped dead when he stepped in front of her.

'I apologise. I did not come to insult you, Rebecca. I came because I need you to answer a question for me.'

His voice sounded so cold, so distant that it was impossible not to compare it to the way he had spoken to her the night before. Then his voice had been full of warmth and desire, echoing with unspoken promises that made her heart race even now to recall it. It made it doubly difficult to understand what was happening.

'What question? I don't understand…'

'Why did you tell me that you are Josh's mother when it was a lie?'

Felipe saw the colour drain from her face and he felt nothing, neither pleasure nor pain. He felt too numb to feel anything. He heard her drag in a little air and still he felt nothing. All his emotions seemed to have died slowly, agonisingly, when the solicitor had told him the truth at last, that Rebecca wasn't the mother of his brother's child.

'How did you find—?'

He gave a sharp downward thrust of his hand which silenced her. 'It does not matter *how* I found out, it is *what* I found out. Josh is indeed Antonio's son, but he isn't yours. His real mother is Tara Lewis. It is her name on Josh's birth certificate, and before you try to deny it I must warn you that Antonio's solicitor has faxed me a copy of the document.'

He gave a small shrug, knowing that he couldn't bear it if she tried to lie to him again. 'Evidently, he needed to see Josh's birth certificate when he drew up the papers appointing you as the child's guardian. He kept a copy of it for his records.'

'Then there would be no point in me trying to deny it, would there?'

The bleakness in her voice seemed to penetrate the numbing layer that had enveloped him and his hands clenched because he didn't want to feel anything at the moment. All he wanted was to get the facts straight and then decide what he should do.

'Tara Lewis gave birth to Josh and subsequently she and Antonio signed papers appointing you as his guardian,' he said flatly. 'Why? That's the only thing I am interested in at the moment.'

'Because Antonio knew that I would always look after Josh.' Once again she had to struggle to drag in a little air, and another pain pierced the wall around his heart.

'And why would you look after him and not his mother? Surely it was her responsibility, not yours?' He gave a dismissive flick of his hand. 'You were nothing to my brother, were you?'

'No, that's not true! I loved Antonio and he loved me. He knew that he could trust me to look after Josh—'

'And he couldn't trust Tara? Is that what you're claiming?' he shot back. Even though he knew it was wrong to let himself be sidetracked at a time like this, it had hurt unbearably to hear Rebecca claim how much she'd loved his brother.

'No, he couldn't trust her! Tara never wanted Josh. When she found out she was pregnant, she wanted to have an abortion. She went to see Antonio and asked him for the money to pay for it!'

The words were flowing out of her now. Felipe tried to harden his heart, but her anguish was almost more than he could bear. He wanted to gather her into his arms and tell her that it didn't matter what she'd done because he would always love her. But deep inside he knew that it *did* matter. How could he ever trust her when she'd lied to him about something so important?

'Antonio was desperate when he found out what Tara was planning. His affair with her had been over for some time by then, and he'd told me that he'd realised it had been a mistake. But having Tara turn up at that point in his life, telling him that she was pregnant and that she wanted to get rid of the baby, was too much for him to cope with.'

She ran her hands over her face and Felipe realised that she was crying, but he couldn't afford to show her any sympathy. He needed to hear the whole story then put it behind him, only it wouldn't be that simple, of course.

'Why couldn't he cope?' he snapped, trying not to think about the future and the fact that Rebecca could never be a part of it now. Once before he'd been deceived by a woman, but this time it was far worse. He had never loved Teresa as he loved Rebecca. His heart ached because there was no way he could deny it.

'If Antonio was old enough to have got himself into that mess in the first place, he was old enough to deal with it,' he said harshly.

'Maybe he could have done if circumstances had been different,' she said thickly. 'But he'd only just found out that he had cancer and the doctors had told him that the treatment he needed would make him sterile. At that stage we were still hoping that he might be cured, but learning that he would never be able to father a child came as a huge blow to him.'

Felipe could understand that. It would have been a bitter blow to him, too, although having children wasn't something he had thought about for a long time.

He closed his mind when an image of Rebecca—her body swollen with his child—rushed into his head. It would never happen now, not after the way she'd lied to him about Josh. Maybe she'd lied about the rest of it as well, about Antonio and the money, the way she seemed to feel about him.

It was an effort to focus because that last thought caused him such pain. How could he believe that Rebecca really felt anything for him when her whole life might be one huge lie?

'And that's when I came up with the idea to pay Tara to have the baby.'

'So it was your idea?' He laughed softly, hoping it would disguise his heartache. 'Why doesn't that surprise me? What else did you plan, Rebecca? Was it your idea to write Tara out of her son's life? You say that Tara was paid to have the baby, but I'm sure you received a lot more than she did. She was the unfortunate victim in all this, wasn't she? Once she'd had Josh then you simply dispensed with her.'

'No, you're not listening to me! Tara never wanted Josh. She had him purely and simply for the money! Why do you think I needed that twenty thousand pounds?'

She looked him straight in the eye and he could tell that she was willing him to believe her. 'Tara threatened to go to court and claim that she'd been coerced into signing over custody of Josh if I didn't give her more money. She'd had nearly every penny of Antonio's inheritance and there wasn't anything left. I tried explaining to her that it could end up with Josh being taken into care, but she just laughed. She told me that she didn't care what happened to him so long as she got the money!'

Felipe could hear the ring of truth in her voice, but he was afraid to believe her. He couldn't comprehend that any woman would have handed over her child the way Tara Lewis apparently had.

He realised then that he wasn't capable of thinking rationally at that moment and the matter was too important to make any mistakes. Josh's whole future was at stake. What it all might boil down to was whether or not he was prepared to leave his brother's son in the care of a woman who had lied to him.

'What do you intend to do…about Josh, I mean?'

His heart ached afresh when he heard the fear in her voice, but he couldn't afford to think about Rebecca's feelings. It was Josh who mattered, nobody else. 'I haven't decided yet.'

'I promised Antonio that I would always look after him,' she whispered brokenly. 'No matter how much you might hate me, please, don't take Josh away from me, Felipe. I…I don't think I could bear it if I had to give him up.'

'Maybe you should have thought about that sooner,' he said bitterly. He shook his head when she went to speak. 'No. I need time to think about this. My only concern from now on has to be Josh. I have to do the right thing for him.'

'Even if that means applying for custody of him?'

'If that is what I decide will be best for him in the long term, then yes, although obviously his real mother's wishes must also be taken into account.'

'Tara doesn't care what happens to him. I've told you that!' she exclaimed. 'Please, please, don't make the mistake of thinking that Josh might be better off with her.'

'You have told me a lot of things, Rebecca. Some may have been true, others obviously weren't.' His tone was uncompromising and he saw her flinch.

'I wanted to tell you the truth, Felipe. Really I did…'

'It doesn't matter now.' Suddenly, he knew that he couldn't bear to hear any more. It wouldn't help to know how much she was hurting and that he was responsible for it. 'The only thing that concerns me now is Josh.'

He turned and walked away. Rebecca was still standing where he'd left her when he reached the end of the terrace and looked back. He let his eyes rest on her for one last moment then carried on, and it felt as though a door had closed and he'd been plunged into darkness.

There was no future to look forward to now. Oh, he would do his utmost for his brother's child. If he did apply for custody of Josh and was successful he would love and care for him to the very best of his ability, but there would be no pleasure in it because Rebecca wouldn't be there with him, helping him, loving him, bringing light and warmth into his life.

How empty his world was going to be without her.

Becky stared after Felipe, wishing with her whole heart that she could make her body obey her. She wanted to run after him and make him believe that she'd wanted to tell him the truth, but she couldn't move. All the strength seemed to have drained from her limbs so that she could only stand and watch him walking away from her. And she knew in that moment that it really was the end, the end of her dreams and maybe the end of her role in Josh's life as well.

Tears clogged her throat but her eyes were dry. The grief she felt ran too deep to find an outlet in tears. Somehow she made herself walk back into the hospital and it was as though she were suddenly a stranger in the familiar environment. Everything was the same as it always had been: the quiet bustle of the ward; the murmur of voices; the smell of antiseptic that hung in the air. The world was carrying on as normal and it was just for her that life had come to a halt. From this point on she had no future to look forward to.

She managed to get through the morning, but it felt as though she were functioning on autopilot. She was programmed to react to various situations and she did. She spoke to Diane and Tim Ryan, comforted parents whose little girl had broken her arm, gave out drugs and checked obs, and afterwards she couldn't recall what she'd done. It scared her to realise that because it was too risky for the patients.

She went for lunch, wondering what she should do. She would have to leave, of course, because she couldn't stay at the clinic now and certainly couldn't continue living in Felipe's house. She would have to go back to England, take Josh with her, see if she could hide him away so that Felipe couldn't find him...

'Becky!'

She jumped when someone called her name. Turning, she stared in bewilderment at the red-haired man who was hurrying towards her. For a moment she had no idea who he was before she realised it was Simon Montague.

'What are you doing here?' she asked faintly.

'I've come to see my cousin—Richard Jeffries. Remember, the chap who broke his neck diving into a swimming pool?' Simon stared at her when she didn't answer. 'Richie said that he'd met you, Becky. You must remember him?'

'I...um...yes, of course. I...I had no idea he was your cousin, though.' She tried to smile but her mouth wouldn't seem to work and she saw Simon look at her in concern.

'Are you OK? I didn't mean to give you a shock, really I didn't.' He looked momentarily uncomfortable. 'I may as well come clean and admit that I knew you were working here. As soon as I heard that Richie was in the Clinica Valdez I made the connection. But I didn't mean to...well, upset you.'

'You haven't,' she said quickly. 'It's not you, Simon. I've just had a bad day....' She bit her lip when she felt a sob rise to her throat.

Simon shot a look along the busy corridor then quickly steered her into an alcove. 'Tell me what's happened. And before you try to deny it, I can tell there's something wrong.' His pleasant face tightened all of a sudden. 'Has Valdez done something to upset you?'

'It's all very complicated,' she began, not wanting to involve him in her affairs.

Simon shook his head impatiently. 'No, you're not going to get away that easily. I want to know what's wrong, Becky. I thought we were friends and I want to help you any way I can.'

Her eyes filled with tears when she heard the concern in his voice. 'Oh, Simon, it's such a mess. I never meant this to happen. All I ever wanted to do was help Antonio and look after Josh.'

All of a sudden the whole miserable story came pouring out. To give Simon his due, he didn't interrupt her even though she could see how shocked he was by what he heard. She wiped her eyes with the handkerchief he gave her and looked miserably up at him.

'I've made a real mess of everything, haven't I?'

'No, you haven't. I can't think of anyone who would have done what you've done.'

It was such a relief to hear him say that. Tears welled from her eyes again. She didn't protest when Simon put his arms around her and hugged her. He gave a deep sigh then slowly loosened his hold on her.

'Now we need to decide what you must do. Obviously you can't stay here so you'll have to go back to England.'

'I know, but I don't have any money for the fare. And even if I do go back, I've nowhere to live, no job…nothing.'

'That isn't a problem. I'll pay your fare and you and Josh can stay with me while you find somewhere to live. I'll be staying in Mallorca for a few days to be with Richie so I'll give you the key to my flat. As for a job, well, they'll take you back at St Leonard's like a shot. They've not found anyone to replace you, so we've been making do with agency nurses when we can get them.'

'Oh, but I couldn't,' she protested. 'I don't mean the job, but I couldn't let you pay my air fare. And as for putting us up…'

'Becky, it isn't a problem! Really.' He took hold of her hands and squeezed them. 'I want to help you but, please, don't worry that you might be giving me the wrong idea.' He shrugged. 'I realise that we can be nothing more than friends, but that's OK.'

'I don't know what to say, Simon. It's so good of you…'

She tailed off when she caught sight of Felipe coming along the corridor. Her heart felt as though it was being slowly squeezed to pulp when she saw the coldness on his face as he spotted her and Simon.

He passed them without saying a word and his very silence was enough to tell her how pointless it would be to go after him. He would never believe that she'd wanted so desperately to tell him the truth.

She took a deep breath but it did nothing to ease the agony she felt. 'Thank you, Simon. I really appreciate this.'

'You don't have to thank me, Becky. I'm happy to help.' Simon stared after Felipe and for a moment she thought he was going to say something before he thought better of it.

'I'll sort out a plane ticket for you. What time will you be ready to leave? I might be able to get you a seat on a flight today if that's not too soon.'

'No,' she said hollowly. 'The sooner I leave here the better it will be for everyone concerned.'

Simon hurried off to make the arrangements while Becky collected Josh from the crèche and took him back to the villa. She packed only the things she had brought with her and left behind all the beautiful toys and clothes that Felipe had provided for him. They weren't hers to take and she wouldn't give him the chance to accuse her of stealing from him.

Tears slid down her cheeks and she dashed them away, but more kept on coming. She picked Josh up and held him close, drawing comfort from the feel of his sturdy little body in her arms.

How long she would be able to keep him was another matter, of course. But whatever happened, she would make sure that he was never handed over to Tara. She didn't really believe that Tara would want him, but there was always a chance that Tara might change her mind if she could see any financial benefit in having Josh.

If it came to a court case she would tell the judge the whole story, present him with all the evidence to back it up and make sure that Josh was placed in Felipe's care. No matter how much Felipe hated her, he would do his best for Josh.

He would give his brother's child all the love that he could never give her.

Felipe made his way to Theatre and scrubbed up. It was a fairly routine operation, the removal of a gallstone laparoscopically—minimally invasive surgery performed through a tiny incision using a laparoscope. It was an operation which he'd performed dozens of times before so he wasn't anticipating any problems, yet he found that his hands were shaking when he turned off the taps

He made himself breathe deeply, but the tremor didn't stop He could feel his muscles bunching and flickering, feel the ligaments and nerves jerking beneath his skin, and realised that he was in no fit state to carry out even the simplest procedure if he didn't manage to control himself. But seeing Rebecca standing there in another man's arms had already tested his self-control to its limit.

He swore softly, fluently, and Domingo, who was standing beside him at the sink, shot him a worried look. 'Are you all right, Dr Valdez?'

'Yes!' he snapped, holding out his hands for the sterile towel Theatre Sister had ready for him. It fell from his grasp and he stared at it lying there on the floor while images played in front of his eyes, images of Rebecca with that man's arms around her, her slender body pressed against his, her face tilted up as she waited for him to kiss her...

Felipe swung round, ignoring the startled looks that Domingo and the nurse exchanged. 'I am unable to continue with this operation. Have Dr Ramirez paged and ask her to take over from me.'

He didn't wait to hear what Domingo said as he strode from the room. Tossing his paper hat into the waste basket, he left Theatre and made his way to the stairs. He didn't stop to change from his scrub suit into his clothes and he saw several members of staff stare at him in astonishment as he passed them.

He had made it a strict rule that everyone must be properly

dressed at all times, but he didn't give a damn about appearances at that moment. He didn't give a damn about anything except finding Rebecca and making her explain what she'd been doing with that man, Montague, and why he had been in the clinic. Was this another one of her schemes, another way to make use of every man she came into contact with?

Anger ripped through him and the fact that it was mixed with a burning jealousy he hadn't believed himself capable of just made him feel worse. He didn't want to be jealous about a woman who had lied to him, but he couldn't stop himself.

He left the hospital and made his way to the villa, knowing instinctively that she would be there. He only hoped that Montague wasn't with her because he wouldn't be responsible for his actions if he found the man in his house.

Rebecca was in the hall and she jumped when he flung open the door. He just had a moment to take in her tear-stained face before he caught sight of the cases at her feet. His eyes skimmed over the battered suitcase and the cheap shoulder-bag stuffed with Josh's nappies and bottles, while a piercing pain ran through his heart as he realised that she was leaving. It took every scrap of strength he possessed to open his mouth and speak.

'Where are you going?'

'Back to London.'

Her voice wobbled and he saw her bite her lip. His hands clenched when he saw that she'd bitten it so hard that she'd drawn blood. He ached to take her in his arms and kiss it better, let his lips heal that tiny wound, but he couldn't do that. He couldn't let himself forget what she had done.

'And what if I refuse to let you leave?' he said hoarsely instead.

'You can't stop me, Felipe.' Her head came up and despite the tears on her cheeks and the pain in her eyes there was a quiet dignity about her that shamed him. 'I'm Josh's legal guardian and until the courts decide differently I'm free to take him back to England, or anywhere else I choose. It goes with-

out saying that you have no hold over me now that I've ter-
minated my contract at the clinic.'

'You know that I'll probably sue for custody of the boy?'
he shot back, stung by that last comment. He had no hold over
her because she didn't care about him. She didn't love him;
his feelings didn't matter; it had all been an act.

'Yes. And if I can't have Josh, I hope you win, Felipe. In
fact, you have my word that I shall do everything in my power
to make sure that you get custody of him.' She brushed a gentle
kiss over the top of the baby's head then looked him straight
in the eye.

'I won't run away with Josh. I won't try to hide him. I did
think about it but I realise that it would be the wrong thing to
do. However, I shall do everything in my power to ensure that
Tara never gets him back.'

She gave a husky laugh and he felt his eyes burn with sudden
tears when he heard the sadness it held, the pain. 'I know that
you will love and care for Antonio's precious son every bit as
much as I would have done. It will be some consolation.'

Felipe didn't know what to say. He'd never dreamt that she
would want to entrust Josh into his care if the child couldn't
stay with her.

Once again his emotions shifted, swirling like sand in a des-
ert storm. Had he been wrong? Should he have let her explain
why she hadn't told him the truth about Josh? Did it *really*
need explaining or could he work it out for himself? Had
Rebecca not told him purely and simply because she'd been
afraid of losing the baby?

Questions raced through his mind and he jumped when she
suddenly bent and picked up her case.

'The taxi's arrived. I'll have to go.' He heard her swallow,
heard the thickness of her voice as she added, 'Don't hate me
too much, Felipe. I only did what I thought was right for Josh.'

She went to the door, murmuring her thanks when he opened
it for her, and it was the fact that she could thank him after
everything he'd said to her that moved him unbearably.

He watched her climb into the cab, saw how carefully she

settled Josh on her lap, how tenderly she held the little boy in her arms, and saw nothing else. Tears filled his eyes and he couldn't see the taxi as it drove away. Maybe that was a good thing. Maybe it would stop his heart breaking if he didn't have to watch her leaving.

Maybe.

CHAPTER TWELVE

'IT'S great to have you back! At least we'll have someone here who knows what she's doing!'

Becky laughed. It was her first day back at St Leonard's and the first person she'd met on her arrival had been Karen. As they travelled up to the IC unit together in the lift, she made a determined effort to be cheerful.

Simon had assured her that nobody knew the real reason why she'd come back to England and she knew that she could trust him. He had been a wonderful support, letting her and Josh stay at his flat then helping her find a place of her own and lending her the money for the deposit.

She'd managed to find a tiny one bedroom flat close to where she'd lived before, so Josh had gone back to the same child-minder. He had settled in straight away and it was a relief to know that he was happy.

As Simon had predicted, the hospital had been only too eager to take her back. They had even waived the usual interview and had simply asked her when she could start. Now all she had to do was convince everyone that she'd returned to London because she'd been homesick and she could start putting her life back together, or as together as it was possible to be in the circumstances.

'I'm sure it can't have been that bad,' she said, trying not to think about what might happen in the coming weeks. Felipe hadn't made any attempt to contact her even though she had written to tell him her new address. However, she intended to keep her word and do everything in her power to help him gain custody of Josh if it came to a court case.

'Simon told me that you'd had agency nurses covering my post.'

'If and when they could find any.' Karen sighed as the lift came to a stop. 'It's easier finding gold in the Thames than it is to find qualified IC nurses, especially paediatric ones. I can't count the number of double shifts I've worked since you left.'

'Really? I suppose that explains why the powers that be welcomed me back with open arms,' she suggested wryly.

'That, plus the fact that you're one of the best IC nurses we've ever had in the unit,' Karen said generously. 'I was really sorry that it didn't work out for you in Mallorca, but their loss is our gain. I only hope that Josh's uncle didn't give you too hard a time.'

'What do you mean?' she asked, her heart sinking. Had something leaked out after all about what had gone on?

'Well, I don't suppose he was very pleased about you leaving after he'd made all the arrangements for you to move over there,' Karen replied, leading the way along the corridor. 'He didn't strike me as the sort of man who would take kindly to having his plans disrupted.'

'No, he isn't,' Becky agreed hollowly. She tried not to think about Felipe too often, but it wasn't easy to shut him out. Now, she sighed as an image of his handsome face swam before her eyes.

She missed him so much! Every day that passed just made it harder to cope. If only he'd let her explain why she hadn't told him the truth about Josh. If she could believe that he didn't hate her, it would help to ease the pain just a little.

'You OK? I didn't say something I shouldn't, did I?' Karen grimaced when she looked blankly at her. 'Simon has been rather evasive whenever I've asked about you. I did wonder if there was more to your return than he told us.'

'Hardly!' Becky summoned a smile, not wanting Karen to start asking any awkward questions. 'I got homesick for good old London. End of story. Anyway, what's been going on here? What happened at the inquest into Rosie Stokes's death?' she asked, briskly changing the subject.

'Oh, it was all St Ada's fault, as we knew it was. Turned out that they'd run out of blood and borrowed some from St

Leonard's until their own supplies arrived. That accounted for the discrepancy in the bar-code.'

Karen was successfully distracted and Becky breathed a sigh of relief as she followed her into the staffroom. 'And how about the mix-up with the blood groups?'

'St Ada's again. They only went and left their most junior trainee to change poor little Rosie's drip.' Karen's face mirrored her disgust. 'She mixed up the blood with some intended for another patient and nobody double-checked. Fortunately, another nurse realised there had been a mistake, so the other poor soul didn't get the wrong transfusion. But nobody followed it up to see what had gone wrong.'

'Incredible!' Becky exclaimed. 'I don't know why people can't just follow the rules. Someone should have checked the trainee's work. Imagine how awful it would have been if Debbie had been blamed for what happened.'

'She was completely exonerated before the inquiry. Danny Epstein—remember him, the boy with endocarditis?' Karen carried on when she nodded. 'Well, Danny's mum saw Debbie settling Rosie in and was able to testify that she hadn't changed the transfusion. She's a lawyer, as it happens, so she was very precise about what she said.'

'How wonderful! I was afraid it would be the last straw and Debbie would ask for a transfer,' she admitted.

Karen laughed. 'Funnily enough, it's done just the opposite. She's far more confident than she used to be. Odd how adversity sometimes brings out the best in folk, isn't it?'

Becky nodded, but her heart felt heavy all of a sudden. Would it bring out the best in her if Felipe took her to court to claim custody of Josh? How would she cope if she didn't have Josh to give meaning to her life? She could never have Felipe now, of course, and the thought of how empty her life might be in the future was almost more than she could bear.

Felipe had taken some time off work because he was more of a hindrance than a help. He knew that his colleagues were starting to wonder what was wrong with him, but he didn't care. Where once the affairs of the Clinica Valdez had been his sole reason for getting up of a morning, he now found himself unable to take any interest in what was going on there.

He appointed one of his senior colleagues as director in his absence and left it at that. If…and it was a very big *if* at this stage…he managed to get his life back on track, he would resume his duties. Maybe one day the clinic would take centre stage in his life again, but at the moment it was Rebecca who had claimed that role.

He missed her so much! Missed the sound of her laughter, the comfort of her silence. He missed just knowing that she was there in the villa. He missed her more than he'd believed it possible to miss another human being, and it was slowly but surely driving him to the edge of despair.

He knew that he would have to do something to resolve the situation before he drove himself completely crazy, but it wasn't until he heard a bulletin on the midday news three weeks after Rebecca had returned to London that he was shocked into action.

He sat on the edge of his chair as the reporter told of a fire which had swept through St Leonard's Hospital in London. There were pictures of the burning building, along with scenes of staff ferrying patients outside. It was hard to take it all in, especially when the reporter mentioned that several members of the hospital's staff had been injured in the blaze.

Was Rebecca one of them? Was she even now lying in another hospital's bed, in pain, maybe dying?

He felt sick at the thought of losing her. He couldn't bear it if he had to live out the rest of his days without the comfort of knowing that she was alive and well somewhere in the world. All of a sudden, it was that thought which drove the confusion from his head.

Yes, she had lied to him about being Josh's mother, but she had done it purely out of fear for the child. She had wanted to protect Josh, make sure that no harm came to him.

Everything she'd done, from promising Antonio to always take care of his son to visiting the clinic that day to ask him

for money, had been done for Josh. She had put the child's
welfare before her own, been prepared to suffer any kind of
hardship so long as the child was happy. Even the fact that
she'd promised to support *him* if he sued for custody had been
typical of her commitment to the boy. Right from the beginning, Rebecca had put Josh's needs before her own.

It was a huge relief to have realised the truth at last, but
terrifying that he might have arrived at it too late. If Rebecca
had been gravely injured, he might never have the chance to
beg her forgiveness and tell her how much he loved her.

He phoned the airport and tried to book a seat to London,
barely able to curb his impatience when he was told there
weren't any available that day. When the ticket agent suggested
making a detour via Madrid he immediately agreed, not caring
how long it took him or how many changes he would need to
make. So long as he got to London and could be with Rebecca,
that was all that mattered.

He could only pray that she was unharmed.

The fire had started in the laundry and had swept through two
floors of the hospital before it had been brought under control.
The accident and emergency department had been gutted as
well as Women's Surgical. It had been a terrifying ordeal for
everyone concerned.

The fact that all the patients had needed to be evacuated had
put everyone under a great deal of pressure. Wheeling seriously
injured people through the billowing clouds of smoke had been
a nightmare. Several of the nursing staff had been overcome
by fumes and one of the A and E doctors had been seriously
injured. A section of the ceiling had fallen on him when he'd
gone back to rescue an old lady who'd been trapped in the
toilets. He'd been transferred to a specialist spinal unit and the
prognosis wasn't good.

The children in the IC unit were transferred to St Ada's
which was rather ironic after recent events. Becky and the rest
of the team from the unit did their best to make the transfer as
smooth as possible, but it was a worrying time for them all.

Moving gravely injured children across London was an ordeal, and she was glad when it was time to go off duty. Sister Reece had told them to report to St Ada's the following day, although whether they would continue to run the department from there was still being discussed.

Becky was exhausted by the time she collected Josh from the childminder. She took him home and put him in his playpen while she changed out of her smoke-tainted clothes. She filled the bath and then to Josh's delight got in it with him, washing them both then playing a game of splash in which she came off worst.

It reminded her poignantly of the time Felipe had helped her bath Josh and had told her about his experiences with the doll, Esmeralda. She could recall the surprise in his eyes when he'd admitted that he'd told nobody else the story.

All of a sudden she was crying. Maybe it was the stress of the past few weeks, combined with the events of that day, but she couldn't seem to stop the tears from pouring down her cheeks. Josh looked at her uncertainly, his small face puckering, and it was that which helped her compose herself. The last thing she wanted was Josh being upset.

'It's OK, darling. Mummy's fine,' she told him, but he still looked unsure.

She climbed out of the bath and put on her old towelling robe then lifted him out and dried him, singing his favourite nursery rhymes to distract him. He looked a little happier by the time she went to fetch his bedtime milk and soon settled down once he'd drunk it. He was drifting off to sleep when she heard the doorbell ringing. She hurried to answer it, not wanting it to wake him.

Becky slipped the chain on the door because she wasn't sure who it would be. Simon had been her only visitor so far, so maybe he'd come to update her about what was happening. She knew that there were concerns about the IC unit remaining at St Ada's so they might have decided to relocate it somewhere else.

All that was whizzing through her head as she opened the

door so the last thing she'd expected was to find Felipe standing outside. Just for a moment she stared at him with her heart in her eyes before she dragged her gaze away.

'What do you want?' she asked hoarsely.

'To see if you were all right. I heard the report on the news about the fire. It said there were people injured…nursing staff…'

She heard him take a deep breath, heard the raw note of fear in his voice when he continued, and it was that which made her heart start to thunder inside her. To hear him sounding so scared shook her to the depths of her being because she didn't understand what it meant.

'I was worried about you, Rebecca. I had to come.'

Felipe held his breath, praying that she would believe him. Knowing that she was safe was such a relief.

He had been so scared on the flight from Madrid, terrified of what he might find when he arrived. He'd taken a taxi from Heathrow, his mind whirling this way and that yet always coming back to the thought of what he would do if Rebecca had been killed in the fire. He couldn't even contemplate living out the rest of his life without her…

'Worried about me? You really expect me to believe that?'

He flinched when she gave a bitter little laugh, felt his stomach roil with sickness when he saw the disbelief in her eyes. He could barely contain his pain when he realised that he was responsible for it.

'Yes. I know you must find it hard to believe, Rebecca, and I understand why you feel that way. I behaved abominably. All I can do now is apologise and hope that you will forgive me.'

'What is the point?' she said in a tone that made him ache because it held so much anguish. 'You hate me because I didn't tell you the truth about not being Josh's real mother. Nothing is going to change that fact, is it?'

'I don't hate you, Rebecca. I never could!' He felt his heart swell with tenderness when he saw the sudden uncertainty in her eyes. He sensed that she desperately wanted to believe him and it was that which suddenly made it easy to tell her the truth.

'I love you, Rebecca. I love you with my whole heart and if you feel anything at all for me, please, let me come in. We can work this out if it's what we both want, I promise you.'

'You love me?' She closed her eyes and he saw the lines of strain that were etched on her beautiful face. 'If this is a trick, Felipe...'

'*Dios!* Do you think I would lie about such a thing?' he demanded. 'I love you. My life is empty without you. I cannot work, cannot sleep, cannot even think! That is why I had to come and see if you were all right. I...I couldn't go on if anything had happened to you.'

His voice broke and he turned away, unable to stand there while she refused to believe him. Maybe he deserved to be treated like this after everything he'd done, but it hurt. It hurt so much!

'Wait!'

He paused, one hand gripping the banister when he heard her call out to him. He couldn't turn, couldn't speak, couldn't do anything except wait and, maybe, hope.

'Don't go. Please. Not yet.'

He heard her footsteps coming along the landing, heard them stop, and still he couldn't move. He seemed to be frozen, waiting for her to say or do something, hoping—praying—that it would be what he wanted so much.

'Did you mean it, Felipe? Do...do you really love me?'

The hope in her voice was the catalyst that unlocked his mind and body, and he turned towards her. He knew that she could see the truth in his eyes even before he answered her question.

'Yes, Rebecca. I meant it. I love you. Really.'

'Oh, I never dreamt...never thought...'

Suddenly she was laughing and crying at the same time but more importantly she was walking towards him. Felipe opened his arms and as she stepped into them he knew he would never let her go again.

She tipped back her head and he could see the love in her eyes as he heard her say the words, 'I love you, Felipe.'

He kissed her then, gently, tenderly, and the moment he felt her lips under his he was filled with certainty. Rebecca loved him. He loved her. They were two constants upon which they could build their future, no matter what happened.

Becky wasn't sure how long they stood there with their arms wrapped around one another. It was only when she heard the front door slam and footsteps coming up the stairs that she realised how public a place they had chosen to declare their love for each other. She stepped out of Felipe's arms, smiling tenderly when she saw the bemusement on his face.

'I think we should continue this in my flat, don't you?'

He blinked and she saw him look around uncertainly before a slow smile curved his mouth. '*Sí, querida.* We are in danger of shocking your neighbours, I fear.'

She laughed softly as she led the way into the flat and closed the door. Felipe reached for her again and kissed her hungrily and she shuddered as she felt desire starting to burn inside her. It was an effort to speak when he raised his head.

'It's a good job we did move. We could have caused a riot out there on the stairs.'

Felipe laughed, taking her hand and pulling her back into his arms for one last kiss before he reluctantly let her go. 'We shall confine our love-making to the privacy of your home from now on, my darling. But first there are things we need to talk about. *Sí?*'

'You mean Josh and Tara and everything?' She sighed when he nodded. 'You're right, of course. It's just that I'm—'

'Afraid that I will not understand?' He looked deep into her eyes and she saw the assurance his held. 'I shall, Rebecca. Just tell me what happened, right from the beginning. We need to put this behind us once and for all.'

She smiled because she knew that he meant it. 'Let's go into the sitting-room, or what passes for a sitting-room. I'm afraid it's rather cramped.'

She led the way, smiling ruefully when she saw the expresion on his face. 'Not the height of luxury but it's served its purpose for the past few weeks.'

'I hate to think of you and Josh having to live here.' He cast an expressive glance around the dingy room then made an obvious effort to ignore it as he sat beside her on the lumpy sofa. Lifting her hand, he pressed a kiss to her palm then closed her fingers over the tingling little spot as though he wanted her to feel the evidence of his love while she related her tale. And in an odd sort of way it helped.

'You said to start from the beginning so I shall. I met Antonio by chance one day when we were both using the local launderette.' She smiled. 'He'd put all his washing in together and one of his shirts had been stained by dye from a T-shirt. I offered to take it home and see if I could get the stains out of it for him.'

Felipe laughed. 'Antonio must have found it difficult doing things for himself because Maria had always taken care of us.'

'He did at first, but he soon learned,' she assured him. 'After that we started going out together. I think we were both rather lonely, to be honest. Antonio had recently split with Tara and my mother had died a few months earlier. My father died when I was a toddler so it was just Mum and me, and we were very close.'

'I wish I could have been there for you,' he said huskily and she smiled at him because it was such a lovely thought.

'I wish you had, too. Anyway, Antonio told me about his relationship with Tara not long after we started going out together. He said that he regretted getting involved with her and believed him.' She sighed softly. 'He never made any secret of the fact that he loved me.'

'And you loved him, too, didn't you, Rebecca?'

She heard the pain in his voice and knew at once what had caused it. She framed his face between his hands and looked deep into his eyes. 'Yes, I loved Antonio, but not the way I love you. He was the sweetest, gentlest man I've ever known.'

Felipe turned his head so that he could brush her palm with a kiss, and she heard the tears that had thickened his voice.

'Thank you for being there when he needed you, Rebecca
Thank you for caring about him enough to make him feel
loved. It helps to know that he had you with him when he
died.'

Her own eyes filled with tears as she drew him into her arms
and held him. 'I only ever wanted to help him, Felipe
Everything I did was for him and for Josh.'

'I know that. I really do.' He kissed her quickly on the lips
then wiped away her tears and smiled at her. 'So, please, tell
me what happened.'

'Tara's announcement that she was pregnant came like a bolt
from the blue. Antonio knew what she was like, that she was
only really interested in money and having a good time. Even
though he regretted having got involved with her, he couldn't
bear the thought that she was going to abort his child, especially when he might never be able to have any children in the
future.'

'And that was when you came up with the idea of paying
her to have the baby?' he suggested gently.

'Yes. It probably sounds crazy to you, but Antonio was so
distraught I had to do something to help him. Finding out that
he had cancer was such a devastating blow, especially when it
turned out to be such an aggressive form.'

'Fibrosarcoma is one of the most difficult cancers to treat
especially if it has spread throughout the body,' he observed
sadly.

'Which was what had happened in Antonio's case. I tried to
give him all the support I could, but there was very little I
could do.'

'You were there for him, Rebecca. That was the most important thing of all.'

She sighed when she heard the pain in his voice. 'You're
wishing that he'd told you, aren't you? He did think about it
We spoke about you a lot, in fact. Even though you two had
argued, he loved you very much, Felipe. He just felt that he
had to face what happened on his own and make his own decisions. He was afraid that you might not let him and that the

time might come when he wouldn't have the strength to fight you.'

'And he was right. I would have tried to persuade him to carry on with the treatment, but now I can see that would have been the wrong thing to do.'

His voice echoed with regret and she squeezed his hand. 'You loved him and Antonio knew that. Never forget that.' She carried on when he nodded, knowing that it would be easier if she stuck to the facts. 'Paying Tara to have the baby seemed like the best thing to do.'

'And she agreed? The promise of money was enough to make her decide whether her child should live or die?'

'Yes, I'm afraid it was. All Tara was interested in was the money, and she made sure that she got as much as possible out of Antonio. She demanded fifty thousand pounds immediately with another five thousand each month for the duration of her pregnancy to cover her living expenses.'

She heard him curse under his breath and sighed. 'There were also credit-card bills and payments on a car she'd bought. Then there was the money she asked Antonio for to buy baby clothes, only she never spent it on Josh.'

'And that's why you had to buy everything second-hand?' He stood up and paced the room, as though he couldn't bear to remain still while he listened to what she had to say.

'Yes. I had a little money left in my savings account so I used that. I'd given up my agency job to look after Antonio and I hadn't been earning for a while so it wasn't very much, I'm afraid.'

'And what about the money Antonio left you in his will?' he asked gently as he sat down again.

'That was for Tara, her final payment for having Josh— another fifty thousand pounds.' She shrugged. 'He didn't trust Tara not to get rid of the baby so the agreement was that I would pay her the money after the child was born. Of course, he hoped to leave enough money for me to take care of Josh, but Tara had drained his account almost dry. Antonio never fully realised how much of it he'd handed over to her, and I never told him because it would have upset him too much.'

'*Dios!* I find it hard to believe that any woman could be so…so callous. Did she not change her mind after the child was born?' he demanded.

'On the contrary. She couldn't wait to get rid of Josh and get her hands on the final payment due to her. She handed him over outside the hospital and I never saw her again until she turned up at my flat, demanding another twenty thousand pounds. I was so scared!'

She started shaking and she heard Felipe bite out something harsh in Spanish as he drew her into his arms and held her tightly. 'Shh, *querida*. There is no need to be afraid. Tara will never get her hands on our precious child. I swear on my life that I shall not allow that to happen!'

'You don't know how wonderful it is to hear you say that.' Becky lifted her face and kissed him lightly on the mouth, let the kiss deepen when he immediately responded. This time the tremor that passed through her owed itself to something other than fear, and she smiled shakily.

'I love you so much, Felipe. Have I told you that?'

'Yes, but I can stand hearing it as many times as you care to repeat it.' His eyes were full of warmth and tenderness, his lips full of love, and every last tiny bit of fear melted away. Felipe would always take care of her and Josh.

He let her go with marked reluctance. 'I love you, Rebecca. I only wish that you hadn't had to suffer the way you have. I only wish that Antonio had told me what was happening because I would have understood.'

She sighed softly when she heard the regret in his voice. 'I'm sure he knew that, but he didn't want your life being disrupted by having to raise his child. You were busy with the opening of the clinic and he said something about you having had to give up such a lot for his sake already.'

Felipe sighed. 'He must have meant when I broke off my engagement to Teresa. He was always a sensitive child and he blamed himself, although there was no need. Teresa was having an affair with a friend of mine and that is why we ended our engagement. She wanted a man who would dance attendance on her and I wasn't prepared to do that when I had my life mapped out.'

'You mean setting up the Clinica Valdez?' she guessed.

'Yes. I gave up everything to achieve my dream. Now I realise that I missed out on so much by doing so.'

'You mean Teresa?' It was hard to keep the ache out of her voice and he laughed in delight.

'No, I do not mean Teresa! My pride was hurt when I found out what had been going on, but my heart certainly wasn't broken. I meant that I had missed out on enjoying things other than my work. Isn't there a saying the Americans use about waking up and smelling the coffee? Well, that's what I never did.'

It was so ridiculous that she laughed. 'I can easily make you some coffee, Felipe, if that's what you want!'

'Wretched woman! How dare you tease a man who has been in such torment?'

'Have you? Been in torment, I mean?' she said huskily.

Felipe smiled at her, seeing the love in her eyes. His heart seemed to overflow because he knew it was all for him.

'Yes, my darling. I have been in the worst kind of torment possible because I had lost the one thing that mattered most to me—you.'

'You haven't lost me. I'm here now and I intend to stay right by your side.' She leant forward and there was a world of promise in the kiss she gave him. 'I love you, Felipe.'

'I love you, too.' He chuckled wryly. 'I was *so* jealous when I saw you with Montague at the clinic that day. I have never wanted to hit anyone, but I wanted to hit him!'

'Poor Simon. He's been a good friend and I hope that you two will try to get on.'

He glowered at the idea then sighed when she gave him a stern look. 'Very well, I shall try. But I am more concerned about what will happen to us—you, me and Josh.'

'I am still afraid that Tara might do as she threatened and

go to court out of spite,' she admitted worriedly. 'I'm sure she will try to demand more money at some point, and she won't be pleased if we refuse to pay her.'

'I do not believe that any judge would find in her favour once you had told them the truth, Rebecca. However, we need to bring this to a proper conclusion. I do not want you spending your life worrying what might happen.'

He kissed her quickly, his tongue teasing so tantalisingly around her lips that she groaned. He knew his expression was more than a little smug when he drew back, but he couldn't help it. Rebecca loved him. He felt ten feet tall and as though he could climb mountains. And nothing was going to spoil their happiness from now on.

'I shall sort everything out. Trust me. And now do you think we can steal a few minutes for ourselves? I have come a long way to see you, Rebecca, and it seems a shame to waste this visit by talking all the time.'

She laughed softly, her grey eyes sparkling as she looked at him. 'I thought talking was good for the soul, Dr Valdez?'

'Is it?' He kissed her once on the lips, then a second time on the jaw, feeling the tremor that ran through her as his mouth moved to her throat and began its descent.

'Oh, yes. Very good…'

He heard her breath catch as his mouth slid over her collarbone and carried on with its journey. All she had on was a towelling robe and the V-neckline was the perfect spot to aim for.

A shudder ran through him when he felt the soft swell of small breasts beneath his lips as they travelled towards their goal. Her skin was so warm and smooth, the scent of soap making his body hum with anticipation. He reached the base of the V and planted a kiss there, smiling when he felt her shiver.

'So, do I take it that you still prefer to talk, Rebecca?' he asked, his lips brushing against her skin.

'I suppose it all depends what other choice there is,' she said huskily, and he had to bite back a laugh of delight when he realised how much effort it had cost her to force out the sentence.

'Then perhaps I should help you make up your mind by showing you what is on offer,' he suggested with a wickedly sexy laugh.

He drew the folds of her robe apart and turned so that he could kiss first one nipple and then the other, hearing the moan that came from her lips. It was such a heady experience that he did it all over again then realised that it was he who was moaning this time.

He stood up and lifted her into his arms, smiling down at her with eyes full of love. 'Talking might be good for the soul, Rebecca, but it does very little to ease the ache in one's body, I fear.'

'Then maybe it's time we did something about that.' She wound her arms around his neck, pulled his head down so that she could kiss him lightly on the mouth then smiled. 'Do you think it might help if we made love? It's only a suggestion, of course. Feel free to disagree if you wish.'

'Oh, I think it might help quite a lot.' He returned her kiss then drew back and looked at her. And he knew that he had never meant anything more in his whole life as he continued, 'I love you, Rebecca. I shall spend my life making you happy if you will let me.'

'Good. Although for a man who isn't keen on words, you do seem to spend an awful lot of time talking,' she said pertly, smiling at him.

'Don't worry, *querida*. I do not intend to say anything else for a long time to come!'

He quickly carried her into the bedroom and laid her down on the bed. Josh was fast asleep in his cot and didn't stir. Felipe undid the belt of her robe and pushed it off her shoulders.

Her body was smooth and firm in the glow from the night-light, her skin gleaming like mother-of-pearl. He was almost afraid to touch her because she looked so fragile, so delicate. But then she reached up to him and her arms were surprisingly strong as she pulled him down to her and held him tightly against her heart.

'Love me, Felipe,' she whispered. 'Just love me.'

'I shall. Always.'

It was the easiest promise he had ever made, and one which he would never break. He would love Rebecca from now until eternity…

Six months later…

'Is that from the solicitor?'

Felipe heard the anxiety in Rebecca's voice as she came into the study where he'd been opening the day's post. He turned and smiled at her, knowing that the past few months had been the happiest of his entire life.

They had been married in a simple, civil service held at the local registrar's office in London before she'd flown back to Mallorca with him. It was what they had both wanted so there had been no reason to wait. Now he pulled her into his arms and gave her a gentle kiss before handing her the letter that had arrived from London.

They had made a formal application to adopt Josh before leaving England. He knew that Rebecca had been terrified that Tara might lodge an objection once their solicitor informed her of their plans, but it hadn't happened. Now he smiled when he heard her gasp of relief as she read the letter.

'See, it is official now. We are legally Josh's parents.'

'I kept wondering if something would go wrong at the last minute,' she admitted with a catch in her voice.

'I know. And it has almost broken my heart, watching you worrying yourself to death.'

He kissed her again, feeling her relax against him as he held her close. 'Everyone knew that it was the best thing for Josh and I had no doubts that it would be perfectly fine in the end. The fact that Tara never bothered to fly back from New York for the hearing proved that she isn't interested in him.'

'I believe she has a new man in her life—a millionaire, so rumour has it.'

'Then she has got what she wanted at last—money,' he said firmly. 'Now we shall forget about her and start to make plans for our future.'

'What have you got in mind?' she asked curiously, tipping back her head to look at him.

'What I have in mind at this minute will have to wait,' he said drily. 'I am needed at the clinic. My colleagues are already talking about the amount of time I have taken off recently.'

'Let them talk,' she murmured, kissing his jaw and smiling when she felt his body immediately quicken.

'Mmm, you can be so very persuasive, Rebecca...' He kissed her quickly then set her away from him and sighed. 'No, I must not be tempted. There is something I want to ask you first.'

'That sounds very serious,' she teased, smiling up at him with her heart in her eyes.

Felipe smiled back. 'It is something I have been thinking about for some time, but I thought it might be better to wait until everything had been finalised. Now we shall be able to have a double celebration.'

Becky shook her head. 'I'm not sure I understand.'

'It is simple, *querida*.' He took her hands and held them tightly as he looked into her eyes. 'I have spoken to the priest at our local church and he has agreed to bless our marriage, if you like the idea.'

'Oh, I do!' She laughed in delight. 'I can't think of anything I would like more, in fact!'

'Good. I also thought that it might be nice to have a party here at the villa to celebrate after the service.' He bent and kissed her lightly on the mouth. 'We can also celebrate the fact that Josh is ours and that nobody can ever take him away from us.'

'That would be wonderful, Felipe.'

She bent and lifted Josh into her arms as he came toddling into the study to find them. There was a light in her eyes when she looked at him that made Felipe's breath catch. 'I can't think of anything I want more than to let everyone share our happiness.'

'Neither can I,' he said deeply. He bent and kissed her, laughing when Josh pushed between them and held up his face to be kissed as well. They both kissed him then Rebecca put him down when he started wriggling.

Felipe put his arms around her as they watched him making a beeline for the desk. There were tears in Felipe's eyes but he didn't try to hide them from her. 'Antonio would be so glad to know that his son was loved like this, Rebecca.'

'He would, and I think he would be glad for us, too.' She turned to face him. 'I love you, Felipe.'

'And I love you, too.'

He kissed her hungrily, held her to his heart and knew that he had never felt more blessed.

He had Rebecca.

He had his brother's son.

He couldn't have wished for anything else!

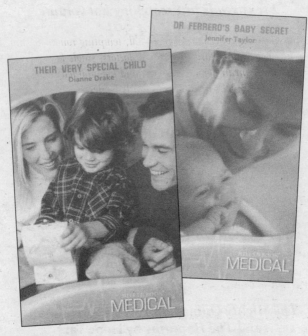

MILLS & BOON®
MEDICAL™
proudly presents

Brides of Penhally Bay

Featuring Dr Nick Tremayne

A pulse-raising collection of emotional, tempting romances and heart-warming stories — devoted doctors, single fathers, Mediterranean heroes, a sheikh and his guarded heart, royal scandals and miracle babies…

Book Five

THE DOCTOR'S ROYAL LOVE-CHILD
by Kate Hardy

on sale 4th April 2008

A COLLECTION TO TREASURE FOREVER!
One book available every month

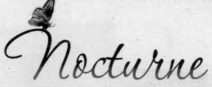

The Regency

LORDS & LADIES

COLLECTION

More Glittering Regency Love Affairs

Volume 17 – 4th January 2008
One Night with a Rake by Louise Allen
The Dutiful Rake by Elizabeth Rolls

Volume 18 – 1st February 2008
A Matter of Honour by Anne Herries
The Chivalrous Rake by Elizabeth Rolls

Volume 19 – 7th March 2008
Tavern Wench by Anne Ashley
The Incomparable Countess by Mary Nichols

Volume 20 – 4th April 2008
Prudence by Elizabeth Bailey
Lady Lavinia's Match by Mary Nichols

Volume 21 – 2nd May 2008
The Rebellious Bride by Francesca Shaw
The Duke's Mistress by Ann Elizabeth Cree

Volume 22 – 6th June 2008
Carnival of Love by Helen Dickson
The Viscount's Bride by Ann Elizabeth Cree

M&B

Celebrate 100 years
of pure reading pleasure
with Mills & Boon®

To mark our centenary, each month we're
publishing a special 100th Birthday Edition.
These celebratory editions are packed with extra
features and include a FREE bonus story.

Now that's worth celebrating!

4th January 2008

The Vanishing Viscountess by Diane Gaston
With FREE story The Mysterious Miss M
*This award-winning tale of the Regency Underworld
launched Diane Gaston's writing career.*

1st February 2008

Cattle Rancher, Secret Son by Margaret Way
With FREE story His Heiress Wife
Margaret Way excels at rugged Outback heroes…

15th February 2008

Raintree: Inferno by Linda Howard
With FREE story Loving Evangeline
*A double dose of Linda Howard's heady mix of
passion and adventure.*

Don't miss out! From February you'll have the
chance to enter our fabulous monthly prize draw.
See special 100th Birthday Editions for details.

www.millsandboon.co.uk